Carol Smith, formerly a lea_____
concentrates full-time on her _____
twelve highly successful nove_____
more information about Caro_ _____, visit her website at
www.carolsmithbooks.com.

Praise for Carol Smith

Hidden Agenda
'Both a thriller – I was hooked by the very first page – and a
gripping story about the power of female friendships. A winning
combination!' Marika Cobbold

'A gripping and beautifully constructed story' Elizabeth Buchan

'Carol Smith has done it again, an unput-down-able thriller with
a twist . . . Smith holds the reader in her grasp from start to
finish, and gives us compelling psychological insights on the
way' Julia Neuberger

Grandmother's Footsteps
'Grandmother's Footsteps . . . will keep you entertained, reading
and guessing all the way to the end' Crime Time

'With its teasing insights into the mind of a serial killer,
Grandmother's Footsteps keeps you guessing until the end'
Sainsbury's Magazine

Unfinished Business
'If a pacy thriller is your thing, Unfinished Business will suit you
to perfection . . . an addictive read' Sunday Express

'A thriller which certainly keeps you turning those pages . . .
gripping right to the end' Daily Mail

Family Reunion
'A gripping read' Family Circle

'Full of action, twists and surprises, this intricate suspense story
offers a fascinating new take on the nature of family ties'
Good Housekeeping

Also by Carol Smith

DARKENING ECHOES
KENSINGTON COURT
DOUBLE EXPOSURE
FAMILY REUNION
GRANDMOTHER'S FOOTSTEPS
HOME FROM HOME
HIDDEN AGENDA
FATAL ATTRACTION
TWILIGHT HOUR

CAROL SMITH OMNIBUS

Without Warning

Vanishing Point

SPHERE

This omnibus edition first published in Great Britain by Sphere in 2009
Carol Smith Omnibus copyright © Carol Smith 2009

Previously published separately:
Without Warning first published in Great Britain in 2006
by Time Warner Books
Published in 2006 by Sphere
Copyright © Carol Smith 2006

Vanishing Point first published in Great Britain in 2005
by Time Warner Books
Reprinted 2005 (six times)
Copyright © Carol Smith 2005

The moral right of the author has been asserted

A CIP catalogue record for this book
is available from the British Library.

ISBN 978-0-7515-4147-2

Printed and bound in Great Britain by
Clays Ltd, St Ives plc

Sphere
An imprint of
Little, Brown Book Group
100 Victoria Embankment
London EC4Y 0DY

An Hachette UK Company
www.hachette.co.uk

www.littlebrown.co.uk

Without Warning

For Joanne Dickinson.
She knows why

Acknowledgements

Thanks, as always, to my wonderful publishers for doing their usual impeccable job. To Sarah Rustin and the rest of the team, especially Sales and Marketing. An additional thank you to Jenny Fry and Helen Gibbs for telling me stories about travelling by Tube which inspired me to write this book. And to Mark Thompson (formerly Metropolitan Police) for his helpful comments on police procedure. Also to my agents, Curtis Brown, for backing me up so well.

Prologue

The first time was almost an accident; an annoying woman, yapping into her phone, pushed in front of a train with the slightest of nudges. In the ensuing hullabaloo it wasn't hard to get lost in the crowd, though later he found the adrenalin fix lingered on. Killing was easy. It gave him a buzz and proved there were certain things that he *could* do.

The Tube was a relatively new experience which got him out of his virtual prison and enabled him to mix with the public at large. The incident had been spur of the moment, the victim chosen because of her manner and the way she ignored the commuters packed all around her. Though he was unable to catch what she was saying, the facial grimaces had been enough. She was overweight and her lipstick was smudged. He found her existence offensive. It took little more than a flick of the wrist to knock her off balance on her fashionable shoes and into the path of the approaching Circle Line train.

Alone and faceless in the milling crowd, he experienced a taste of what could be achieved. Next time he would come prepared and select his target more precisely.

Part One

1

The worst part was not being able to sleep, but he'd more or less given up on that since they'd started reducing the morphine that killed the pain. What he thought about most was the blinding flash and the disintegration of Finch's head when the booby trap he had failed to detect had blown up in their faces. In the months that followed he had tried to remember precisely what had led them to that spot. That particular spot, at that time, with its terrible denouement. For once his intelligence had proved faulty, the worst crime any surveillance expert could commit. Killing anyone was traumatic enough. To sacrifice a trusted partner was more than he could live with, even now.

Andy Brewster, ex-SAS, had returned from Baghdad a stretcher case, not entirely expected to walk again or even pull through. For months, as he'd lain in a hospital bed, slowly regaining the use of his legs, he'd gone endlessly over the nightmare scenario that would haunt him the rest of his life. He and

Finch had worked side by side for an unbroken seven years. The trust between them had been absolute though, naturally, never referred to. Yet Brewster had blundered and Finch had been killed; he knew the image would never be expunged. There were moments still when his courage almost failed and he longed to follow his partner into oblivion.

But Brewster was made of sterner stuff, despite the sweating and panic attacks; as his spine was fixed and his legs improved, so too did his fighting spirit. He knew he owed it to both of them to get back in the saddle as fast as he could to justify Finch's meaningless death by continuing with the fight. He had no inclination to do anything else, even if he'd had the choice. His fluent Arabic and knowledge of Islam had led him, via the Ministry of Defence, to this role as an undercover cop. Life on the edge really suited him best: he liked to stay constantly on his toes. His firearms training and specialist degree had led him to some of the world's hottest spots. He had kept super fit and emotionally free and worked out regularly in the gym. At forty-two he had been at his fighting best.

Not any more though. Since Iraq he'd had to learn to walk again. Now he could manage without his sticks, though occasionally used one to get around when the pain was at its most intense. He rapidly weaned himself off the drugs, having seen how pernicious such a habit could become; was determined not to give in to terrorists. He had begged to be allowed to return to work, to leave the confines of the hospital, which was rapidly driving him out of his mind with a suffocating ennui. Also to help him repay the debt, to give back something in recompense for having been the unwitting cause of the wasteful death of his friend.

*   *   *

After much deliberation and the usual red tape, they'd seconded him to the Metropolitan Police, working plainclothes on the transit system, using his espionage expertise in the fight against terrorist crime. It was not a job he particularly relished yet it fell within his limited scope until he had fully regained his strength and been given a clean bill of health. At this time of year, at the height of the season, with the tourist invasion beginning to peak, anti-terrorist skills like his were at their most essential. And it certainly beat a desk-bound job, a death-knell to the active career he fervently hoped he would some day be able to resume.

His initial reaction to Burgess, his new partner, had been cautious in the extreme. After what he'd seen happen to Finch, he'd have far preferred to have worked on his own, for the symbiosis between partners is crucial and he wasn't yet ready to bond again. But police regulations said he must have one and Burgess possessed credentials he couldn't replicate. At first they'd regarded each other with caution, then taken a walk to break the ice, and Brewster, rather to his surprise, had found himself quickly won over. Despite the fact he was trained to kill, Burgess had such an equable nature that it only took a matter of days for them to become trusted pals.

They had settled down to a steady routine that varied little from day to day. Brewster hated the Underground, missed the exotic delights of Baghdad, but his new companion made it easier to adjust. Furthermore, there was no denying that Burgess certainly knew his stuff. Like it or not, they were stuck with each other, certainly till the end of the season. The job was tedious but had to be done. One blink and a deadly device could go off or something nasty be hidden beneath a seat. And at least it beat mouldering away in retirement like so many of

7

his former colleagues. He enjoyed being part of the ebb and flow of the city's daily life.

What he hadn't expected though, quite so soon, was to witness first hand the terrible damage a train can do to a person beneath its wheels.

At first it had looked like an accident: the victim had stumbled and lost her balance as the rush hour crowd surged forward, out of control. It had meant total closure of the Circle Line for the minimum two and a' half hours it took for the police and emergency services to come through. They had raised her carefully from the track and placed her remains in a body bag. It was only when they turned her over that what had happened became apparent. Deliberately killed in the rush hour crowds, yet no one appeared to have seen a thing. At least, no witnesses had so far come forward.

The few they'd questioned had noticed nothing. All they recalled was the usual swirl of people pressing forward as the train approached and then the blood-curdling scream. It had taken the transport police an age to curb the panic and calm them all down. It wasn't a bomb or a terror attack, just a horrible, meaningless tragedy caused by too many people on the platform at one time.

'I blame the council,' an official declared. 'If it weren't for this damned congestion charge people would still be using their cars and these incidents wouldn't occur.'

But then, of course, they'd discovered the knife and the Metropolitan Police were drafted in.

2

It was ten to nine and the platform was packed. The Underground system was still snarled up by Friday's horrible murder. All the papers had carried the story though none appeared to have any real lead. A bank cashier, who had worked in Moorgate, had fallen beneath an Underground train while talking on her mobile to a friend. It now turned out that she had been stabbed, incredible with so many people about. Beth loathed the Tube, especially in rush hour, but at this time of day it was the preferable option. The traffic along the Bayswater Road would be at its usual standstill. Duncan kept urging her to take a cab but she knew, from grim experience, how hard that could be. Compared to hers, his journey was simple: two stops anti-clockwise to Gloucester Road. If he felt in the mood, he could easily walk, as occasionally in the summer he did. He liked the stroll over Kensington Church Street, with its rows of classy antiques shops.

Beth shoved her way along the platform to be closer to the Baker Street exit, and surged with the crowd when the train came in, disgorging a sprinkling of tourists. She wriggled her way to a corner by the doors, trying to avoid too much bodily contact. The journey was only five stops but absolute hell. She was used to it now, had been doing it for years since she took the decision to give up her catering career. Running a shop was hard enough but not nearly as stressful as wedding receptions or boardroom lunches for stuffy men in suits.

The woman standing opposite was familiar: Beth had noticed her many times before. She also travelled to Baker Street every morning. They would climb the steps to the street side by side but not, by so much as a glance, acknowledge each other. Typical of the Brits, she thought; in almost any other city in the world they'd be swapping jokes and on first-name terms by now. Except for New York, where they'd be cursing each other in a frantic jostle to reach the turnstile first. Beth grinned; one day she'd surprise them both and venture a tentative 'Good morning'.

Celeste was also aware of Beth, a pretty woman who was often privately smiling. She envied her; from the wedding ring it would seem that she wasn't alone in the world. She looked like someone at peace with herself who paid little heed to the laughter lines, her thickening waist or the first faint touches of grey. Not so Celeste, who hated herself as much as she hated life in general, had done so since the catastrophe that had stopped her career before it had even begun.

She had once lived the life of a pampered princess, spoilt and indulged by adoring parents who had given her every advantage in life, including an opulent home. No expense had ever been spared; she had ballet classes and deportment lessons and her clothes, like her mother's, were couture made in Paris. Her future, it had been assumed, was already completely mapped out. With looks like hers, plus the family name, she was destined surely to shoot to the top. Stardom was hers for the taking, once she was ready. She had grown up haughty and condescending, aware of the admiring looks but too aloof to acknowledge her would-be suitors.

Until the terrible thing occurred, after which her life had drastically altered. Instead of becoming a movie star, she'd been forced to quit RADA in her second year and now was stuck in this tedious job that she felt was unworthy of her talents. It wasn't fair; it had not been her fault that the sole inheritance they'd left was the house, these days shabby after years of neglect, plus the problem it contained. For, no matter how much she disliked her work, going home at night was the hardest part, having to deal with a situation from which she could never escape.

Consulting hours were 9.30 to 5. She must get a move on or else she'd be late. It was seven minutes to Devonshire Place then another five down to Wimpole Street. With luck, she'd be there before His Nibs and have the coffee on by the time he arrived.

They were late that morning leaving the flat, because they'd stayed up too late the night before and Alice had said they must first make things shipshape for the cleaner.

'You are *so* middle class,' scoffed Julie from Bradford, running her fingers through her spiked-up hair and checking her iPod was properly charged for the journey. In her ultra-short skirt and cork-heeled wedges, she was the epitome of groovy chic. She worked in women's features for the *Daily Mail*. Alice's male friends found her slightly alarming.

11

'Then go on without me,' Alice said calmly, rinsing glasses and stacking plates. She had been taught, from an early age, always to clear up after herself and not leave a mess for the cleaner to have to deal with.

Which was something Julie could not comprehend. 'Why keep a dog and bark yourself?' she said.

Alice smiled. It was hard to explain but, nevertheless, she dried her hands, removed her apron and relented. They were lucky to have a cleaner at all but that was what sharing a flat entailed. For a small extra cost, it gave them domestic freedom. Onslow Gardens was close to the Tube; they would be there in just a few minutes. They discussed what to do about supper that night, then went their separate ways.

The *Daily Mail* was only two stops away. If it weren't for the height of her heels she could almost have walked it. It was a stroke of luck having Alice to share with; though earning quite well for her twenty-two years, Julie was an inveterate shopaholic. And Kensington High Street was packed with clothes; it was only lucky that her hours were so long. If she didn't love the job so much, she might well have packed it in.

She had served her apprenticeship on a Bradford paper then moved to London as soon as she could. Had been living in the YWCA when, fortuitously, she'd met Alice on a typing course and the two of them had become friends. Alice was posh, in a low-key way, and worked in a bookshop, which was badly paid but the only thing she had ever really wanted to do. When her flatmate got married, she'd invited Julie to move in. They were chalk and cheese but got along well, mainly since Alice was so easy-going and Julie put a bit of zip into her life.

Julie herself was fiercely ambitious and longing to have her own by-line. She was good at the job and a very hard worker though inclined to be confrontational which put up her colleagues' backs. Apart from Alice, her friends were mostly male. She hung around the bars with them after work.

Wilbur and Ellie got on at Tower Hill, having started their sightseeing early. With only five days before moving on, Wilbur was keen to fit everything in, though secretly Ellie preferred a more leisurely pace. She would have preferred to have seen some street life, not just the tourist sights. That was her husband all over, however; he was not yet used to not having a business to run. It was just one stop to Monument, after which, she had a nasty suspicion, he was going to expect her to tramp around all day.

He had studied the map over early breakfast and made a list of the things he wanted to see. St Paul's Cathedral came top of his list and then, surprisingly, the Bank of England, whereas Ellie would have liked to browse in Spitalfields market or cross the river to the new Tate Modern and take in some art after having a leisurely lunch. But Wilbur, at seventy, had in no way eased off. She wasn't sure she'd survive another four days.

Her married life had not been eventful: two daughters, now grown, were all she felt she'd achieved. Chippewa Falls was pleasant enough and she'd made good friends there over the years, but Wilbur's retirement had meant a considerable change. In place of a quiet domestic life, baking and cleaning and bottling preserves, she now had him home all day, getting under her feet. Golf still occupied much of his time and that was a heaven-sent blessing, but his presence interfered with her charity work and the coffee mornings she ran for the church and meant she had a lot less time for herself and her cultural activities. Along with being his general factotum, she was now his social secretary as well.

'We're here,' he announced. They had reached their stop. Ellie obediently fell into step behind him.

Margaret changed trains at Victoria station, heading for Kensington High Street. She was making a tapestry cushion for the den and needed to buy more wools from Ehrmanns, the only place she knew of that still supplied them. She loathed the crowds, wasn't used to them, but at least today the Circle Line wasn't too packed. A smiling busker came through the carriage, playing guitar rather well. She gave him a pound. After Haywards Heath, it was quite a culture shock. She came into London so rarely these days, for urgent shopping or to see an exhibition. Since Jack had died she had been on her own. The boys were both busy with their careers and neither daughter-in-law seemed to care for her much.

After she'd done her bit of shopping, she'd walk through the park to the V&A or else get back on the Tube for the two-station ride. She must start heading home by mid-afternoon, before the early rush hour got under way. The train was usually packed after that and she wanted to be sure of a seat. There'd been a nasty incident the previous week that had hit all the front pages. A woman had fallen in front of a train; it was even suggested she might have been pushed. Margaret shuddered. At times life was very unpleasant. She missed not having her husband around, hated entering the empty house knowing there wouldn't be anyone there to greet her. She took out her book; it was only four stops but she couldn't wait to finish the last few chapters.

3

Imogen enjoyed a long lie-in, something she did a lot these days. She was rarely home before half past one and her mother said she could do with the extra rest. She rose at eleven, had a leisurely soak, then called her friend Alice on her mobile phone.

'Hi,' she said, biting into a peach and stretching out on the sofa to chat. She was part of the chorus of *Anything Goes* and wasn't required at the theatre till a quarter past six.

'Can't talk now,' said Alice, sounding rushed. She ran the bookshop almost single-handed with only part-time help.

'So call me back,' said Imogen benignly. The problem with working nights was the empty days.

She scrambled eggs in her mother's pristine kitchen, trying hard not to make a mess. Since Beth had given up catering, they mainly ate out. Then she settled down to watch *Cash in the Attic*, keenly observed by two hopeful dogs, slavering for a snack.

'Come here, you.' She tugged one over, dropping a kiss on its satin-smooth snout. The dogs belonged to her stepfather, Duncan, and often went with him to work. She loved the setup now; her mother had never seemed happier.

Beth, in the shop, was working flat out, serving a queue of early lunchers who came in droves every day at this time in search of her famous homemade snacks. Though primarily a delicatessen, the shop also had an area at the back which laid on a grazing menu for famished shoppers. The work was hard but preferable to cooking. At least she now had her evenings and weekends free.

She took a breather to call her husband, to check how his day was going.

'Good,' he said. They had saved a Burmese cat's life.

'That's wonderful, darling.' He was a brilliant vet, as immersed in his career as she was in hers. The pivotal point of her life had been when they'd met.

'I have to get back.' They both worked hard but liked to make contact whenever they could. Imogen laughed and called them soppy, but only ever with a twinkle in her eye. Life had improved for her as well when they'd finally got it together.

They arranged to eat at home that night and Beth made a note to take something back. There was a movie on he wanted to see which suited her fine as well. With Imogen out six nights a week, their cosy twosome had been restored. She missed her daughter and worried about her but also enjoyed being back in honeymoon mode. It made her feel young and frisky again. She hoped she'd get home in time to wash her hair.

'Bye, darling,' she said. 'See you at seven.'

'Can't wait. I'll try not to be late.'

*　　*　　*

Their first appointment was a teenage girl with a nose too large for her delicate face. She'd been brought by an overbearing mother who did all the talking and made one thing clear: she wanted her daughter fixed for her social debut. The doctor tactfully said very little but carefully scrutinised the patient before taking preliminary Polaroids for his own use. He smiled at her, which helped her relax, and made her lie back on the comfortable couch while he flashed a series of slides on the screen before her.

'It is your choice,' he said. 'There are several that would suit you. You'll be beautiful, I promise, when I am done.'

The girl, overwhelmed with embarrassment, carefully studied each picture. Then turned her head to look at Celeste, still hovering in the doorway. 'I'd like to look like her,' she whispered and the mother nodded her approval.

'What do you think, Celeste?' asked the doctor, accustomed to patients reacting this way. 'That's why I keep her around,' he explained, with a wink. 'She's a great advertisement for my work.' A tired old joke; Celeste merely smiled and went back to her case notes. The only part of the job she could bear was witnessing the happiness surgery could bring. With a smaller nose that child would be transformed, might even end up pretty. The mother was right; the ugly duckling deserved the chance to become a swan. The details were discussed and a date was set. They could fit her in at the start of next year which would mean she'd be fully recovered in time for her ball. Celeste gave the mother a list of dos and don'ts – no alcohol, avoid these foods – and promised to phone a few days in advance to remind them of the appointment.

'Don't worry,' she said as she saw them out. 'Dr Rousseau is world famous. Without doubt, the best plastic surgeon we have in this country.'

'Well, if you are anything to go by,' said the mother. The daughter was far too timid to speak at all.

Celeste gave her enigmatic smile and stood at the top of the stairs to watch them leave. They shared the elegant house with three other surgeons.

The next one in was a much older woman with the tight strained look of a habitual addict; she was far too thin, with a startled Bambi look. When she filled in the forms, Celeste was proved right. A surgery junkie, destroying herself. She really believed that no one out there would ever notice. Celeste showed her in to talk to the doctor, then closed the door and returned to her notes. He would set her right, being deeply committed to making his patients look better not worse. Which, in this case, would require considerable tact. She made more coffee – it was almost eleven – then studied herself in the glass. If only her life had turned out as intended, she wouldn't be here, in this menial job, paying lip service to spoilt rich women and emotional cripples.

Two perfect murders had made him restless. The buzz in his head stopped him sleeping. He got up early and went downstairs. While the kettle boiled, he opened a drawer and stared at the rows of gleaming knives, carefully stored in their green baize slots, untouched for so many years. He tested the blades with a practised finger and found them as sharp as they had been then, a sensation that made him shiver and feel slightly giddy. He closed his eyes and his senses whirled, stirred by the memory of what they could do. The moment of impact, the scream, the blood; the release he felt when the blade went in, as smoothly as slicing through butter. He had watched her fall and the blood gush forth in a foaming arc that had soaked his hair. He closed his eyes in an effort to block it out.

He had started to sweat at the recollection, so made his coffee and took two pills to try to calm himself down. He had felt the moment it punctured her lung, the hysteria of the crowd as she toppled forward. Had watched the train as it neatly sliced her in two. There'd been panic then and such pandemonium that he'd had no reason to hurry away. He had hung around to see what happened next. Since childhood that was what he had been: a silent observer on the sidelines of life. A watcher whom no one had ever even noticed.

But now he had a new incentive. It was growing late and time to go. He picked up his bag, slipped his sunglasses on and let himself out of the house.

By the end of the day, as they headed home, Ellie found herself distinctly flagging. Though twelve years older, Wilbur took the pace in his stride, seemed scarcely out of breath. By Victoria station the train was packed, the evening rush hour well under way, and a nice young man with excellent manners stood up and offered his seat. For a moment Ellie thought it was Wilbur who should sit but she knew his pride wouldn't countenance that. Wisconsin males went out of their way to take proper care of their ladies. It would almost have been a duelling point should the young man have offered it to him.

'All right, dear?' He smiled down at her, his broad face flushed in the stifling heat. He removed his plaid jacket and loosened his tie. She could see he was heavily perspiring.

'Here, give me that.' She held out her hand and took the jacket, leaving Wilbur free and unencumbered, studying the map.

'Tomorrow,' he told her, 'we will go upriver to look at

Greenwich and Canary Wharf. I am sure you would like a nice ride on a boat. And afterwards we'll go to Hampton Court.'

She nodded and smiled. At least on a boat she'd be sitting down and she liked the prospect of seeing a royal palace. But it wasn't enough. It was her trip too, and inside Ellie was seething. Europe had always been one of her dreams, something they'd never been able to do. The kids were too small or they hadn't the money or Wilbur was too busy with his golf. They were finally here but nothing had changed. Wilbur was making all the decisions, barely aware that his wife might have preferences too. Tonight they had tickets for *The Lion King*; he had heard that the show was not to be missed and he'd booked the Strand Palace for a meal afterwards.

Though unimaginative, Wilbur meant well. It was not his fault that their tastes were so different, though it might have helped if he ever stopped to listen to what she had to say. He treated her, as he always had, as the child bride he had snatched from her studies, without ever stopping to think that she still had a brain. But the train was already at Gloucester Road. She rose and followed him once again for the arduous evening slog down the Cromwell Road.

4

In those long arid months while he'd lain in bed, encased in plaster, unable to move, Brewster's awareness had been a living nightmare. Over and over he had replayed the shattering explosion of the booby trap, the moment when the bomb had gone off, blowing their jeep to pieces. How he'd survived was a mystery; he had dragged himself from the wreckage with oil in his hair and blood all over his face and clothes. Finch's blood. Those of the team who had also escaped had covered him as he crawled away and later an army helicopter had airlifted him to safety. The rest of that period remained a blur. He only knew how lucky he was to be alive.

Later, after they'd moved him to Bournemouth and a nurse started pushing him out for walks, the sting of the salt in the air had begun to revive him. The skirl of the gulls had a soothing effect so that, after a while, he could sleep again. Nature was aiding the long slow haul to recovery. Though the terrible image of what had occurred was etched indelibly into his brain. From that point on, he was emotionally barren.

It was during that time, as he practised walking, that Brewster had taken up painting. As a boy he had been an accomplished draughtsman, though in the tough circles he moved in then such skills had been dismissed as being sissy. He'd forgotten about it for several decades until an elderly aunt came to visit, bringing a child's set of crayons and a sketchpad.

'Something to help you fill in the hours.' She remembered the Christmas cards he had drawn as a child.

Brewster, startled, had muttered his thanks then shoved the package to the back of a drawer. These days he couldn't even read, he was so despondent. But then, as he idled, with time on his hands, and the bright clear light from the sea had inspired him, he delved back into the drawer and rescued the pad.

At first he started with simple things: a chair, a jug, an arrangement of flowers, even a sketch of the chambermaid when she came in to change the sheets. Later he sent out for charcoal and paper, the thick matt kind he remembered from school. And a slim tin box of watercolour paints and a bunch of sable brushes. The nursing staff were pleased with his progress; his constitution improved along with his art. Also, to his surprise, his spirits. The future no longer seemed quite as grim. He was slowly beginning to live again, not before it was time.

'Are you planning to sell them?' another patient asked.

'You have to be out of your mind,' he growled. But, nevertheless, the remark raised his spirits and made him that much more determined. Painting helped him focus his mind and expel the nightmares. In his darker moments, since he'd been discharged, his mood swings were mirrored in what he produced. It slowly began to dawn on him what a great catharsis art was.

Since he'd moved to the Metropolitan Police he hadn't had time to start painting again. Till now he had not felt the need.

Once the morning rush hour had slackened off, Brewster and Burgess came into their own, working methodically through the train, permanently on the alert. They acted as if they were ordinary passengers and kept a very low profile. Occasionally they would alter their pace and sit for a while to rest Brewster's leg and keep an eye on what was happening around them. They concentrated on the comings and goings, who got on and off at each stop. Brewster's memory was photographic; once he registered a face, he rarely forgot it. Commuters had their own regular patterns, depending on their destinations. In a couple of weeks he started to recognise people.

They began at Cannon Street, where they were based, and did the whole circuit clockwise. At the City stations it was bankers in suits, frenetically gabbling into their phones as they scurried off, always late no matter how early. Temple was barristers carrying wig-bags; Embankment the bulk of the tourist trade. The river boats and the London Eye as well as the bridge to the Festival Hall. They travelled in herds and, when they got off, the air felt that much fresher. Westminster was Parliament, which meant more tourists, including the ones en route to the Abbey. St James's Park was the passport office, where students and all sorts of backpackers swarmed, then Victoria – one of the main-line stations – where the carriages filled up again. Sloane Square was shoppers and ladies in hats, with their braying voices and silly laughs. Brewster winced; more than anyone else, he loathed well-bred women like that. It took him back to his early days as a hoodlum from the north.

At Gloucester Road a busker got on, methodically working his

23

way through the train, expertly playing guitar Bruce Springsteen-style. He glanced at the cops, who gave nothing away. Brewster stopped himself just in time from flicking a coin in his cap. These days buskers were becoming a menace, Romanian gypsies the worst of the lot. Kids as young as eight or less with instruments they couldn't play. In his uniform days he would caution them but they took little notice. Begging, for them, was a way of life; he had learned to turn a blind eye. This guy, however, was the real McCoy, with a soaring talent that startled Brewster and took him back to the days of his youth when he'd played in a student band. This guy had a story he'd like to hear; he was sorry to see him move on.

At the end of the carriage sat a grave young man, impeccably dressed in a business suit, apparently reading the *Financial Times* but never once turning the pages. Brewster watched him and wondered where he was heading at this time of day. He looked a typical City type yet had stayed on through all the obvious stations. It seemed an odd time to be going home. At least he didn't have a backpack.

South Kensington was museum traffic; masses more shoppers at High Street Ken. By now both partners were feeling peckish so they'd take a break at Notting Hill Gate. This was already their second time round this morning.

It was sobering to think that, among all these masses, someone was out there playing dangerous games with a knife.

When he saw the damage the train had done, Brewster had almost thrown up. Death was one thing, but mutilation . . . the mental image of Finch exploding triggered the images in his head and brought the nightmares back. Yet by the time she fell under the wheels, the bank cashier was almost certainly dead.

Someone had knifed her so hard in the back, it had pushed her under the train. The killer had taken a terrible risk of being caught on closed-circuit TV but, as it was, the cameras had failed to record it. All that showed up on the grainy footage was a moving mass of people packed tight and the sudden confusion as the train pulled in.

Brewster wondered who would take such a risk when a back-street stabbing would have done the job. Surely only a certified madman would chance it. They had brought in the people closest to her, her boyfriend and colleagues at the bank, then let them go because they had alibis. Kimberley Martin was just a statistic. He filed the interviews away.

5

Dancing was in Imogen's blood. Both her parents had been on the stage; it was how they had first met. Beth had not wanted her to turn professional, had herself given it up at roughly that age and taken the far more sensible step of learning to cook for a living. But in matters like that her ex, Gus Hardy, invariably prevailed. His daughter, he said, was born to dance, with her mother's height and his own agility. Although, these days, he stayed mainly on the coast, he kept in touch and watched Imogen's progress with pride. From a gawky child she had grown into a woman, slimmer than Beth and more finely boned, with glossy dark hair and those great trusting eyes that came from her father's genes. Gus was right to be proud of his daughter; they both were. And the marital split seemed not to have damaged her at all.

She got on brilliantly with Duncan too, a secret relief to Beth. His knack with animals included kids; he had guided Imogen through her teen years as if she were his own. Beth's sole regret, which she kept to herself, was that she'd not managed a baby with him. Her childbearing years had been almost over by the time they had first got together. Imogen, though, was an absolute joy. Beth loved it that Imogen still lived at home, dreaded the time, which could not be far off, when she finally spread her wings and flew the nest.

The journey to the National Theatre could not have been more straightforward. Imogen took the Tube to Embankment then walked across Hungerford Bridge. The sun was brilliant, though starting to sink as she elbowed her way through the rush hour crowds. Her mobile rang; Alice at last, finally returning her call.

'I'm on the train,' said Alice primly, at which they both shrieked with mirth. The silly cliché had become their code. Thank God for friends who were on your wavelength. No need to mention the quaking nerves; they had been together since infanthood. Alice always understood these things.

Imogen gradually slackened her pace, her phone still pressed to her ear. Every few yards along the river live acts performed for the strolling crowds, part of the free street the-atre of the South Bank. There were acrobats and performance artists, doing all manner of dangerous things. If it weren't for the fact she was due on stage, she'd be strongly tempted to hang around. She loved the ambience of the place, especially in summer.

Posed on a box beneath the trees a living statue was doing his thing, bronzed all over and eerily still, even his eyeballs unmoving. Unlike the angel and the painted clown, this one wore very male attire, with boots and breeches and gauntleted gloves like an old-fashioned aviator. Imogen paused to look at him, finding the blank eyes disconcerting. He could have been genuinely made out of bronze, showed no sign even of breathing. She looked at him and he looked back. Something about that unwavering stare unnerved her. There were mimes in most of the tourist spots; she saw them whenever she travelled abroad. Clever, maybe, and often inventive, but still decidedly creepy.

'I'd best get on,' she said to Alice, having lost her desire for an intimate chat. 'The curtain goes up in less than an hour and I've still got my make-up to do.'

They made a date for later that week; then Imogen, still experiencing a thrill, proudly walked through the doors of the National Theatre.

Margaret retraced her tracks to Victoria, keen now to catch her train and be gone. She had bought her wools and another canvas that should keep her occupied into the winter or, at the very least, for another few months. The Arts and Crafts exhibition had been lovely, providing inspiration for things she might do. Room by room, she was sprucing up the house; it kept her busy and stopped the endless brooding. She'd converted Jack's den into her sewing room and often went up there in the afternoon for a long luxurious read. Her love of books had proved a great solace and helped fill in the empty hours. She glanced round at her fellow travellers. Whereas once they would have been reading papers, now it was paperback books. Due, no doubt, to the cramped conditions but excellent for the book trade.

It was also hot; she dabbed at her neck, relieved to be leaving town. A few hours in this stifling city was as much as she could endure these days, though she also found herself energised by the crowds. She had always been the active one, while Jack had preferred to potter at home. It was quite an event when she got him to come into London. The familiar misery rose in her throat. His death had been dreadfully sudden. Just as they'd faced their golden years he was gone.

A blind man and his dog got on; she contemplated giving up her seat but a young man in a dark City suit beat her to it. She watched as the blind man carefully settled, wondering how he could manage on his own. There were all kinds of loneliness in the world, something she'd never thought of. He was rather striking, tall and well built with an interesting face and sensitive mouth. He wore black glasses with opaque lenses; the dog was an Alsatian. She stooped to pat it and it licked her hand. Jack would have liked a dog but had been asthmatic.

Alice and Julie met for a pizza at the Pheasantry, where they could sit outside. It was almost July and the days were long though by this time pleasantly cooler. Julie was late, which was nothing new, held up, she said, by an editorial crisis. She enjoyed her job, as Alice did hers, had her sights fixed firmly on one day having her own column. She was wearing one of her very short skirts with wedge-heeled sandals that tied with bows. Her hair was artfully waxed into spikes which gave her the look of a cockatoo. She was pretty, in a rather offbeat way, though inclined to spoil the effect by being too abrasive. Alice admired her sardonic wit but knew that others found her hard to take. She drank too much and was then inclined to get vicious.

Imogen at first hadn't warmed to her at all, jealous, perhaps, of the two girls' closeness since Alice had always been her own best friend. Lately, however, she was coming round and starting to find her tremendous fun. Julie was fearless and often outrageous whereas Alice, even at the best of times, could be prim.

'Hiya!' said Julie, flopping down and instantly lighting up, another habit that Alice's friends couldn't stand. Alice ordered a tuna salad, Julie her favourite American Hot. With a bottle of house red and two glasses of water.

'How are things?' Julie wanted to know and Alice filled her in on the state of the book trade. Sales were poor and increasingly sluggish; the supermarkets threatened to close the independents down. She might even end up losing her job but books were where her heart had always been set. One day she was hoping to write herself but was far too modest ever to let Julie know that.

Julie asked how Imogen was and Alice said they had spoken an hour ago. 'She works terribly hard,' she said with pride. 'Eight performances every week, plus daily rehearsals and having to keep herself fit.'

'But she doesn't work in the mornings,' said Julie, who would herself have occasionally liked to sleep in. She was a party girl who stayed out late and drank far more than was good for her. And the writing part of the job could be very exacting. She made it look easy by knocking things off but rarely mentioned the research that lay behind it.

She was slightly in awe of Alice's friend, with her supple body and stunning looks and the type of skin that is just as good without make-up. Since Imogen was dancing almost every night, Julie had not really got to know her. But she liked what she saw and envied Imogen's talent. She had seen the show a couple of times and hoped to do so again, but felt awkward even suggesting it in case Alice felt she was pushy.

Alice, however, could read her thoughts and was touched by Julie's sensitivity. 'I'm seeing her later this week,' she said. 'If you'd care to tag along.'

They finished their meal and then drifted home through the lustrous foliage of Chelsea. They would probably watch a DVD and open another bottle of wine. It was great to be single and independent in the summer of 2005.

It was almost eight when Celeste got home, having taken a detour through Selfridges, not that she needed any new clothes or, indeed, had anywhere to wear them. The house was silent as she opened the door; all she could hear was the grandfather clock and the distant thrum of the fridge motor ticking over. The air was stale, the windows all shut, and the scent of decay and yesterday's lamb hung heavily in the air. She carried her packages through to the kitchen and switched on the kettle for a cup of tea. There was vodka chilling in the freezer drawer but the later she started on that, the better. She would eat her palm hearts and beetroot salad and check what was on TV.

He was out as usual; his door was closed but she knew he wasn't there from the absolute stillness. Over the years she'd become adept at picking up on the slightest sound. Even his breathing at times could drive her crazy. She'd been blessed with looks that might have made her fortune but instead served only as a magnet to fools who believed that happiness lay in superficial perfection. If they knew what she did, they'd think twice before wasting their money.

She changed out of her working clothes and into her ancient

kaftan. There was nothing but *Big Brother* to watch and that she could easily do without. With a sigh, she collected the bottle from the freezer and took it upstairs for an early night. With luck, she wouldn't even hear him when he came home.

6

The boat was breezy but Ellie kept quiet. It was better than having to walk all day and she found its gliding progress oddly soothing. It was fully packed, with every seat taken, so she dared not leave hers for even a second for fear of having it snatched. Wilbur, as usual, was striding around, taking endless photos that no one would look at but might prove a conversational topic back home. She watched him as he stood at the prow, the breeze from the water ruffling his hair, a fine-looking man though sixty pounds overweight. His military bearing belied his true status, glued to a desk for most of his life, running the business inherited from his forebears. Nothing glamorous about fertiliser except that it had kept them in style for most of the thirty-eight years they had been married. He had always thrown his weight about, the more so now he was retired. His booming baritone competed with the commentary that she, for one, was straining to hear. Had he been nearer she'd have asked him to shush but, for once, he was keeping his distance, enabling her to pretend she was travelling alone.

The couple beside her had brought their lunch. 'Bit breezy today,' said the woman.

'Indeed,' said Ellie, producing a scarf and wrapping it tightly round her ears to keep them from dropping off. The boat was heading for Canary Wharf and then on to Greenwich where the *Cutty Sark* was moored. After that they would catch the next one back, all the way down to Hampton Court for Ellie to get a glimpse of the palace, though they'd have to move pretty sharpish. Another day without proper sustenance; she wished she had also thought of bringing a picnic. The man went down to the bar for drinks and offered to bring Ellie something back. They thought she was on her own. Would that she was.

'Thanks, but no,' she said with a smile. 'My husband will fetch me something later.' He was leaning comfortably on the rail, chatting away to a couple of men, clearly throwing his weight around, oblivious of her needs. With an audience he'd be happy for hours. She decided to move inside, away from the breeze. She pointed him out to the friendly woman and asked her to kindly let him know where she'd gone. She might have told him herself but couldn't be bothered.

'Men,' said the woman, with a complicit smile.

'Indeed,' said Ellie as she left.

The downstairs lounge was hazy with smoke but at least she was out of the wind. And now could easily hear the commentary. She settled in a corner and loosened her scarf; what she'd really like was a cup of tea but the fifty storeys of Canary Wharf were fast bearing down upon them. Time to move; Wilbur was beckoning, having finally noticed her absence. No peace for the wicked. She rose to her feet and wearily went to join him.

Julie, for once, was in on time since she had a very tight copy date and prided herself on always meeting deadlines. As she rode the long escalator up to her floor, her mind was buzzing with feature ideas. Her copy was due in at noon and she still hadn't thought of an angle. Cautious Alice, who was conscientious, admired this devil-may-care attitude; one of the reasons she so much liked sharing with Julie.

'I'd never have the courage,' she said, 'having always been such a tedious swot. At school I did my weekend homework on Fridays.'

'That's what it's all about,' explained Julie. 'Living on the edge.' She needed the last-minute panic to make it work. It was one of the reasons she was so good, the constant ability to think on her feet. She relied on her fertile and active brain to get her through any crisis. It was ten by the time she had sorted her mail. Two hours till deadline; well, she'd been in tighter spots. She walked to the window and gazed out at the church, desperately seeking inspiration.

'If you've nothing better to do with your time,' said Rupert Lascelles, the theatre critic, 'you might care to help me out with a spot of research.'

Julie gave him her slant-eyed look. She wasn't a bloody researcher. Nor, for that matter, was she part of his team.

'Don't worry,' said Rupert, who knew her well. 'I'll see that you get a proper credit.' Money, too; there'd be cash in hand. Julie, he knew from experience, drove a hard bargain. He dumped a pile of buff folders on her desk. 'It's part of a series I'm working on for Hallmark. With luck, there will also be a tie-in book.'

Julie liked Rupert, who was caustic but brilliant and whose savage one-liners made her laugh. 'Deal,' she said, 'on one condition. Give me a subject for a fast four-hundred-word filler.'

'Ladies' fashions at Wimbledon this week? What the Williams sisters are wearing. Or else the Live8 concert in Hyde Park. There has to be some sort of hidden agenda. Those guys can't be that altruistic.'

'Wicked!' said Julie. How naff could one be, but celebrity pieces never failed. And Venus was tipped to win the championship again. Four hundred words on how cool she was would beautifully fill the slot.

The shop stayed open till half past nine, though Beth only rarely stayed there that late, an advantage of being the boss, she was fond of saying. Her team was efficient and able to cope. There were far fewer people around at that hour, mainly locals buying their supper or office workers in search of something to eat. The grazing room did a fairly brisk trade which also boosted regular sales as customers often then bought food to take home. The shop specialised in cheeses and charcuterie, own-baked breads and patisserie as well as superior wines and homemade truffles.

Tonight, however, would be an exception. Beth had stayed late in order to audit the books. At this time of year, when the pressure was off, she always did an in-depth stocktaking, making lists of things to cancel or replace. She liked this chore, even though it took hours, since it gave her a sense of how well they were doing. She had built the business from scratch and was making it work. On nights like this, when she got home really late, the last thing she wanted was to have to cook, so they almost always ate out.

It was hot when she finally wound down the shutters and the street still thronged with people. Summer in London in weather like this was almost like being in Paris or Rome. There were café tables out on the pavements and packs of young people round the pubs. She stopped to buy some cut-price flowers for the house.

She considered waiting for the 27 bus, then decided it would take too long. She needed to get home by the fastest route. They would drink outside on the patio tonight and book a table for after ten. As she wandered towards Baker Street, she dreamily savoured what she would eat, the special pasta at Assaggi or seafood at Kensington Place. Life with Duncan was a lasting delight because they had so many tastes in common. And never ever were short of things to discuss.

There were people milling around at the station, more than usual at this time of night. Beth heaved an utterly weary sigh; the last thing she needed when she was so tired was another bloody hold-up. She reached the turnstiles, travel card ready, but before she got there she saw the board. Long delays due to an incident, it read. The service was suspended.

Another horrible death, it turned out, only five days after the last one.

7

This time the murder was not at rush hour but at 8.47, when things were much quieter, before the theatre and restaurant crowds came out. Another young woman, again stabbed to death. She'd been standing alone on Baker Street station, presumably waiting for a Circle Line train; pretty and stylish, perhaps in her thirties, chatting cheerfully on her phone, just like the previous victim, Kimberley Martin. Several passengers claimed to have seen her, though none had been witness to the actual attack which must have occurred straight after the train she hadn't got on had pulled out. Brewster and Burgess arrived at the crime scene five minutes after they got the call. This time they were official, not undercover.

There was quite a lot of blood on the platform but, since the body was not on the track, the transport police had just taped off the area and temporarily closed the station. The body lay spread-eagled face down, the knife protruding from the small of her back.

'Did you check the cameras?' was Brewster's first question. Temporarily out of action, he was told.

Goddammit! He instantly lost his rag. He loathed such plodding incompetence. Did none of this crappy system ever work? What was the point of closed-circuit TV unless it bloody well functioned? he asked. The station official shrugged. These things happen.

The victim was slim and in very good shape; her phone was lying beside her. Brewster bagged it and handed it over. A police technician would rush it to the lab.

'Have you looked in her handbag?'

Not yet, he was told. They'd been waiting for Brewster to give the instruction. He slid on a pair of latex gloves and carefully opened the snakeskin bag: Chanel, he noted; presumably well off. He'd expected it to be empty. Her wallet, however, appeared untouched, and contained a hundred pounds in cash as well as a row of credit cards, one of them gold.

'Check her out,' he said to the team then followed Burgess back to the scene of the murder.

Mary Ellen Goddard (Meg to her friends) was a City banker from New York. She had worked in London for the past two years and rented a flat in the Bayswater Road, to which she had been returning when she was killed. She was on the phone to her boyfriend at the time, letting him know she was running late. He had started cooking when he took the call, and was now being treated for shock.

'What was the likely motivation?' Nothing appeared to have gone from her bag and she still had her Rolex watch and a pair of pearl earrings. She even carried her passport: not very wise.

Whatever the motive, she'd been struck so hard the blade

had severed her spinal cord. This was more than just a bungled mugging. It could be that she was followed from the bank, which was situated in Liverpool Street. So what was she doing at Baker Street, waiting for a train?

'Simple.' Brewster now knew his stuff, having done a crash course on the Circle Line. 'The train she didn't get on was Hammersmith bound.'

Which threw no light on who might have wanted to kill her. He made arrangements to talk to her boss and also the grief-stricken boyfriend, once he was up to it. Both knife and phone were now with forensics, though Brewster wasn't expecting much. The only prints they could ever match were those they already had on file and, so far, no modus operandi was apparent.

Brewster had digs in Meadow Road, a row of small houses by a council estate, close to the Oval cricket ground, handy for those rare occasions when he could snatch a few hours off. For the sake of convenience, since they worked as a team, Burgess was currently staying there too, which made things that much simpler. There was a park close by where they liked to stroll; stretching his legs helped to ease Brewster's pain and also focus his mind. There were kids on swings living normal lives; he would stand and watch them enjoying themselves and wonder where his own life went wrong and why his personal relationships didn't work out.

He had never been attracted to family life though realised now he'd have liked a son, one he could teach to bowl a googly or play guitar as well as Eric Clapton. One he'd have definitely headed off from getting involved with the police. Brewster's father had been a miner, granite-jawed and emotionally stunted, who had disapproved of his only son's progression to the SAS.

A waste of an education, was his view, an adult version of cops and robbers that would doubtless one day result in his premature death. But Brewster had never been much of a student, had veered towards cricket and playing the blues. His move into the SAS had been mainly a gesture of puerile rebellion.

But the active life had suited him; the danger had kept him on his toes. It had taken him all over the world where he'd picked up an alternative education; fluent Arabic and firearms training as well as surveillance work. A career that offered a constant challenge but had not equipped him for civilian life. At forty-two, his time was almost up. He had no idea what he'd do if forced to retire.

Nor was there anyone to share his life. He had made a point of travelling light, keeping himself emotionally free, perhaps the only way he could handle the job. In his youth he had played the field, yet always remained uncommitted. There were times he longed for a kindred spirit with whom to share his most intimate thoughts, his hopes and aspirations. Finch had been more than a working partner, had become his buddy and trusted friend. His death had left a hole in Brewster's life that he didn't expect to fill.

The second murder brought the nightmares back. He couldn't shake off the recurring image of that lifeless body in a pool of her own blood. The first might have been more graphically distressing but this one really drove home the point. That night he got out his easel and started to paint.

From charcoal sketches and watercolours he'd slowly progressed to using oils. Gone were the delicate well-observed touches; he found release in bold primal colours and violent images from his tortured subconscious. With a cigarette stuck in the corner of his mouth, he attacked the canvas with lethal fury in an effort to rid himself of the day's frustrations. By the time he stopped for a late-night drink, a hefty whisky to help him sleep, the band of tension inside his head was easing.

Two similar murders within a few days, both at stations on the Circle Line, with no attempt made to cover up the crime, at either end of the day. Both victims female and working for banks, though from entirely different backgrounds, east London and New York. Both in steady relationships. Both the boyfriends with alibis. Both struck in the back with considerable force by expensive finely honed knives. Both talking on their mobile phones at the time of the attack.

Two in five days might be bad enough but what they needed, to establish a pattern, was a third.

8

He was all fired up by the third time he killed. His palms were clammy, his heart rate fast. He had caught her so totally unawares, she hadn't had time to scream. He had chosen the knife with obsessive care, testing the blades till his fingers were bloodied. When he struck and felt it slide in, his reaction was almost orgasmic. At last he understood about life, was belatedly achieving his manhood.

He stayed around while they called the police; had nothing to fear having fixed the cameras before striking. There was only a dribble of people about, all intent on their own affairs. It was possible to be invisible if you tried. He'd inhaled her essence as he closed in, silently on his sneakered feet. Had she caught him watching, he'd have known how to reassure her.

Her various aromas had almost unnerved him, taking him back to much happier times. The cream, the powder, the expensive cloth, the gleam of the pearls against her skin. Somewhere inside his skull a prism had shattered. His choice of prey had been fairly random; this station was one of his hunting grounds. He had spent a couple of hours in the waxworks from which he found he could learn a lot. Then walked in the park and watched the young couples at their business. So much had been denied him all his life. Now it was his turn to get a piece of the action.

He had left at speed and picked out his quarry, alone on the station platform. She looked so serene in her chic pink suit as she chatted contentedly on her phone. He hated her china-doll prettiness, knew that he must have her.

The worst part was always the journey home, especially after she'd stayed on for drinks or someone had persuaded her out for a meal. Stage-door johnnies, her mother called them, referring back to her own misspent youth, but Imogen only ever went out with people she already knew. Though she certainly had no shortage of invitations.

Since childhood she'd had it drummed into her never to take stupid risks or talk to strangers. Duncan had made her promise to call if she ever found herself stranded and in need of a lift. He could be there in twenty minutes, he said, since traffic at that hour was negligible. But Imogen felt that to call him would be wimpish, proof that she wasn't yet ready to live on her own. She loved being part of her mother's ménage but should soon be thinking of moving on. Alice and Julie seemed to have so much fun she was vaguely considering sharing with them. Alice had been suggesting it for some time. She was twenty-two, with her life before her. When the show closed, she'd have to sort something out.

Now, however, at the height of summer, it was worth the

journey to get home to Notting Hill. The house was spacious, she had a whole floor and few house rules to abide by. No noise after midnight was the paramount one. If she wanted company later than that, she just had to keep it down. No one she knew had parents like hers which was why she had little incentive to leave. But dancing at the National Theatre was widening her horizons.

The final curtain was at 10.35 and it took her at least twenty minutes to sort herself out. There were usually backstage visitors around which meant that, even if they weren't for her, she was often kept chatting at least for another half-hour. After that came the walk across the bridge which was usually still busy. She loved the spectacle of the river at night, with St Paul's Cathedral all lit up and the South Bank ablaze with its numerous busy venues. She had once been to Venice and liked that too but the Grand Canal was not nearly as grand as the Thames.

The last train home was at ten past twelve; Imogen usually caught it with ease. By that time most of the crowds had dispersed and only a handful of stalwarts remained, slumped in corners of carriages, often asleep. Occasionally there was a rowdy drunk but she'd grown adroit at avoiding them. The easiest way was to move to another carriage. Notting Hill felt immediately like home, the air there that much sweeter. She never felt threatened; she ran up the station steps with a lightening of heart. The streets were still busy and there was lots of traffic, and the two-minute walk home to Chepstow Villas had never bothered her at all.

Tonight she found her mother still up, with the weak excuse that they'd just got in and she'd been setting the breakfast table for the morning. She seemed relieved when Imogen arrived and gave her a long unnecessary hug.

'Mum,' said Imogen, 'I'm not a child. In five years I'll be the age you were when you had me.'

Beth simply laughed. 'Allow me,' she said, 'to worry about my baby girl if I want to.' She didn't mention the appalling newsflash, that another young woman had been stabbed to death on the Tube.

There was no one waiting up for him. When he got home in the early hours and crept up silently to his room, nothing stirred in the house. There was sometimes a light from beneath her door which probably meant she was sloshed again, but she never showed any concern for him or checked that he was all right. The first thing he needed to do was shower and rinse away the evening's excesses. He had travelled around on the Tube for hours, slowly coming down from his high.

He was still too aroused to be able to sleep so, draped in a towel, went down to plunder the fridge. She always kept it stocked with food, the very least she could do for him. There was ham and salami, half a cold chicken and a hunk of his favourite bread. He searched for the vodka but she must have got it upstairs. So he turned his attention to the well-stocked cellar and selected a bottle of finest claret, too good to squander like this but what the hell? He needed it; he was still unfulfilled as the thirst for danger grew stronger daily. She needled him with her chilly contempt. One of these days, if she didn't watch out, she was going to push him too far.

9

The shop had been Duncan's inspiration, created because he felt Beth was working too hard. It was ten years now since they'd got together but things had happened so fast it seemed far less. The catering business had been great fun but had meant her working relentless hours, which might have made sense as a single parent but not now. Wedding receptions and boardroom lunches had certainly kept the wolf from the door but divided her from her sexy new husband; not smart. Once they were married, which happened quite quickly, she never wanted him out of her sight and the trekking around and endless late nights had totally worn her out.

So, based on her tireless obsession with food, Duncan came up with his master plan. Situated in Marylebone High Street, flanked by an enclave of gourmet restaurants, the shop had become a magnet for foodies in search of ingredients they couldn't locate elsewhere. Palm hearts, pomegranates, chocolate truffles. A wide variety of cooking oils, and breads still warm and crusty from the oven. It was a feast for the senses from the moment it opened, and right up until they closed the shutters they did a very brisk trade. 'The Food Emporium.' That said it all. Word spread rapidly; the columnists gave it high marks.

At first Beth found standing all day a strain but soon got herself into shape. She and Duncan would jog round the park, rising at dawn in the summer months and still creeping out when the winter mornings closed in. Hyde Park was only a stone's throw away, as well as the mansions of Palace Gardens Terrace where oil sheikhs and football moguls now had their homes. They loved to wander down the gated street, towards the palace full of minor royals, then on to Kensington High Street, bustling with shoppers.

'Happy?' he'd ask as he squeezed her hand.

'Deliriously so,' she'd reply.

'Whatever happened to Vivienne?' asked Jane, still Beth's closest, most enduring friend. 'Do you keep in touch? I don't hear her mentioned these days.'

'We swap Christmas cards,' Beth said guardedly. 'And her cats are still registered with the practice.' Duncan saw her at least once a year, when her pampered darlings came in for their jabs, but no longer bothered to mention it when he did. That episode of Beth's life was closed; she wasn't proud of her out-of-wedlock liaison. But she hadn't, of course, known Vivienne then, her sole excuse for the way she'd behaved; also Duncan had not yet entered her life.

'And Georgy?'

'Occasionally. She's a loyal friend. She was here for the opening of *Anything Goes*.'

Georgy, another name from the past, these days was really more Imogen's friend. She tracked her career with genuine interest and spoilt her whenever she could. She had started off as a dancer herself before moving on to photography. These days she ran a photo gallery in the meat-packing district of New York.

'Did she ever marry?'

'Not so far,' said Beth. Georgy had carried a torch for her own ex.

'What is she – forty?'

'Younger,' said Beth. 'Mid to late thirties, and I must say she still looks great.'

A whole decade. Could it be that long? So much had happened since then to them all, yet the memories still remained fresh as well as painful. Beth felt she was now a different person; older, maybe, but also much wiser. She had never been tempted, since her happy second marriage, to so much as glance at anyone else. The house, the business, her beloved daughter. She had them all, plus the man she adored. Fate had been kind to Beth; she was content.

Not so Celeste, bitter and sad, for whom just waking was an ordeal. She had spent the whole of her life in this house and in just a few years would be forty. Yet all she had to show for it were the lines of disappointment etched into her face and a mouth that was hardening into a narrow line. Once she'd been fêted for her startling looks; the photo albums downstairs bore witness to that. The child of a famous theatrical pair, Sir Edward Forrester and Esmée Morell, she had always taken it for granted she'd follow in their footsteps.

Esmée Morell was the darling of her age, undisputed queen

of the London stage. Famed for her wit and vivacity, her performances had always been sell-outs. Even at fifty, she was offered the starriest roles. Her marriage, too, was legendary; they had played together in the *Dream* at Stratford. She was well into her thirties by then but he had stopped her in her tracks.

'All it took was a single glance,' she never tired of boasting. 'God knows, by then I'd been in and out of love as regularly as the swing doors of a pub. But when dearest Teddy appeared, that was it for us both.'

He was slightly camp, which was part of his charm, and a stunningly handsome man. Tall and distinguished as a diplomat, he towered over his fragile wife who was, in reality, tough as old boots, though careful never to show it. He towered, she gushed; they were made for each other. No one else, not even their children, got so much as a look in.

Celeste no longer looked at the pictures; they were locked away to keep her from further pain. For eighteen years she had hogged the limelight until, without warning, the music had stopped. It was over, though the world never knew what had happened. People had offered her money to talk but she maintained a resolute silence. Those days were dead, which was no bad thing. The older she grew, the more she saw how warped her childhood had been and how corrosive. There were still some questions that needed answers but she'd put it all in the past. They'd imprisoned her in a living tomb from which she would never get out.

Rupert's idea for a TV series was hardly revolutionary but the faded cuttings he had thrown together immediately had Julie hooked. *Theatrical Legends* was the working title, to be aimed at a mass television audience, primarily in the States. He'd included a handful of obvious names – Valentino, James Dean and Garbo – along with a handful less well known whom Julie had not even heard of. Her role as researcher was to flesh out their lives and try to fill in any gaps. This was the sort of project she loved, which could prove more fun than her regular work. The gossip angle attracted her and a TV credit would look good on her CV.

Tonight she had brought the folders home since the office was not conducive to much concentration. She lay in bed and flicked through the contents, instantly absorbed. The more she read, the more involved she became. She knew little about the London theatre, having grown up in a celluloid age, and her Yorkshire childhood had not included culture. Actors, to her, meant movie stars; she had never even seen a Shakespeare play. But *Theatrical Legends* had caught her fancy; starting with Sarah Bernhardt, she was hooked.

It was almost like a detective series; some of the cases were particularly intriguing. It amazed her how many big stars simply dropped out of sight. Lauren Bacall was occasionally in the news but Gloria Grahame had faded right out and spent her final days in a Liverpool slum.

'Who on earth was Esmée Morell?' she'd asked Rupert, never having encountered the name before.

'Esmée Morell and Edward Forrester were titans of their age,' he said. 'In their day as famous as the Redgraves are now.'

'So how come I've never heard of them?'

'Neither ever made a film. They were thespians in the grand old style, adored by the theatre-going public.'

'Why are they on this list?' asked Julie.

'They died within a few weeks of each other, both still at the height of their fame. For no known reason, it appears to have been hushed up. It is up to you to try to find out why.'

Her eyes grew heavy; it was time for sleep. It was ten minutes after midnight. She'd devote her weekends to the bulk of the work, which Rupert was keen to get finished fast. Tomorrow she'd draw up a list of old films and order the DVDs. She had always been a movie buff; the project was right up her street. She stuffed the cuttings back into their folders and stacked the lot on the bedside table. A monochrome photograph fluttered out and she checked the back to see who it was: a wasp-waisted beauty in a cartwheel hat covered in ostrich feathers. Nobody Julie recognised. Though the pose looked Edwardian, the date was 1979.

Esmée Morell, the caption read. *Playing the lead in Pygmalion. Opposite her husband, Edward Forrester.*

10

Kimberley Martin was from Walthamstow. Brewster went down there alone. The streets were anonymous, like his own part of town; it took him a good ten minutes to find the house. Despite the heat, all the curtains were closed; an obvious place of mourning. He felt apologetic for his intrusion. The mother showed him into the lounge; the father, who worked on the buses, had gone in to work. Her eyes were puffy and red from weeping. She offered him tea which he declined. He would not take up much of her time, he said, awkwardly patting her shoulder. It was the part of the job that he liked the least but something that had to be done.

Had Kimberley any dubious friends? The questions were purely routine. Was it possible she could have been in some sort of trouble?

No. Her mother was adamant. Kim had always been a very good girl, just promoted at work and with excellent prospects.

The interview took less than an hour; he could see he was adding to her distress. At least they had managed to keep the newshounds at bay. He scribbled some notes then left her to it, inadequate in the face of such grief. What sort of a world was this? He often wondered.

Next on his list was the banker's boss. He wasn't expecting more luck there but it should be less distressing. Brewster sighed as he walked to the car. He hated the suffering of innocent people. On occasions like this he could wish himself back in the battle-zones of Iraq.

As he drove through the grimy congested streets, he contemplated the teeming masses that make up the colourful sprawl of London's East End, sanctuary to all kinds of refugees who, over the centuries, learned to live together, respecting each other's beliefs and embracing their cultures. Only a very few dissidents, fired by prejudice or warped beliefs, occasionally rocked the boat with violent behaviour. There were eight million people in Greater London, considerably swelled at this time of year by tourists. And among those masses was a frenzied killer who'd committed two murders in less than a week.

Back at his easel later that night, Brewster ran through in his mind where they'd got so far. Two nasty murders, five days apart, both young women talking on their phones. Both, as it happened, working for banks. Both on the Circle Line. There had been a report of an accidental death, again a woman in the rush hour crowd. Although there had been no suggestion of murder, it fitted the same MO. She too had been using her phone. Could there be some connection?

The painting he'd started was rapidly growing as he slashed and stabbed at the canvas. He had chosen colours that were garish and bright, in some places harsh on the eye. They helped release a force within him that assuaged the anger in his soul. Red for blood and the carnage on the track; purple and indigo for violent death. Even the evenings were growing shorter as the summer seeped away. Scarlet and black for Finch's head as the booby trap blew him to smithereens.

A final whisky before he turned in. Nevertheless, he would probably not sleep.

11

Much to Margaret's irritation, the colours were not precisely right. The dyes were obviously from a different batch. It would mean another trek into town, the last thing she really wanted to do. The garden needed her full attention; it was her memorial to Jack. But the work on the den was almost complete; all that remained to be done was that dratted last cushion. The weather was glorious so she'd give herself a treat and turn the chore into a proper day out. She checked the listings to see what was on and decided the time had come to visit the Globe. She had read a lot about what they had done. Today, while there wasn't a cloud in the sky, seemed ideal for watching an open-air performance. She booked a ticket for the matinée – *The Winter's Tale*, a play she didn't know. It was scheduled to end around twenty to five which meant she could comfortably catch her train home before the worst of the evening rush hour started. She thought about asking a friend along but could think of no one likely to be free whose company she could bear for so many hours. Haywards Heath was nice enough but hardly overflowing with kindred spirits. She had lost her dearest friend when her husband died.

To fit in the wool shop before the show she would have to start making tracks right away. She picked out a neat linen lavender two-piece that Jack had always particularly liked, and a pair of sensible flat-heeled shoes for a leisurely stroll along the river. Her spirits had risen by the time she set off. She was suddenly looking forward to the jaunt.

It was the Diefenbakers' last day in London; they still had lots to fit in. Ellie felt quite wrung out after Hampton Court. Though dying for a chance to look at the shops, she had meekly followed where Wilbur led; had looked at enough old buildings to last a lifetime. Today they were heading to Parliament Square and, after that, on to County Hall to see the aquarium and ride on the London Eye. Ellie, who had no head for heights, would sooner remain on terra firma but knew from experience that Wilbur would simply not listen. They only ever did what he wanted. She had given up arguing long ago.

So 'Yes, dear' she murmured, praying for rain. Treacherous, maybe, but at least it might get her to Harrods.

But the sun blazed forth and the tourists swarmed. He made her walk across Westminster Bridge after they'd had a whistle-stop tour of the Abbey. She was only grateful that Parliament wasn't in session. By the time they arrived at County Hall, Ellie was virtually dropping. She would kill for a coffee and a nice sit down but Wilbur was striding in front, as always, and before she knew it they were passing through the turnstile.

The aquarium was impressive, she couldn't deny it, though

she'd never really had much time for fish except when served with hollandaise sauce and some lovely crispy French fries. Which reminded her how hungry she was; they'd been at it all morning, with no time for lunch, and it would, when they'd done the Eye, be well after four.

'Come along,' said Wilbur briskly. 'Don't start flagging now. There'll be time enough for napping on Eurostar.'

The new Globe Theatre was fabulous, an exact reconstruction of how it had been when Shakespeare was alive. Since the actual performance didn't start till two, Margaret went round the exhibition to get her into a suitable mood for the play. She was glad she had come. The weather was perfect, and she was feeling quite light-hearted. Her one regret was not having Jack there to share it. As students they regularly queued for the Old Vic; she'd seen numerous fine performances there, including the young Richard Burton in his heyday.

The seats were narrow and had no backs which meant she had to concentrate, though she still found it hard to understand the play. She took a break and wandered outside to eat an ice cream and look at the boats, then strolled back just in time for the second half. She liked the authentic informality, though in Shakespeare's day they'd have eaten oranges, not ice cream. Or was that Nell Gwynn? Margaret really didn't know. To her relief, the final act turned into a bit of a pantomime, with everyone singing and dancing and getting married.

Margaret, her spirits now fully restored, spilled out into the street with the rest and started retracing her steps towards Waterloo station. She lingered awhile beneath a bridge to thumb through the tables of second-hand books. This stretch of the river was reminiscent of the left bank of the Seine. Further along, close to the National Theatre, there were acrobats and high-wire artists performing bravely in front of an eddying crowd. She'd have liked to stay longer but checked her watch. She didn't want to miss her five o'clock train.

Along the river living statues posed. A clown, an angel, a Tutankhamen, all of them showing no sign of life to a quite disconcerting degree. They might be clever but they spooked her slightly. She had an urge to creep up and say boo, to check just how good their reflexes really were. At the flick of a coin, they would break the pose and make an elaborate bow. The Tutankhamen was especially good; she stopped for a moment to study him. His face was concealed by a golden mask that had a fixed expression. It was a curious way to earn a living. Why couldn't he get more regular work? Having raised two children, she did not really approve.

She longed to stop for a cup of tea, even though it meant cutting things very fine. Then she remembered that no one was waiting at home; she need not hurry back. She could stay on in town for as long as she liked and catch a later train. Her car was safely parked at the station and no one ever got mugged in Haywards Heath. But her heart wasn't in it; she had had her day out, and the gnawing grief was setting in again. She decided, after all, to call it a day.

There was much activity on the South Bank as Wilbur and Ellie shoved their way through to buy their tickets for the London Eye then join the endless queue. Wilbur, at last taking pity on her, told her to go and sit under the trees and buy herself whatever she liked from the kiosk. So she bought a coffee and a chocolate bar and settled comfortably on a bench; a minor triumph that made her feel heaps better. With the weight off her feet, her spirits rose; at last she had time to relax and look around. She loved this city, despite its size, regretted now that they had to move on. Just as she was growing acclimatised, he was whisking her off to Paris.

There was street entertainment all along the river, with a jazz band playing quite close to her. She relaxed in the sunshine and waved to Wilbur, making slow progress along the queue. Her eyelids started to droop so she closed them. She was, after all, on vacation.

Once he became aware of them, they seemed to be everywhere, solitary women of every age, wistfully searching, he felt, for something undefined. He detected a sadness in their eyes that matched the emptiness of his soul, a gnawing hunger for something he'd not yet achieved. Standing here, as he often did, he studied them as they wandered past, aimlessly, with nowhere specific to go. Since that first sharp thrill he was hungry for more, on the alert for another easy target, growing increasingly restless each time he struck. No need to stick with the young and brash. A door in his memory opened a crack and he glimpsed, for a second, the past he tried hard to suppress.

A woman in lavender paused to look, fair and pretty in a faded way, her mind clearly set on other things; in no particular hurry. She was roughly the age that *she* must have been then, the day when his world crashed around him.

A flash of sunlight, a flurry of commotion, an arc of blood, as the blade went in, that had spattered his face and matted his hair; he recalled the rusty smell. For a second he felt himself growing faint as his hands went clammy and his heartbeat quickened, but he managed to steady himself before he fell. He felt the urge coming on again, a strong compulsion that made him shake. He tensed his muscles and focused on keeping his balance. No matter what, he must not lose control. He took deep breaths till the panic attack had subsided.

Someone was watching. Ellie woke with a start and sat up quickly in case Wilbur wanted her. But there he stood, still in the queue, having only advanced about twenty yards. She waved to him gaily and he waved back. She still had that feeling of eyes upon her though when she turned to look there was no one there. A tremor of fear shuddered down her spine. She gathered her things in a bit of a hurry and went to stand beside Wilbur.

The ride was better than she had expected. The wheel seemed hardly to move at all. And there was enough room in the glassed-in pod to allow you to walk around. The panorama spread beneath them took in a large part of Greater London. The higher they went, the wider the view. Ellie, forgetting her fear of heights, squealed as she recognised places.

'Look!' she cried. 'There's Buckingham Palace.' And the Houses of Parliament close to them. And the river, winding like a silver ribbon past Canary Wharf and the Isle of Dogs and down to Hampton Court in the other direction. Wilbur took loads of photographs with his new and expensive digital camera. He'd have endless enjoyment for the rest of the year, boring them all with his picture shows.

After the apex came the slow descent, gliding smoothly down towards County Hall. As the pod moved gradually closer to the ground, the wheel continued its ceaseless motion. A couple of uniformed guards stood by to help the passengers get off.

'Here, love, give me your hand,' said one and Ellie stepped daintily on to the platform, assuming Wilbur was following right behind her. Later it wasn't quite clear how it happened; perhaps he was too engrossed with his camera, but, right at the very last moment, he stumbled and fell.

'Whoa, there,' said the uniformed official. 'Take it easy, old chap.' He tried to catch him but Wilbur was heavy. His bulk almost flattened the man.

It could have turned out to be really nasty, but one of the guards pressed the button and stopped the wheel.

'Are you all right, sir?' He tried to help but Wilbur was scrambling back to his feet, annoyed at making such a fool of himself in public.

'Absolutely,' he said abruptly, waving the fellow away. Leaning heavily on Ellie's shoulder he limped along the walkway to the steps then, slowly and painfully, made his way down to the ground.

He stood for a moment, testing his balance, then slowly crumpled like a building collapsing and sprawled across the footpath, unable to rise.

Margaret, passing and seeing it happen, swiftly stepped forward and offered her hand. 'I trained as a nurse,' she explained to Ellie. Then, when he failed to get back on his feet, she advised him to lie there and not try to move. 'Wait while I summon the ambulance people.'

It didn't look awfully good.

12

When obliged to drop out of drama school, Celeste's only option was to look for a job. She had no other training, could not even type; all that was going for her were her looks and some timeless couturier clothes. She tried to sign up with a model agency but was told she was too small for the catwalk, though they'd try to get her some advertising work. The money wasn't great but kept them alive. The outlook was fairly bleak though at least they had a substantial roof over their heads. When her parents died, they left almost nothing, had given the future little thought. Celeste's whole life was, in theory, mapped out. They just hadn't paid her RADA fees, though had luckily left the house in trust for the boy.

Esmée had been a gigantic snob which was where the bulk of the money had gone. Never saved, just frittered away on cocktail parties, designer clothes, tickets for Glyndebourne, Ascot outings and lavish house parties in the south of France.

The Tite Street house was a social hub where only the well connected were welcome. Rich or famous, preferably both; her address book bulged with illustrious names she could drop. She had passed this snobbery on to her daughter who baulked at the thought of a suitor who wasn't top drawer. At eighteen she could have had her pick; the heir to a dukedom, a baronet or two. She had turned up her nose at them all.

The shock of losing both parents at once had thrown Celeste temporarily off balance. For a while her future looked very dicey but she had no choice but to soldier on. Someone had to put food on the table; her brother, at the time, was only eight. When the advertising work fizzled out, she got a job in a department store, demonstrating sewing machines and, later, Kenwood mixers. It might not be acting but did draw a crowd; the personnel people were pleased. But she quickly grew irritated by mindless shoppers asking the same dumb questions all the time while their husbands tried to grope her. She packed it in and went back to reading the job ads.

The post of receptionist filled the bill, as much as anything could do. At least she got to wear her nice clothes and to work in a classier part of town. Her inborn snobbery had not reduced one bit. Dr Rousseau was heavily French, with elaborate Gallic good manners. He was suave and silky, as befitted his profession, and appreciated her glamorous looks. The five-storey house was split up into suites with a different surgeon on every landing, each with his own backup staff, and a general administration team on the ground floor. It was decorated in muted good taste in keeping with the fees they charged. Celeste, not given to casual small talk, was on nodding terms with the other employees, mainly women of quiet refinement doing parallel jobs. Now and again she had lunch with one but they never particularly hit it off. She couldn't help letting her attitude show, that she found such employment demeaning. But it covered the bills and got her out of the house.

Beth occasionally saw her in the street, wandering aimlessly in her lunch hour, sometimes pausing outside the shop as if thinking of venturing in. Beth resolved that, if she ever did, she would boldly introduce herself. Something about the stranger's bleakness touched and also intrigued her. Though rarely out of sorts herself, Beth recognised a tormented soul. Her clothes were classic, her jewellery minimal, she seemed never to have a hair out of place. Yet among the crowds in Marylebone High Street, she always looked totally lost. She reminded Beth vaguely of a woman she'd known with whom she had shared a traumatic experience. Vivienne Nugent, a society beauty, had had that same look of suppressed despair, despite the expensive and pampered life she led. These days they only rarely met, though once they had been good friends.

Which was why Beth was drawn to this younger woman, based on a feeling of unresolved guilt. Friendship became more precious as one grew older. And since their paths appeared destined to cross, she would take that first step and introduce herself.

The curse of beauty was underrated. Celeste saw proof of that every day. In they came, troubled and insecure, malcontents chasing a cherished dream, convinced that whatever was wrong in their lives could be fixed by a surgeon's knife. Now and then it was worth what it cost, as with the deb with the overlarge nose, hoping to be transformed by the time of her ball. But mostly they simply deluded themselves by assuming that beauty

71

was the ultimate prize. Celeste knew only too well how wrong that was. Had she been able to turn back time, these days she'd choose to be ordinary but happy. Her sensational looks had brought her only disappointment. She'd been set apart from an early age, since other girls only envied her and boys were too scared to try to chat her up. The admirers she had dismissed with scorn had gone on to marry plainer girls, while she was still on her own with no one to love her.

Nobody noticed her any more, except the occasional randy old man, and the patients who looked at her with detachment. The desolation of her private life was known to only a few. Because of her situation, she had no friends. She had many times thought of running away but the burden her parents had landed her with could not be abandoned because she had a conscience. For years she'd assumed that her prince would one day come and carry her off on his milk-white steed. That dream had long been locked away with the photos.

Julie was full of her television project which was taking increasingly more of her time. The deeper she delved, the more enthralling it became. She brought home videos and DVDs and Alice would order a takeaway while they sat up late with a bottle of wine soaking themselves in old films.

'This is loads more fun than reading,' said Alice, who usually had her nose in a book and hardly ever went to the pictures at all. 'I confess I've missed out on most of these classic movies.'

'Which is why Rupert dreamt it up. The series is aimed at people like you who don't know your Garbo from your elbow.'

When Imogen dropped in after Sunday lunch, having walked from home to stretch her legs, she was startled to find them both slumped in semi-darkness. 'What in the world are you watching?' she asked, plonking herself on the sofa beside them. She removed her sneakers to allow her toes to breathe.

'*Hangover Square*,' said Julie abstractedly, busily scribbling notes.

'Linda Darnell is on her list,' Alice explained, making room for her. The kettle was boiling; she was about to make a pot of tea.

'I've always fancied George Sanders,' said Imogen, 'though shouldn't you both be outside on a day like this?'

'You are starting to sound like your mother,' said Alice, laughing.

Out of deference to Imogen, they switched the film off and Julie produced a bottle of wine. 'Drink?' she asked, with corkscrew poised.

'Please,' said Imogen. 'I really shouldn't but, what the hell, it's Sunday.'

'Thank God for people who drink,' muttered Julie. Alice and her perpetual tea. She was secretly slightly in awe of Imogen and wanted the chance to get to know her better. Stardom thrilled her to her Yorkshire roots; she had never encountered a professional dancer before.

'I can't believe you walked all that way. Shouldn't you be relaxing at home?' Julie never took exercise at all if she could help it.

'It's part of a dancer's daily regime and walking through the park is more fun than just doing basic stretching.'

Julie told her about her project and Imogen was intrigued. She found all aspects of show business fascinating.

'Who are the people you're doing?' she asked. Julie passed her the list. Imogen skimmed it and, just like them both, stopped at the name of Esmée Morell, one she didn't know at all; odd since it was her profession.

'She's the one who interests me most,' said Julie, handing her the photographs. 'Most of the others are fairly straightforward but with her I keep drawing blanks.'

Imogen studied the pictures closely. 'She was certainly very pretty,' she said. 'I tell you what, why not come backstage and talk to some of the cast? You never know. It's a very small world.'

'Thanks,' said Julie, secretly thrilled. 'She's the one I am finding the hardest. And my deadline is creeping closer.'

'What happened to her?' asked Imogen, curious. Normally things like that were easily looked up.

'Nobody knows, which is why she's included. That's the main thrust of the series.'

'Do you have her on DVD?' asked Imogen. 'I'd really like to see her in action.'

'No,' said Julie. 'That's the crazy part. She never appeared on the screen.'

'So why is she in the series at all?'

'In her day she was a colossal stage star who seemingly vanished overnight. Nobody knows what happened.'

13

Brewster and Burgess were back on the beat, patrolling the Circle Line. The tourist invasion had reached its peak; the trains were stifling, with too many passengers sweating and swearing as tempers stretched and frayed. It was no way to travel at this time of year; even a dog would rebel.

Methodically they checked every carriage, taking the occasional break to sit and study the fluctuating crowd. Observation, Brewster knew, was vital to the surveillance process. The traffic flow at different stations was something he now understood. At the major ones, like King's Cross and Victoria, they lingered longer and were more alert. Burgess's expertise was bombs; Brewster cared more about human interaction.

As he idly watched Burgess doing his stuff, minutely examining every seat, Brewster pondered the criminal mind, specifically what might trigger the actions of a psychopathic killer. Take, for instance, a woman on her phone. Raised voices drew immediate attention though a whisper could have the same effect. Someone speaking *sotto voce* gives the impression of having something to hide. It is only human nature to want to eavesdrop.

But where to start looking, he had no idea. What they badly needed was another lead. Though it was hardly kosher to wish for another murder.

Gradually there were certain people whose faces started to strike a chord. Since most commuters keep regular hours, a pattern slowly began to form of who was travelling from A to B at what time. Not everyone would make that connection; Brewster was specially trained. Several times they encountered the busker who clearly had his own regular patch. The policeman in Brewster wondered if he had bothered to get himself a licence. He also saw several homeless people who seemed to spend the whole day on the Tube, most of them fast asleep or else heavily drugged.

They took their breaks at different stops to vary their observation points. They even occasionally rose to street level and walked for a couple of blocks.

Off duty, Brewster listened to jazz or drifted down to the local pub to sit in the corner with a couple of beers, absorbing the atmosphere. The way to know a community was to act invisible and simply listen. This pub was basic, all spit and sawdust, with excellent ale and a dartboard always in use. Women occasionally came on to him but Brewster hadn't a problem with that. A cop couldn't really stay undercover without attracting a degree of interest and his vanity, though in some ways dented, on that score remained intact. At times he ached for some human contact but was not yet ready to socialise. He came here partly for relaxation but also for basic research.

He wondered, as he so often had, what motivated a person to kill and if that something could then turn into a habit. He had many times been in the line of fire but only ever in the course of duty. The few occasions he had pulled the trigger had been strict emergencies. But that was war, for which he'd been trained. He'd been fighting for a justified cause. The solitary chancer, acting alone, was another matter entirely. This one appeared to be doing it for kicks, knowing there was an even chance he'd be caught.

Brewster studied his fellow drinkers, all of them, except him, in friendly groups. Did it take a loner to be a killer or could they ever lead ordinary lives? The Yorkshire Ripper had a wife who had sworn she knew nothing about his crimes.

Time to leave. It was getting late. His brain functioned best when he'd had sufficient sleep.

14

It was several hours later, well into rush hour. Margaret had stuck around in case she could help. Wilbur had been taken to St Thomas' Hospital, only yards away; the stretcher had arrived in minutes. She sat with Ellie in the cafeteria, awaiting the doctor's verdict. She hadn't the heart to abandon her at such a time.

'We're supposed to move on to Paris tomorrow.' Ellie was scared and unable to cope, unused to having to make decisions herself. She sipped at the coffee Margaret had bought her, twisting her handkerchief in distress.

'Wait till you hear what they have to say. It could be that he's OK after all. It was a nasty tumble but he may be no more than bruised.'

Privately, though, she was not convinced. She had seen the awkward way he had fallen and feared this might be the start of far worse to come.

'Tell me about yourself,' she said, tactfully trying to change the subject. The Diefenbakers were from the Midwest which was all she knew so far. Ellie was wearing a velvet jacket over a printed cotton dress, with a cameo brooch at her throat like a much older woman. But a paperback by Anita Shreve was peeking out of her bag, which suggested her clothes belied her taste in fiction. A pretty woman when she wasn't so fraught, with delicate bones and a clear, almost girlish, complexion.

At first she was at a loss for words. Her eyes flickered nervously round the room, awaiting the summons that never seemed to come. 'They are certainly taking their time,' she fretted. 'It doesn't look very good.'

Margaret explained about the NHS, that it had been greatly maligned. The waiting lists were incredibly long but in a matter of urgency, like this, they were able to streamline things fast. She refrained from adding that, in the States, they wouldn't have picked Wilbur up off the street until they'd seen proof that he had sufficient insurance. Nothing like that had been mentioned here. They had lifted him carefully on to the stretcher and admitted him straight away.

Gradually Ellie loosened up and ceased her endless fidgeting. Again she remembered how famished she was so Margaret went to get her a sausage roll. She was in the queue when a woman appeared, carrying a clipboard and looking for Ellie. As soon as she found her, she led her away and Margaret promised to wait. She was hungry too but would stick around until she was certain this poor lost soul was properly taken care of.

Wilbur's hip was severely fractured; they were going to have to keep him in. It seemed bizarre that a simple fall could have caused so much damage. There was nothing that Ellie could do for a while; he was under heavy sedation and the doctors were waiting to have a look at his X-rays.

'If you come back around ten,' said the nurse, 'we should be able to give you more information.'

There was a noisy bistro at Waterloo station in which Margaret had eaten several times. It was always packed with after-work drinkers, plus the early pre-theatre crowd, but the food was good and the service friendly and, very quickly, the noise level dropped as the tables began to clear. They found one in a distant corner and Margaret immediately ordered a bottle of wine.

'I think you could do with a drink,' she said, ignoring Ellie's feeble protests. The American woman was in shock and could do with a bit of a booster.

Ellie was not a habitual drinker but the Sauvignon Blanc helped to steady her nerves and the menu on the blackboard was very enticing.

'If you're really hungry,' suggested Margaret, 'you couldn't do better than the bouillabaisse.' And when Ellie didn't know what that was, she described it.

Ellie was cautious. It sounded very foreign, but she did like fish and was now completely famished. 'If you think I should,' she said cautiously, so Margaret summoned the waitress and ordered it twice. She had given up hope of that early train so, provided she didn't leave it too late, was now resigned to an evening in town in one of her favourite eateries. She topped up their glasses then settled back to try to get to know her new friend better.

*   *   *

The obvious place to start was the Internet but Julie had little success with that. There were references to the Forresters but only in listings, without any personal details. A chronology of their leading roles (they'd been especially busy in the fifties and sixties when Esmée, especially, had been the toast of both London and New York) but, frustratingly, nothing about their private lives.

'Where else can I look?' she wailed to Rupert, hating to seem such a useless wimp, ashamed at being unseated at the first fence.

'Don't ask me, duckie,' was his caustic reply, as he concentrated on today's review of last night's disastrous opening. 'What do you think I am paying you for? Now run along, dear, and stop interrupting my muse.'

He was right; she shouldn't have bothered him. In her lunch hour she slipped across to the library and immersed herself in the theatre section, hoping to be enlightened. Not much there either; just volumes of reviews with occasional mentions of Esmée in the footnotes, mainly giving only chapter and verse of roles in which she had starred. The fact that she'd married Edward Forrester was also scarcely alluded to. A veil seemed to have been drawn over both of them.

Julie returned to the *Daily Mail* and, on an impulse, phoned Imogen who, she knew, was usually home at that time. With nothing to do.

Imogen, idly painting her nails and watching a vapid Australian soap, was only too delighted to be interrupted. Julie outlined her problem and Imogen thought.

'She must have performed at the NT,' she said. 'Everyone who was anyone did so in those days. Let me talk to the folks backstage, some of whom have been there for yonks, and see what they can come up with.'

She had nothing to do till that evening's performance so would get there early and nose around. She was growing tired of being idle; it was good to have something to do.

Margaret stayed as long as she dared, then dropped Ellie back at the hospital before taking the taxi on to Victoria station. She wrote down her number before she left, wished Ellie luck and urged her to stay in touch.

'Call any time and I really mean it,' she said as she hugged her goodbye. Their meal together had been a success; she had really enjoyed their conversation once Ellie was over the initial shock and able to turn her mind to other things. With a couple of glasses of wine inside her, she'd revealed a bright and intelligent wit. When she talked about life in Chippewa Falls, a wicked glint came into her eyes. She made it sound quite a lot like Haywards Heath. Despite the fact she had lived there all her life and was therefore a fixture in the town, she confessed she'd never quite felt she fitted in. Church affairs, jam-making and such were all very well when the children were small but these days, now they had both left home, she found more and more that she needed some space. The worst thing that could have happened was her husband's retirement.

'I like to read and Wilbur does not. And now he is constantly under my feet. I don't mind admitting I miss the days when he was away at the office.'

Margaret laughed. The complaint rang bells though she'd never had any such problem with Jack. They'd had so much in common; she missed him badly.

'How long has it been?' asked Ellie softly, gently patting her hand. She could see the unnatural brightness of Margaret's eyes.

'Almost a year now,' Margaret told her, taking out a tissue and blowing her nose.

'There is nothing to beat a good marriage,' said Ellie. 'And at least you still have your children.'

Margaret pulled a face which made Ellie laugh. She told Margaret about the classes she took in renaissance history and visual arts. It meant a lot of essay writing but she managed to fit it all in.

'My husband thinks I'm quite mad,' she said. 'But as long as he gets his meals on time, he graciously allows me to do my own thing. Only in my own time, of course. Running the house comes first.'

Margaret was impressed as well as surprised that this quiet woman had such an internal life. It made her feel guilty that all she did now was loll around on the sofa and read, or listen to music and plays on Radio 4. The garden was really her only hobby; she ought to get into London more. With a friend like Ellie, with similar tastes, she would make it a regular thing.

Much as she would have loved to stay, she really had to catch that train. As it was she only just made it in time to the station.

15

The hotel desk clerk, whose name was Tom, could not have been more sympathetic. He had no problem with extending Ellie's stay and also offered to exchange their tickets and explain the situation to the travel people. There was no reason why the tickets to Paris should not be transferred to a later date.

'I assume you do have insurance,' he said but Ellie confessed that she didn't know. Wilbur always took care of details like that.

She tried not to panic. He was in safe hands and the doctors assured her that, all going well, he should make a complete recovery. She wasn't sure what to tell the family, though Monday was Independence Day and she'd have to make a call and talk to them then. She decided to play it down a bit in case one of her sons-in-law should fly over, which would be even worse than just having Wilbur to contend with. Now that she'd found a kindred spirit, Ellie was getting a whiff of freedom, which she liked.

She went to see him, in a public ward with his leg slung up on a special harness like an exhibit in the Natural History Museum. It was Saturday morning; according to their schedule they should by now have been en route to Paris. She brought him a pile of magazines though, throughout their marriage, he had never been much of a reader. He mainly just skimmed the financial news before devouring the sporting pages. A typical man, or so she privately thought.

'I've a good mind to sue,' were his opening words. 'As soon as they let me out of here, I intend to call my lawyer.'

'Yes, dear,' said Ellie in her dutiful way, only now starting to comprehend that they had her tyrannical husband a virtual prisoner. She even had to fetch him a bedpan because he wasn't allowed to move. The nurse said he would be in for at least three weeks.

After a while he told Ellie to go; he had never had much of an attention span and his wife's doleful face was starting to grate on his nerves.

'Don't just sit there,' he growled at her. 'Take advantage of the money we're wasting. There's no point hanging around in that dismal hotel.' He warned her, though, to watch her spending and to keep a careful note of everything. London was an expensive city; the much looked-forward-to trip was a total disaster.

Back in the street, having done her duty, Ellie had nothing she needed to do. The sky was clouding, and it looked like rain. The last thing she felt like was walking. She could either trek back to Waterloo or cross the bridge to the Underground. A taxi approached so she flagged it down.

'Harrods,' she told the driver.

*   *   *

He remembered little about his early childhood except that certain aspects stood out in sharp relief because of the echoing silence. The house was vast, like a mausoleum, except on the nights when the world flocked in and all the doors were flung open to welcome the guests and their hangers-on. In the two main reception rooms the rugs were removed and the floors wax-polished for the dancing, while the curtains were taken down and steam-cleaned then carefully rehung. The brass and silver were vigorously polished and the huge chandeliers sprayed with gin. An army of florists spent whole days garlanding every room.

They came in their hundreds, the great and not so good; actresses, barristers, politicians. Stars from every branch of the performing arts. Occasionally even minor royalty; she had been adept at sucking up and the hint of a title was enough to get her fawning. The fires with their scented logs were lit and myriad candles flickered. A string quartet played discreetly from above.

The children, of course, were banished upstairs but watched the proceedings from the darkened landing until an irritable nursery maid chivvied them off to bed. They saw the visitors milling beneath in their sumptuous clothes and exquisite jewellery until the moment a hush descended and the hostess made her grand entrance. She was fond of hats, even in her own home; they added some grandeur to her tiny person and accentuated the delicacy of her features. Hats and gloves were her signature note, with tightly laced boots to show off her legs. She gushed and gleamed and fluttered her fingers, smiling coquettishly at the crowd until someone encouraged her to give them a song and she took up her place at the piano.

Which was when her daughter would be summoned down and together they'd sing a cute duet, the child immaculate in virginal white with socks to match and highly polished shoes.

He would kneel and watch them doing their stuff, the candlelight gleaming on his sister's hair as she pranced and performed as outrageously as her mother. The little snob. Then all the ladies would preen and purr and crowd round them to compliment the child and clasp her to their bosoms. He never could make out what they said but it curdled his stomach every time. To this day he could not expunge the taste of his bile.

Nobody ever took notice of him; few even knew he was up there. Sooner or later the maid would find him and drag him back to his room again, this time carefully locking the door and pocketing the key. All these years later he still had that room, now entirely from his own choice. There were empty bedrooms on every floor, damp and decaying from years of disuse, but still he considered the attic his den and haven.

When they were gone, which was most of the time, the house retreated into itself and the crowd of liveried part-time servants dispersed to their other jobs. Only a skeleton staff remained while both his parents were on the road for sometimes as long as several months at a time. The reception rooms were no longer lit; the furniture was covered in dust sheets, while the brass and silver gradually lost its lustre. They lived upstairs on the top two floors with only a governess and a nursery maid to see to their daily needs and teach them their lessons.

They were both dead now, which was just as well. The images kept him awake at night but only when he remembered; he normally blocked them. He had hated them then, hated her still, yet was locked with her into a bond which there could be no breaking. This house, which had ruined all their lives, still shielded the secret that could not be told. He would go to his death before he ever revealed it.

* * *

Wilbur was right about the hotel. Their room was cramped, with an uninspiring view of the busy Cromwell Road traffic. The other guests were mainly tourists, American women in crimplene pants and uniformly white curly hair, like sheep. Mostly they only stayed a few nights, then another contingent would take their place. More Americans, Japanese; sometimes even Germans. Ellie, seated in the tiny lounge with her coffee and the morning paper, would watch their luggage trundling in and out. Lost without Wilbur barking orders, she wasn't quite sure what to do with herself now she was cut adrift. She'd completely surrendered her independence when she married him thirty-eight years ago, and although she knew money was hardly a problem, she wasn't sure how to access it. He had never allowed her a credit card of her own.

When she needed something, she had to ask; he kept tight control of the purse strings. He also insisted on keeping her passport; the only time it was ever in her hands was when they passed through immigration, after which she had to give it back. Wilbur put it down to prudence; Ellie was less sure. But here she was now, stranded in London, a sprawling city that scared her to death, separated, for the first time ever, from her over-uxorious jailer.

Harrods had virtually blown her mind, making her feel like an ant in an Eastern bazaar. So many people and so much stuff; she had wandered through ladies' fashions until her head spun. She treated herself to the luxury washroom, guilty at frittering an unnecessary pound on something that elsewhere in the store was free. But Wilbur had urged her to have a good time, so why not? She was surely worth it.

While looking for gifts to take home to the children, she found a quiet restaurant on an upper floor and paused for a sandwich and a cup of tea. She was all shopped out and had nowhere to go. She longed for someone to talk to.

'Will there be anything else?' asked the girl, hovering politely with the menu.

'A glass of white wine,' declared Ellie boldly, remembering that supper with Margaret. After which she would take a tour on an open-top bus.

16

Lucy Tucker was getting married. Her female colleagues at Lambeth Council were sending her off in style with a raucous hen night. After champagne with the boss in the office, they straggled in disorderly array along the riverside walk of the South Bank, after their ringleader, Dawn, who was walking with Lucy. Lucy, in her purple boho dress, was decked out in style in a bridal veil with a bouquet of lilies and roses in her arms. The rest of the group wore quivering antennae tipped with glittering silver balls. It was Tuesday evening and still very warm; she was taking off three days to prepare for the wedding.

They drifted along among the crowds, past the Festival Hall and National Theatre, towards the Oxo Tower where they had a reservation. All ten were well into party mood, Lucy's nuptials an ideal excuse for a rave-up. They lingered by each of the various living statues, passing comments, some of them lewd, forgetting in their fevered state that they could be overheard.

The one who all of them voted best was a shimmering Tutankhamen, as still as if he were really dead, his face concealed by a gilded mask, hands folded against his chest. The box he stood on was a cubic foot, the marvel being that he didn't even wobble.

'Wow,' said one of them. 'Look at that. See if you can get him to move.' Fall off his perch was what she meant. Dawn deftly flicked him a coin.

For a very long moment he didn't react then slowly, like an automaton, he bent at the waist in a perfect bow, hands still folded.

The girls all clapped. He was out of this world. 'Do it again,' they shrieked. How did he manage to stand so still for so long?

'Lucy,' said Gail, who had brought her camera, 'let's get a shot of you with the pharaoh. Go and cosy up to him and I'll chuck him another coin.'

Lucy, still draped in her wedding veil, minced up to him on her stacked-up shoes and coyly nestled her head against his chest.

'Kiss him!' they screamed and she turned to comply, but when she peered into his gilded mask the eyes behind it were fiercely alive and burned with malevolent hate.

She backed off like a scalded cat as a bolt of terror shot through her. 'I think it's time to move on,' was all she would say.

'What?' asked Dawn as they drifted away. But Lucy wouldn't explain.

The trendy restaurant, as always, was packed, with a celebratory ambience that completely restored Lucy's spirits. She was getting married. They checked her flowers into the cloakroom but not the huge box, done up in silver with ribbons and bells, that two of their number had valiantly lugged from the office. After they'd eaten and the dishes were cleared, more champagne was ordered. Which meant the speeches and the presentation of the microwave oven for which they had all chipped in.

'Thanks,' said Lucy, who couldn't cook. 'That's one of my problems solved.'

'So now we move on to the bedroom,' said Dawn. 'The gospel according to Jerry Hall.' A second package, this time bright red, revealed a sexy nightgown.

Three of them went to the cloakroom together and came back, after a lengthy pause, cracking up at some secret joke that it took them a while to divulge. They had seen this guy who was really neat, sitting alone at the end of the bar, film-star good-looking and dressed head to foot in black. They all craned to look but could not make him out; the area round the bar had really filled up. They amused themselves by laying bets as to which of their number would be the one to pull him.

'Not you, Lucy. You're disqualified.' The management requested they keep it down.

Sexy Leanne, the elected one, with her short tight skirt and incredible legs, glossed her lips and tousled her hair then wandered to the bar to check him out.

'Gone,' she reported on her return. No one there answering his description. Somehow, amid all their mitherings, he had managed to slip away.

Most of the group were catching buses. Dawn and Lucy and a couple of others walked together to the nearest station, Blackfriars. Lucy was heading for Monument to change at Bank for the Central Line which meant a long trek through a complex of tunnels to catch the last train home to Theydon Bois. They helped her with her packages and waved as she struggled on to the platform still decked in her bridal veil. It was well past midnight. There wasn't much time, and she still had to get through that maze of passages. Faintly squiffy from all she had drunk, with her wilting bouquet stuffed under one arm, she now regretted the stacked-up shoes and considered taking them off.

There were very few people around at that hour; the brightly lit complex was virtually deserted though she felt much safer down here than up on the street. The box was so heavy it weighed her down and, from time to time, she had to pause. Now she wished she had splurged on a taxi; she was getting married, for heaven's sake. She stuffed the nightgown into her bag and dragged the box along by its ribbons, accompanied by the irritating jingling of minuscule silver bells. As she hurried along the endless passages, she had the feeling she was not alone. She turned a couple of times to check but could see no one behind her. Only eight minutes; she doubted she'd make it. She ought to have asked him to pick her up. But that was no way to begin a marriage; she'd deliberately left her phone switched off. Start as you mean to go on, her mother had said.

At last she reached the escalator that led up to the Central Line. She balanced the flowers on top of the box and steadied it all with one hand. Still two minutes in hand; she might just make it.

There was movement behind her, she was positive now. She turned and a man had come into view, just setting foot on the escalator behind her. Lucy was gathering her things together – her handbag, the flowers and the cumbersome box – when the hem of her long boho dress got caught between two of the moving stairs. There was only a matter of yards still to go; she tugged at the fabric in panic. There were rapid footsteps behind her now; thank God, he was coming to help her.

'Thanks,' she said as she felt him close. 'All it needs is a mighty tug.'

His breath was warm on her cheek as he leaned towards her. It was only when the knife went in that Lucy realised how wrong she had been.

Her body was found by station cleaners a long time after her train had left. She was lying in a crumpled heap, the hem of her dress very badly torn, her presents and flowers strewn around her, the bridal veil soaked in her blood.

The cop who called next day at the town hall was older and handsome in a lived-in sort of way. The girls, still heavily traumatised, were summoned, one by one, to be interviewed. He walked, Dawn noticed, with a very slight limp but had intelligent eyes. He asked her to tell him exactly what had happened.

'She was fine when she left us,' said Dawn, alarmed and very much on the defensive. 'She got off the train at Monument.' The murder had occurred at Bank. The stations were part of a complex and interconnected.

'Had she been drinking?'

He had to be joking. A hen night? 'We all had,' she said. 'She was getting married on Saturday. We were giving her a send-off.'

'And she was wearing a bridal veil? And carrying a bouquet?' he asked.

He clearly didn't move in their circles. Where had he been all his life?

'Did anything you can think of happen that might have led

95

to her sudden death? Anyone else, outside your group, who might have been involved?'

Dawn shook her head. She had no idea. They were simply a group of colleagues from work who got together now and again for a drink or two and some laughs.

'She seemed very happy,' she added, somewhat lamely.

The cameras had managed to catch it this time, had recorded her struggling, first with the box and then with the hem of her skirt when it got snarled up. They were focused on her as she tried to free it, had caught the frustration on her face which turned to relief – and later terror – as she neared the escalator's end. The dark-clad figure who had followed her up at first appeared to be coming to her aid. Until he'd whipped out the bowie knife and moved so fast, all they got was a blurred impression. The technicians were working to try to sharpen the image.

'Were you aware of a stranger about?'

'No,' said Dawn. 'It was just us girls.' The guy the others had giggled about completely slipped her mind.

'Right,' said Brewster, checking his notes. 'That's all I need from you for now.' He still had another eight to get through, each as paralysed as the last, as well as the stricken bridegroom-to-be out in Essex.

'Let me know if you think of something. And, whatever you do, be careful.'

17

It was 8.51, the platform was packed and Dawn was still in a state of shock as she waited for her train at Aldgate station. What had happened to Lucy had left her reeling; the news had still not entirely sunk in though that stony-faced cop hadn't helped. He had spoken to each of the girls in turn, reducing a couple to desperate weeping. They had started the evening on such a high. It seemed that it must be the Circle Line killer who had now struck three times in less than two weeks. What had just been a newspaper item had now come gruesomely close to home. If only they hadn't left her alone with all that champagne inside her. Dawn shuddered to think that they all could have wound up dead.

It was 8.53. With luck, she would get to work in time for a natter. The rest of the group were feeling as shaky as she was. From the tunnel came a resounding explosion. Dawn was blown off her feet.

* * *

Ellie had made an early start. She still had so much to fit in. To think that Wilbur had really believed they could get to know London in a single week. The more she saw, the more she longed to stay on. She had loved going round on the open-top bus, which had shown her new areas to explore. Wilbur had seemed detached last night; irritated, even, that she was there. He was chatting to the man in the neighbouring bed; he made her feel she was intruding. So she'd only stayed a couple of minutes while she checked on his progress with the nurses. They reassured her that his hip was healing, and that he would be coming out within weeks. So, with a kiss and a girlish wave, Ellie left the hospital, feeling as though she had just been let out of school.

Monday had been Independence Day and she'd dutifully telephoned home, though she wasn't sure till the very last minute how much it was wise to reveal. Wilbur, she'd told them, had trouble with his knee and was having a medical check-up. They were all together at one daughter's house; she could hear the clatter of plates and everyone laughing.

'Is he all right, Mom?' They were screaming out greetings.

'Yes, dear,' she said. 'As soon as we get there, we'll send you a postcard from Paris.'

Today she was braving the British Museum which not been not included on Wilbur's schedule. But she wanted to see the Elgin Marbles; the story had always struck her as so romantic. Melina Mercouri. She remembered the fight and had also read Byron on the subject. She felt slight guilt at being out and about but, as Wilbur had said himself, there was little point moping around in that dreary hotel. Tom, the desk clerk, was not yet on duty but his stand-in told her the best route to take. Circle Line to King's Cross, he said, then change to the Piccadilly Line for just one station to Russell Square. She would not be able to miss the museum, which was vast.

At 8.57 she reached King's Cross. She was slightly early, but it didn't matter; she would take a leisurely stroll through Bloomsbury and look for the house where Virginia Woolf had lived. King's Cross station was in absolute chaos, with people screaming and rushing around and police making announcements over megaphones, imploring the crowd to stay calm.

'What on earth's going on?' she asked, grabbing the arm of a passing stranger whose face was bloody and clothes were all covered in soot.

'Bomb,' he said urgently, shaking her off. 'Terrible carnage underground. I'd move, if I were you, as fast as I could.'

So Ellie ran, not knowing where to, losing her handbag along the way and bumping into people in her panic. No one was interested in her; they were concentrating on getting out too for fear of another explosion underground. There was pandemonium everywhere, with sirens blaring and a huge police presence, many of them with sniffer dogs, some even carrying machine guns. It was a scene straight out of a World War Two film, with fleets of ambulances everywhere and bodies on stretchers with their faces covered up. Ellie ran as far as she could, until she was totally out of breath, then collapsed on a bench in a leafy square and wept.

9.17. Beth was running late but her staff would be there to open the shop. Though she usually tried to be first in, it was one of the perks of being boss. The train was packed, as it always was, and she glimpsed the wistful face of the beautiful stranger. How odd. If Beth was late, then she must be too. Perhaps at last they would finally speak. This train terminated at Edgware Road. She would have to change platforms and switch to the City Line—There was a colossal explosion and the train ground quickly to a shuddering halt. The lights went out; they were left in total darkness.

Beth could smell smoke in the putrid air. 'What's happened?' somebody screamed. A man at the end of the carriage reported seeing flames.

'Fire!' The word went round in a flash and people started to panic. Some of the men took off their shoes and tried to shatter the window glass; others were trying to lever open the doors.

After ten minutes, which seemed eternal, the lights came back on and there was an announcement. There had been an incident at Edgware Road and everyone must stay calm. They were going to evacuate the train as swiftly as they could. 'Leave your baggage and stay in an orderly line.' They were told to be careful walking on the track because of the live rail.

The beautiful woman, her face chalk-white, pushed her way through and clutched Beth's arm. 'Please may I come with you,' she begged. 'I think I'm about to have a panic attack.' She was certainly shaking and sweating profusely and looked on the verge of collapse.

Beth took her arm. 'Breathe deeply,' she said. 'It seems they've got everything under control. Follow me and yell if you need any help.' Thank God she was wearing trainers today, with a pair of flip-flops stuffed into her bag. She looked at the other woman's elegant shoes, obvious doubt on her face.

'Should I take them off?' The heels were high, hardly the thing for negotiating a tunnel. 'Do you think there will be another explosion? I'm feeling slightly wobbly.'

'Put your head down.' Beth tightened her grip and could feel her shaking like a frightened bird. 'We can only be a matter of yards from the station.'

Whatever it was must be very bad or they'd never have asked them to leave the train. The smell of burning was now intense; people were screaming in terror. And then Beth saw the westbound train with the front all gone and the roof blown off. There were bodies and wreckage all over the track; she tried very hard not to look. This was more serious than she had thought. She dug in her bag for her mobile phone. She had to let her colleagues know where she was. She also wanted to contact Duncan and reassure him that she was safe.

Her phone was dead. She couldn't get a signal.

'The system must be blocked,' someone said. 'This looks very much like a terrorist attack.'

Part Two

Part Two

18

The bombings had come out of the blue with no advance intelligence warning. MI5 had received no message that al-Qaeda was planning an attack. The reverse, in fact; only four weeks earlier, the intelligence level had been reduced because the threat was judged to be at its lowest since 9/11. On the very morning of the bombs, in fact, the Metropolitan Police Commissioner had gone on air to boast that London was the envy of the policing world when it came to countering terrorism.

'I am absolutely positive,' he said, 'that our ability is there.' Though, on a graver note, he added that sooner or later an attack was bound to happen. Vigilance must be of prime importance. He implored the public to stay on the alert. There were ugly forces at work in the world which was now a restive and dangerous place. Britain was, after all, no longer an island.

In less than two hours four bombers had struck, timed to

go off simultaneously, three on the Tube and one on a bus, all in the central London morning rush hour. Fifty-six were killed and seven hundred injured, with the grim expectation that these numbers would rise. There were several theories about the catalyst, the most favoured being the G8 summit where the key world leaders were currently gathered in Scotland.

Brewster, however, with his specialist knowledge, had his own ideas about motivation. The day before, on 6 July, the capital had been in festive mood at the news that it was to host the Olympic Games. The television footage from Trafalgar Square showed Londoners celebrating in time-honoured fashion and could have been all that was required to spark off the suicide bombs.

There was likely to be a second attack; Brewster had seen the pattern before and London had always been an obvious target. The financial district, within the square mile, was where they were likely to focus their fire, the area where they could do the maximum damage. Despite the ring of steel that was in place, this time they might send in a car-bomb or, even worse, a loaded petrol tanker. Brewster would have liked to take command but his walking wounded status prevented that. Besides, they told him, he'd be far more use if, on this occasion, he stayed out of the line of fire and supervised the overall surveillance.

A car dropped him back at Meadow Road; Burgess should be there already. He had been on his feet since the early dawn, was at Aldgate almost as soon as the bomb went off and had been at Scotland Yard ever since, conferring with his bosses. His leg was hurting and so was his head. What he needed now was a handful of pills, washed down by a shot of single malt to help him endeavour to sleep.

*　　*　　*

106

One thing was sure, their assignment was suspended; the Circle Line was temporarily closed. The damage at Edgware Road and King's Cross would entail much heavy-duty engineering, before which they still had the delicate task of digging out the bodies. It was slow and disheartening excavation work, much of which had to be done by hand since even the tiniest scrap of evidence had to be carefully preserved. Brewster offered his services again but was rigorously overruled. His Iraq experience could be put to better use.

So it was back to a desk in Cannon Street until they had further information, knowing the odds were that al-Qaeda would probably strike again. His file on the Circle Line murder cases was relegated to his bottom drawer while a couple of uniformed cops took over the routine investigation.

It didn't stop Brewster thinking, though, as he lay in bed attempting to sleep. The gruesome murder of Lucy Tucker was the third he had half expected. Again the victim was a pretty young woman on her own, slightly drunk which would make her an easier target. The dark-clad assailant had seemed spare and fit as he came up behind her, offering help. She had looked relieved and spoken to him. She wouldn't have known what hit her.

Because of the timing of her death, it got submerged in the coverage of the bombs. Londoners now were on full alert, which was the only good thing about it. The killer should find it harder to strike again.

19

It took Beth a while to contact Duncan, the queues for the phones were so long. And when she got through, he hadn't heard about the bombs. He had strolled across the hill with his dogs and been in surgery ever since. They only summoned him to the phone because she was obviously crying.

'What on earth's the matter?' he asked in alarm, and when she told him he said he'd be straight over to collect her.

'Don't,' she said, getting a grip on herself. 'I only wanted to let you know I'm all right. It's like a battle station here.' She glanced round the hotel lobby, strewn with survivors with blackened faces, some of them with their clothes in shreds, all of them obviously shell-shocked. 'In any case, you'd never get through.' The sound of sirens was deafening. 'All I wanted was to tell you how much I love you.'

Celeste, nearby, was watching Beth but couldn't make out what she was saying. She could see, though, that she had now lost her cool and was in a highly emotional state. This was the woman who had helped save her life by taking her firmly into her care and leading her out of that hellhole of a tunnel. Beth wiped her eyes when she finished the call and gestured helplessly to Celeste. Then smiled and stumbled across and gave her a hug.

'I am sure things will be all right,' she said. 'I just needed to let my husband know. As soon as you're up to it, let's get out of here.'

Celeste, unaccustomed to physical contact, pulled back sharply and almost lost her balance. 'Thanks, but there's no need,' she replied rather stiffly. Then, more graciously: 'I don't know how I'd have managed if you hadn't been there.'

'Nonsense,' said Beth, 'though I must admit we came very close to being blown up.' She was quick enough to catch Celeste as she fell. 'Take your time,' she said to her calmly. 'I'm going nowhere till you're OK. And then you're coming home with me.'

Outside it was raining hard. The street was blocked by the emergency services and policemen were diverting all other traffic. They were going to have to fend for themselves but at least they were both still intact.

Ellie stopped crying and looked around. The square was eerily silent. A couple of pigeons came waddling up, obviously hoping for something to eat, but she had nothing to give them; her bag was gone. She had somehow lost it in her frenzied flight, too panicked to know what she was doing. There had been an explosion, the man had said, and there might be more to follow. He had told her to leave so that's what she'd done, too terrified to first get her bearings, and now she hadn't the faintest idea where she was. She also had no money at all, nor map, guidebook or travel card. She had even lost her umbrella and now it was raining. She could not even call for help since she didn't have a phone.

All around her were wailing sirens as police cars sped by, with flashing lights but there wasn't a soul on the street apart from herself. So, since she had no idea where she was and her legs were still decidedly shaky, she decided the simplest thing to do was stay put. The rain had increased but she didn't care. Compared with what she had just been through, being soaked to the skin was the very least of her worries.

She was almost back to herself again when the air was split by the most colossal bang and a cloud of pigeons rose vertically from the trees. Another bomb and extremely near; this time there could be no doubt. Police in a passing car drew up and shouted at her to move away. It wasn't safe to stay where she was. There had been another bomb, was all they would say.

At last she encountered another pedestrian who told her a bus had blown up nearby. Round the corner from where she'd been sitting thirty people were reported dead. The transport system had been suspended. The only way to get home was walk, which was fine by Ellie since she had no money. The woman directed her to Oxford Street which was thronging with office workers doing the same.

When he finally surfaced, having slept in late, the streets were unusually deserted. For a second he wondered if it was Sunday but it wasn't. Though it had rained quite recently, the sun was bright and making the pavements steam. He slid on dark glasses and headed towards the station.

Terrorist bombs on the Tube, said the newsstands and now he saw that the station was closed. Sloane Square was virtually deserted except for the taxis. Since he had no means of discovering more, he decided to call it a day and go home. He would find out later, when she got back, details of what had occurred.

The fridge, always her preserve, was empty. Usually she shopped on a Thursday night. If he got hungry, he could get a sandwich from the Indian grocery round the corner. They were usually slightly stale but he had no choice. There wasn't a language problem there since they hardly spoke English anyway and paid no attention at all when he came in.

He drifted upstairs and, to his delight, found that for once her door wasn't locked. Which meant she must have left in a hurry; she was very seldom so careless. Though he had a duplicate key of his own, he preferred to keep that a secret from her. Knowledge was power; he had learnt that a long time ago. She had always been tidy, pathologically so, with everything neatly put away and all her bottles and jars lined up in straight rows. Tight-arsed cow. He fingered each one, unscrewing the lids to inspect the contents, occasionally spitting inside with malicious glee. She still used their mother's dressing-table set. He caressed the bristles of the silver brushes and held them against his face. They still had that faint sweet powdery smell he always associated with *her*.

He smoothed back his hair and studied his face, then massaged it gently with Crème de la Mer before perfecting his eyebrows with her tweezers. They might have been twins, people often said that, only he was ten years younger. He chose the foundation that suited him best and skilfully blended it into his skin, then fluffed it gently with her swansdown puff. A touch of colour just under each cheekbone and a thin line of kohl to

112

enhance his eyes. His lashes hardly needed mascara but still he carefully applied it.

Pleased with what he saw in the glass, he turned his attention to her closets, running light fingers along the rails of expensive designer clothes. She was still the size she had been as a girl which meant that they fitted him too. He selected one of his favourites and slipped it on. Piled in boxes on the highest shelf were the hats their mother had famously worn. He stood on a chair and moved them all down to the bed. For twenty minutes he tried each one on, posing and flirting in front of the glass, until he was satisfied with the total effect. Then, making a sweeping theatrical bow, he blew kisses to an imagined audience. *Voilà – ladies and gentlemen – Esmée Morell!*

And then he laughed – oh, how he laughed – until fat tears rolled down his face, streaking the artfully applied maquillage and ruining the illusion. He ripped off the hat in a fit of hysterics and hurled it against the wall.

Ellie was flagging by the time she reached the park, glad at least to be wearing comfortable shoes. She crossed Park Lane by the underpass, then followed the signs to the Albert Memorial which was roughly in the right direction and ought to get her home. The rain had slackened and the sun was out. Away from the traffic, her spirits revived. The truth was she hardly missed Wilbur at all, had given him scarcely a thought since the bombs went off. Safe in his sanitised hospital ward, the odds were he wouldn't even know what had happened. He had his new pals and his poker games and a band of nurses to look after him. It amazed her how fast he'd become institutionalised.

Maybe she had been wrong all these years to give in quite

so easily and allow her husband to take control of her life. It took two to make a relationship work and, despite her silent rebellion, she wondered now if she might have been hard on him too. She had married so young, had not thought things through; had only in her later years begun to regret having not completed her degree. Yet who was to say she couldn't do it now? Talking to Margaret had opened her eyes to the possibilities that still remained outside marriage. If Wilbur could find other interests, so could she.

What she'd really lacked, since the children left, was a close and compatible female friend who shared her interests and sense of humour and didn't rely only on shopping and gossip. She found her neighbours trivial and dull, with their concentration on domestic things. Few had interests beyond their families and home. The women she knew in Chippewa Falls were fine for coffee mornings at the church but entirely lacking in intellectual challenge.

Margaret Gillespie had rejuvenated her, with her caustic humour and lively wit and droll way of looking at things, despite her underlying melancholy. Within just a few hours they had talked like old friends and discovered numerous interests in common. She had also been frank about her grief. Ellie suspected she might be lonely too. With a new resolve, she quickened her pace, determined to waste no more time. Like it or not (and she did, a lot) she and Wilbur were stuck in London, so should both make the best of it in their separate ways. She didn't begrudge her husband his poker: he had always gambled a bit on the side and at least, she'd joked, it was better than other women. It was not his fault things had turned out this way and if it made things easier for him, let it be.

She, however, had new aspirations and a brand-new friendship she wanted to pursue. As soon as she reached the hotel she would make that call. It was only then, with a sickening jolt, that Ellie remembered she had lost her bag with Margaret's phone number in it.

20

The reading group simply hadn't worked out. Margaret had found the other women vapid. It was not their fault; they were pleasant enough but largely tied down with toddlers and mortgages, few of them even as much as half her age. She'd enjoyed it at first since she'd badly needed a change of scene, something to get her away from the echoing silence. They had introduced her to Margaret Atwood and later to Zadie Smith. But mainly they discussed their problems, the potty training and sleepless nights, and Margaret had finished with all that long ago. Not even being a grandmother could revive her interest in baby care. Neither of her children lived near or included her in their daily lives. Except, of course, in the run-up to Christmas or when they were in need of a babysitter.

'Don't you carry your grandchildren's pictures?' The group were appalled by her nonchalance. To them it didn't seem natural that she appeared not to want to show them off. What sort of grandmother was she?

'No,' she said, not at all embarrassed. She hadn't even done it when her own kids were small. Too much flashing of baby pictures to her smacked of shallow boastfulness. Haven't I done well, was the implication.

She stuck it out for a couple of months, then made her excuses and left. She preferred to do her reading alone and not waste valuable time on trivia. Her mothering years were long since past. Now she faced a future on her own.

Card games had never been her thing so she also eschewed the bridge club. Haywards Heath was certainly socially rich. There were coffee mornings and bric-a-brac sales as well as tennis and bowls. After Jack's death she was swamped with invitations. But as the novelty of her loss wore off, so too did the telephone calls. If she chose to keep her own company, that was all right. She knew her neighbours thought her standoffish, which worried her not a bit. She'd had a long and successful marriage in which both partners had been well matched. She missed Jack's conversation most, and that could never be replaced.

So instead she threw herself into gardening, which had previously always been his domain, finding a new enthusiasm for it. They had lived there only a couple of years but the back-breaking work was already done. What remained was principally general upkeep, which she found unexpectedly soothing. She had started browsing through gardening books and swotting up on plants she didn't know.

'Blimey!' said Graham, her older son, when he caught her weeding on hands and knees. 'If the old man could only see you now, he'd be gobsmacked.'

She laughed. Fair game, she had left it to him in order to give him an engrossing hobby. She'd been pretty sure, had she tried to pitch in, that his own commitment might wane. He had faced retirement with gritted teeth, was not temperamentally suited to taking things easy. It had been up to her to provide him with targets: she had once even got him to ice a cake. As it happened, of course, it had not lasted long. At the age of sixty-two he had suddenly died.

Now, as Margaret mowed the lawn, she remembered Ellie Diefenbaker, whose husband had had that unfortunate fall which had interrupted their trip. She felt sudden guilt; it must be a week yet she'd still not got round to phoning to check how things were. Especially since those terrible bombs. Being right in the thick if it, with her husband stuck in a hospital bed, the American woman must have been petrified.

The meal they'd shared had been a real treat once Ellie was over the initial shock and the wine had eased her tension. They had found they had quite a lot in common, including a wry and subversive humour. If it weren't for the thousands of miles between them, they were surely destined to be friends. Though she hadn't taken to the husband at all, the type of boorish bully she tried to avoid. The antithesis of everything Jack had stood for. Time was passing alarmingly fast and, at this age, it was increasingly rare to find a new kindred spirit. As soon as she'd put the mower away, she would call the hotel to check up on Ellie and see if she'd like to get together again.

On the long trek back to Notting Hill, Beth attempted to get Celeste to talk. Now was the time to find out more about the mysterious stranger. To start with, they simply discussed the bombs, which looked like being a terrorist attack although, from what they had overheard, the authorities so far had no proof it was al-Qaeda.

'Do you suppose they'll attack again?' asked Celeste, still visibly shaken. 'I certainly won't be using the Tube again.'

'Don't let the bastards get to you,' said Beth, restored to her normal spirits. 'We can't allow them to frighten us or else their tactics will have worked.'

She had lived through some pretty hair-raising things but this was no time to be bringing them up. She'd been stalked by a psychopathic killer who had almost succeeded in finishing her off. To this day she had the dent in her skull to remind her.

She talked instead about safer things, the second marriage, the Marylebone shop, the daughter who was a dancer. 'She's in the chorus of *Anything Goes*. One of these days I'm hoping we'll see her on Broadway.'

Celeste had very little to say. Their conversation flagged. Inside she was churning with bitterness and regret. This confident woman seemed to have it all, even the talented daughter. There had been a time when her mother, too, had nursed such glittering hopes.

'I trained as an actress myself,' she said.

Beth wasn't surprised. With looks like that, given any acting ability at all, she would have been a natural. She waited politely to hear the rest but Celeste had relapsed into brooding silence. It was a good five minutes before she went on.

'I got into RADA. They said I had talent.' The statement appeared to embarrass her.

'What happened?' asked Beth, with genuine interest though not wishing to pry.

Celeste gave a brittle and humourless laugh. 'Life, I suppose you could say it was. Both my parents suddenly died and there wasn't enough money to cover my fees. I had to leave in my second year and get a job.'

Beth was appalled; what a terrible thing. 'Were there no grants at that time?' she asked.

'It wasn't that simple,' Celeste said grimly, regretting having brought it up. 'Let's just say that the legacy they left has entirely blighted my life.'

21

Burgess had really come into his own, working round the clock so that sometimes Brewster hardly saw him for days on end. Because of his specialist expertise, he had been seconded to the bomb squad, sifting through the debris from the recent carnage. He was highly proficient at what he did though few would have cared to have his job. He was always the first one on the scene, fearlessly leading the way down the burned-out tunnels. It was dangerous work and he was heroic, showing no sign of reluctance or fear. It was certainly nothing that Brewster would fancy doing. When Burgess came home, he reeked of smoke, combined with a more pervasive odour that took Brewster back, with a sense of distaste, to the scene of his own booby trap. There was no disguising the smell of death, which took much sluicing to get rid of.

Brewster spent most of his time at his desk, poring over the news reports or watching endless footage from hidden cameras.

Stuff about the bombers was emerging; all four were now proved dead. Suicide bombers, trained by al-Qaeda. He watched the coverage of their final journey, four British-born Muslims from the north, one of them deeply into his faith, two of them cricket mad. Casually dressed, they all had backpacks containing bombs preset to go off at precisely the same time. They also carried credit cards and other forms of identification, hoping to claim a spurious glory after their martyrdom.

Three of the bombs had exploded as planned, killing forty people as well as the bombers, and injuring over a hundred. The fourth man, apparently having screwed up, wandered for almost an hour through the streets before climbing aboard a bus and blowing it up. Witnesses spoke of his obvious agitation; too late he appeared to have changed his mind. Four young fools seeking paradise; it was hard for a Western mind to grasp such baffling motivation.

Life was brief and increasingly precious. The stronger he grew, the more Brewster acknowledged that. For a period after he'd been blown up, he had felt all incentive to live drain away, had lain for months in a hospital bed, indifferent to his fate. There wasn't a soul in the world left to mourn him. He would die, as he'd lived, all alone. But as his wounds began to heal, so did his spirit revive. Dead was bad; it was better to live. With each new day that resolution strengthened.

Random murder was mindless and cruel and didn't discriminate. Many among the bombers' victims had been of the Muslim faith. Risking his life, as Brewster had done, was designed to preserve democracy. There were times when a tyrant force, like Iraq, must not be allowed to prevail. Murdering civilians on the Tube was every bit as criminal. Terrorists had to be caught and stamped out before they could strike again.

But suicide bombers hunted in packs. The Circle Line killer was a solo act who had claimed three lives in less than two weeks, at intervals of a few days. In his way, he was even more lethal than those who at least had their crazy beliefs to support them. No one could tell when he'd strike again. Brewster decided to disinter the file.

He talked routinely to the girls again but not one of them came up with anything new. There was no dispute over facts or times on the night of Lucy's murder. He drove all the way out to Theydon Bois, to interview the shattered bridegroom, who he'd never really thought was a likely lead. The killer was almost certainly a stranger taking advantage of Lucy's inebriated state. She had made an exhibition of herself with her bridal veil and the silver box with its trail of tinkling bells. The station was almost deserted at the time, and its passages were very well lit; her progress was easy to follow on the closed-circuit television footage.

She had liked a laugh, the fiancé said, the nice young man with his stricken face, and always got on well with the crowd at work. She'd intended to keep on working, he added, at least until they started a family. At which his voice cracked and he couldn't say anything more.

22

Imogen was just out of the shower when Beth and Celeste walked in. The rain had finally stopped and the sky was bright.

'Mum!' shrieked Imogen, wild with worry. 'I heard the news from Julie. Thank God you're safe.'

Beth embraced her then turned to Celeste. 'My baby girl,' she explained.

Imogen laughed. She might look fourteen in her towelling robe with her hair dripping wet, but was in fact a grown-up twenty-two. Tall, like her mother, but finer-boned, she had a dancer's elegant posture. Celeste regretted having mentioned her own past, would like to take some of it back. She wasn't accustomed to talking to strangers though Beth, from the first, had made her feel like a friend.

Beth cleared her daughter's breakfast dishes and stacked them efficiently in the machine, then asked Celeste if she'd like a drink. She, for one, was gasping.

She carried a bottle of wine outside and pulled up a couple of garden chairs. 'Has Duncan rung?' she asked her daughter.

'Yes, and he's on his way home.'

Imogen went upstairs to dress and Beth raised a glass to Celeste, 'I think we can honestly say we deserve this. Is there anything urgent you ought to be doing, calls you might like to make?' she asked. 'I am sure my husband will drive you there if there's anywhere you should be.'

'No,' said Celeste. There was nothing that mattered. She had called the doctor from the hotel lobby and told him she wouldn't be in. Which was fine with him since all his patients had cancelled.

'Great,' said Beth. 'Then you'll stay for lunch.' She settled back in her chair to soak up the sun.

Duncan joined them, a rugged Australian with humorous eyes and a greying beard and the sort of handshake to make a woman feel fragile. He crushed Beth in a tight embrace and nuzzled his face in her neck. Although he tried to make light of it, it was clear he had been severely rattled.

'Thank God you're all right. I was worried,' he said and Celeste was pierced by a shaft of envy when she saw the love in his eyes. This woman certainly had it all: the kid, the house, the flourishing business and now this adoring man. Yet she must, at a guess, be pushing fifty and was nothing special in the looks department except for the glow she exuded from knowing she was loved.

Beth popped inside to knock up a meal while Duncan did the honours with the wine.

Julie hadn't even started out when news of the bombings came through. A colleague had rung to check that she was all right.

She was dying to get in there and hear things first hand but the man instructed her not to move. It wasn't safe; her presence wasn't essential. Julie instantly took offence; her job was every bit as vital as his. But her colleagues in Features were being sent home. The paper had ordered a fleet of black cabs since it wasn't safe to use the Tube, much of which wasn't running anyway.

'You can write about it from home,' he said, in an effort to pacify her. 'Why not go out and get some first-hand impressions?'

Julie brightened; a good idea. If she was quick, she could get in ahead of the *Mirror*. First, however, she made herself coffee and lit her first cigarette of the day, then settled down to watch the TV coverage. Within an hour of the bombs on the Tube, a number 30 bus exploded, killing a lot more people. Julie's enthusiasm rapidly waned; the vox pop interviews could wait. She would stick around here to see what happened next.

Meanwhile, she checked that Alice was safe and practically everyone else she could think of. Beneath her brassy exterior, Julie's heart was solid gold, though she wouldn't have cared to let anyone know that. Her call woke Imogen, who hadn't yet heard and immediately worried about her mother.

'I'd better get off the line,' said Julie. 'Call me when you know.'

Now was clearly not the time to ask Imogen if she had managed to dig up anything about the mysterious and fabled Esmée Morell. She got out her folder of notes, however, and mulled them over while she listened to the news.

Duncan kept the radio on to catch what was happening on the news and find out if there had been any more explosions. Imogen had to leave by five to get to the National Theatre on time. Duncan said he would drive her whenever she wanted.

'You're not going in?' said Beth, alarmed.

'I have to. The show must go on.'

'Surely not tonight,' said Beth. 'Who in the world will venture out? I wouldn't have thought it worth them opening at all.'

'That's not for me to decide,' said Imogen, born with the theatre in her blood. She had never missed a single performance so far.

Duncan offered Celeste a lift home. It wasn't out of his way, he said. 'Unless you'd rather stay on for supper. We can even find you a bed for the night if you're nervous of being alone.'

Celeste, unused to such kindness, was touched. 'Thanks, but I have to get back.' She still had the grocery shopping to do, had left the house empty of any supplies, though the news was now saying that most shops had closed early.

'Come again soon,' said Beth as they left. 'I am really glad to have got to know you at last.'

Chelsea was only a mile or so and the roads were surprisingly empty. People must be doing as Beth had said and staying home.

'I hope they'll come to the show,' wailed Imogen, hating the thought of an empty house.

'Don't worry,' said Duncan, 'I'll stick around and check things out before I leave. And I'll come back after it's over to pick you up.'

When they saw Celeste's house they were both impressed. It was huge and imposing, in Edwardian brick, with a handsome porch that added a touch of grandeur. All the curtains were partially drawn as though they had caught it napping.

'Crikey!' said Imogen, leaping out. 'Surely you don't live here alone.' It looked as large as a small hotel and must need considerable upkeep. She'd have liked to have had a look inside but Celeste was not forthcoming.

'More or less,' she said obliquely. 'I was born here.'

Duncan went round to open her door and Celeste emerged with the poise of a model, graciously allowing him to take her hand. He walked her across to the imposing porch and waited while she searched for her key. 'Are you sure you'll be OK?' he asked and she nodded.

'Unusual woman,' he said thoughtfully, heading now towards the river. 'Out of some bygone age. She seemed unreal.'

Imogen wasn't listening, though. She was staring back at an upstairs window where she could swear she had seen a curtain twitch. Celeste had implied she lived on her own yet somebody up there had been watching.

23

Margaret never did get round to phoning Ellie; her daughter-in-law, Amy, rang requesting a favour. They had Glyndebourne tickets for Saturday night, a work thing to which they should really go. She wondered if Margaret would come and take care of the children.

'Stay the night, of course,' she said in her abrupt, slightly grudging way.

Thanks, thought Margaret grimly, though didn't say it. Still, she hadn't seen them in quite a while and, away from their parents, the children were fine. Graham would come and collect her, said Amy, but Margaret preferred to be independent. She would drive herself over in the afternoon and take the kids out somewhere local for a treat. So there went the restful weekend in the garden she had planned.

Never mind, she mustn't be selfish; they were, after all, Jack's grandchildren too. Her crusty manner belied a generous heart.

She sincerely hoped that, when her grief was less raw, she'd be able to be a proper granny again. She forgot all about poor lonely Ellie stuck, for her sins, in that dreary hotel, wondering how to get to the hospital to beg the ghastly husband for a handout.

By Sunday things appeared back to normal, except that the Tube was still closed. We Are Not Afraid, the posters proclaimed, and Londoners came out in droves to emphasise that message to al-Qaeda. Chelsea was going about its business. The restaurants had all opened again and the King's Road shops were doing their usual brisk trade. Families out for a Sunday stroll daw-dled along the riverbank or crossed the Albert Bridge to Battersea Park. It was impossible to cow the spirits of Londoners, many of whom had survived worse things than this.

In the house in Tite Street it was business as usual. Celeste was preparing the Sunday lunch. It was one tradition she insisted on maintaining. The only sounds in the cavernous rooms was the ponderous tick of the grandfather clock and the sizzle of sausages burning in the pan. She was slightly unsteady on her feet, having knocked back three sherries in quick suc-cession as she vainly tried to mash the watery potatoes. The sprouts were already overcooked. Their sulphurous smell per-vaded the whole of the house.

She had only learnt to cook by default since they could no longer afford the staff and neither cared very much about what they ate. For eighteen years they had lived this way, subsisting on an unvarying diet, abandoned by the hangers-on who had endlessly sponged off their parents. She did it all, since he offered no help, though only ever with deep resentment. Occasionally she would get out the Hoover but left the grandiose reception rooms to decay. There was no point, since they never entertained, in trying to maintain the splendour of their youth. Most of their time they spent apart, closeted separately behind closed doors in their different states of quiet desperation. What he did up there she had no idea, though she strained her ears to catch even the slightest movement. He was never up by the time she left and almost always out when she got home. They rarely sat down to eat together apart from this regular Sunday charade, a parody of normal family life.

Now, as she served the uninspiring meal, he stood there nursing a glass of claret with his customary blank stare.

What he wanted to know was what she'd been up to and who this man was who had driven her home. A big man, burly, with a greying beard, who had opened her door and helped her out then taken her arm protectively as he walked her across the street. He had watched them talking outside the house and had seen the way she'd looked up at him with a smile so luminous it knocked ten years off her age. He lost sight of them when they entered the porch but he had a graphic vision of him kissing her. The idea appalled him, almost made him want to throw up.

Minutes passed and the man reappeared, casually raising his hand in salute, returning to the car against which a pretty young girl was now leaning. His daughter, perhaps, with long dark hair and the lissom figure of a beauty queen. She was showing considerable interest in the house. It was years since he'd known her have any sort of boyfriend. Even the idea made his flesh crawl with rage. Although he detested her much of the time, she remained his only kin as well as his lifeline. His deepest fear, which he couldn't face up to, was that she would finally have had enough and walk out. He wouldn't be able to deal with that, would do whatever it took to prevent its happening.

He knew very little about her work, despite the fact he had followed her there several times. She kept that part of her life quite separate, rarely discussed it and never brought anyone home. He was jealous because she had somewhere to go, could hold down a job and earn money. He deeply resented still being dependent on her. He had lurked outside inconspicuously, a talent he'd polished to almost an art form, and watched a succession of people go in, mainly female.

So where had she suddenly found this man, with his sleek smart car and beautiful daughter who must be around his own age? Perhaps he had brought her to look at the house with a view to marrying and moving in. A ready-made family: there was certainly room. But what would they do about him? Now he wept and his tears were real. He would not allow it to happen.

He was in a mood, she could tell from his stillness and the mutinous stare as she served up the food. He was sick, she knew, of being a social recluse. This was not the way they had been brought up. Their childhood had been affluent and pampered, the house a magnificent work of art, its doors always open to the world. The world of the rich and famous, at least; the unclean masses were not included. Sir Edward Forrester and his lady did not know the meaning of democracy. They had always lived way beyond their means, in a manner they felt they owed their adoring public. The parties they gave had been legendary, the house the focal point of bohemian London.

They had shown off Celeste from the age of three. Dressed in a pretty party frock, she would be invited down to entertain the guests. She was used to being at the centre of things, knew how to smile and curtsey cutely, even sing a song when invited to. She had lived the life of a pampered princess with the whole of her life mapped out for her. With that name and those looks, there was no way she could fail.

Until the son and heir had arrived, which was when the public pageantry ceased. Since that single appearance at Drury Lane, Oberon Forrester had not been seen until his mother's funeral, eight years later.

She was in the kitchen, rinsing the plates, when she heard a great shattering of glass. She closed her eyes in apprehension; what now? He had hurled his wine glass against the mirror, the Venetian one that was worth so much. Part of her heritage too, she wanted to remind him.

Having made his point, he was smiling now. Don't tangle with me, was the message. Though unable to cope with the rest of the world, he always unerringly knew which buttons to press to upset his sister.

24

It was late on a Monday afternoon and Brewster and Burgess, for once off duty, sat in the stands at the Oval cricket ground, watching the England team warm up for the forthcoming Test Match series. Australia was fielding a formidable line-up but this year the British were optimistic, with Freddie Flintoff, their new white hope, in superlative form. It was long overdue that the Ashes came home, which today took precedence in Brewster's mind. What he cared about most was the team's maintaining its form. As the light diminished, they called it a day and the players trooped off the field. Brewster rose and stretched his legs, one still aching more than it should, automatically checking his phone for messages.

'Come on, old chap,' he said to Burgess, quietly snoozing at his side. 'Time to pack it in for the day. Tomorrow we're going to need all our wits about us.'

At which, on cue, his mobile rang: the duty officer at Cannon

Street. Brewster listened for a few terse moments. Then: 'Hold it right there,' he said. 'We're on our way.'

The woman who entered the interview room looked strained and haggard, as well she might. It was she who had found the latest body, sprawled backwards on a marble staircase, a surgical instrument dropped beside it in a spreading puddle of blood. It could be just a random killing but the sketchy details resounded in Brewster's brain. He nodded to the witness to sit, checked his recording device was on, made a note of the starting time then asked her for her details.

'Name?'

'Celeste Forrester.'

'Address?'

'Tite Street, Chelsea, SW3.'

'Age?'

'What business is that of yours?' she almost spat.

Brewster, surprised, glanced up at her and, for the first time, registered her looks. For a second he thought he might have seen her before. No matter what trauma she had just been through, there was no denying her flawless beauty or the great soulful eyes that instantly drew him in. Nor, he now noticed, the curve of disdain on her chiselled upper lip. He hesitated then left a blank. She was right; it was hardly relevant. He moved on.

'Occupation?'

'Receptionist. I work for a doctor in Wimpole Street.'

'Which was where the incident took place?'

'Correct.'

Even the memory made her cringe. For a moment she shuddered and closed her eyes, trying to blank it out.

He gave her time to compose herself while covertly stealing a closer look. Five foot four he would say, at a guess, with a perfect figure displayed at its best by the classically cut designer suit, set off by expensive pearls. Definitely class; he wondered why she'd be doing such a menial job. Fallen on hard times perhaps; no doubt a messy divorce.

He laid down his pen, leaned back in his chair and requested politely that she continue.

'No hurry,' he said. 'Please take your time. But tell me every detail you can remember.'

It was twenty to six but Celeste was still there, updating case notes the doctor needed for an early consultation the following day. She took no notice when the doorbell rang – Miranda worked until six o'clock – but when it rang again she pressed the buzzer. The doctor had already left, had a regular Monday-night session at the clinic. Celeste went on working and gave it no further thought.

After a while she paused to listen and, hearing no voices from below, decided she'd better check that all was in order.

'Hello,' she called from the first-floor landing. 'Is there anyone there?' When no one answered she went downstairs to look.

Which was when she discovered Miranda's body, sprawled backwards across the marble stairs, her throat neatly slit from ear to ear, the scalpel lying beside her. The blood was appalling, all over the stairs with splashes up the cream walls. She closed her eyes at the memory. What she recalled most vividly was the look of pure surprise on the dead woman's face.

'So what did you do?' Brewster asked.

'Screamed,' she said. And instantly called the police.

Celeste would never forget that scene, the mellow sunlight of early evening shafting between the heavy drapes to spotlight the corpse on the stairs. Miranda Perkins, who was fortyish, had worked in the practice for fifteen years. Not a friend but a long-time acquaintance, a woman of cheery disposition who chatted a lot on the phone. It made no sense, had happened so fast that the killer had slipped away without being seen.

They would have to look into the dead woman's life. Miss Forrester's too, thought Brewster.

She wasn't an easy woman to fathom, with her chilly façade and haughty eyes, though in her youth she must have been a knockout. Not that she wasn't quite ravishing now, with a timeless iconic beauty. Brewster found her hard to get out of his thoughts. As he went about his evening chores, grilling a steak while he watched the news then catching up on his paperwork to a Dizzy Gillespie CD, he ran through the interview over and over again. He went upstairs to the attic room he had set aside for his painting. He did his best thinking at this time of night with the phone switched off, a whisky beside him and a paintbrush in his hand.

The signs were all there, though did not yet add up, that this could be the work of the Circle Line killer. The viciousness of the knife attack, fuelled, he imagined, by uncontrolled rage, combined with the boldness of the choice of scene. Not the Underground, which was closed, but Wimpole Street in the middle of rush hour when shoppers and office workers were streaming home. To ring the bell and demand admittance displayed a level of reckless boldness that commanded Brewster's grudging respect. And to have left no trace behind except the

142

victim. It had none of the signs of an accident waiting to happen. It must have been planned.

No trace apart from the murder weapon, wiped clean then left at the scene of the crime. An obvious choice in a houseful of plastic surgeons.

25

Celeste hadn't slept. She was far too stressed, her head in a constant state of turmoil. The world appeared to be crashing about her ears. First the bombs and those terrible scenes she knew would stay with her for the rest of her life and now the horrible murder of poor Miranda. The bombs had been bad but the blood was worse. She was stuck with a mental image she couldn't erase.

Dr Rousseau was kindness itself and suggested she might like to take time off while she came to terms with both traumas. 'You must not blame yourself, my dear, for being the one who opened the door. The crime rate in this city goes up every day.'

Celeste was startled. She felt no guilt, just utter revulsion at what she had seen and how close she had come, once again, to destruction. It had also brought back Sunday's events and her nasty little brother's ugly tantrum. The worst thing she could imagine now was to be cooped up in that hateful house with its shady and devastating history. Had she been able, she'd have sold it long ago and moved to something smaller and modern, where she could live in comfort on her own and make some semblance of having a normal life. But her parents had left it in trust for their son. Without his consent she was powerless to act and she couldn't afford to buy a place on her own.

Instead of a break, what she needed was to talk, to clear her head and get her perspective back. Cautiously, she telephoned Beth.

'I don't suppose you are free for lunch,' she said.

They met in a restaurant convenient for them both; quiet, discreet and not crowded. Beth, who was a regular there, had booked the best table in the window and waved when Celeste walked in.

'Good to see you.' She gave her a hug. 'How are you feeling now?' Celeste, she thought, looked pallid and very strained.

Celeste said she was over the bombs and filled Beth in on the murder instead. Beth was appalled; she'd read nothing about it in the papers. She listened in silence to the horrifying story, watching Celeste's composure crack.

'She wasn't exactly a friend,' she said. 'I didn't really know her that well. But we'd worked together for a number of years and to come across her like that on the stairs . . . ' Her eyes welled up with impromptu tears. Beth took hold of her hand. 'The worst part is, it was I who let him in. The murderer, I mean. Someone rang from downstairs so I pressed the buzzer.'

You could have been the victim, thought Beth but had the

sense not to say it. The scenario was quite grim enough as it was.

'So what happens now?' she asked Celeste. 'I assume the police have been on to you.'

'They have,' said Celeste, abruptly back on her guard. 'They hauled me in first thing this morning to answer the usual routine questions. There wasn't a lot I could tell them, though. Let's hope that's the end of the matter.'

She is holding something back, thought Beth, who was far too canny to probe. Sooner or later she would spill the beans, which was doubtless what this lunch was about. She indicated to the waitress that they were ready.

Julie's project had caught Imogen's fancy; she was suddenly keen to find out more. She loved a good whodunit and this was real. She had most of her mornings and afternoons free and nothing specific to fill the time before the evening performance. She had asked backstage at the National Theatre but not come up with anything much apart from one of the dressers remembering Esmée, though only just.

'I was hardly more than a kid at the time and she was a major star. I only remember how difficult she was.'

'In what way?'

'Oh, the usual,' said the woman, who must have been somewhere in her forties.

'Have you any idea what became of her?'

'She died at the height of her fame. It hit the headlines for twenty-four hours, something to do with a child, I believe, but after that she was yesterday's news. Typical of show business.'

'And her husband?'

'Sir Edward. He was really sweet, a damn sight nicer than she was. He died too, very shortly after. It was said, of a broken heart.'

'That's it?' said Julie, when Imogen told her, intrigued yet also disappointed. She had hoped the National Theatre might have yielded more.

'Have you thought about looking for their graves?' said Imogen. 'If they lived in London, they shouldn't be hard to find.'

Julie, the journalist, hadn't got that far. She resented Imogen's being so much on the ball yet had to agree it was a brilliant idea.

'Find the graves,' said Imogen sagely, 'and who knows where else it may lead.'

'What are you suggesting I do? Exhume them?' asked Julie sarcastically.

'The graves should give you the names of their next of kin.'

Julie pondered; she could be right. She could kick herself for not thinking of it first. Actors that famous must be listed somewhere.

'It's not the fact that they lived,' she said. 'It's how they came to die. Suddenly and before their time. Why was it all hushed up? Esmée Morell was right at her peak. She took the lead in *Follies* that year, which won a Best Musical award.' She had done her homework.

'Right,' said Imogen. 'I've nothing else to do. Let's get our spades and go and excavate.'

Lunch progressed and, as Beth had predicted, Celeste began to open up. She was visibly shaken by something, not only the murder.

'This cop,' she said, as she toyed with her food. 'Treated me like a piece of shit. Barely gave me the time of day, just asked a lot of dumb questions.' Especially her age, which had really riled her, though she didn't exactly know why.

'What was he like?' Beth was hot on the scent, aware there were things Celeste still wasn't saying.

Celeste considered. 'He was rude,' she said. But had had the most disturbing eyes, steely and concentrated. At first he seemed not to notice her at all, certainly not as a woman. And that was something she wasn't used to; most men gave her a second glance, even now. 'He behaved as though I wasn't in the room, as if he was asking his questions into thin air.' He had scarcely even looked at her, the part that had hurt the most. He had damaged her pride; she would find it hard to forgive him.

He was tall and thickset with a rugged face and a scar, dissecting one cheek, that she found disconcerting. A man of action; she could tell by his handshake when he finally escorted her to the door. In addition he walked with a limp, though it didn't appear to impede his movements. A man who had known mortal combat. She found that sexy.

'What sort of age?'

Celeste considered. Mid to late forties she would guess. He had not been wearing a wedding ring though she'd kicked herself for noticing that, especially since he had made her feel so inconsequential.

'He acted as though I didn't exist, just another routine statistic wasting his time.' Celeste took a hefty gulp of wine. The pallor of her cheeks had gone; her eyes were now bright with anger.

'Well, he certainly made his mark,' said Beth, amused to be able to prove her theory. Celeste, aroused, revealed an astonishing beauty.

Celeste flushed slightly. 'It wasn't like that. But he almost made me believe he thought I had done it.'

'You!' said Beth. No wonder she was mad. 'How in the world could he justify that?'

'I was the only person in the house at the time, apart from poor Miranda. Plus I was the one who let the murderer in.'

'Come now,' said Beth. 'You're overreacting. Was he cute?' she added, with a knowing smile. There was more to this tirade than pure indignation.

'What, in my youth, we'd have called rough trade.' Celeste's expression was hard to read and she hadn't answered the question.

'So what happens next?'

'I haven't a clue. I just hope he'll leave me alone.'

26

Talking to Beth hadn't really helped. Celeste's emotions were all over the place. She couldn't stop thinking about the cop and his cool analytical eyes. It was a good ten years, at the very least, since a man had had such an effect on her. She didn't know whether to be mad or hurt, to cry or break his balls. Dr Rousseau, watching her shrewdly, was aware she seemed very much out of sorts. Miranda's death had clearly upset her profoundly. Since she refused to take time off, there wasn't a lot more he could do. He invited her out to dinner but she refused.

Dr Rousseau was a man about town, a Frenchman to the core. Though in his late sixties, he was well preserved and prided himself on his immaculate grooming. Whether he'd ever been married wasn't known but he squired many ladies to the opera and ballet and occupied a bachelor flat in nearby Devonshire Street. His photograph often appeared in the press, at fund-raising dinners or opening nights, and his list of patients read like Debrett or a first-class passenger list. Not, though, that he would ever divulge it. The keynote of his success was discretion. That and his skill with a knife.

Celeste intrigued him and always had, not only for her dazzling looks but also for her enigmatic reserve. She had worked for him for eleven years, yet he still knew almost nothing about her. He had seen her house, had once driven her home but not been invited inside. Though always polite, she shut him out, keeping him firmly at arm's length. No messing around with the staff was the implicit message. Which seemed a waste since both were single and she'd be a social adornment he'd like to flaunt. When he pressured her for information about the way she filled her time, she only ever gave him sketchy answers. Working hours were committed to him; she'd often accompany him to the clinic or even work a Saturday shift when justified by his caseload. Other than that, though, she kept to herself. He had tried, on numerous occasions, to woo her but was always met with tactful resistance. Which, to any red-blooded male, could only be a turn-on. One day, he was still determined, he'd win her trust.

Now, though, she sat at her desk and brooded; he couldn't manage to raise a smile. She went about her duties as though in a trance.

Beth conceded that Celeste was strange. A refugee from a time-warp. Yet something about her defensiveness touched her profoundly.

'I don't believe she has any friends,' she said to Duncan that night at dinner. 'She always looks so sad on the Tube and clung to me like a drowning rat the day the bombs went off.'

'You should see the size of her house,' said Duncan. 'I cannot believe she lives there alone and Imogen swore she saw a curtain twitch.'

'She probably keeps a mad aunt in the attic or else a Brazilian fancy man. With looks like hers, I can't believe that she hasn't a secret in her life.'

'Beautiful, yes, but not flesh and blood. A little too perfect to be mussed up. Give me a real woman every time.'

Beth laughed and dodged his lecherous swoop. 'Yet she's definitely hiding a secret,' she said. 'I think I'll ask her to lunch on Sunday, if that's OK with you.'

'She was only here a week ago and you saw her again today Surely the two of you don't have that much in common.'

'You'd be surprised,' said Beth with a wink. 'I have a feeling she may be lonely. I thought I might try introducing her to Richard.'

Duncan roared. 'Don't you ever give up? Besides, he's still got the hots for you.' Richard Brooke was a well-known painter whom Beth had known most of her adult life, had even helped finance at the start of his career. These days, however, he lived in France though kept his studio on the canal. Beth was endlessly trying to find him a wife.

'They wouldn't get along,' said Duncan. 'She's far too uptight for the likes of him. Can you imagine her in that filthy studio?'

'You never know. It takes all sorts. And maybe he'll want to paint her.' A nice little earner on the side that might open up new vistas for her. And possibly him; he had been on his own far too long.

'What is it about you,' asked Duncan, embracing her, 'that always wants to put people in pairs? You're worse than Noah. At least he was saving their lives.'

'It's because I am so happy myself, I want to spread it around,' said Beth, flinging her arms round his neck and kissing him long and hard.

'Break it up, you two,' said Imogen, drifting in from the garden. 'You are far too old to be messing around like that.'

Later, on the phone to Alice, she asked her to come on Sunday too. 'We could do with a bit of lightening up. My mum's inviting another of her strays, met in the bomb disaster, can you imagine?'

Beth's Sunday lunches were legendary, the hottest ticket in Notting Hill. A throwback to her catering days, she loved having people round her table. Since the shop took up most of her energy now, she tried to restrict entertaining to weekends. All were welcome, the more the merrier as far as she was concerned. If Celeste could come, she would build the guest list round her.

Beth's call helped to raise Celeste's battered morale; she still felt badly about the cop and the brutal way he had taken her through all those questions. What hurt the most was his studied indifference. He'd behaved as though she weren't female at all. Lunch on Sunday would make a nice change and get her out of the house. Oberon, for once in his life, would just have to learn to cope on his own. She would buy him something he could microwave and leave explicit instructions. It was time he learnt to fend for himself. He wasn't remotely a needy child any more.

She was sitting wondering what to wear and if she should

have her colour done when her phone rang and it was Brewster, the cop, saying he needed to talk to her again. He had further questions that wouldn't keep. He was sorry to disturb her.

'When?' she asked, inexplicably shaking.

'Tonight,' he said. 'What time do you knock off work?'

27

He caught his breath when she entered the room. She was even more ravishing in the flesh than in his tormented dreams. Cool, serene and immaculate, she scarcely glanced at him as he lumbered clumsily to his feet and offered her a chair. She was the kind of woman that, all his life, he had found distinctly intimidating: classy and aloof, way out of his league. He shuffled his papers while she settled herself, then, with an effort, regained control and began the interrogation.

How close had she been to Miranda Perkins?

Not close at all, said Celeste. They had been little more than acquaintances, with no real contact outside their work. Even there they did not do much more than pass the time of day.

So, no socialising outside hours?

None, said Celeste. She had told him that. With mild irritation, she watched him scribble a note.

What did she know of Miranda's life?

Virtually nothing, Celeste replied. Just that she lived beyond Baker Street. Wembley or Northwick Park, she thought. With her mother. She also knew that she sang in a choir.

Boyfriends?

How would I know? Celeste shrugged. Privately, she thought it unlikely but didn't want to be mean about the dead. Certainly not to this arrogant cop who seemed to be out to get her. Miranda had been nice enough, friendly, chatty, slightly overweight. She spent a lot of time on the phone, gossiping with friends.

What friends?

There was no way Celeste could know that. Not only had they not been close, they hadn't even worked on the same floor.

Brewster paused and looked at her, his eyes, as before, expressionless, seemingly impervious to her charms. Not that Celeste could give a damn. He could tell she found him boorish and unappealing and couldn't wait for the interview to end. She was growing tetchy and tapping one elegant shoe against the other. Nice ankles, he thought, then looked away. He refused to allow her to get to him. He caught her surreptitious glance at the clock.

Not so fast, thought Brewster, hardening. She wasn't getting away like that. There was something about the frosty bitch that got right under his skin. He would keep her here as long as he damn well pleased.

'Did you ever have any kind of falling out?'

Her eyes grew wider; she was genuinely shocked. 'Of course not. I've told you, we hardly knew each other.' Miranda was older by several years and had been in the job that much longer.

They had lunched together a couple of times but found they had little in common.

'You came from different backgrounds,' said Brewster.

She looked at him with her chilliest stare, meeting his challenge head on. If he wanted answers, he must ask direct questions; he could not expect her to improvise. The intensity of his scrutiny was starting to unnerve her, though she'd die before she let him realise that.

'Tell me, Miss Forrester,' Brewster said, leaning forward with narrowed eyes. 'Who do you think might have wanted her dead? Or, for that matter, you?'

'Me?' said Celeste, caught completely off guard. 'Where on earth do I come in? I thought we were here to talk about Miranda.'

'You were the one who opened the door.' The only person around at the time.

He doesn't believe my story, she thought, suddenly chilled to the bone.

'Take your time.' He was on to something. Her eyes were wild and she kept on looking around. The more distressed, the more beautiful she became. He was right; she was covering up.

'I have nothing to add,' she said, suddenly hostile. 'I must go now. I'm late as it is.'

'Sit down,' he commanded as she started to rise. 'I'm not through with you yet.'

He stood up and perched on the edge of the desk, his eyes now slits of steel. 'Someone entered the house that night with murder on his mind, yet no one saw him come or go and he left no obvious traces. Miranda's throat was savagely slit yet you, just one floor up, heard nothing. No raised voices nor sounds of a struggle. Not even the click of the door as it closed. How do you explain that?'

Celeste stared back in startled silence. One of her eyes had begun to twitch. She looked like an animal at bay. He found himself unexpectedly moved which had not been on the agenda.

'Don't you find that strange?' he asked. 'That the murderer should have rung the bell at a time when everyone else had left and you weren't usually there. You let him in and she got killed. Mission accomplished – or was it really? Might it have been that he simply killed the wrong person?'

'What exactly are you trying to say?' She looked one degree off breaking point.

'Just,' said Brewster in a milder tone, 'that you had a narrow escape.'

He stood at the window and watched her leave, slightly thrown by his feelings. Part of him was sure she was hiding something yet another, perversely, was on her side. One thing he was convinced of, though, she would never willingly see him again. The consternation in her eyes had been sharpened by dislike. Before she left, he had handed her his card.

'Call me at any time,' he said, 'should anything else occur to you that might help.' Or, he almost added, if you need to talk.

There were things about this latest crime that didn't entirely match the others. Someone had taken a massive risk by ringing the bell and walking in at a time in the afternoon when the street must have still been swarming with people. At a time when the doctors could well have been there, not to mention some of their patients. Whoever it was would have certainly left prints, yet both doorknob and weapon had been wiped clean, which indicated that the killing had been premeditated.

Brewster doodled on his pad. What kind of person would act like that? A psychopath or an imbecile or someone desperately seeking attention. Unless, of course, that was not what had happened and the ice maiden was holding something back.

28

Tom helped her out when he came on duty by providing Ellie with a bus map. It was complicated but could be done; they leaned like conspirators on the desk and worked out the most direct route. He lent her money for a travel card, with a pound or two extra to cover her needs. She wouldn't have asked but had no other option. Wilbur had always kept her short of funds. She suspected it was to keep her from straying, another thing about him she didn't like. He might mean well but rarely showed it. Too often he'd publicly humiliated her. She took a book to read on the bus and a folding umbrella in case it rained. She headed first for Victoria station after which, according to Tom, the journey was easy.

Travelling by bus was a new experience though she'd liked the one with the open top. She was now too scared to go upstairs because of what happened in Tavistock Square. She loved the view from Westminster Bridge (Wordsworth had written an ode to it) though shook a little when she found herself facing the Eye.

Wilbur was absorbed in a poker game with three kindred spirits he had somehow drummed up without getting out of bed. He made it clear that she wasn't welcome, was interrupting the game. He had heard about the bombs, of course, yet remained unnaturally detached. His bones were fusing though he still wore the harness and had to use a bedpan. Ellie wanted a private talk; there were things she was not prepared to discuss in front of a group of old codgers she didn't even know. This was the longest apart they had been since their marriage.

Grudgingly Wilbur laid down his cards while she drew the curtains round the bed. Their conversation was stilted and dull. She tried to make light of her King's Cross ordeal but he only showed any real interest when she mentioned the loss of her bag. Then he blustered and called her a fool. It was just as well, he pointed out, that he'd never allowed her a credit card of her own.

Ellie responded with her customary mildness and requested funds to keep her afloat. The hotel bill he could settle himself but she needed cash for her daily expenses. He told her she'd have to get it herself; he had left their passports and traveller's cheques locked in the hotel safe. What cash he had he needed here for his now twice daily poker games. Everything else would go on his hospital bill. He was getting off lightly as it was since his treatment was covered by the NHS and all he would have to pay for was his bed. She wondered if he still intended to sue and, if so, who would be his target. British Airways, who owned the Eye, or perhaps the City of Westminster for having uneven pavements. But she knew enough not to go that way. It would only set him off again and that she could do without.

'Don't carry too much money,' he said. 'Since you can't be trusted not to lose it. And keep a detailed note of what you spend.'

It was her money too, though she didn't point that out. Her mind had already detached itself and was thinking of other things. Since they wouldn't now be going to Paris, she intended to spend to her heart's content. There were numerous shops that she longed to explore without an old Scrooge of a husband holding her back.

Once on the bus with her book on her lap, Ellie's spirits revived. The odds against being in another attack must be high. It was mid-July, she had nothing to do except see the sights and enjoy herself. She was even becoming expert at getting around. First she'd have tea at Fortnum & Mason, something she'd always wanted to do, after which she intended to look at clothes. Tomorrow there was the V&A where she could linger as long as she liked. And later she'd try another Kensington restaurant. She settled back to read her book and, when she turned to the place she had marked, discovered the slip of paper with Margaret's number. It hadn't after all been in her bag.

Celeste sounded agitated when she called, apologising for the interruption. She had seen the cop again and things weren't looking good. He had made her feel she was under suspicion, was scared he was going to arrest her.

'What?' said Beth, profoundly shaken. 'He has be out of his mind.' It was clear to anyone with a brain that Celeste was refined to her fingertips, apart from which she would not have the strength to slit anybody's throat. Beth remembered how frightened she'd been by the bombs, that she'd very nearly fainted. Sensitivity such as that could not, she was certain, mask a callous killer. 'Why on earth would he think that?'

'Circumstances,' replied Celeste. 'I was the only one on the scene at the time of Miranda's death.'

'And?' said Beth.

'And I buzzed him in. I ought to have gone downstairs to check. I just assumed she had stepped away from her desk.'

'Don't let the bastard bully you,' said Beth. 'Would you like me to talk to him?' She always stood up for the underdog, something her friends found endearing though occasionally intrusive. But Celeste was aware Beth's intervention might make matters worse. She had seen in the cop's reptilian eyes that he had it in for her big time.

'So what are you going to do?' asked Beth. 'Do you want to come over and stay with us?' In any case she'd be there for lunch on Sunday.

'I don't see how that would help,' said Celeste. 'If I disappear, it might only make matters worse.'

Beth thought about it and saw her point. But at least she need not face him alone. 'Would it help if I came too?' she asked.

Celeste, alone in her Wimpole Street office, found her eyes suddenly welling with tears. She wasn't accustomed to anyone giving a damn. But no, she said; it was out of the question. Though she'd turned to Beth in her moment of panic, she didn't want to take the risk of letting her into her life.

'That's kind,' she said, 'but I can't allow it. You have your family to worry about. I simply wanted to get it off my chest.'

'What do you think he'll do next?' asked Beth, aware of the customers waiting to be served, knowing she should hang up.

'I haven't any idea,' said Celeste. 'He seems to be playing at cat and mouse.' She was sure he got a kick out of jerking her strings. 'I suppose he will just keep his eye on me until they come up with another suspect.' The thought filled her with unspeakable dread. She hadn't really thought things through until now.

'Try not to worry,' said Beth consolingly, raising her eyebrows to one of her staff to let her know she'd be free at any minute. 'Once they've dug into Miranda's past, they're bound to come up with other leads. Who knows what murky secrets she may have been concealing.' Though, from what Celeste had told her of Miranda Perkins, it didn't seem awfully likely.

'Thanks for your support,' said Celeste. 'Promise you'll visit me in jail.' She tried to make a joke of it though wasn't very convincing. If they dug into Miranda's past they were likely to do the same to hers. The thought chilled her to the bone.

The doctor was showing a patient out and would soon be in to hand her the notes. She would have to go but Beth had helped calm her down.

'Are you all right?' Dr Rousseau noticed she seemed upset as she ended the telephone call. She was still chalk-white.

'Yes, fine,' she said, 'thank you. Would you like some coffee? It must be about that time.'

It was after five, and she was tidying her desk when the call came through she'd been dreading all day.

'Miss Forrester,' said Brewster benignly. 'I think I may have been too hard on you and that we should probably have another talk.'

She gripped the phone, too scared to speak, certain it was a trick.

'I am sorry to call so late,' he went on, 'but is there a chance you'd be free tomorrow for a drink? If you can't make that, perhaps some other time?'

'No,' Celeste said weakly. 'Tomorrow will be fine.'

29

As a birthday treat for her very best friend, Imogen got Alice a private box for a Saturday matinée of *Anything Goes*. As an afterthought, she asked Julie too, liking her more since their recent collaboration. Of course, they had both seen the show before, had been invited to the opening night and were at the party Gus Hardy threw for the daughter of whom he was so proud. But the show had been running for almost a year and Alice adored the music. She had even bought the cast recording which she played whenever she had the chance. Julie liked to make fun of her, though, in truth, enjoyed it too.

'It's over by five so come backstage and then we'll go out for an early supper.' Imogen had a rare night off; an understudy would cover for her. She hardly ever had time to socialise now.

Julie was pleased by the invitation, having always felt slightly excluded from their close friendship. Also she welcomed the chance of a snoop backstage. She didn't quite know what she hoped to find out but needed to get the atmosphere right to help make Rupert's TV presentation come alive. She also very much liked the idea of rubbing shoulders with the stars. The theatrical life appealed to her. She wished she had Imogen's talent.

The performance, as always, was a total sell-out and the audience roared and stamped their applause. The cast took five curtains which, for a matinée, was almost unprecedented.

Imogen, still wearing her soaking tights, had her hair tied back and was creaming her face.

'Be with you in a second,' she said, offering them both champagne.

Alice perched but Julie wandered, inhaling the evocative greasepaint smell. A handful of celebrity faces were crowded into the dressing room where two of the leading players were holding court. This was the life the Forresters had led, adulated by the crowd and mixing regularly with their peers in backstage settings like this. What had happened to cause them to drop out, right at the peak of their glittering careers, to such an extent that nobody knew where they'd gone?

Imogen was ready so Julie wandered back, more determined than ever to find out the truth.

It was another marvellous summer's night and the riverside walk was bustling with life. The world and his wife were having an evening out. The street entertainment was there in force, jugglers, acrobats, trapeze artists, even a jazz band playing under the trees. When London puts on a show, it does it in style. There was also Imogen's personal bugbear, living statues of all descriptions, posed every few yards along the public footpath. The girls stopped and stared at each one in turn, giving them marks out of ten for their costumes and the effectiveness of their silent performances. Some of them were very impressive indeed.

'I find them distinctly creepy,' said Imogen, 'though what they do is incredibly hard. To stand that still for hours on end is even more tiring than sentry duty. At least the guards don't have to pretend not to breathe.'

'Why,' asked Alice, who could be censorious, 'do they do it at all if they have so much talent? Why not go and get themselves proper jobs?'

Imogen laughed. 'They are resting actors and this just another performing art. Give them credit for dedication and having the guts to stick it out. I know that I, for one, couldn't possibly do it.'

'Also you must admit they are cute,' said Julie, who always had an eye for the boys. 'Look at the beauty of that face. Is it male or female? I confess I really can't tell.'

Beautiful, yes, but also weird. Imogen found the unwavering stare disconcerting.

They were all the same with their intrusive glances and the way they giggled among themselves. He hated them all, these vacuous women; what did they knew about art? They talked about him as though he weren't there and, despite the fact it was what he intended, their callous indifference made him mad, the more so since he could barely make out what they were saying. The tallest one, with the long dark hair, looked vaguely like someone he had seen before. Whoever she was, he would certainly know her again. The other one too, with the red spiky hair and a skirt so short he could almost see up it, laughing bawdily, not like a woman at all. She was over made-up and smoking in public as if it were socially accept-able, which it was not.

The women who'd raised him had not been like this, had taught him manners from an early age: not to whisper and certainly never to point. To treat other people with respect. But he had grown up in a different milieu, where manners were important and nobody swore and ladies were ladies, and acted accordingly instead of parading like half-dressed strumpets, showing the world all they'd got. The one he still lived with, whatever her faults, was always flawlessly coiffed and groomed with her elegant well-cut clothes and inherited pearls. She would never be been seen out dressed like that or make such a show of herself.

But, despite all this, they excited him too with their brazen laughter and come-hither eyes. They provoked a hunger that was new to him and which he found hard to control. Let them mock him then turn their backs. They would find he was not so easy to shake off. Before they knew it, they'd regret their rudeness and discover they'd bitten off more than they could chew.

Julie's project was steadily progressing. She had filled in the backgrounds of most of the stars on her list. She was getting nowhere with the Forresters, though, despite having trawled through the British Library website. In their time, both husband and wife had been celebrated. Julie found many reviews of their starring roles. She'd played everything from Titania to Medea progressing, as the years went by, to Dolly and Lady Macbeth. In her early fifties she had starred in Sondheim, earning the show a Best Musical award, after which she had completely dropped out of sight. Frustratingly, her bibliography said almost nothing about her personal life.

He had played Jimmy Porter and Hamlet, spanning the decades between the two with varying roles, because of his looks, as a foppish upper-class toff. They had acted together whenever they could and, at the peak of their fame, were rarely apart. They had mixed in celebrity social circles and their hospitality was legendary. At last she located their London address: Egremont House in Tite Street, Chelsea.

The first thing she did was check the phone book but nothing was listed for that address. Just thirteen Forresters spelt that way in the whole of Greater London. Julie pondered; she could try them all but would probably just make a fool of herself. They had both been dead for eighteen years and nothing was known of their children. Most likely they'd married and moved away and were living anonymous lives. But at least she now knew where to look, which was a start.

Celeste was preparing for her date with Brewster; he'd suggested they meet in the Royal Court bar. It was not very far from where she lived; he had chosen it for its convenience. It was years since she'd had any kind of date, if that's what this meeting was really about. She was not convinced it would not turn out to be a trap. She couldn't keep her heart from pounding or settle to anything for very long. She racked her brains and ransacked her closets for precisely the right thing to wear. Chic but casual was her style, especially on a hot summer's night. She owned up to finding him very attractive. She had to get it just right.

Having gambled on nobody's being at home (he was usually out on a Saturday night) she drifted around her room in her slip, sifting through armfuls of clothes. She checked them all out, on their padded hangers, arranged according to colour and season, and tossed a few of them on to the bed for donation to the local charity shop. She would not be seen dead in anything outmoded despite her lack of a social life. She loved the feel of couturier clothes, which she'd always taken for granted as her birthright.

In the end she settled for stark black silk with patent sandals to give it a lift. That with her pearls should do the trick, if only she knew what he was after. He had looked at her in a searching way and the steel in his eyes had seemed somehow softer. The fact they were meeting in a bar made her less apprehensive. She showered then carefully made herself up, resisting the lure of a shot of vodka. Tonight she certainly needed her wits about her.

30

So tonight was the night. They were meeting at seven. He was slightly surprised that she hadn't cancelled. He looked at himself in the bathroom mirror and fingered the prominent scar on his cheek. It was fading slowly, helped by his tan, but to him still looked very unsightly. He shaved with care, then splashed on cologne. For personal reasons which slightly confused him, he wanted to look his best. The evening was hot so he wore a blazer, teamed with grey pants and a plain white shirt. He decided to travel by public transport; the car might appear too official. He wasn't quite sure what his motives were apart from wanting to know her better. Something about her fragile beauty had started to touch him profoundly. Put at its basest, he recognised a damaged kindred spirit.

There was something enigmatic about her; underneath he was sure she was not what she seemed. She worked in a relatively menial job yet, he would bet, had been destined for better things. She'd been hostile when he'd questioned her, unwilling to answer even routine questions except in the barest of monosyllabic grunts. She had flared up when he had asked her age, though he now conceded that she had a point. He was totally out of touch with the fairer sex. They had started badly but perhaps tonight he could get things on to a more even keel. He had spent too much time cross-examining thugs. He needed a softer approach.

'Night,' he called out to Burgess as he left. Usually they spent the weekends together but on this occasion he preferred to operate alone.

He deliberately got there ahead of time and ordered a double Scotch. He positioned himself at one end of the bar to be instantly visible when she arrived. He wondered now if he'd done the right thing, expecting a woman of class like her to enter this place on her own. But at least he had come all the way to Chelsea. He reminded himself that it wasn't a date; they still had unfinished business that needed unravelling.

Celeste was a studied ten minutes late, though the walk could have taken only half that time. He rose to his feet and politely extended his hand. He wanted to tell her how great she looked but wasn't sure it would go down well. Instead he simply asked what she'd like to drink. She chose white wine and he topped up his Scotch, then led her over to a quiet table. He saw the way men looked at her. Up close she was even more stunning than he had remembered.

'How are you?' he asked, once they were settled. 'Are you coming to terms with what happened?'

'As much as I can. I still can't sleep. But at least the image of Miranda's face no longer haunts me at night. Though, I confess,

I still feel terribly guilty.' She sipped her wine, clearly ill at ease, fiddling nervously with her pearls. Now they were face to face again the situation felt awkward.

Brewster switched to another tack. 'Tell me about yourself,' he said. 'Where you come from, that sort of thing. The kind of childhood you had.'

She looked up, startled, caught unawares. For a second he thought she might even walk out. A wash of colour highlighted her delicate cheekbones.

'Why should you want to know about me? It's Miranda, surely, we are here to discuss. I can't see where I fit into the picture.'

'You were the last one to see her alive. And you worked with her for a number of years. As you yourself said, it was you who opened the door.'

For a moment Celeste stared into her glass, then raised her great luminous eyes to his. 'I have told you all I know,' she said. 'Please believe me.'

He wanted to do so but sensed that she lied. Though to what degree, he was still unsure. Again he noted that one of her eyes was twitching.

He refrained from lighting a cigarette though he always thought better when he smoked. 'Let's imagine,' he said, leaning back, 'that Miranda was not the intended victim. That whoever it was who slit her throat, by accident got the wrong person.'

Now she was pale and avoiding his gaze. He knew for certain she was holding something back.

'Why do you work for a plastic surgeon? You're not the receptionist type.'

'It pays the bills,' she said with a shrug. 'I wasn't trained to do anything else and have no one else to support me.'

'Divorced?' he asked, risking her wrath, and watched her jaw tighten slightly.

'No,' she said. 'I was never married.' *Not that it's anything to do with you.* 'I really can't see where these questions are leading.' *Cut to the chase,* she implied.

'Answer them, please. Where did you grow up and what sort of school did you go to?'

'My family has always lived in Chelsea. I was privately tutored at home.'

He'd been right about the pedigree, then. She was bona fide top drawer. The haughty manner and poise were indeed inbred.

'What was it that your father did?' Undoubtedly he had been self-employed. Probably didn't work at all if you took account of the daughter.

She was so long answering that Brewster wondered what she might be concealing. He was in no hurry and relaxed with his drink. He liked the ambience of the bar. This meeting was out of working hours; he had all the time in the world.

At last she looked him straight in the eye. 'Both my parents were on the stage. Edward Forrester and Esmée Morell. In their time they were quite well known.'

If she'd hoped to impress him, it hadn't worked. Neither name meant anything to him.

'Still alive?'

'No, both dead for years. Nothing interesting there, I'm afraid. Thank you for the drink. I must go. I hope I've not wasted your time.'

He had touched a nerve. It was time to quit. He dropped his card on the bill. He knew precisely when to back off, when the suspect was showing sudden signs of panic. He would do his research then bring her back in to answer further questions.

They stepped out into the busy street and Brewster offered to get her a cab but Celeste said she'd rather walk, it was very near. Despite her protests, he insisted on escorting her home. On the corner of Tite Street she held out her hand.

'There's no need to come any further,' she said. 'I'm just down there, half a block away. Here is the best spot for you to get a taxi.'

He tried to argue but she turned away, unexpectedly chilly and withdrawn. Whatever it was she was covering up obviously meant a lot. He watched her as she walked away, calm and in total control of herself, without a backward glance. She didn't even turn when she reached her house, just paused in the porch while she found her key, closing the door in his face. He heard the click. Brewster, reluctant to call it a night and now even more intrigued by Celeste, advanced discreetly on the other side of the street. There was something about her, he wasn't sure what, that had caught him in a vulnerable spot so that now he had an urgent desire to get to know her better. Not just as a murder suspect; privately, as a woman.

He stayed in the shadows, impressed by her home which was grander than he had ever imagined, especially for a receptionist living alone. He watched her progress through the house as she turned on lights and then switched them off, until she appeared at a second-floor window, pulling the curtains shut. The show was over yet still he lingered, lighting another cigarette. He found it hard to tear himself away.

Right at the top, in what must be the attic, a gentle flickering light appeared. A light so pale it was probably a candle, wavering in front of the window. Not strong enough to show anything much except the dark outline of a motionless figure. He stayed there, watching, until the light went out.

31

Alice couldn't make it after all; her parents expected her home. But, even so, Beth had ten for lunch that Sunday. She cooked a dish of succulent pork that positively melted in the mouth, garnished with roast potatoes and baby parsnips. Duncan had chosen a fine Bordeaux that enhanced the delicacy of the roast. To start with, Beth had made them artichoke soup.

Celeste, at first, felt the odd one out since everyone else seemed to know each other but they all made an effort to make her feel at home. Duncan greeted her like an old friend and asked, with real concern, how she was feeling.

'Much better,' she said but did not expand, could not explain how her outlook had subtly altered. She badly needed to talk to Beth and catch her up on last night's encounter which had turned out not to be the date she'd expected. He'd been very affable and looked good in plainclothes, yet in the end all it turned out to be was a slightly veiled attempt at further interrogation. Apart from that, she was looking great. Despite the fact she had hardly slept, her eyes were bright and her skin translucent, a transformation from how she had looked the first time Duncan had met her. A striking woman, he now conceded, slightly less weird than he had previously thought.

Beth and Duncan seemed ideally matched, warm and generous hosts. From the frequent looks she saw them exchange, it was clear they were still very much in love. Celeste, unusually, found herself empathising. It wasn't a feeling she had known first hand, not even in her tempestuous youth when scalps came two a penny and she'd scorned them all. Then men had been mere commodities, to be used, discarded and instantly forgotten. In her heyday she had broken numerous hearts. Today, however, she felt oddly chastened; still not clear about how things had gone last night.

Richard Brooke, an eminent painter, was seated next to Celeste at lunch and she sensed, from the rapt attention he paid her, that she hadn't entirely lost it. Two men in less than twenty-four hours. Her old self wouldn't have even noticed but Beth, aware of her slight agitation, assumed that Richard had scored.

Later, however, in the kitchen where she followed Beth to offer a hand, Celeste was almost bursting to unload.

'I saw him again last night,' she said 'He took me out for a drink. Though it wasn't so much a date as an interrogation.'

Beth was startled. 'The cop, you mean?' Could it be the relationship was hotting up? Surely he couldn't really think Celeste was a killer?

'He asked me loads of personal questions quite unconnected

with Miranda's death. I seriously think he has me down as a suspect.' She didn't add that she fancied him, had found his aggressive male presence attractive. Had wished it had been a genuine date that might have turned into more.

'How did he leave things?'

'In the air. Though I have no doubt I'll be hearing from him again.'

It was early evening when she wandered home, and the bells of St Luke's were ringing. She felt like a stupid schoolgirl, all het up. For a few brief hours she had sensed romance, had indulged herself in the impossible dream, when all the time he'd been trying to trap her into giving herself away. *He thinks I did it, killed Miranda.* The enormity of the realisation almost stopped her in her tracks. He had sensed she was attracted to him and used it as a weapon against her. By delving into her secret past, he was finally showing his hand. She was suddenly scared; he was a very tough man who would stop at nothing to track down a killer. He had worked in war zones; she knew that from his scars.

She was sick of continually carrying the can for what had happened all those years ago. Her career, her marriage prospects, her life had all been sacrificed to the one end, covering up and protecting the family honour. They were decently buried and forgotten while she still hid in that terrible house, having to keep herself to herself and her profile as low as she could, in constant fear of the knock on the door she was scared would one day come.

As she entered the house, she knew he was home though nothing except the clock's steady ticking disturbed the somnolent silence. She hadn't lived with him all these years without being able to sense his malevolent presence. She still took care of his basic needs, as she had for most of his life. But now he was grown with a life of his own, though she knew very little about it. He remained her personal albatross, hung like a boulder round her neck. Whenever happiness threatened to strike, he always contrived to destroy it.

She had no idea how he spent his time; when she left for work he was still asleep and when she came home he was gone. The only time they sat down together was for Sunday lunch, as they always had, but which today she had left him to eat on his own. It had been ready for him on a plate in the fridge with clear instructions as to how to heat it. When she checked, the plate was in the sink, along with the crystal goblet he had used. He never lifted a finger to help, something she'd given up worrying about, the result of being first spoilt and later neglected.

Used to it, though, after all these years, she dropped her handbag and wrap on a chair while she tidied the kitchen and carefully rinsed the glass he should not have been using. All they had left was this dwindling inheritance. They'd already been forced to sell some of the pictures. Once it was gone, she didn't know how they would cope.

When he rose at noon and found her not there, he flew into a terrible rage. Sunday lunch was their special time which, throughout their lives, had been a kind of ritual. She had left a note saying she'd gone out for lunch and telling him how to heat the cottage pie. She had set the dining-room table for one, with a damask napkin and a rose in a glass, and the sherry bottle on its silver coaster.

To hell with that. He hated sherry. Why did she treat him

like a child? He went down to the cellar again, to plunder more of his father's claret, then selected an eighteenth-century glass goblet from which to swig it down. He liked the finer things in life; it was, after all, how he had been brought up. As he sat at the table in the cavernous room, with the sunlight streaking through the heavy curtains, he studied the rose and uncomfortable memories began to filter through from his subconscious. The house had always been filled with flowers, one of his mother's particular foibles. She had made a personal statement out of arranging them herself. His mind clicked back to those opulent days when the house had been at its glorious best as, indeed, had his very gregarious mother. Celeste was a pale imitation of her and had cut their excesses after she died. He resented that and the way that she kept him imprisoned.

Recently she had been going out more; he had glimpsed her with that man and his beautiful daughter. She had only said that he was a friend but she had no friends, as far as he knew. Certainly none he'd ever met. The house was impressive and surely a bait for any loner with marriage in mind. She was long past her best but even he could see she still retained some of her charms. He would not allow her to marginalise him by bring strangers into their closeted life. His fingers tightened round the stem of the glass. He would sooner break her first.

He had killed the woman just to show who was boss, slitting her throat from ear to ear. The thrill he'd derived from watching her bleed was better than any of the ones before. He had simply dispatched the others in a hurry. This one he had watched die. He had not expected there to be so much blood. Slicing through the jugular had produced a fine spray which soaked his T-shirt and matted his glossy black hair. He would use the lavatory close to the station to clean himself up and change his clothes. He always carried his leather bag, containing the tricks of his trade.

She had needed that lesson to bring her to heel, to remind her what he was capable of. And yet she was out, for the first time ever, leaving him to eat alone on a Sunday.

Last night he had waited until she came in, had stood at the window and seen the guy, skulking like a fugitive in the shadows. He was slightly shorter than the one before, had not had the telltale beard, yet had stuck around for at least ten minutes, lighting one cigarette from another, like a lovelorn schoolboy after a bitch on heat. He would not allow her to act this way; it was not the way she'd been raised. If the lesson he'd taught her was not enough, he would show her the full extent of his rage. She must not even think about walking out.

He wolfed down the pie which she'd bought from Marks and followed it with cheese from the fridge. Then finished the bottle and went upstairs to wreak a little more havoc.

When she saw the damage he had done to her room, she almost abandoned him then and there. Her drawers were all open, their contents displayed, as though a burglar had been through them all, taking nothing but mutilating all he could. Her perfume bottles had been thrown at the wall so the place smelt like a brothel and the expensive lotions and creams she used had been smashed and ground into her Persian rug, another legacy from her mother's boudoir.

Her clothes had been casually strewn on the floor and some were ripped where he'd tried them on in too much excitement to treat them with proper care. The hats were scattered all over the room. She wept profusely as she gathered them up and tried ineffectively to repair the damage.

He was out of control. She'd not seen him this bad. She had no idea what had brought it on but a terrible thought she had tried to suppress no longer seemed quite so far-fetched.

32

Margaret was delighted when Ellie rang, as well as very contrite. She had meant to be in touch, she said, but circumstances had intervened. She hoped the news of Wilbur was better and that he would soon be out.

'Perhaps we can get together again before you return to the States,' she said.

'That's precisely why I'm calling,' said Ellie. 'I want to invite you to lunch.'

Since she still hadn't seen the Elgin Marbles, they arranged to meet at the British Museum where she had heard the restaurant was very good. She said she would book a table for Thursday. Wilbur was being discharged the following day.

Ellie was managing well on her own, with the help of Tom and her travel card, but lacked a congenial companion to do things with. Margaret was right on her wavelength, she felt; she'd enjoyed her conversation and quirky humour.

Money had ceased to be a problem since she'd got her hands on the traveller's cheques. She could replicate her husband's signature well enough to fool a cashier. She had also liberated her passport and the travel tickets that Tom had exchanged. It did seem a terrible waste not to use them but as soon as Wilbur was back on his feet he planned to fly straight home.

Julie had a dental appointment, her regular check-up in Markham Street, so since she would be in the neighbourhood it made sense to look for Egremont House. None of her colleagues would notice her absence; they'd all be glued to the opening of the First Test. Her teeth were perfect, which was no surprise, so she got out after a scrape and polish and zigzagged towards the river in search of Tite Street. It wasn't far. She was there in five minutes and strolled the few blocks down from Tedworth Square, checking out every house. Some had numbers but this one did not, at least from the details on the Internet. She saw a blue plaque for Oscar Wilde and another, nearby, for James Whistler but nothing for either Esmée Morell or her husband Edward Forrester. It was blazing hot and good to be out; better than being stuck in that air-conditioned building. If anyone checked she would say she'd been doing research.

She got to Dilke Street and found the sketch-club then stopped an old man and politely asked if he'd heard of Egremont House. Indeed he had; he lived in the street. They were standing almost outside it. He pointed towards an imposing building in Edwardian brick with an ornate porch that Julie had mistaken for a hotel.

'Do you know if anyone lives there?' she asked, not quite believing her luck. 'Indeed,' said the man, 'though it looks deserted, I occasionally see people coming and going.'

'But you don't know their names?'

'I do not,' he said. 'But a young man is sometimes there at this time of day.' He checked his watch; it was half past two. He was on his way to buy a paper.

Julie thanked him then, drawing a deep breath, walked up to the big front door and boldly rang the bell.

Lunch at the British Museum was great, the restaurant a triumph. Their table looked over the central courtyard and the menu was unusual and eclectic. Ellie asked Margaret to choose the wine; Wilbur didn't like her to drink, found it unbecoming in a woman. But now she was out from under his thumb, she intended to do as she darned well pleased. It was good to have found a kindred spirit in London.

Margaret asked how Wilbur was though, in truth, she couldn't care less. The little she'd seen of the grumpy old boor did not incline her to improve on the acquaintance. She already had the impression from Ellie that he must be a bit of a trial to live with.

'Cantankerous,' said Ellie frankly. 'Though he's taken it all surprisingly well.' She told her about his band of cronies and their peripatetic poker game, at present focused round Wilbur's bed since he was unable to move. 'It's exactly like a men's club,' she said. 'Without the brandy and cigars.'

Margaret laughed. She could well imagine, though Jack had not been remotely like that, having always rather preferred the company of women. She told Ellie a bit about life in Croydon and how they'd moved further out when he retired.

'I like the house but it's lonely,' she said. She hadn't expected him to die.

They talked a little about their children and Margaret pulled a slight face. Two boys, she said, with ambitious wives with neither of whom she saw eye to eye. 'I think they consider me slightly past it. Except, of course, when they need a babysitter.'

Ellie laughed. Her thoughts entirely; both her daughters were much the same. 'They think they're all so modern and with it, despise the mothers like you and me who had no option but to stay at home and give them so much of our time.'

The wine was a Chilean Chardonnay which went very well with the seared-tuna salad. Ellie commended Margaret on her choice.

They moved on comfortably to other things, including their mutual love of books. They shared, it emerged, several favourite authors, obviously liked the same things. Margaret told her about the reading group and what a non-starter that had been. Ellie talked about life in Chippewa Falls.

'At least you're not far from London,' she said. 'Imagine living, as I do, out in the sticks.'

Their conversation flowed so freely, they were both amazed when they saw the time. Margaret had a train to catch and Ellie must make her nightly visit to Wilbur.

'Now that he's almost better,' she said, 'he is back to being a grump again. Though he's bonded in a major way with those other pathetic old fools.'

Margaret laughed at Ellie's directness. She certainly pulled no punches. She regretted that they lived such a distance apart. Ellie mentioned the Paris trip, now sadly consigned to the rubbish bin. 'As soon as Wilbur can walk,' she said, 'he insists on going straight home.'

'Well, please stay in touch and come back soon.' Margaret realised, to her surprise, how much she was going to miss her amusing new friend. 'And next time you're over, you must come to Haywards Heath. It's hardly swinging but does have its own rustic charm.'

They hugged and went their separate ways. It was only at Victoria station that Margaret discovered there had been more bombs which had luckily failed to go off.

He was checking the weather before going out when his eye was caught by two people outside, talking in the street. An elderly gent he knew vaguely by sight in conversation with a girl in a very short skirt. She was waving a piece of paper around and glancing at all the houses. To his consternation, the old gent turned and pointed straight at where he was standing. He was saying something and she was nodding, then he turned and shuffled away. At which point, to his absolute horror, she stepped into his porch.

He skipped out of sight with a quickening pulse and flattened himself against the wall, as if she could see him up here on the attic floor. Something about her seemed vaguely familiar; he had seen that spiky red hair before as well as the skirt that could hardly be classed as decent. His heart beat faster and his hands were clammy. He could not imagine what she wanted with him or what that nosy old bastard could possibly have said.

He went downstairs very cautiously in case she peered through the letter box. She looked the sort who would stick her nose where it definitely wasn't wanted. Then it clicked where he'd seen her before: Saturday night near the National Theatre. She had wandered by with two other girls, one of whom he'd seen hanging around this house. The tall one with the long dark hair had been in the car that brought Celeste home. The daughter of the bearded man he suspected was a suitor.

He could see her outlined against the glass as she stood there, waiting for someone to answer. For all he cared, she could stand there all day, though it stopped him going out. He moved with stealth into the kitchen and waited for her to leave.

He was suddenly gripped by colossal rage; they should mind their own business and leave him alone. They were vermin, every last one of them, and needed to be wiped out.

33

Tamara, Lady Fermoy-French came bowling out of Daphne's late, after a very long lunch with her three dearest friends. Dottie, Annabel and Plum were up from the shires on a shopping spree, culminating in their annual reunion at one of the hottest watering-places in town. Tamara was wearing a Pucci two-piece and was slightly unsteady on her feet. Tonight was cocktails with the Peruvian ambassador. She ought to be home at the latest by six in order to get dolled up. But first she had a gift to buy; her husband's niece was getting married and had her list at Peter Jones (the china department, of course).

The afternoon was bright and hot; the streets were alive with shoppers. She tripped along on her Manolo Blahniks, oblivious of the covetous stares at her heavily manicured and bejewelled hands. Her husband, Peregrine, scolded her for flaunting his wealth quite so blatantly but what was the point of having it at all if you kept it locked up in the safe? Though no longer in the first flush of youth, she desperately tried to fend off age with strenuous exercise regimes as well as the surgeon's knife. Not a nice woman; Lady Fermoy-French had an ungenerous heart.

At Peter Jones she scanned the list, silently sneering at some of the choices. So many of the young these days possessed no concept of style. Still, it saved her having to trawl the shops and waste time making decisions. She settled on six matching cereal bowls (the bride was only on her husband's side) and ordered them to be sent the following day. Then she drifted through the linen department to check out the latest stock.

She really ought to be heading home but first she needed the ladies'. These lunches were Sisyphean affairs; her bladder was not what it had been. The store had just had a total makeover; she had not been in there for almost five years, since the building work had begun. But they wouldn't have shifted the cloakrooms, surely, halfway up the stairwells, in between floors.

She tidied her hair and checked her teeth, then sprayed on some Cartier cologne. She was only a two-minute cab ride from Eaton Square. These embassy functions were a crashing bore but Peregrine liked her to look her best so tonight she would wear the Saint Laurent satin as a foil to the emerald choker. In one of the cubicles the cistern flushed and someone was washing their hands beside her, though Tamara was too self-absorbed to spare a glance.

It was twenty to six; the store closed at seven. If it weren't for the function, she might have continued to browse. Filling in time was always a problem for a woman who'd never had a job, apart from sporadic fund-raising gigs for her husband. She picked up her bag and turned to go, then froze when she saw who (or what) was standing beside her.

Her heart started palpitating wildly. 'Kindly allow me to pass,' she said. Perry was right: she should not have worn so much bling. She could tell from the smile that things might well turn ugly and prayed for a saviour to intervene. But, by this time in the late afternoon, the ladies who lunch had gone home.

Tamara faced her nemesis alone, too petrified even to scream.

Her body was found by a security guard, doing his rounds before locking up. She was pinned to the wall beside the basins, the knife had gone in so deep. The look on her face was of frozen horror, her mouth a rictus of pure disbelief. Whoever had done this had virtually scared her to death. But for what purpose? She hadn't been robbed; her rings were intact and the Prada bag she had dropped remained unopened. She wasn't even young and pretty, and carried no mobile phone.

Panic ensued; the police were called but the body could not be moved till forensics had been. The big question was, had the cameras caught it? On this occasion they had, which at least was something. The store's refit had been long and costly. The entrance to the ladies' loo was guarded by cameras in all directions. Anyone entering or leaving should therefore be seen.

The evidence had to be passed to the police where it landed inevitably on Brewster's desk. Another bloody murder, he groaned. What the hell was going on?

He was working late that Tuesday night, scrutinising endless data in an attempt to check out Celeste's antecedents. Before he asked her further questions, he needed to know as much as he could if only to catch her out if she was lying. It wasn't a job he very much liked. He still hadn't totally made up his mind, was drawn to her in a way he found unnerving. He badly wanted to prove himself wrong but the process had to be gone through.

'Send it straight through,' he said wearily, when told that the tape was on its way. At least this time it might give them some sort of lead.

They gathered in the projection room in front of a magnifying screen, Brewster and his team of highly skilled experts. Coffee was brought and they all sat round, recording machines and notebooks to hand, intrigued to find out why the guard had been so freaked out.

The SOC report began with stomach-churning close-ups of the body, skewered to the wall and covered with blood, hands spread out as if imploring, face contorted with terror. The clothes were expensive, if overdone, the jewels the genuine thing. Yet nothing at all had been taken, said the report.

'Some kind of vengeance killing, do you think?' A jealous wife or over-importunate suitor.

They looked at each other and Brewster shrugged. She was surely too old to provoke a *crime passionnel*. But the savagery fitted with the Circle Line killings and, since it hadn't reopened yet, there could be a possible fit. Where else do you go when your stamping-ground is temporarily cordoned off? And the damage wrought by the knife was in a similar league. Even Brewster was finding it hard not to gag.

'OK,' he said, when they'd seen enough. 'Now let's look at the TV footage.' He drained his coffee mug, longing for whisky, and lit an illicit cigarette.

The film was clear and of excellent quality, though showed

only a flight of stone steps either way, leading up and down from the cloakroom positioned between the floors. For a very long time nothing happened at all. On the whole, as one of the team observed, shoppers use escalators rather than stairs.

'Or else the lifts. They're a lazy bunch.' Unless they wanted to pee.

They began to mutter among themselves until a figure popped into view, climbing the stairs in desperate search of the loo. Another long pause until she emerged.

'What do they do in there?' one asked. The cameras could not see beyond the closed doors.

'Breach of privacy,' explained the technician, embarrassed as if it were somehow his fault.

'I'd sooner watch paint dry,' said a weary detective.

'Wait,' ordered Brewster, suddenly alert. A slight dark figure had come into view, racing up the stairs on nimble feet.

It vanished abruptly into the cloakroom and thus was immediately lost to sight. Male or female? None of them knew; like a rat up a drainpipe, they said. After which there followed a lengthy pause, fifteen minutes or even more.

'Can't you speed this thing up?' asked the man from forensics.

Then, just as they were about to drop off, Lady Fermoy-French made her appearance.

She was in the cloakroom quite a while.

'Probably having a natter,' one said.

'A fag more likely,' said Brewster, lighting up.

The door at last opened but the figure which emerged was not that of Lady Fermoy-French but the previous arrival who'd been in there a good half-hour. Slim and dark was all they could make out; it might have been male or female. Whoever it was ran lightly up the stairs without ever glancing towards the cameras.

'Fast forward,' said Brewster urgently. But the rest of the tape was blank. That, apparently, was the end of the show.

'Nothing more happens till a later tape,' explained the technician. 'At six fifty-five the guard goes in. And finds Lady Whatshername skewered to the wall.'

'So now, at least, we have glimpsed the murderer. It can't have been anyone else. We just need formal identification. Run it through again,' said Brewster.

When the slim dark figure appeared on the stairs, Brewster leaned forward in his chair. 'Try for a close-up of the face,' he said. Something was tugging at the edge of his memory. Somewhere, not very long ago, he was almost certain he'd seen that person before.

The technician zoomed in as far as he could, then advanced the tape slowly, frame by frame. The killer appeared to have short dark hair which was all they could clearly make out. Next would come the interminable wait until Lady Fermoy-French appeared. And after that another long gap till they saw the killer again.

'This is no good. It's a total charade.' The team were all longing to call it a day. Yet they'd seemed so close to a genuine breakthrough.

'Wait,' said Brewster, suddenly inspired. 'How did the murderer leave the store? Walked on up to a higher floor then took the escalator down.'

'Or the lift.' But Brewster was no longer listening. He was hellbent on following a hunch.

By eleven p.m. he was almost dropping though still resolved not to quit. By then the forensics team had left and only the weary technician remained, valiantly checking through endless footage of film.

'I can't believe there's so much of it,' said Brewster. 'How many escalators do they have?'

'Fourteen now,' the man said glumly. 'Basement to the eighth floor.'

'Go on then,' said Brewster, dying for a drink but settling instead for a cigarette. He was starting to droop; he needed to keep a clear head.

And that's when he saw it, the face in the crowd that sent a bolt of electricity through him and made him doubt his sanity for a second. Calm and poised and exquisitely dressed, there was no mistaking that startling beauty as she rode the escalator down towards the ground floor.

'Again,' he said. They reversed the tape and ran it over and over until he was sure. It seemed she had been in the store at the time. Just as she'd been on the spot when Miranda was killed.

He sat and sweated, severely shaken. Although he'd initially suspected her, their latest meeting had given him pause. He had started to feel very drawn to her since that evening in the bar. Now, however, there was no turning back. He had a duty to perform. Having made his decision, he stubbed out his fag. Whatever romantic feelings he had, at heart he remained a high-principled cop. The job would always come first. The team had dispersed but that was tough luck. He put through the order all the same.

'Bring her in as fast as you can. Better take reinforcements.'

Part Three

34

It was six in the morning when the doorbell rang; Celeste was still asleep. She tried at first to ignore the sound, turned over and buried her face in the pillow, but the insistent banging of the knocker too convinced her there was someone at the door. She dragged herself over to the window. What she saw stopped her heart in her chest. Two police cars with flashing lights parked untidily right outside with four uniformed officers standing around. With a dog. She couldn't see who was at the door.

'Open up!' commanded a voice. She grabbed her robe and hurtled downstairs to try to stop the commotion. The last thing she needed was the neighbours in on the act.

There were two of them waiting in the porch, a man and a hard-faced woman.

'Celeste Forrester?' she asked, displaying her badge. 'We have a warrant for your arrest. Please get dressed and accompany us to the station.'

Celeste stared blankly. It must be a joke, though the woman showed not the slightest sign of humour. And the dog looked very threatening indeed.

'There must be some mistake,' she said. 'What is it I am supposed to have done?'

'You'll find out the details once we get to Cannon Street,' said the grim-faced woman.

Cannon Street was where Brewster worked. Celeste was suddenly gripped by terror. She had always suspected he didn't believe her; now it seemed that he was going to charge her.

'Give me five minutes,' she said with dignity and swept back up the stairs. She wouldn't bother waking Oberon, not that he would have cared. She didn't want Brewster knowing of his existence.

She came back regal and perfectly groomed. 'The detective inspector is a friend of mine,' she said.

The policewoman stared at her stonily. 'It was DI Brewster who sent us,' she said. She practically frogmarched Celeste to the car and pushed her in with a hand on her head. The dog came to sit beside her, baring its fangs.

Here they were again, face to face, though in quite different circumstances. Brewster was back in uniform, with a grave and inscrutable expression. He didn't even rise to greet her, but remained at his desk, engrossed in his work, without glancing up.

'Be seated,' said the lady cop, then stood to attention by the door. The atmosphere in the room could be cut with a knife.

'For goodness' sake,' Celeste said sharply. 'Won't somebody please tell me what this is about?' She was chilled to the bone by the atmosphere in the room.

His eyes, when at last he looked at her, were bloodshot and his face was drawn. He had been at his desk all night, since he issued the order. Before he spoke, the policewoman read out her rights. 'Do you want a solicitor?' she asked.

'Not till I know why I'm here,' said Celeste.

Brewster, who appeared to be sunk in thought, still had not uttered a word. Now he finally looked at her and she saw from his eyes that the news was bad.

'Murder in the first degree,' he said in a wooden voice.

'Miranda Perkins?' She couldn't believe it.

'Tamara, Lady Fermoy-French,' he replied.

He had to admire her brazen front and she did look a million dollars. He tried to remain detached but found it hard. Celeste just sat there, stupefied, unable to take it in. She certainly did have style, he gave her that.

'At approximately five fifty-five,' he said, 'yesterday evening at Peter Jones, you stabbed the victim to death with a kitchen knife.'

The colour drained from her flawless face; she positively gasped with surprise. Her great dark luminous eyes beseeched him to tell her it was a cruel joke. He found it hard to meet her gaze. She had somehow managed to break through his defences. Yet he had proof she had been there at that time.

'What have you to say?' he asked, switching on his recording machine.

'Nothing at all,' Celeste said stiffly. 'Except that I didn't do it. I have never even heard of the woman before.'

'I'm afraid we have it on film,' he said, his voice controlled and ice-cold. Please don't lie, he wanted to add. Or else I won't be able to help you.

Celeste absorbed this for several seconds. Then: 'Show me

the evidence,' she said. 'I didn't go near the store yesterday.' Which was not entirely true, in fact. He saw she knew that she was bending the truth.

'What time did you leave work?' he asked.

'Around five-thirty.'

'And went straight home?'

'I did,' she said. 'Baker Street to Sloane Square by way of Victoria.'

'Bringing you straight to Peter Jones.'

She couldn't deny it so said nothing.

'At approximately the time the murder was committed.'

Her eyes flashed sparks. 'But I didn't do it. I wasn't even in the store.'

'Can you prove it?' He badly wanted her to win. 'I'm afraid, Miss Forrester, the closed-circuit cameras do not lie.'

Celeste stayed silent; she had no defence. He saw her inwardly crumble. Her life had been hexed right from the start; she couldn't see any way out of it though by now, of course, she was figuring out what had happened.

'Any more questions?' She faced him full on, her beauty piercing him to the core.

'None,' said Brewster. 'Take her down. We are holding you in custody pending further inquiries.'

The cell was awful and smelt of Vim with an undercurrent of urine. They offered Celeste a solicitor again. She refused.

'What are you going to do?' asked the warder, a woman with a compassionate smile. 'Is there anyone we should notify that you are here?'

'No,' said Celeste. 'Except my boss. Tell him I won't be in for work and that I am very sorry.'

She wrote down his number, then contemplated. She really had no idea what to do for the best. She asked how long they would hold her there; a maximum of four days, said the warder, after which, by law, they were bound to let her go unless they formally charged her.

'I would like a change of clothes,' she said, 'if I'm going to be here that long.'

They gave her a prison overall and provided her with a toothbrush. They offered to pick up things from her house but she declined. She sat in silence and thought about it, trying to work out what to do, wondering how Oberon would cope when she didn't come home. And how he would ever find out where she had gone.

Brewster was also sitting in silence, still not entirely convinced of her guilt. If only the cameras hadn't caught her, she might well have got away with it. He knew he shouldn't ever think that way but, in this case, couldn't help it. She had seemed so defenceless in the interview room, vulnerable and afraid. And yet . . . he thought of what she had done, two women brutally hacked to death, probably several more. He wondered about her motivation and whether or not she was just plain mad. She certainly showed no sign of it but nor did she show remorse.

He wandered down to the detention block and studied her through the two-way glass. Even in prison regulation clothes she retained her dignity and poise. She sat staring into space, lost in an inner world. He would insist she get a lawyer, the very least he could do for her. The evidence against her was pretty damning.

35

He didn't emerge till almost noon, shattered by what had occurred. The adrenalin buzz he always got was invariably followed by a similar low. He wouldn't experience a high like that until he did it again. He showered and dressed, then went downstairs where he found the fridge almost empty. Provisions had sunk to an all-time low but tomorrow was Thursday when she did her big shop. Occasionally he requested things but didn't, as a rule, much care what he ate. He kept himself at minimum weight, could exist on very little.

He tried her door on the way back up but found it, as usual, locked. She was furious at the way he'd behaved, daring to tamper with her things, though still apparently hadn't twigged that he had a duplicate key. He didn't feel much like going out but was far too restless to settle. The weather was good so he thought he would go for a walk.

He didn't go far, just loafed around, confining himself to the

Chelsea backstreets, drawn like a homing pigeon to Peter Jones. The latest murder had made the headlines: 'Society hostess stabbed to death.' Her picture was there on all the newsstands, brassy and overdressed, with shifty eyes. He felt another adrenalin buzz; the bitch had certainly had it coming. People like her should not exist, putting on airs and flashing their wealth. Greedy, superficial and cruel. He knew her kind from his childhood.

Celeste was concerned about how he would cope but dared not risk the police discovering there was anyone else in the house. If she answered no questions, she might hold them off until the statutory four days were up and they had to let her go. They couldn't hold her indefinitely since she, for one, knew she wasn't guilty and therefore what evidence they had must be faulty. He'd been up to his tricks again, of course, had deliberately landed her in this mess out of spite. Though fully grown, he was still a spoilt child who flew into tantrums of thwarted rage if anyone tried to stand in his way or stop him doing what he liked.

She understood and sympathised. Nature had dealt him a very low blow and she'd been his champion since the day he was born. Their parents had grossly neglected him, had not looked after his welfare at all but turned their backs on a situation they were unable to handle. These days they would have been in court by now. Lately his behaviour had started to grow worse; she no longer knew how to control him. One of these days, if he hadn't already, he would go too far and they'd have to lock him up.

Julie was deeply immersed in her project and enjoying the research. Her main concentration was fixed on the Forresters now. There was definitely some sort of mystery there; the trail went cold right after their deaths and no one she'd found knew anything much about them. A theatrical knight and his glamorous lady; some scandal appeared to attach to them though what it had been she hadn't been able to uncover. In the end she sought out Rupert and asked him point-blank.

'What do you know about Esmée Morell?'

He looked up with an abstracted smile, busy writing his column. 'Very little, which is why I enlisted your help.'

'So why include her if her life is so obscure?'

'That's the whole thrust of the series. *Theatrical Legends.*'

She told him she had located the house, the scene of their celebrated salon, though hadn't established if anyone still lived there. 'Nobody ever answers the door and the place looks totally empty and neglected.'

'Have you thought of breaking in?' he asked, not entirely kidding. He had chosen Julie for her journalist's nose and gritty determination.

'I suppose I could set the place on fire and see who comes rushing out,' she said. Then gave him her brightest smile and returned to her desk. She wouldn't give up. She enjoyed a challenge, was determined to see the thing through. Was especially keen on the promised TV credit.

Later Rupert stopped by her desk and handed her a card. *Leonard Beamish – Actor*, it read. 'A fellow I know from the Garrick,' he said. 'Give him a buzz and say I told you to call.'

'Who is he?' asked Julie suspiciously. Not a name she had ever heard.

'One of the old-style theatricals who made his career in rep. Does endless bit parts on television. You'll certainly know the face.'

'What's the connection?'

'He acted with them. Played Puck at Stratford the season they met. Has always been a little in love with Esmée.'

Julie took the card impatiently. 'Anything else you've omitted to tell me?'

'I saw him the other night,' said Rupert. 'But it totally slipped my mind.'

When evening came and she still wasn't home, he really started to panic. She was out so little, especially at night, and never before without giving him warning. He was getting hungry now but had nothing to eat. With luck she had moved her big shop to tonight. He raided the fridge for the last bit of cheese and also uncovered an ancient tin of sardines. No bread, no eggs, not even milk. A very poor show altogether. He would order himself a takeaway if he could.

He paced the unlit reception rooms then made his nightly descent to the cellar. If he couldn't eat, he might just as well get plastered. His father may not have left him much but had, without doubt, possessed a superlative palate. He stood there, gazing at the once well-stocked shelves, now seriously depleted, selected a bottle of Grand Cru Muscat and ceremoniously pulled the cork. Of the very few pleasures allowed him in life, drinking came high on the list.

Because of the way they had lived and the fact that they were often on tour, his parents had seen very little of their children. Except on nights when they entertained and wanted to show them off, but after his infant years he'd been kept out of sight. Celeste would go down in her party frock, the image of her mother, they said, and do a dance or sing them a song; the visitors found her cute. He, alone and unseen on the stairs, could never have properly taken part but he'd loved the show of it all, which had seriously thrilled him. She had always been the favoured one, her daddy's darling, her mother's pet, which meant she had, inevitably, grown up a bitch.

Esmée Morell, with her fabled charm, underneath was a selfish and callous woman, caring only for her personal fame and the husband on whom she doted. It suited her to have a pretty daughter to emphasise her own glamorous looks, but as Celeste grew older she turned on her too. She raised her to be ruthless and hard, carelessly tossing her suitors aside, promising that there were better ones yet to appear. She studied their backgrounds with scrupulous care, only welcoming into her house the ones she considered the best, by which she meant rich.

Glass in hand, he went back upstairs and switched on the drawing-room lights. The grand piano on which she had played had been silent and shrouded all these years. The antiques were dusty, the mirrors tarnished. No one any longer polished the brass. It was all just junk; he could see that now, tawdry and meaningless possessions. If they sold the lot and moved away, they could have a very much better lifestyle. But he was too scared to consider such a change or even stand up and face the world. He blamed it all on his mother.

•

36

The summer was showing no signs of letting up. Beth felt in serious need of a break. Richard had asked them to his house in France and she desperately wanted to go.

'Any time will suit me,' he said. 'I plan to be there all summer.'

Jane and Alastair were also invited; it could be a lot of fun. Richard was an exemplary host provided they let him get on with his work. He was putting together an autumn exhibition.

'Bring Imogen too.' The house was huge and Richard was her godfather.

'I can't,' she wailed. 'The show will still be running and they'd never allow me time off.' Not that she would want it, either; she was proud of being in such a great production. Every performance was fully sold out right to the end of the season.

'Good,' said Duncan, though with a grin. 'You can look after the dogs.'

'Oh, darling,' said Beth. 'Will you be all right?' She hated the thought of her stuck in London on her own. 'Perhaps you ought to ask Alice to stay.' She could even bring that awful Julie. In this hot weather they might enjoy having access to a garden.

'Mum,' said Imogen, her regular cry. 'I'm not a child any more.'

But they still hadn't caught the Circle Line killer and there'd just been another horrendous murder in, of all unlikely places, a classy department store. Though Beth was too smart to mention that. Her daughter was right; she had to live her own life.

When she had still not returned by morning, he came out in a cold sweat. From childhood she had looked after him and now was his only lifeline. He was seriously hungry, with a splitting head, the result of too much wine. He looked for an aspirin without success. He couldn't believe she would just walk out, despite the number of times she had threatened to. She loved him really; in his heart he knew that. She would not abandon him now. As he would never abandon her, even were he to have the option. They were joined at the hip and always would be. Both had grown up knowing that.

Then he remembered how he'd trashed her room and damaged some of her precious things. He had the right: in a way they were his things too. If he wanted to wear his mother's hats, it wasn't for her to interfere. But this time he had possibly gone too far. He remembered shattering her crystal bottles and grinding the shards into the beautiful rug. He gnawed his finger and thought about it. If he knew where to look, he would go and find her. Until he remembered the latest thing he had done.

He popped round the corner and bought a paper, something he'd never dared do before; just handed the man the right change and hurried away. On the second page was a tiny item in the right-hand column of just-breaking news. 'Suspect Held' was all it said. But he knew.

'My mum's had this totally mad idea,' said Imogen on the phone to Alice. 'They are off to France in a couple of days and don't want me here on my own. She suggested you might come over and stay. Bring Julie too. You could help with the dogs.'

'Whatever's got into her?' asked Alice, who'd known Beth Hardy most of her life. 'She can't still imagine you need a babysitter.'

'You know what she's like.'

'I do,' said Alice, but the thought of that lovely spacious house was enticing; the garden too at this time of year.

'It's the murders,' said Imogen. And today's nasty news of the second lot of terrorist bombs. Even though they hadn't gone off, London was now a very dangerous place.

'Tamara, Lady Fermoy-French,' mocked Alice, 'sounds rather like Danny La Rue. Out of one of the glossy mags, slashed in a ladies' loo.' Something about it was deliciously absurd. Especially in a department store. Neither of them could help chuckling.

'She was ordering something from a wedding list,' said Imogen. 'The essence of the bourgeoisie. Which only goes to prove you can't be too careful.'

Exactly her mother's thinking, of course, which was why she'd suggested that the girls should move in. They discussed it further and Alice agreed; staying with Imogen was always fun and would also mean a slightly shorter journey to work.

'What about Julie?'

'I'll ask her,' said Alice. 'But don't be surprised if she says no.' Julie had not been the best of company since getting

219

involved in the Hallmark series. She was out all hours or else reading late. Her bedroom smelt like an ashtray.

Survival had to be his first concern now that he knew she was not coming back; not, at least, before he had starved to death. He might have overplayed his hand, just hadn't thought through the repercussions; wanted to scare her and let her know how far he was willing to go. He had been alarmed by those two young women – three, he now remembered; there had been a fair one too. It seemed they were closing in from all sides. He had seen the tall one several more times on her way to the National Theatre. It surely could not be coincidence that two of them, on quite separate occasions, had been standing right outside his house, showing rather too much interest.

Later he'd seen all three together and they'd paused to watch his act and laugh. Admiration he took in his stride but laughter he could not cope with. He did what he did for the adulation, had absorbed the need with his mother's milk. They hadn't really seen him, not at any of those times, but he had most certainly taken them in. And would not forget their faces in a hurry. He closed his eyes and the blood was there, swirling around in his consciousness, making his breath come in short sharp gasps, the palms of his hands cold and clammy. The spots were gathering in front of his eyes; if he didn't sit down he would faint. Later, he'd feel the ache in his groin and know he was ready to do it again. Thus it had been since the accident in the house.

Rather to Imogen's surprise, Julie said she would love to move in. She was tired of the stifling heat in central London. It was also only a walk away, over the hill from the *Daily Mail*, closer even from the flat she shared with Alice.

'It'll be all right. She's improved a lot.' Alice was well aware of her flatmate's failings.

'Don't worry,' said Imogen. 'There's bags of room. And, to tell the truth, I like her far more than I did.'

Julie had cut her partying down, was showing a slightly more serious side. Had got them watching old films with her at weekends. She was slightly starstruck by Imogen's house but dutifully pulled her weight by walking the dogs.

After she died the police had come but had managed to keep the press away because of his age and the manner of her death. There had been a thorough investigation after which he had spent three years in a home until his sister turned twenty-one and reclaimed him. They had taught him nothing; he had rebelled. They'd been glad to see the back of him when she had agreed to act as his legal guardian. Slowly, as other stories took their place, the rumours had started to fade away. His father died in a matter of months, of a broken heart it was said. Nothing was proved and no charges brought because he was then still a minor.

Celeste had dropped out of acting school though, in truth, she had never really shared the gift. He was the one who, had he been able, was born to perpetuate the family name. A reason for his endless rage. Through a freak of nature he had been denied his birthright.

There was a Marks & Spencer in the King's Road which had to be his initial target. He was all fired up to attempt the difficult mission. After doing deep-breathing exercises, he took his bag and donned his dark glasses then set off in pursuit of something to eat. Milk and bread were the main essentials; cheese and fruit, too, if he had enough cash. He had some savings of his own but had never before had to fend for himself. He had no idea how much things cost; had never been shopping before. But people did it, it was part of life. He would just be careful to choose the shortest queue.

37

She worried about how he'd cope alone, having never before had to do so. In the eighteen years they had been on their own they had virtually never been parted. Except, of course, for his years in an institution. She thought of him now, in that tomb of a house, packed with memories he'd sooner forget, with no way of finding out where she was or if she had simply walked out. It had crossed her mind to do so any number of times; there had been occasions, as he grew older, when he'd almost driven her crazy. But the bond between them was very strong. Both knew in their hearts that, no matter what happened, she would always be there to protect him.

He'd be traumatised when she didn't come home, trapped in his own living purgatory, marooned with nothing to eat or drink, unable even to call for help or pop next door to a neighbour. She wondered if she should spill the beans but then they would only arrest him. And this time round he would get a much heavier sentence. She couldn't forget what a sweet kid he'd been. Only circumstances had caused him to change.

The night in the cell had been horrendous. She couldn't imagine how she must look. The friendly warder brought her a tray of breakfast.

'How long are they going to keep me here?'

'Until they have some answers,' said the warder. 'Four days is the legal maximum without a formal charge.'

Four days was too long to leave him alone. There was no predicting what he might do. She wished there was somebody she could trust. She had never felt more alone.

'When do I get to see DI Brewster?'

'When he's good and ready,' was the reply.

She was right; he thought she was guilty. The idea appalled her.

Brewster had been unable to sleep. He could not get her out of his mind. Although it was he who had issued the warrant, he still found it hard to believe she had killed. It wasn't only her fragile looks; everything about her was privileged – the way she moved and dressed and spoke. It simply didn't add up. They brought her back to the interview room for another confrontation but this time he found it hard to meet her eye. Any rapport they might have established had died when he had her arrested.

He asked more of his repetitive questions; she answered the same as before. She stuck to her guns; it seemed he could not touch her. She had not been in Peter Jones when that woman was killed. Nor had she murdered Miranda either, despite being on the spot. There was something she was holding back; he couldn't think what it could be. If only she'd open her heart to him, he would do all it took to save her.

Having failed to get anything out of Celeste, Brewster arranged to meet her employer, the doctor for whom she had worked for eleven years. Dr Rousseau received him in his elegant office, stylishly dressed and impeccably groomed. Brewster was struck by the softness of his hands. He was courteous and engagingly French as well as one hundred per cent on her side. No, he said, there could be no doubt. The woman he'd worked with so long could not be a killer.

'She has far too much *savoir faire*,' he said, 'to put herself in that sort of position. A lover, maybe, but – *tiens* – another employee?' It was clear he was more than a little in love with her.

They could find no link between the two women beyond shared office space. The staff confirmed that they had never been close. Their social backgrounds were worlds apart; there was no need to say more.

What was her background, Brewster wanted to know. What did she do before working for him? The doctor gave an eloquent shrug. It was so long ago he could not remember. Would it be on the files? Why, no, he said. Receptionists didn't have records.

'And her home life?'

That was the baffling part for such a sensational woman. 'None, as far as I am aware.' He only knew that she lived alone in what had once been her family home. She seemed to have little social life. Kept herself very much to herself. A shocking waste. Both men agreed on that.

*   *   *

On the way to the car, it came back to him. The night he had walked Celeste home. He had half expected her to ask him in; it was Saturday night and not yet nine. She had made an effort to look her best so why had she changed so abruptly? Both were single and unattached; at least, that was what he had understood. And he had been offering the hand of friendship, feeling he'd been too tough the first time round. They'd been chatting easily till they reached her street when all of a sudden she held out her hand, told him she'd be all right from that point and hurried off without another word.

Baffled, he'd wandered along behind her and stood on the other side of the street, regretting not being a touch more assertive instead of letting her go like that. Which was when he'd seen the flicker of light from a window on the top floor. There was obviously someone else in the house, so why had she not said so?

He went back to see her in her cell and asked the question point-blank. He might be intruding but to hell with it. She was under arrest for suspected murder. If she didn't answer his questions, he wanted to know why.

'Does anyone share your house?' he asked. She was looking drawn and unwell.

'No,' she said. 'I told you that. When are you going to let me go? It is very inconvenient being in here.'

'But after you left me, I saw a light. I stood outside your house for a while. To check that you were all right.' He felt slightly foolish.

She stared at him blankly but didn't respond except that her eye was twitching again. It was almost like a lie-detector. She needed to learn to control it.

'Are you suggesting I imagined it?' He had an irresistible urge to shake her. He wished she would get a grip on herself. Her life was on the line. 'Or a ghost maybe?'

'Perhaps,' she said. 'The house is very old.'

38

The voice that answered when Julie called was petulant and shrill.

'Yes?' it said, as though he were hard of hearing.

'Mr Beamish?' It couldn't be him; by now he must be as old as the hills.

'Who wants him?' he asked, suddenly sounding guarded.

Julie acted on inspiration. 'I am calling on behalf of Hallmark,' she said.

That did it. Immediately the petulance faded. 'Ooh,' he said, sounding decidedly camp. 'Tell me more.'

Julie grinned. They were all much the same. The smell of big bucks brought them running. 'I'm working on a new series,' she said. 'And was rather hoping you might be able to help me.'

The rest was easy. He agreed to meet and invited her over to his Wandsworth flat. 'Ought I involve my agent?' he asked.

'No,' said Julie. 'Not at this stage.' She didn't want to risk losing him. 'I'd far rather talk to you first, if you don't mind.'

He could see her whenever she liked, he said, so they made a date for the following week. For her it would mean taking time off work but this was more important. At last she seemed to be getting somewhere. She prayed he'd deliver the goods.

The morning after her lunch with Margaret and the shock of the bombs that had failed to go off, Ellie was due to go and pick up Wilbur. She had packed some clothes for him in a bag, with slippers because of his injured hip, and asked the porter to kindly get her a taxi. First, though, she rang the hospital to check that everything was on schedule.

'One moment,' said the duty nurse. 'Sister would like a word.'

Ellie hung on for several minutes until the sister came on the line. 'I'm afraid,' she said, 'there are slight complications. He won't be leaving today.' And made an appointment for Ellie to see the consultant.

'Something's come up,' said the affable man, twinkling with bonhomie. 'The bones have fused quite splendidly and he's able to walk with the help of two sticks. Soon, if he keeps up the exercises, he shouldn't have any more trouble.'

'But?' said Ellie, keen to get to the point.

'We need to do some more tests. The sugar content of his blood is high. It seems he may have contracted diabetes.'

'Why would that be?' Ellie asked. It had never been diagnosed before.

'He is overweight. He will have to make drastic diet changes.'

'Which means?' she said.

'That he'll have to stay in for at least another week. Maybe more. Until we have regulated his blood sugar level.'

Something disloyal clicked in her brain and she heaved a secret sigh of relief. Though she did her best to conceal it from the doctor.

Wilbur, however, seemed not to mind; he was already into his poker game and, as usual, made her feel she was intruding. 'Better to find out now,' he said. And get it free on the NHS. All he thought about was money. She had started to despise him.

So what was she going to do for a week? Wilbur apparently wasn't bothered. She could entertain herself, was becoming an expert. More to the point, she still had his cheques and the Paris tickets that had been deferred. She kissed him lightly then hurried away to share the good news with Margaret.

Amy was getting on Margaret's nerves with her selfish impositions. It was late July and the kids were under her feet. Margaret considered she more than pulled her weight; it wasn't within a granny's brief to look after them all the time. She read to them and took them out and stood in whenever her daughter-in-law went away with her work. But she was allowed a life of her own, which they often seemed to forget.

Much of her time she spent in the garden, especially nice at this time of year, and at night she had a lot of books to catch up with. Although she had dropped the local reading group there was an on-line one she liked in Saturday's *Times*. She was currently working her way through Thomas Hardy.

But when the phone rang and it was Ellie, she was more than willing to be disturbed. Yesterday's lunch had cheered her up and renewed her appetite for life. Ellie filled her in briefly on Wilbur's health then made her bold suggestion. A week in Paris, all expenses paid. How about it?

Margaret didn't need to think twice; it was just the tonic she needed. Although she insisted on paying for herself. We'll discuss that later, said Ellie. It was Saturday morning; they would leave on Monday. Margaret rushed off to sort through her clothes and drop a message of false regret to her importunate daughter-in-law. Ellie, delighted, went out to buy a guidebook

By the following day she had still not come home though news of the latest murder was all over the papers. There was a lot about Lady Fermoy-French and the terrible way she had met her death but all the police were reported as saying was that they were holding a suspect. No further details, but of course he guessed what must have happened. He didn't know what he would do if they came to the house. Sooner or later she was bound to crack, which meant he must make a contingency plan. Once she could prove she was in the clear, they were bound to start delving deeper. He didn't know what he would do when they came, apart from refusing to open the door. And in that event it could only be a question of time before they returned with a warrant.

Although he missed her and feared for her safety, he had also always resented her. She was able to hold down a job and live a more or less normal life. Frustrated, as he usually was, he read her mail and spied on her, scared that one day she'd have had enough and leave him. In the past two weeks he had seen her with two men, neither of whom he knew anything about. Both appeared to be after her; one had been hanging round the house. Without him she might have had a future, some children, got married, been happy. But what sort of man would take her on with him as part of the package?

He paced the house with nothing to do, not daring to risk

going out. He was too upset to do anything much except drink. From time to time he went to the window in the hope of seeing her on her way home but the quiet street, as usual, was deserted. When night came, he dared not switch on the lights but huddled alone in his attic room, biting his nails as he desperately searched for a plan. The time to leave would be in the night, though he had no idea where he'd go.

He was far too strung up to be able to sleep but when bedtime came and she still wasn't home, he decided to give it a go. He went to the window for one last look and his heart almost stopped in his chest when he saw a police car parked outside.

39

Beth had popped out for some last-minute shopping. They were catching the afternoon ferry to Dieppe. Most of the packing had already been done. Duncan was getting the car filled up. Imogen sat on the stairs with the dogs, waiting for her new housemates to arrive.

'Now try not to do too much partying,' said Beth, when she bustled back, arms full. 'Remember you need your beauty sleep. And that goes for all of you.' She need not worry too much about Imogen, who'd be at the theatre six nights a week, though she still didn't like the thought of her travelling home alone. She worried more about Julie, who had always struck her as brash and shallow. Not an obvious friend for Alice whose mother, she knew, felt much the same. Still, she was glad the girls were willing to housesit her daughter. Not that she'd put it like that, of course. Imogen would have killed her.

'The same applies to you,' said Imogen. 'Be careful on those

French roads.' She almost wished she was going too but would have more fun, she was pretty sure, staying here unchaperoned with her friends. Alice looked forward to the washing machine while Julie was planning to perfect her tan. Though she was sorry the dishy stepfather wouldn't be around.

'Now, be sure and ring us if there's anything at all.'

'Stop worrying, Mum,' said Imogen. 'Go and have that well-earned rest and forget all about the shop and me. Remember, if all else fails, we have the dogs.'

'I know, I know, but you know how I am.'

'I do,' said Imogen, hugging her.

Duncan took her aside before they left. 'Don't forget to phone,' he said. 'I know she fusses but you're still the centre of her life.'

'I know,' said Imogen. 'I promise to behave. Now go and get on that blasted ferry or else you'll ruin our orgy for tonight.'

She was waving them off when the girls arrived, spilling boxes and packages out of the cab, Julie lugging a crate of red wine, Alice carrying a pot plant.

'Oh dear,' said Beth, as they drove away.

'Shut up and relax,' said her ever-loving husband.

'What do you want to do next?' asked Imogen, after they'd done the Portobello Road and eaten lunch at the local Pizza Express.

'When are you due at the theatre?' asked Julie, still envious of Imogen's glitzy life.

'Not till six. We have plenty of time. We could always take a stroll down Kensington High Street.'

'I can do that in the week,' said Julie. It was where the paper was situated. 'If you don't mind, I'd prefer to go back to Chelsea.'

'Fine with me,' said placid Alice who was always easy, whatever it was. There was nothing she wanted to buy but so what? She liked hanging round in this jolly threesome, was glad her two friends were finally starting to click

'Do you mind if we don't go shopping?' Julie astonished them both. She was like a magpie when it came to clothes; there were things in her wardrobe with the price-tags still on. Alice had never known her pass up such a chance before.

'What is it you want to do?' asked Imogen, who had no preference either way. It was fun to hang out with Alice and her flatmate. Though she'd had her doubts about Julie at first, she was rapidly starting to like her a lot. She was full of zip and always raring to go.

'Some detective work, if you really don't mind. I have found out at last where the Forresters actually lived.'

There was a police car sitting outside the house, though it drove away when the girls arrived. Probably having their lunch, said Julie, and now off to watch the cricket. They drifted past but the house looked abandoned, even more than it had before. The brass on the door badly needed a polish and the mat was a disgrace. There were buttercups and grass growing up between the tiles in the porch.

'It's a shame,' said Alice, 'that they've let it go. It must have been glorious in its day.' She imagined it with its windows agleam and a footman waiting by the open door as the carriages rolled up and the guests arrived.

'Hang on a minute!' said Imogen suddenly. 'I swear I've been to this house before.' She stood quite still till it all came back. The night of the bombs and that woman, Celeste. Only that time she'd only seen it for a few minutes. 'I don't think

I ever heard her last name. I'll ask my mum next time we speak.'

'Did you do anything about finding their graves?' Alice asked. Seeing the actual house made it suddenly more intriguing.

'No,' said Julie. 'There hasn't been time.' But she told them about Leonard Beamish. 'I'm going to see him on Monday,' she said. 'He sounds a bit of an oddity.'

'I would guess they are buried in Brompton Cemetery,' said Imogen. 'We could check that out. Or else at the actors' church in Covent Garden.'

'What are you going to do?' asked Alice, falling in with Julie's purposeful stride. They had walked the length of the block and now were heading back.

'I shall ring the bell and play it by ear which seems to make the best sense. If there's no one there, I shall leave my card and hope that someone will contact me.' If that should fail, she was hoping Beamish might come through.

Julie rang the bell and, when nothing happened, scribbled a note on her business card and dropped it through the tarnished letter box.

Alice sat on the warm brick wall and closed her eyes in the afternoon sun. 'It must have been wonderful in the old days, living in such an elegant street, surrounded by artists and writers.'

Julie and Imogen swapped a glance. There went Alice, the dreamer, again. Still, she did have a point. It seemed ludicrous that such a magnificent house should be left to decay.

They had finally left. He had checked all morning and at last the police car had driven off. He had no idea what they could have wanted since he hadn't opened the door. But they'd sat

238

there in shifts throughout the night, presumably ringing the bell at times. He didn't know since he'd been upstairs in the attic. Now, however, it was afternoon and the watch had not been replaced. It might be because of the weekend or else they had simply given up. Either way, he was glad they had gone and was able to breathe more freely. He couldn't stand being cooped up like this so would head straight back to his usual patch. The South Bank was crowded on Saturday nights. There had been more bombs but no one seemed terribly scared; he hoped to make a killing.

Still no word from her but he'd given up. Sooner or later they would let her go or else they would have to charge her. He showered and shaved, feeling much better, then packed his bag for the evening shift. The itch was beginning to get much worse and would soon be beyond control

He was daily growing more confident since he'd crossed the barrier of learning to shop. He had counted his money and had enough to keep him going for a week or so. He had never done anything for himself; all his life he had been looked after. Those in the know still thought him subnormal but nothing was actually wrong with his brain. Celeste knew that, which was why they stuck together. He had never cooked but had often watched her; knew how to heat a frying pan and use the microwave. And now he knew he could also shop, the walls of his prison were really starting to fall.

Wearing dark glasses, he checked the street in case the cops had returned. What he saw instead, with a sickening jolt, was something that stopped him dead in his tracks. All three harpies were right outside, one of them sitting on his wall.

40

Suicide bombers had struck again, this time with no casualties since none of the bombs went off. The police put it down to incompetence. Somebody somewhere had royally boobed which meant they now had a number of leads and were rapidly closing in. The gang had been caught on CCTV, easily recognised and now under siege. The media frenzy was at its height; Londoners, glued to their screens, were watching it avidly. Brewster, whose area of expertise it was, was in overall charge of the operation. Burgess had also come into his own and was out there controlling the crowds.

It meant that they'd had to put on hold the murder inquiry they were working on. The suspect they'd taken in was still in detention. Despite the fact that they had her on film, she still refused to co-operate, and, without more evidence, they might not be able to charge her. Before this latest emergency they'd done all they could to reason with her yet, unbelievably, she was still refusing to talk. Burgess had been to the house with a team but no one appeared to be living there now. If it weren't for the suspect's original statement, and the fact it was there they had picked her up, the place might well have been derelict, it looked so completely uncared for. All the windows were firmly shut, unusual at this time of year. The paint was flaking; the window glass looked wobbly in the frames. The team had taken a quick look round but, until they'd been issued with a formal warrant, there was nothing they could do to gain admittance.

Remembering the flicker at the upstairs room, Brewster put a round-the-clock watch on the house but no one was spotted going in or out during that time. Every room remained in darkness; nobody ever answered the bell. In the end he called the surveillance off. The patrolmen were needed for the terrorist round-up. Why she refused to co-operate, he still couldn't figure out. Nor could Dr Rousseau explain though he was obviously loyally on her side.

What troubled him most was his own state of mind; his head was in a turmoil. Something about her wistful beauty had really succeeded in getting to him. He was developing stronger feelings than any he'd experienced since his youth. He feared it might be the first stirrings of love. He hoped not.

Sir Peregrine Fermoy-French was a fop in the old Edwardian style. Thirty years older than his trophy wife, he still affected the air of a man who spends most of his time at his club. Brewster was ushered in by a maid who'd have taken his hat if he'd had one. The baronet stood by the empty fireplace sipping a glass of dry sherry. He pointedly didn't offer one to Brewster. Nor did he invite him to sit.

'Mind if I take the weight off my feet?' Brewster wasn't

242

impressed by this snobbery nonsense. An inherited title did not equate with a serving member of Her Majesty's forces, especially one who'd been wounded in active service.

Sir Peregrine grunted but could hardly refuse, though he still didn't offer Brewster a drink. Not that he would have accepted one while on duty. He pulled out his notebook to underline that this visit was strictly official.

'Tell me,' he asked, 'can you think of anyone who might have wanted to harm your wife?'

'Almost everyone, I'd say, old chap. Beginning with yours truly.' If that was humour, it left Brewster cold. The man was vile; he wished he could run him in.

'Chapter and verse, please,' he asked him formally, tapping the notebook with his pen. 'I understand Lady Fermoy-French was a bit of a socialite.'

'You can say that again.' Sir Peregrine laughed as though it were not his wife who was under discussion. His dead wife, what's more. He might have shown some respect. 'She was out so much I rarely saw her, not that it made much difference. The stuffing went out of the marriage a long time ago.'

'How did she spend her time?' asked Brewster, refusing to be drawn. From the little he knew of the latest victim, she had been well matched with this ghastly man.

'Oh, the usual stuff. You know what they're like,' said the baronet, topping up his glass. 'Shopping, gossiping, playing bridge. Sitting on endless committees frittering time.'

'Would you say she was popular?'

'Hardly,' he said, with a sniff of disdain. 'Her sole claim to fame was as my wife.'

Brewster paused then cut to the chase. This was going nowhere; the man was a boor and a fool. If there'd been a way to implicate him, he'd have done it like a shot. Patiently, he tried another tack though it really hurt him to do so.

'Does the name Celeste Forrester ring any bells?' He tensed as he spoke the name aloud.

The baronet, barely listening, shook his head. 'I could never tell any of her friends apart; they were all as vacuous as each other. Now I must fly.' He looked at his watch. 'Lunch in the City with my broker.'

A hollow man with a celluloid heart. Brewster gave him his card. 'If you think of anything, let me know.' But he knew he was wasting his time.

Brewster had reached another dead end. He felt angry and frustrated. Despite the fact that they had her on film, he could find no link between her and the victim. Yet the peculiar viciousness of the attack bore all the signs of the work of the Circle Line killer.

41

The address in Wandsworth was a purpose-built block, 1930s and slightly seedy but decidedly atmospheric. Julie arrived there with time to spare to get the feel of the neighbourhood and savour its ambience. A natural journalist from birth, she knew the importance of getting the details right. She rang the doorbell precisely at ten and a voice she recognised from her call demanded, in stentorian tones, who was there.

'Julie,' she said, then, remembering her cover, 'from Hallmark Television.'

He buzzed her in and was waiting to greet her, a gnomish man in a shiny suit with a poorly disguised toupee. Leonard Beamish was as she'd imagined, an ageing Puck who had failed to fulfil his potential.

'Enchanted, I'm sure.' He ushered her through to a minute sitting room where a couple of couches occupied most of the space. He offered her tea and went to make it, leaving her free to look round and make herself at home. Despite the weather, the windows were shut and the atmosphere decidedly musty. It was like a time-warp from an earlier age. There were antimacassars on the chairs and a rubber plant badly in need of a dust. The walls were covered with fading sepia photos.

'Ah,' he said, coming up behind her. 'Me in starrier days.' He was holding a tray with a dainty cloth, a teapot in a knitted cosy, a couple of Jubilee cups and saucers and a plate of ginger biscuits. He placed it all fussily on the table and plumped up the cushions for her to sit.

Today she had taken the wise precaution of toning down her image. Instead of her usual garish persona, with garments deliberately chosen to clash, she was dressed like a sober office worker in her plain grey interview suit. Her hair, instead of its usual spikes, was brushed back smoothly behind her ears and the whole effect was enhanced by black-framed glasses. They'd have died in the office to see her like this but Julie was an instinctive pro. She needed to put this man at his ease before starting on the questions.

She glanced again at the photographs, in most of which he appeared. Clowning around or striking a pose, he had clearly missed the dramatic roles because of his lack of stature and high-pitched voice. His hair was faded but had once been red; his eyes were pale blue and bloodshot. As he poured the tea she smelt peppermint on his breath.

'So,' he said, once they were settled, politely passing the ginger nuts. 'What is it you want from me? I'm all ears.'

Which he was indeed, an odd little man with the cosmetic smile of an erstwhile imp whose dentures didn't quite fit. Julie had brought a fat folder with her to emphasise her professional status. She sensed she might be stepping on delicate ground.

'It's good of you to see me,' she said. 'And of course you will be reimbursed for your time.' Rupert had not mentioned expenses but she felt it struck an authentic note. She was having fun working herself into the role.

'No need,' he said, and his smile was broad. He sat like a nervous interviewee, fingers entwined in his lap.

He thinks I am offering him work, she thought, wondering how she could let him down without too much damage to his ego. She flicked through the file while she organised her thoughts, fearing to mess things up at this crucial stage.

'I wonder if you could tell me,' she said, trying to sound as impersonal as she could, 'what you know about the actress, Esmée Morell.'

His eyes bulged and his jaw sagged slightly; she feared he might swallow his plate. Whatever he knew, it was clear she had caught him off guard.

'Goodness,' he said. 'You have got me there. It's been years since I even thought about her. What exactly is it you are after?'

Julie dramatically lowered her glasses and looked him directly in the eye. 'As much as you can remember,' she said. 'In particular, when and how she came to die.'

'Mum,' said Imogen, when Beth rang in to check how things were going. 'What was the name of that woman you had here for lunch?'

'What woman?' asked Beth, in holiday mode, who entertained a lot.

'The beautiful one you met on a train. On 7/7, the morning the bombs went off.'

'Oh,' said Beth. 'Celeste Forrester. You've met her a couple of times.'

'What do you know about her life apart from living in a very big house on her own?'

'Almost nothing. She doesn't say much.' They mainly talked about the murder and the cop.

'Do you happen to know who her parents were? If her mother was an actress?'

'No,' said Beth. 'Though it wouldn't surprise me. What's this all about?'

'Just something Julie's doing for the paper. I'm helping her with research.'

'So it's working out?' Beth was relieved though hoped the awful Julie wouldn't lead her astray.

'Absolutely. We're getting on fine. She's got a wicked sense of humour.'

We may have cracked it, she wrote in a note which she left on the kitchen table for Julie. Since Celeste was indeed a Forrester, they must be getting close.

Esmée Morell, a name from the past. At first that was all he said. Julie knew, though, from his instant pallor, that he was holding things back. She held her breath and said nothing at all while he sank into a deep reverie. He gulped his tea, then scratched his head; she feared for the safety of the toupee. His eyes were focused on the middle distance. He seemed to forget she was there.

'Esmée Morell,' he eventually said, and she had the feeling he was faking fast. 'The most charismatic woman I've ever known.'

The plunge taken, he turned to face her, almost defiant in his stance. The colour had returned to his cheeks; the pale-blue eyes were fired. He had, however, misjudged Julie, who almost always gave better than she got.

'Mind if I go to the little girl's room?' she asked.

The bathroom was another cliché, though in no way was she surprised. Huge framed portraits of long-dead monarchs, interspersed with signed photos of stars. One of them, right above the cistern, was signed flamboyantly with Esmée's name, with a row of kisses, and inscribed to 'dearest Lennie'.

Julie discreetly washed her hands and plastered her hair back behind her ears. She was definitely getting somewhere now; felt she might be closing in on the truth.

42

As a child he had been adorable, with his soulful eyes and appealing smile and a wistfulness that practically broke your heart. Celeste was ten when her brother was born and right from the start, as a matter of course, had made herself responsible for his welfare. The rejoicing in the house had been great; at last the son and heir had arrived. Madame had fulfilled her ultimate dream; her family was now complete. Trumpets sounded and the press went wild but, rather than putting her nose out of joint, the son's arrival helped to aggrandise Celeste. With the baby carriage to push around, she found herself even more in the spotlight. The christening was held at St Paul's, Covent Garden where plaques to both her parents were now displayed. They would, of course, have preferred the Abbey but, as things turned out, that was not to be. The hubbub that heralded Oberon's birth was, ironically, the start of their gradual decline.

Most of theatrical London was there, including a handful of megastars who flew in specially for the occasion, two of them as godparents. Esmée, already slightly wobbly on her feet, had stood at the font in one of her hats and her vibrant trill had resounded throughout the church. The paparazzi were waiting outside when the band of luvvies spilled into the graveyard and Sir Edward voiced some well-chosen words to welcome his longed-for son. Another Forrester. Everyone cheered. May he continue the illustrious thespian line.

The rejoicing, alas, had not lasted long. The idyll rapidly faded. Despite his beauty, as the baby grew the realisation had gradually dawned. He was not quite as perfect as he had seemed at first. Esmée, almost demented with grief, abruptly turned her back on the child, banishing him to the upper floors and trying to pretend he didn't exist. At first she admitted the fault was hers though she later rescinded that story. She'd had German measles which was no big deal. She had ceased her drinking for the full nine months. All it had been was an accident of fate. Later he had come to share that opinion. But it *was* her fault, there could be no dispute. She should never have let him be born. It was no life at all for any living creature, especially one with his intelligence and looks. The biggest waste, though, was of his inherited talent.

Celeste gradually took over the care of him, along with a battalion of nursery staff, none of whom stayed long out of pure frustration. Her parents were very seldom home, being usually either on tour or performing in London, and neither now would acknowledge their only son. Used, as they were, to adulation, flawed perfection was something they could not accept. Celeste was too young to understand quite what a burden she had taken on: a lifetime's devotion that ended her own career.

Now, as she languished in her cell, she reflected on all those wasted years. If only her mother could have come to terms with what was no more than a quirk of fate, her own life might have been happier too and the ultimate tragedy avoided.

This time he'd exceeded even himself, landing her in a situation from which she could not see any easy escape. Short of blowing the whistle on him, something she was resolved not to do, she would have to remain in custody until they formally charged her. Or let her go; without evidence they could not hold her for more than four days. And though Brewster said he had visual proof, in fact he was mistaken.

Beamish had acted with both the Forresters, starting at Stratford in 1969 in Trevor Nunn's acclaimed *Midsummer Night's Dream*. She played Titania, Forrester Oberon and Beamish a critically applauded Puck. He was just seventeen at the time; it was his first break.

'That was the season they got together,' said Beamish. 'My God, she was hot. She played her in a diaphanous gown, which was pretty daring, considering her age. The magic between them was electrifying. Sex just oozed from their every pore. By the end of the season Esmée was pregnant. They married two months later.'

His eyes were misty with a strong emotion. He'd been more than a little in love with her himself; the effect, he said, she'd had upon most men.

'Tell me about her,' said Julie gently, careful not to destroy the mood. She switched on the small recording device she had brought.

Leonard Beamish was off in a trance; the words came tumbling out. 'The attraction between them was sex incarnate. The

253

audiences lapped it up. It was like the pull between Burton and Taylor. I have never seen anything like it before or since.'

'And the child?' At last she was making progress.

'A daughter. Celeste or something fancy like that. Conveniently born in a gap between productions.'

Julie waited but he had dried up, back in his own emotional past. 'The wedding,' he said at last, 'was amazing. *The* event of the social year. Everyone who was anyone came. I was the pageboy who carried the ring.'

'You're kidding!' said Julie, stifling her mirth.

'Indeed I am not,' he said huffily. 'I was lovely then, at just seventeen. Small for my age. They said I looked younger. I could have been the next Nureyev, you know.'

Julie said nothing, let him ramble on. Once he had got it out of his system, she would bring on the heavier guns.

Ten years later their son was born. Esmée, by then, was in her late forties and the life she lived had not been conducive to conception.

'She was hardly ever at home,' he explained. 'The daughter was raised by the household staff. The Forresters were the king and queen of the stage. When the boy was born she went wild with delight. They named him Oberon to commemorate their first meeting.'

He described the occasion at Drury Lane when Esmée had brought the new baby onstage and held him aloft like a sporting trophy to the clamorous applause of the crowd.

'Another Forrester male is born,' she had proudly announced to the audience. 'To follow in his father's distinguished foot-steps.' Then, handing him to her beaming husband, she blew air kisses to the balcony. Somewhere, up in one of the boxes, her ten-year-old daughter was looking on. In eight years' time she would be at RADA herself.

'Esmée always lived life to the full. It was one of the things her fans most enjoyed.' Beamish clearly had never been able to exorcise her ghost. 'For a week or so he went everywhere with her, as pampered as a lapdog. She enjoyed the role of devoted mother and hammed it up as much as she could. Until, one day, she realised how ageing it was. The baby was relegated to the wings and never again seen in public. Esmée reverted to playing the vamp. The world forgot she had children.'

'But what really happened? There has to be more.' Julie was growing impatient now. 'She can't just have given the whole thing up and vanished into thin air.'

'She died,' said Beamish, with misty eyes. 'At the absolute pinnacle of her fame. The papers all carried the story but then went silent.'

'Silent?'

'Silent. The world forgot. And five weeks later he was dead too, of cancer activated by a broken heart.'

'What happened?'

'An accident at home. She tripped on the stairs while arranging flowers and stabbed herself with her pruning shears.'

Even tough Julie recoiled at that. 'My God, what a horrible way to die! Surely they could have saved her? She was in her own home.'

Beamish said no. 'She was all alone. By the time she was found it was too late.' Crumpled at the foot of the stairs, the blade still stuck in her throat.

'But the children and the domestic staff?'

'Celeste was at RADA, in her second year. The boy saw it

happen but was only eight. There was nothing he could do to save her. He watched her bleed to death.'

'Wait a second,' cried Julie, disbelieving. 'He was old enough to have raised the alarm. He must have known about 999, could have simply run into the street for help. Eight is fully *compos mentis*, hardly a child any more.' The story simply didn't add up. Part of it must be missing.

'Ah,' said Beamish, suddenly sly. 'It wasn't quite that simple.'

43

It was days since he'd last had a full night's sleep; the Circle Line case was destroying his peace of mind. He couldn't stop thinking about Celeste and what he could do to exonerate her. Even though she refused to co-operate, he still had a feeling in his gut that she was holding something back, though he hadn't yet worked out what. He wondered if she was shielding someone, which seemed the most likely scenario. Though what she hoped to achieve, he couldn't imagine. Again he drifted over to Tite Street and stood long minutes outside her house, remembering the night he had lingered there once before.

He stared up at the attic window where he had fancied he'd seen a light. Nothing there now but a blank façade with the curtains three-quarters closed. He rang the bell but nobody came, then stooped and peered through the letter box. All he could hear in the cavernous silence was the distant ticking of a clock. To gain admittance he would need a warrant but hadn't enough yet to justify that. Her face on film might place her in the store but not the murder weapon in her hand. They needed evidence to back it up: at the very least, a link between her and the victim. He could only hold her another two days, after which he was legally bound to let her go.

The simplest way forward would be if she'd learn to trust him.

She was pale and defiant yet beautiful when the warder ushered him into her cell. Whatever happens, don't screw this up, he prayed. The prison overall did her pasty skin and unwashed hair no favours, yet still she managed to stop the blood in his veins. He had never known anyone like her before. She rose from her seat on the hard narrow bed and received him like a society hostess without a hint of recognition. He had locked her up like an animal, thereby forfeiting any rights. She made it clear she resented this intrusion.

And yet they'd come close to falling in love, or so he sincerely believed. She had got to him in a way no other woman had. All his life he had trusted no one, especially since the booby trap, yet something about her defiant beauty touched the void in his heart. They were both emotionally crippled, it seemed. Not the best basis for love, perhaps, though he, at least, had been willing to give it a try.

Now here they were, in a prison cell, on opposite sides of the law. She facing charges of multiple murder; he there to put her inside if he could.

'Sorry to disturb you,' he said, indicating that she should sit. 'I've just looked in to check that you are all right.'

The ice in her eyes chilled him to the bone. 'Why are you really here?' she said. 'I have told you what little I know.'

'I need proof that you didn't commit this last murder. Remember, we have your face on film. Without some assistance from you, we can't let you go.'

'I wasn't even in the store,' she said. 'I have told you that several times. I was still travelling home at the time that woman was killed.'

'But in the vicinity of the store.'

'Along with several thousand others. Whoever the cameras caught, it wasn't me.'

Her indignation was so convincing, he almost believed she was telling the truth. But until she could prove she had not been there he had no other choice but to think her guilty. Which meant there could be no future in their friendship.

44

They caught the eight o'clock Eurostar, having met at Waterloo. Margaret had left at the crack of dawn to get there from Haywards Heath in time; Ellie was so fired up by the trip, she wanted to cram in as much as she possibly could. She was thrilled at the chance to see Paris after all. Wilbur, despite his parsimonious streak, always believed in pampering himself so had splurged on first-class tickets. Ellie and Margaret, excited as schoolgirls, faced each other in the exclusive seats and were instantly served with a glass of champagne before a lavish breakfast.

'This is certainly the life,' said Margaret, who at home would only have tea and toast. They had never travelled first class, especially after Jack retired. They had always looked for economy deals though had seen quite a lot of the world.

Ellie had never in her life before been to a country where she didn't know the language. She would not remotely have dared do it on her own. Their fellow travellers were businessmen, working on laptops or engrossed in the papers. The carriage had the feeling of a reading-room, and Ellie and Margaret lowered their voices, though could not prevent the occasional shriek of merriment bursting out. Poor old Wilbur, stuck in his bed. Ellie was sorry about the diagnosis although, if it led to his losing weight, it could only be for the best. All his life he had been a glutton and in recent years had been piling it on. She had given up trying to lecture him because he would not listen.

The waitress offered them more champagne, which both of them declined. They didn't want to be tipsy before they even got there.

He was just recovering from the shock when he spotted the card on the floor by the door. Julie Hudson of the *Daily Mail*. 'I would very much like to talk to you. If you would ring me at this number.' Brazen hussy; he cautiously checked but the street was now blessedly empty.

He was traumatised and began to shake. This was not something he'd handled before. Though Saturday nights saw his richest pickings, he cancelled his evening plans. They were closing in; he had seen it coming, though from another angle entirely. His sister's love life he could control. A national tabloid he could not. Sweating and scared, he withdrew to the cellar to pull another expensive cork and sit in the dark, away from prying eyes. His world was disintegrating all round. He might as well drink the lot.

Later, once he felt slightly calmer, his fighting spirit came surging back. There were very few people who had ever scared him; they did not include a sluttish girl. He knew it wasn't the long-haired one whose path he had tracked several times to the theatre. It must be the one with the spikes and short skirt. She had the look of a journalist. Well, Miss Hudson of the *Daily Mail*, now he knew where he could find her.

The hotel Wilbur had booked was small but beautifully situated, close to the Place Vendôme and the Tuileries gardens. Ellie suggested a second room but Margaret said she was happy to share. It was far more fun when travelling with a companion.

'If you're sure you don't mind.' Ellie was pleased. She was nervous of being alone in a foreign hotel. Suppose she needed to talk to the maid or ask for anything in the night? She wasn't used to travelling solo, was glad to have Margaret with her.

Despite the breakfast they'd had on the train, both were feeling peckish again so they dumped their bags and went straight out to get a feel of the city. It was Paris at its most alluring. The sun was high; their spirits too. They settled at an outside table and ordered two glasses of wine.

'*Vin ordinaire*. That's all right over here.' Margaret was still in charge of the drinks and Ellie more than content to let her order.

Margaret had been to Paris before, many times in her student years and fairly frequently ever since as she loved to browse in the galleries and museums. It was fun to be here with an ingénue who was wide-eyed with wonder at all the sights. Ellie made an enchanting companion, a mixture of girlish innocence and an insubordinate guile. Her observations made Margaret smile. She had clearly been married to Wilbur long enough. The demure appearance concealed an impressive intelligence.

She also knew a lot about art; Margaret was privately dazzled. She had, she explained, done an arts degree, though had never actually graduated since Wilbur had swept her off down the aisle before she had finished the course. In those days he had been very persuasive and, at least in her parents' eyes, quite a catch.

'The problem with Chippewa Falls,' she explained, 'is that it's stuck in a bit of a rut. Fine for baking pies and raising children but in no way intellectually stimulating.'

Here in Paris, with its bustling streets and all kinds of experiences waiting to be sampled, Ellie was finally coming into her own. London had been wonderful too but there she had been constrained by Wilbur. Margaret was an inspiring companion, energetic and knowledgeable, prepared to walk for miles without a murmur. Even the pavements, Ellie found, in Margaret's company seemed less hard. She was starting to open up like a Japanese flower.

Margaret admitted to being lonely; Ellie that her marriage was not up to scratch. Over quiet meals in cosy bistros, both let down their guards and poured out their hearts to each other. They ought never have moved from Croydon, said Margaret, but they hadn't known then that Jack would die. They had planned it as phase three of their lives, an exciting new beginning.

'He worked so hard, took so little time off, it seems unfair that he should have died so soon. He was a lovely man. I wish you had known him. I know he'd have taken to you.'

What would she do, Ellie wanted to know, to try to expand her horizons? Gardening, sewing cushion covers and babysitting for unappreciative children was not nearly enough for a woman not yet old with so many outside interests. Margaret laughed. She could not disagree. She had spent much time herself considering just that.

'Now that I've met you,' she confessed, 'I see what I mainly lack is a friend. Not just someone for shopping and coffee but a genuine kindred spirit.' Someone to go to the pictures with and discuss whatever might be troubling her. Someone to join her on cultural trips like this.

Ellie wholeheartedly agreed. She felt very much the same. This Paris trip had opened her eyes to what life untrammelled by a husband could be like. She had telephoned Wilbur several times and he'd grumbled a lot but patently did not miss her. The treatment was working, his blood sugar was down. They had it under control. He would be quite sorry to leave, he freely admitted.

'I hate to say it,' confided Ellie, 'but he's like an albatross round my neck. He has retired but I am more shackled than ever.' She had once suggested he iron his shirts and he'd looked at her in bewilderment. Household chores were a woman's domain. She had never once known him clear the dishes or even make himself a cup of coffee.

'He expects to be waited on hand and foot even though he has nothing much else to do. Slavery went out with Wilberforce but my Wilbur seems not to know that.'

They laughed, clasped hands and ordered a second bottle.

Margaret told her more about Jack and the cake he had iced one Christmas and Ellie said he'd deserved a medal for not being gender-bound.

'From all I've heard,' she said, 'you were very well matched.'

'We had a lot of interests in common. Liked walking and archaeological digs. When he retired we joined the National Trust.' She really should have kept up the visits but found it lonely doing things on her own. 'Next time you're over, perhaps you would join me on some outings.'

Ellie's regret, which she'd never told Wilbur, was having to give up her college degree. 'I'm not sure it would have made much difference but at least I'd have letters after my name and could maybe get a job in a museum.'

'You could do that now. It's never too late, not with adult education.' Margaret fancied training as a Blue Badge guide. It took two years and meant intensive study but would certainly get her out of the house and, indeed, enable her to meet new friends.

They finished their meal then, arm in arm, went off to see the Picasso museum, after which they planned to stroll along the Seine.

The actors' church in Covent Garden. It did make excellent sense. Imogen, whose heritage was the theatre, had thought of something that Julie had not. Of course that was where they'd be buried; she'd bet on it now. She left the office sharp at six, after making arrangements to meet colleagues later, and took the Underground to Covent Garden. It was still very hot; the Piazza was buzzing with street performers out in force. The first one who really caught her eye was a mime. He stood in one corner, not on a box but on his own like a marionette with his sad, white-painted face. He drooped, like Chaplin beneath a lamp-post, waiting for someone to work his strings and when Julie stopped, amused, to admire him, he rolled his heavily made-up eyes and gave her all he'd got. She loved it. He was the real thing, as Marcel Marceau as they came, by far the best she had ever seen in London. If he'd had a cap, which he didn't, which seemed odd, she would have made a donation.

She found the church with no trouble at all, right in the middle of theatreland, a masterpiece by the architect Inigo Jones.

Inside it was spacious and filled with light as the setting sun cast its rays through the glorious windows. Julie moved slowly down each aisle, carefully reading each wall-mounted plaque, anxious not to miss a single one. She found Vivien Leigh and Edith Evans and a host of other illustrious names. Now that she knew that the daughter was living she had very strong hopes she would find the son. Rupert should be pleased with her. She felt she might be close to winning the jackpot.

45

The mime was there when she left the church, having found what she had been looking for, only this time he had moved considerably closer. He showed no sign of being alive, was slumped, hands in pockets, against a railing, his deadpan face with its great tragic eyes focused blankly into space. Beneath each eye he had painted a teardrop and his scarlet mouth drooped in abject despair. He wore a red-striped matelot shirt, black pants and neat white gloves. His hair was covered by a curly wig, traditional in the old-fashioned way. Perhaps he was performing somewhere nearby.

She was meeting colleagues for supper at Orso's so made her way slowly across the Piazza, still thronging with tourists and workers on their way home. Imogen's hunch had turned out to be right. Both the Forresters were buried there, though their plaque simply gave the briefest of details with no mention of progeny. Still, it was a start: the dates were there. They had died, as Beamish had said, within weeks of each other. So what had happened to their son if the daughter still lived in the house? Julie felt really fired by the progress she'd made.

One of her colleagues from the paper was moving on to higher things. A bunch of them were throwing an impromptu party. There were twelve of them seated round one table and the noise they made was stupendous. The other diners at this hour were mainly headed to the theatre and appeared not to mind. Julie was wearing her shortest skirt and highest heels for the occasion. The two other women in the party left early. Julie could drink as well as the blokes and the wine was certainly flowing that night. The management brought replacements as fast as they could. It was gone eleven by the time they dispersed, so Julie headed to Leicester Square to catch the tube to Notting Hill.

He was there again as she crossed the Piazza, this time juggling balls. A small crowd stood around him, cheering him on. Julie liked his doleful face, which never seemed to alter its expression. She wondered what it would take to get him to smile. This time he did have his cap on the ground so she tossed him a couple of pounds as she passed; she hoped she would see him again.

There were acrobats performing nearby and a Creole jazz band playing in Jubilee Market. It was Tuesday night; the place was jumping even as late as this. The hot summer's night was fragrant with incense and the candyfloss smell of cheap tobacco. Julie loitered, enjoying the ambience, and on an impulse stopped for another drink. This was the city she'd adopted when she'd managed to make the break from the north. As soon as she could afford the rent, she hoped to move into Soho. She sat outside with her glass of wine and tapped her foot to the lively music. She was thrilled with where she had got with her research. First thing tomorrow she would talk to Rupert. She hoped he would let her help with the book. This could well be the big step forward she needed.

It was time to go or she'd miss her train. The fastest route was down Maiden Lane. The crowds were thinner there and it was darker. A figure stepped suddenly out of the shadows, the white-faced mime, still wearing his gloves, his face fixed into a tragic mask, accentuated by the painted teardrops. Julie, startled, stopped dead in her tracks. For a second he'd really scared her.

'Hello!' she said, once she'd caught her breath. This surely had to be more than coincidence. She wondered if he had followed her. Unless, of course, he was a different mime.

He didn't respond to her friendly greeting, just stood there, blocking her progress in the narrow lane. Then slowly he started to back away, beckoning her with one white-gloved finger until he vanished round the corner into an unlit courtyard. Julie laughed, enjoying the game, which was doubtless part of his act. He was probably a student from drama school earning money in the vacation. Soon he'd unmask and they'd have a good laugh, might even manage another drink if she caught the night bus home.

There was a restaurant across the courtyard with bursts of laughter from within. The whole world seemed to be partying tonight. Julie went with the flow. Laughing herself, she followed him, away from the lighted street and into the shadows. What a lark. She would tell the girls and they must come here again another evening.

*   *   *

Just for a moment she thought she'd lost him till a lamp picked out his white face. He was standing silently waiting for her in the corner.

'Hang on, I'm coming,' called Julie gaily, tripping across the cobbles on her high heels. This was turning into quite an adventure, a filler for the paper maybe. A touch of authentic Dickensian London for the readers. There was obvious movement inside the restaurant, which must be heading for closing time. Soon the diners would issue forth and the moment would be lost. She moved up close and touched his arm to let him know she was there.

For a long rapt moment he stared at her and she stared back at his dead-white face. Even this close she could not make out exactly what he looked like. His hair was concealed beneath the wig; his hands by the tight white gloves. He stood with a dancer's rigid pose, his feet in their black ballet shoes turned out. There were big dark circles round his eyes and tiny comma-like eyebrows. It must take him hours to apply all that paint. She wondered if he went home like that or had somewhere he could change. His mouth was fixed in a downward arc. She had a sudden desire to make him smile.

She trusted him instinctively; he was part of the night theatre. So when he beckoned again she obediently followed. Into the shadows, away from the lamp; she wondered if he'd reveal himself, whether perhaps he was someone she knew simply having a laugh. She moved a bit closer, flirtatiously, prepared for whatever he had to offer. But still he beckoned and, what the hell, there were plenty of people about.

Just for a moment she thought he would kiss her until the light glinted off the knife and she knew, too late, she had badly misjudged him. Then he laughed, oh how he laughed, as the blade went in and she crumpled at his feet. He stood there silently guffawing and the garish arc reversed itself. The mournful eyes now revealed their dislike. He stepped over her body in his ballet shoes and faded into the night.

46

Detective Inspector Brewster arrived in a big official car though, to both girls' surprise, was wearing plainclothes. He stopped in the doorway and patted the dogs, who bounced around him with waving tails and none of the fake aggression they sometimes showed.

'What lovely animals.' His smile was broad, his handshake agreeably firm. Though he walked with an almost imperceptible limp, both of them found him very attractive despite the scar on his face.

Imogen led him to the drawing room, having shut the dogs in the kitchen, out of the way. Brewster seated himself in an armchair and the girls perched side by side on a couch. They were both so young, he thought, and so vulnerable. It sickened his heart that these things should occur. Life in London grew daily grimmer. He looked around and admired the room, then courteously asked them about themselves. Was gravely impressed that Alice sold books and that Imogen was a dancer.

'I will certainly come to your show,' he said. He might even invite Celeste. It was early days, he was well aware, and they both had a lot of bridges to mend but he still had hopes that they might make it once she was cleared of suspicion. He would have to release her now, knowing she could not have been implicated in Julie's death, though she still had a lot of explaining to do, not least how her face had been caught on camera when she swore that she hadn't been in the store. This, however, was far more urgent. He would sort things out with Celeste when he had the time.

After some more congenial chat, he pulled out his notebook and turned to Alice.

'You shared a flat, I understand, with the victim, Julie Hudson.'

Alice nodded and gave him the details. He could see how shattered she was. When the squad car had arrived in the middle of the night, neither of them could believe the news, even though Julie was out a lot and occasionally drank too much. The police had gone first to Onslow Gardens and the downstairs neighbour had directed them here.

Brewster asked how she'd first met Julie. Alice told him about the typing course.

'So you must have known her well,' he said. 'Was she, perhaps, your closest friend?'

No, that was Imogen, Alice explained, which was how she came to be living here while Imogen's parents were away in France. All she and Julie had been was flatmates, though of course she'd been very fond of her and was horrified by her death.

'And did you spend much of your time together? Apart from living beneath one roof.'

'Quite a lot,' said Alice, considering. 'We ate at home maybe once a week and hung around together at weekends.'

'So you knew each other's friends,' he suggested, scribbling her answers in his notebook.

'Not really,' said Alice. They had moved in quite different circles. The only ones she had met were men, usually connected with her work. The *Daily Mail*, she told him, which Brewster knew.

Something about him warmed Imogen's heart, even now when she was so shaken. He gave the impression of strength and stability, both qualities she admired in Duncan. No wonder her mother had married him. Men like that were quite rare these days. Knowing Brewster was on the case made Imogen feel far less threatened. Her mother was insisting on coming straight home although she had begged her not to. She had Alice here as well as the dogs. And now they had this policeman.

Brewster was thinking how cute they were; bright and gutsy and brave. Despite the horror of their close friend's death, they appeared to be coping remarkably well. He was glad the parents were coming home. It was just conceivable these girls might be targets too. He leafed through his notes while he thought about it; when Imogen offered him coffee, he gladly accepted. The murder, he'd guess, was most likely random, a pretty girl on her own late at night, lured into a dark cul-de-sac and knifed.

But you never knew. This latest attack bore all the hallmarks of the Circle Line killer. The vicious stabbing, the blood, the screams, close to a street that was thronging with life, just yards away from a packed and popular restaurant. The murderer must have nerves of steel and seemed to be making a show of it. Either he was growing careless or else he wanted to be caught.

Imogen could add very little. She hadn't really known Julie well though had lately started to like her a lot, had been helping her with some research. She began to cry; it was hard to take in even now, after more than twenty-four hours. Alice leaned over and touched her hand; they were clearly very close. Brewster was glad they had each other. After he'd been through the rigmarole, the routine questions that had to be asked and might possibly lead to something, he closed his notebook and settled back. You learnt more, he'd found, from informal chat. He had been in this game a long time now and knew which buttons to press

Imogen brought the coffee in and the dogs came thundering back. They slavered and wagged but were well behaved. At a word from her, they crouched down. It was excellent that she had them here, both as company and protection. Brewster had checked and the house seemed commendably secure.

'Right,' he said, when he took his leave. 'I want you both to promise me one thing.' He handed each of them his business card. 'This is my direct line,' he said. 'Call me any time, night or day, if you think of anything or feel scared. I promise you I'll pick up.'

'Thanks,' said Imogen, showing him out. 'But you don't have to worry. We've got the dogs.'

As if they'd be any protection at all against a madman with a knife.

47

'We have to go home,' said Beth in France. 'We can't possibly leave them alone without any protection.' Duncan was on to the ferry company but apparently not making very much progress. There was some sort of strike that they couldn't explain; his French was still far short of the local patois. He hadn't even got Richard to translate since he'd gone to Toulouse to see the picture framer.

'They are both grown up.' Duncan did have a point. Plus the dogs would look after them. He had absolute faith in his Weimaraners who were tougher than they seemed. Right now his priority was his wife who had worked all summer without a break and had been through that ghastly experience with the bombs. He couldn't have borne anything happening to her. Although they had now been together ten years, she remained the focus of his life. 'They can come out here when they get the

OK.' A detective was seeing them both that day. 'Richard has said all along that everyone's welcome.'

Beth mulled it over then talked to Jane who had been there for several days. 'Will you think me a bad mother if I don't go home?'

'I can't really see why they need you there. Duncan is right: they're no longer kids. They are both professionals, with jobs to do, who may even cope better on their own.'

So it was settled. Jane usually won since she brought a new perspective to things. Duncan stopped trying to book the ferry, promising Beth that, if need be, he would fly her home in a couple of hours instead of going by car.

Imogen felt she was being watched as she left for the theatre that afternoon. She shrugged it off as part of the trauma caused by Julie's murder. The Circle Line was running again. She was determined to chance it. Alice was also back at work: there was no point hanging around in the house. It might help her come to terms with it all if she had something to do.

'Feel free to call if you need to talk,' she had said before leaving for the shop. She normally didn't like personal calls while she was serving customers but these were unusual circumstances; they badly needed to support each other. The thought of returning to Onslow Gardens filled Alice with utter revulsion. Both, however, were level-headed. Some blame must surely attach to Julie for staying out late and having too much to drink.

Imogen had walked the dogs then carefully shut them in the kitchen, Alice would let them out when she got home. Her mother had rung a couple more times, to check that things were still all right. Duncan was taking them out to lunch while

Richard was back in his studio, working. It sounded normal and very relaxed. The last thing Imogen wanted to do was get her fretting again.

But she still had that feeling, kept glancing round in case there was someone following her, but all she saw was a mass of people going about their business. In the Tube she found she couldn't concentrate, kept checking to see who got on and off, though no one seemed to be taking much notice of her. At this time of day, in the late afternoon, the carriages were relatively empty. She would be at the theatre by the time the real rush hour began.

Hungerford Bridge, though, was already busy. There were more pedestrians on the bridge than traffic on the road. Imogen pushed her way through the crowd, anxious to be at the theatre on time, still with that eerie sensation of being watched. Her mother had jokingly warned her about this. The star syndrome, she called it. Once you have made it, it never lets up; you can no longer call your life your own. The fact she was only in the chorus appeared not to register with Beth. Imogen felt inconspicuous yet the eerie feeling persisted.

After the show she experienced it again, though the South Bank was pulsating. She paused on the steps and looked around. People were strolling along the river on their way home from an evening out. The audience from the Festival Hall mingled with that of the National Theatre to make it doubly busy.

Very close to where she stood, a small crowd was grouped around a mime, laughing and applauding his various poses. Dressed in black with a red and white T-shirt, he battled against an invisible wind, then was dragged along by a forceful dog, his face a mask of desperate bewilderment. Imogen wandered over to watch, forgetting, at least for a moment, her preoccupation. The mime was better than the living statues; at least he displayed real skill. He wore thick white make-up, with painted teardrops beneath each black-circled eye, mournful and staring like a crazed raccoon, and small surprised eyebrows like commas. He wrestled with imaginary balloons as if they were going to carry him off. Imogen chuckled and clapped very hard. He was good.

In lighter spirits she set off home, over the bridge where the crowd had now thinned, towards the welcoming lights of Embankment station. Thoughts of Julie and her terrible death still weighed heavily on her mind. If only she hadn't gone drinking that night on her own.

Alice should have been home some time, waiting up for her with the dogs. They would eat late supper and catch up on each other's day. Imogen loved having Alice to stay. Apart from being her childhood friend, Alice was someone to whom she could talk openly about these paranoid fears. Her mother would only have made a fuss and stopped her travelling on the Circle Line, but Imogen felt it was nothing much more than the shock of a close friend's death.

Halfway across the bridge she stopped and had another quick look round. Right at the end, from where she had come, a slight black figure was advancing fast, carrying something bulky in his hand. Everyone else was in couples or groups. Only Imogen seemed to be on her own.

You are being neurotic, she told herself, then impulsively pulled out her phone and punched out Brewster's number.

Just as he'd said, he answered at once.

'I'm probably just being silly,' she said. 'But I have a persistent feeling of being followed.'

'Just keep on coming,' said Brewster calmly, 'and try not to lose your nerve. Don't look round or attempt to confront him. Whoever it is may be dangerous. Move quickly but don't draw attention to yourself. We'll be waiting for you at the station.'

48

It seemed as though he came out of nowhere, from the darkness of the railway arches alongside the entrance to the Underground station. She didn't immediately know who he was, a tall man in an anonymous raincoat, wearing dark glasses even at this time of night. He gripped her elbow, which was how she knew it was him.

'You startled me,' she said, alarmed, instinctively backing away. She had spent the whole day in a nervous state. This cloak and dagger stuff did not improve things.

'Sorry,' said Brewster, 'if I startled you. But we think we may have a possible lead. It's vital that we should not be seen together.' He drew her stealthily into the shadows. 'Tell me precisely what you think you saw. Have you any idea who it might have been? Perhaps an acquaintance of Julie's?'

Imogen ruefully rubbed her arm where his fingers had gripped her too hard. Detective Inspector Brewster seemed unusually tense.

'It was nothing really,' she tried to explain, regretting now having made the call, sure that he must think her a total fool. 'It was just that I have the weirdest sensation that someone is constantly watching me. And you did say we should call you at any time.'

She looked around for Brewster's partner, knowing they usually worked in pairs.

'He's over there,' he said, understanding at once. 'Keeping an eye on the exit.'

He led her further into the gloom, which hardly improved the state of her nerves. She knew very little about this man except that he had appeared when Julie was killed. On that occasion, she now recalled, he had not worn uniform either.

She edged away. 'It's all right,' she said. The station was teeming with late-night travellers. 'I can manage now. Thanks for coming so quickly. I am truly sorry if I've wasted your time.'

'Look,' said Brewster, grabbing her again. 'We are here entirely for your protection. This isn't a game. There's a killer at large and, until he's caught, you are none of you safe. Keep your eyes peeled and call me whenever you need to. I can't overemphasise the importance of that.'

'Why me?' asked Imogen, startled and shocked.

'Partly because you were Julie's friend. And also because . . . well, you fit the general description.'

'Description of what?' Now she really was scared.

'Of his other victims.' He'd have thought she'd have known. He offered to see her on to the train but Imogen laughed in his face.

I am not a child, she almost said but could see he was far from being amused. And she had been scared, she couldn't

286

overlook that. Julie had died. It was good of them to come. If someone was on a killing spree she didn't want to end up one of his victims.

Alice was in the kitchen reading, the dogs lying peacefully at her feet. She'd adapted easily to Chepstow Villas, but then it was almost her second home since she had spent so much time there in her youth. There was something delicious keeping warm in the Aga; the smell of it was divine. She had even deferred having supper herself until Imogen got home.

'I saw the cop again tonight,' said Imogen, opening a bottle of Chablis. 'I called him and he met me at the station.'

'Why?' asked Alice, instantly anxious. She hated Imogen being out late every night.

'I got scared,' said Imogen, 'crossing the bridge. I had the sensation of being followed.' Eyes upon her was how it had felt, though, in such a crowd, how could she possibly tell? 'I'm sure it was just an emotional reaction in the aftermath of Julie's death. I look for murderers everywhere now, though don't know how I would recognise one. I doubt they look any different from you or me.'

'Thanks,' said Alice, tasting the wine and nodding her head in approval. She knew precisely what Imogen meant, had felt spooked herself when she got on the Tube.

She carried the casserole to the table while Imogen got out the plates. Unlike Imogen, Alice was perfectly house-trained. Imogen sniffed with appreciation. Home felt good, especially with Alice here. The house was spacious, with plenty of rooms, yet the kitchen had always been its heart. Even without the presence of Beth, she could wrap it round her like a chinchilla scarf. The dogs, the Aga, the tick of the clock, the ingrained aromas of legendary meals all contributed to its aura of complete domestic calm. Here, not only because of the dogs, she always felt totally safe.

'Your mother rang to see how things were. I told her there was no need for alarm. I think I finally convinced her that she needn't hurry home.'

There she went, scurrying across the bridge, the flibbertigibbet with the streaming hair and a face that was almost as beautiful as his own. He let her go, was in no special hurry; enjoyed this new game of cat and mouse. He knew where to look for her; there was no great hurry. He leaned on the parapet, gazing down at the river. One simple dive was all it would take to find the blessed release he had endlessly yearned for. He had felt that faint urge throughout his life but lately things had subtly started to change. He'd experienced a thrill he had never imagined when he'd shoved that unknown commuter under a train.

The thrill of killing had made him mature. He was no longer the boy who was hidden away. Since he'd started roaming the streets at night and doing his thing on the Underground he had suddenly found his place in life, his fulfilment. At first he'd selected them randomly, from the sheer frustration of seeing them happy, watching them laughing into their phones, regardless of those around them. The second one, which they had realised was murder because of the knife jutting out of her back, had started a brouhaha in the press that had got him really fired up. Too long had he been anonymous, deprived of the platform that was his by right, the child of performers he longed to emulate.

All those evenings spent sitting on the stairs, invisible to the glittering crowd, watching his parents entertain and his sister showing off. How he had longed to be one of them, to take his natural place at their side. To become the star he had always known was his birthright. But now he had found his natural bent, life was beginning to be worth living. He could choose them now and take his time. With each one he killed he felt a growing catharsis.

He had finished his business for the night. Now it was time to go home. To an empty house with nobody there, where he could do as he damn well pleased, eat his meals in the dining room, get drunk in his father's cellar. Mount the stairs knowing she wouldn't be there, use the key he ought not to have and let himself into the paradise of his mother's inherited things. He had worshipped her from an early age, yet she had cast him aside. Too busy to learn to communicate; too arrogant to accept she'd been wrong. He was only allowed in her presence as a concession.

He had been there the day of the accident, had sat and watched her bleed slowly to death. Had seen she was mouthing something though didn't know what. Afterwards he had stroked her hands, had arranged her skirts as they should have been. Had brushed her hair and restored it to its coiffure. She had looked so helpless, like a broken doll, while he, for the first time ever, felt fully alive.

The sight of her lying there on the stairs, her hair all loose and soaked in her blood, had released an image in his brain he endlessly tried to perpetuate. Death was good. It had caught her in her full glory.

49

They had let her go, he had seen to that, on the condition that she made no attempt to leave town. She was off the hook but only just. Numerous questions remained that would require answers. Especially how she'd been caught on closed-circuit TV. He was out there waiting when she emerged, standing beside the official car with only the driver and one uniformed officer to accompany them on the ride. She was pale yet still very much in control. He held the door open while she got in, then took his seat beside her. He suspected she'd sooner have gone by taxi but today that was not an option. They rode in silence. It was late afternoon. The sky was still bright though the sun would shortly be setting.

She stared abstractedly out of the window as though hungry for her freedom. It was four days since they had taken her in, and she wore the same clothes that she'd worn then. In the interim she had been in prison garb.

After a while, he broke the silence, unable to stand the atmosphere any longer.

'Will there be anyone waiting at home? A family member, perhaps?'

She hesitated then shook her head. She had left so abruptly in the early hours, snatched from her bed like a criminal, that no one knew except her employer who was loyally standing by her. They reached the house, which appeared shut up. Brewster recalled the flicker of light he had seen.

'Would you like me to come in with you?'

She thought for a second then shook her head. But he felt instinctively that she was gradually thawing. When he asked if he might see her later, she said yes.

'Come back in a couple of hours,' she said. 'Give me time to freshen up.' She suddenly smiled. 'I am not about to jump bail.'

'Take as long as you like,' he said. 'I'll meet you at eight in the restaurant on the corner.'

In Cannon Street he reviewed the case. It very much looked as though they were back to square one. If she wasn't guilty, and he now believed it, then a dangerous killer was still at large and he had no answer to the burning question of how she'd been caught by the cameras. It was only her word, he could not overlook that, yet instinct told him she was telling the truth. He planned to use the kid glove treatment in order to get her to talk.

They met in the local bistro at eight. She had washed her hair and changed her clothes and generally cleaned herself up. The smile she gave him seemed genuine.

'How are things at home?' he asked.

'Everything's under control.' She seemed warmer now and

292

more relaxed away from the grimness of that prison cell. As well she might; she was free again, or would be when she'd given him satisfactory answers.

'This has to be off the record,' he said. 'But, without prejudice, I believe in your innocence. I will do all I can to get you off but only if you are honest with me. I like you too much to watch you rot in jail.'

At that she grinned and her eyes lit up. At last it appeared he might be making headway.

The menu came but Celeste couldn't eat. She was far too strung up for that. She knew she was going to have to confide in him; there was no other way. He ordered oysters and steak tartare with a fine red wine to accompany it.

'You must build yourself up,' he told her with a smile.

He waited until she appeared relaxed, then started in with the questions. He could only help her, he said again, if she would learn to trust him. She fidgeted with her oyster fork while she struggled with a decision. Then raised her luminous eyes to his and started to fill him in on the missing pieces. He was, she explained, her younger brother, the only family she had left. Then she told him the whole wretched story, starting nine months before his birth with her mother's bout of German measles which had effectively ruined his life.

As a child he had been endearingly sweet, with a trusting nature and a gentle spirit. She had cherished and protected him and, for a while, it had worked. His mother's death had traumatised him; he had seen her fall, unable to help in any way. Celeste had come home in the late afternoon and found him still sitting on the stairs, with Esmée all covered in blood, her throat slashed open. At first she thought she had broken her neck until she had seen the pruning shears. Flowers

293

had been one of her mother's passions; she liked to arrange them herself.

They had managed to cover the whole thing up. The press only knew she had fallen. But her father had guessed the truth and could not forgive him. He had issued a statement. The case was closed. The child was sent to an institution where he'd stayed until she turned twenty-one and became his legal guardian. The deal was he had to stay under her care, but then there was nowhere else he could go.

Five weeks after Esmée's death, Sir Edward died too of virulent cancer, accelerated, it was said, by a broken heart. Celeste was left with a shattered future and a pile of debts she worked hard to pay off. Most of this she related to Brewster though not the most crucial part. When he asked her where her brother was now, she told him she didn't know.

'So was it your brother in Peter Jones?' He had noted the slightly androgynous look of the slim dark figure they'd seen racing up the stairs.

'Perhaps. We do look rather alike and he has always had a thing about dressing up – a throwback to our mother.'

He had always been mad. She saw that now. Driven to it by his stunted childhood and a tragic twist of fate.

'What am I going to do?' she asked.

'Leave it to us,' said Brewster.

It was after midnight; the street was deserted. He groped for his key when he turned the corner then stopped abruptly in his tracks. The house, which was usually shrouded in darkness, tonight was a blaze of light. His heart started beating wildly with shock. It seemed his fortifications had been breached. The drawing-room chandeliers were ablaze as well as the lights on

294

the staircase. Someone was in there ahead of him. He could only hope it was her.

She was standing at the top of the stairs, the moon back-lighting her like an apparition, wearing one of her mother's diaphanous gowns. She held a heavy silver candlestick in case, perhaps, he might be an intruder. He dropped his bag and peeled off the wig, unwrapping the scarf from round his face, revealing the garish make-up. He was glad and relieved that she was there. He relied upon her completely. His face broke into the smile that was so like hers.

'They are on to you,' was all she said. 'If I were you I'd get out of here before they bring a warrant for your arrest.' There was genuine pity on her face as she turned and went into her room.

Wait, he wanted to say to her, making a lunge towards her door. But when he tried it, he found it already locked.

50

The Paris trip seemed to hurtle by, and before they knew it they were back on the train, agreeing to do it again some time, circumstances permitting. They had worked the city until they dropped, seen all the galleries and museums, even been up the Eiffel Tower and shopped in the Champs Elysées.

'I am really going to miss you,' said Margaret.

'Me too,' said Ellie glumly.

Tomorrow Wilbur would be discharged and they'd fly straight home to Chippewa Falls. She looked forward to seeing her grandchildren again but not to very much else. It would mean returning to the old routines, with Wilbur under her feet even more since he wouldn't be playing golf again for a while.

'I expect the baby has grown,' she said before falling into a grave and thoughtful silence.

Margaret attempted to cheer her up but was feeling equally glum. They had had such good times and really clicked. It seemed a pity they lived so far apart. They were served an elegant three-course meal with an interesting choice of French wines. Ellie began to brighten up; the sparkle returned to her eyes. They chatted a bit about what they'd seen, in particular the Picasso museum in its seventeenth-century house.

'I would have liked more time there,' said Ellie. 'There was too much to see in one visit.'

She reminisced about her arts course, the painters she had studied. Margaret's plan to train as a guide had activated an idea in her head. 'If I lived in London what I'd most like to do is work at the V&A.'

She fell silent again for a while until, outside Lille, she had her epiphany. With heightened colour and a tightened jaw she sat bolt upright in her seat, looked at Margaret fair and square and said: 'I am not going back.'

'What?' said Margaret, who was reading the guidebook, having not quite taken in what Ellie had said.

'I am going to tell Wilbur I am not going home, that I'm staying on in London. He has had the best years of my life, though never appreciated the fact. Now he can learn to look after himself. I am quitting.'

'You're crazy,' said Margaret, but Ellie's mood was infectious. They ordered brandies and toasted her resolution.

Wilbur was waiting when Ellie arrived, bringing him his street clothes. He paid the bill with a credit card and shook the matron by the hand. No hint of a present but that was Wilbur. Ellie did the honours with chocolates and flowers. They had done a wonderful job for him; he was able to walk with a couple of sticks. He would only need them until he'd recovered his balance. The nurses stood and waved him off as Ellie assisted him into the cab. The moment they'd turned the corner, he started complaining.

He had hated the food, the bed was hard and at night he had found it difficult to sleep because they kept the lights on. They had given him pills to knock him out then woken him at a ridiculous hour to ask if he needed a bedpan and give him more pills. They had not approved of his poker games because it impeded the hospital's daily routines. He was putting this matter into the hands of his lawyers.

Yes, thought Ellie, but they'd taken him in and seemed to have worked an extraordinary cure. Not only was he able to walk but he had dropped ten pounds in weight. They had put him on a special diet, excluding most of the things he liked but pointing the way to a much more healthy future. And, as Margaret had pointed out, they were only charging him for the bed. All the medical treatment came free, courtesy of the NHS which Ellie knew was grotesquely overworked. But there was no point trying to point this out. Besides, she was long past caring.

They ate an indifferent dinner in the dismal hotel. The dining room was crowded with yet more tourists. Ellie sat silent while Wilbur talked, pontificating about the food, the weather, the traffic noises and the hefty bill. They wouldn't be staying here again. He was going to complain to the travel firm. Ellie reflected how kind Tom had been but still didn't utter a word.

Back in their room, as they started to pack, she announced that she was leaving him. She had thought about it long and hard and would not reverse the decision. To start with, he didn't take in what she'd said, was preoccupied with the snooker game on TV. But when her words finally did sink in, he simply dismissed them with an incredulous laugh.

'What are you going to live on?' he asked when at last he saw that she really meant it. He had been through her Paris expenses in detail and queried every small bill.

'On half of what you are worth,' she said. 'Unless you let the whole matter drop. In which case I'll settle for my living expenses to keep me afloat while I look for a job. After which I don't need a thing from you. I intend to stand on my own feet.'

After Wilbur had left for the airport, spluttering yet unwilling to risk missing his flight, Ellie phoned Margaret to tell her how it had gone.

'I did it,' she said, 'and he took it badly. Is still recovering from the shock. I have hung on to the traveller's cheques which should keep me afloat for a while.'

Margaret was shattered but also amused. There was far more to Ellie than met the eye. 'How are you going to live?' she wanted to know.

'I'm not entirely destitute. Though he believes I am. I have got a few paintings at home that are worth quite a lot. He thinks I'll be back in a couple of weeks, unable to hack it on my own. But he's mistaken. I've never felt better in my life.'

Lovely Tom, who had been so kind, would help her find a cheap room somewhere until she had fully worked out her future alone.

'You know you can come and stay with me.' Margaret was secretly overjoyed.

'I was rather relying on your saying that,' said Ellie.

51

It was Saturday night and a sell-out show. Only two weeks to the end of the run and tickets for *Anything Goes* were now like gold dust. Lots of people who were really big time were due backstage to pay their respects and celebrate a truly outstanding production. There was talk of renewals and fat new contracts, as well as a transfer to Broadway next year. Imogen knew that she had to stay on, even though she felt nervous of travelling home so late. Duncan would have told her to take a taxi, since he couldn't be there to pick her up, but in that vicinity at that hour taxis were even harder to come by than tickets.

Tonight, unusually, she was dressed to the nines. Normally she changed into sweat pants after the show. But Alice insisted she must look her best, since the paparazzi would be there in droves and the moguls that mattered present. She had borrowed sandals from another dancer, in which she could scarcely walk, just a couple of diamanté straps with higher heels than she'd ever dared try before. The dress she had bought for the occasion was so low cut that it felt obscene. She had searched through her mother's closet for a pashmina.

'It's important you look the part,' said Alice, uncharacteristically clued up. 'If you are going to make it to the top.'

The mime was there, right outside the theatre. Imogen passed him as she went in. Doing his act with the balloons and the dog. She stopped for two minutes to cheer him on, thinking of him as a kind of good-luck charm. Something about his droll appearance got to her and cheered her up. On impulse, she dropped a fiver in his cap, certain he must be aware of her. It was hard to know from that deadpan face, but struggling thespians should always be there for each other.

Now here she was, at a quarter to twelve, full of champagne and on top of the world, urgently needing to leave to catch that last train. Originally Alice had wanted to come but had had to cry off as her brother was getting engaged. Besides, she'd already seen the show several times. Normally Beth and Duncan would be there, but they were still in France.

She said her good nights, then slipped away, as if to a waiting limousine. The dress and the heels were not quite the thing for crossing the bridge late at night. A powerful breeze was coming off the river. It felt as though there might be a storm; she noticed in passing that the mime had gone. Although there was virtually no one about, she couldn't shake off the feeling of being followed.

Embankment station was almost deserted. She caught the train by the skin of her teeth, slowed down by the unaccustomed height of her heels. Alone in the carriage, she finally relaxed. Only eight stations to Notting Hill Gate, followed by a two-minute hobble to the house. She had nothing planned for the following day and could do with a long lie-in. In the afternoon she would take the dogs to the park.

A couple got in at Westminster then off again at Victoria. Imogen, feeling slightly squiffy, closed her eyes. The train pulled out of the station then stopped. Its engine shuddered, gave a kind of sigh, then died. She opened her eyes in sudden alarm, caught a glimpse of a figure at the end of the carriage that definitely hadn't been there before, and then the lights went out. There was absolute silence apart from her heartbeat, hammering frantically in her chest. She strained her ears for sounds of movement but couldn't hear anything at all. Petrified, she grabbed her phone, and, as she was searching for Brewster's number, the lights came on again.

In the darkness, he had moved closer to her, a black-clad figure with a chalk-white face, and was standing motionless, drooping from a strap, staring at her with melancholy eyes. Imogen felt almost faint with relief; it was only her friend, the mime. He wore the same outfit, the candy-striped T-shirt under a clinging black one-piece jumpsuit, and his painted mouth turned down in mock despair. Imogen smiled and greeted him but he neither said a word nor moved a muscle.

There was something creepy about him now, just hanging there like a marionette with nobody working its strings. She had given him quite a hefty tip; surely he must remember her. Could that conceivably be why he was here? It seemed absurd to remain in character with an audience of only one. She pulled her mother's pashmina closer and smiled again but he still didn't move. By now she was starting to find him faintly disturbing.

She rose to her feet and edged away, wishing she wasn't wearing the sandals, then moved to the end of the carriage, phone in hand. Brewster's number was still lit up. She punched it in then turned back to face the mime, who'd advanced several yards and also altered his pose.

Brewster answered on the second ring. She was badly shaken by now. What had seemed a joke was starting to be very frightening. She was stuck in a tunnel with a crazy person who refused to speak or acknowledge her. If the lights went out again, she would die of fright.

'I am on the train,' she virtually whispered, turning her back so the mime couldn't hear. At which point the engine growled back into life and the train inched slowly forward. 'Just beyond Victoria station.' He had somehow managed to come even closer without her seeing him move. 'I am on my own and there's someone who's starting to scare me.'

'Listen very carefully,' said Brewster calmly, not even sounding surprised. 'We are waiting for you at Sloane Square station. The train's almost here; I can see its lights. Try to stay calm, just get off quickly and take the escalator up to the street. Don't worry. We'll have you covered. There is nothing to fear.'

The lights of the station were now in sight; Imogen moved to the door. The mime still hung there, not moving a muscle except that his painted mouth had reversed into a terrifying grin.

Because she had only just caught the train, leaping into the very last carriage, she now was faced with the length of the platform before she could reach the exit. She stumbled slightly on the stupid heels, glancing around her for signs of life, aware that the mime was right behind her, gaining rapidly on her in his ballet shoes. Where was Brewster? He'd promised to be here. Her heart was in her mouth.

'Stop!' a voice ordered through a megaphone, and there he was, in uniform this time, accompanied by a fierce-looking dog wearing a yellow flak jacket.

'Run,' Brewster told her, 'and don't look back. Just get yourself up to the street. The rest of the squad is waiting there. You have nothing to worry about now.'

Imogen took her sandals off and ran like a deer on her dancer's feet, along the platform and, in one graceful leap, on to the escalator.

She didn't know what was happening behind her. All she could think about was not getting killed.

Brewster and Burgess watched the train pull out and Imogen running for all she was worth, followed on silent feet by the weird-looking mime. The empty platform stretched before her but, boy, how that girl could move. He was fast but she was faster. Brewster remembered the one in the veil, who could never have stood a chance.

He raised his megaphone again. 'Stop!' he ordered. 'Or else I'll shoot.' There were armed policeman waiting outside, as well as Celeste, who'd been brought along for formal identification. The mime never faltered, just continued to sprint, pacing Imogen like a predatory beast even though she was now on the escalator and he couldn't possibly catch her.

The dog was straining so hard on the leash that his front paws were off the ground.

'Go get him, Burgess!' said Brewster, raising his gun.

The dog went off with the speed of a cougar, grabbed the mime's arm and tried to wrestle him down. The fugitive struggled and hit back wildly, lashing out with a lethal-looking knife. Then went on running with the dog still snapping at his heels.

'STOP!' ordered Brewster one final time, then raised his pistol and took aim.

52

For them, of course, it meant the end. There could be no future together. What she'd missed out was the most significant part. Though the verdict was bound to be misadventure, Brewster's action had irrevocably damaged what he'd been hoping to salvage from what they had had. He knew that for sure, from the look on her face when they had broken the news.

He stood outside the coroner's court, leaning against his car. Not the official one today; he had come as a private individual to offer sympathy and pay his respects to the dead. A smattering of newsmen were gathered outside to hear the final verdict. The sky was murky; it looked like rain and matched the feeling in his heart.

With a swish of tyres, a Rolls-Royce pulled up and parked discreetly fifty yards away. Dr Rousseau nodded to Brewster but kept his distance. At least it meant she would not be alone; he wished the pair of them well. He was glad to know she'd no longer have to struggle.

If anyone were to carry the blame, it was Esmée Morell for contracting German measles which had left her unborn foetus permanently damaged. A perfect baby in every other way, his slow responses had become apparent only as he approached the age when normally he would start talking. Since his parents were wholly preoccupied by the pursuit of their starry careers, it had fallen solely upon his sister to help him learn to communicate. Nobody else had noticed or even cared. When the deafness was medically diagnosed and it was clear that he would never become an actor, his parents had turned their backs on him.

Celeste was the one who had taught him to sign and later also to lip-read. With proper care he might have lived a far more useful life. Instead he grew up a social outcast, held back from normal development because of his mother's distaste. All Esmée cared about was perfection. First, through jealousy, she had ruined her daughter, then, later, destroyed her son.

An usher appeared on the courthouse steps. The morning session had ended. He carried a statement to read to the press, declaring the verdict as misadventure, just as Brewster had predicted. They pressed round him to shake his hand but could do nothing to ease the ache in his heart. He had sacrificed his emotional future by doing his duty as a policeman.

Celeste appeared, on her lawyer's arm, and the doctor stepped forward to greet her. Grief had added immeasurably to her beauty. She stood in silence in her plain black suit while the lawyer made a brief public statement, then followed him down the steps to the waiting car. When she reached the spot where

Brewster was standing, she walked straight by as if he were not even there. He stood and watched as they drove away. She never even turned her head.

Of course there had been an official inquiry but his service record remained unblemished. Oberon Forrester had been killed while resisting arrest. Since Brewster had now been passed as fit, he'd asked permission to return to Baghdad where he felt his firearms skills would be better employed.

There were things, however, to clear up first, not the least of which was one final walk with his partner. He would miss the playground and his dreams of having children, but the biggest hurt would be saying goodbye to Burgess.

Vanishing Point

Acknowledgements

My thanks, as always, to my publishers, Time Warner, for doing their usual immaculate job. Especially to Joanne Dickinson, my editor, Sarah Rustin and the rest of the team including, of course, the Sales and Marketing people. Also to my agent, Jonathan Lloyd at Curtis Brown.

Prologue

A leaden sky and relentless rain; Belgium in February could not have looked more bleak. Frankie, slumped in her chilly carriage, stared out across the railway tracks and resolved in her heart that, if she moved on, it would be to a warmer climate. Her chilblains throbbed and her muscles ached; her throat felt decidedly scratchy. Normally she would have used the truck but, at least till they fixed the fan-belt, she was going to have to do without it on these monthly expeditions.

The train was halted outside the station, awaiting a signal change. If it didn't move soon, she might well perish with cold. With a grinding lurch it shuddered into life as another one, with mud-splashed sides, moved sluggishly past on the opposite track, the cause of the delay. Frankie mechanically zipped up her jacket and wound her scarf tightly round her throat as she watched the empty carriages racketing by. The sooner they got into Antwerp, the better. By now her teeth were rattling in her head so she thought she might treat herself to a cup of tea. She could do with a little

1

time to herself, away from the others, for quiet reflection. She had recently heard that her mother had died and, although they had been estranged for years, unwelcome memories had come flooding back that she'd tried all these years to suppress.

Which was when she saw it, the face in the window, moving slowly past, just feet away; an image etched into her brain for the past thirty years. The unmistakable face of her lover: the vivid blue eyes and black curly hair that haunted her nightmares as well as her waking thoughts. The face of a man she had loved and lost, which had irrevocably blighted her life.

The face of a man she knew to be dead for she had killed him herself.

Part One

1

It was one month earlier. The start of the year; early January and biting cold. Cabbages, turnips, carrots, beets: traditional Flemish fare, with celeriac thrown in as a special treat. Frankie was in charge of the vegetable garden. She planted them, hoed them and yanked weeds out between them, then bodily wrenched them from the soil and sluiced them down at the standpipe in the courtyard. At this time of year it was not pleasant work; her hands were raw and chapped, with swollen knuckles. Her chilblains ached so she couldn't sleep and now she was fairly sure she was getting arthritis. The only thing going for this arduous lifestyle was that, all things considered, it beat prison.

It was Magda who had coaxed her into making this decision, Magda to whom she also owed her life. When her sentence was up and they let her go, Frankie, facing a total abyss, had seriously considered ending it all. She was tired of having to keep battling on, had died when he did, at least in spirit. But the older woman, doing her job, had kept her under close supervision and, by not letting her out of her sight, had stopped her harming herself. Later, when they talked about it and Frankie revealed the depths of her despair, it was Magda who'd urged her to take herself in hand and not waste the precious gift of life on something that should, by now, be over and done with.

'You learnt your lesson and you paid the price. Now is the time for a fresh start.'

Frankie couldn't really argue; what Magda said was true. She was twenty-four and had nobody else, except the mother who had betrayed her and this brusque, compassionate Polish woman on whom she had learnt to depend. So when Magda had first mooted her plan – worn out by the prison service herself, she felt in need of a total change – Frankie had gone along with it. Together they'd moved to Lier, outside Antwerp, where they now shared a cramped but picturesque cottage. Not just a cottage but part of the Beguinage, an exclusive commune that was mainly a spiritual retreat.

When Frankie thought back to her privileged childhood, it still amazed her that life could have altered so much. The prosperous Wirral, where she had been raised, had in no way prepared her for hardship like this. Her family home had a tennis court; she had even owned her own pony. Her life had been rosy and much indulged, until she had done the Terrible Thing after which she'd become a social leper, entirely ostracised. Why, Chad had asked her, that first time they met, had she risked so much to make a rebellious statement? She had been through it all, many times before, and never come up with a plausible answer, but his eyes were amused (she'd say even admiring) and the smile he flashed had entirely melted her heart. Because . . . she had started to say, then faltered. It was to be several weeks till she told him the truth.

The walk from the station had soaked her right through but she was now well inured to constant discomfort. Her boots were leaking, her woollen mitts sodden; all she wanted to do was rip off her clothes and soak herself in a steaming tub. With piping-hot chocolate, whipped cream on the side, and someone to towel her dry. No chance of that; her smile was fixed as she raised the latch of the barn and pushed open the door.

Of the seventeen inmates, eleven were fixtures and most of them present this wintry afternoon. The barn, still with its original beams, was vast and draughty and smelt of lingering smoke. There were hurricane lanterns placed here and there, to cope with the rapidly vanishing light, and a cluster of beeswax candles in the hearth, not yet lit.

'You're back!' said Magda, looking up with a smile. 'Can it be that time already?' Her bobbins clacked as her skilful fingers worked at the intricate lace. Sister Mary broke off her reading while Sister Agnes was working in clay. An audiotape of pan pipes enhanced the feeling of harmony. A group of women working with their hands, united in a close sisterhood. Suddenly Frankie felt safe.

7

They asked, as they always did, about the market, and this time she could report complete success. She felt like a child before her elders as she proudly related what she had achieved. 'The onions were a particular hit. I could have sold many times more if I'd had them with me.'

'So learn,' said Magda, regrouping her pins. 'And next time you'll know to take more. Perhaps when the truck is back on the road. Would anyone care for tea?'

Later, once they had laid aside their work, they all moved closer to the hearth while Berthe scrabbled around in search of matches. They took it in turns to prepare the evening meal and two of their number were already in the kitchen, chopping carrots and jointing rabbits for the stew. Berthe found the matches and lit a taper.

'Excuse me,' said Frankie, suddenly chilled. 'I must go and change my clothes or I'll catch pneumonia.'

Despite all the therapy she had been through, the sound of a striking match still made her feel faint.

2

Cristina Calvão was in a lousy mood but that was nothing unusual. Yvette, her surly recalcitrant maid, had been late coming up with her café-au-lait and it had not been as hot as she liked, while the croissants were rubbery and stale. In addition, Cristina had chipped a nail and her favourite manicurist was fully booked, or so the lying receptionist would have her believe. It was all too tiresome; she slammed down the cup, spraying coffee all over the starched linen sheets. It was nearly noon. She would soon have to dress and go to meet Claude at Le Crillon for lunch to try to talk him round about the wedding. Cristina had lived in Paris twelve years, since she'd tired of the glitz of Brazilian nightlife and hooked up with an older man wealthy enough to support her. One of the things she liked best about Claude was that he was Catholic and indissolubly married. She had never intended to tie herself down and place all her eggs in the same restrictive basket – until she encountered Rocco Pereira and flipped. Which had been, she was obliged to admit, the story of her life.

He was a racing driver of international fame, sexy, Latin and twelve years younger than herself, which made an exciting change from Claude's ageing flesh. They had met in Rio at Carnaval and soon were hitting the tabloid headlines as well as all the hot celebrity nightspots. In Brazil, that was; word had not yet reached Paris which was why it was so essential she now look her best. She slithered out of her satin pyjamas, dropping them carelessly on the floor, and scrutinised her naked body, which only served to sour her mood even more. In recent years, since she quit the catwalk, her panther-like beauty had sagged and blurred. She no longer enjoyed making love with the lights on, another reason she clung to Claude who was, despite his numerous faults, a gentleman to the core.

How he would feel about this latest liaison, Cristina could not predict. Furthermore, she could not care less, had fallen in with his wishes all these years and now felt she'd earned the right to take a stand. It suited his lifestyle to keep her on the side, devoting his Mondays to Thursdays to her, then motoring home to his château at weekends to play the uxorious husband. He knew she occasionally saw other men; he was not unrealistic. But to hear that she contemplated marrying again might very well be the final straw and would require an element of finesse. Fortunately Cristina was expert at this, had spent her adult years negotiating. What Rocco would think was another matter. She would cross that bridge when she had to. She had not survived all these years on her beauty alone.

With a final scowl at her thickening waist, she flung open the doors of her spacious closets and tossed great armfuls of clothes all over the bed. For today's performance she must look just right, neither provocative nor too showy but understated and winningly demure.

'Yvette!' she screeched down the stairway to the maid. 'Come up here at once and get me dressed.'

Her outfit of choice had to be discarded; the seam beneath one arm was ripped and had gone unnoticed till now. Of course she laid all the blame on Yvette, though she herself had thrown it aside the instant she heard the stitches snap and knew she had put on weight.

'I can fix it, madame,' said Yvette but there hadn't been time. Claude would already be at the table and he hated her to be late. So she settled instead for an understated two-piece, cut on the bias for a slinkier movement, which stopped right on the knee to display her legs. She twirled and frowned, then removed her briefs; visible panty line would destroy the effect. Jewellery was the next requisite, tasteful and not overdone. She yanked out drawers and riffled through boxes, strewing their contents all over the dresser for Yvette to tidy away when she had gone. Diamonds, Claude said, were vulgar at lunchtime and pearls not Cristina's thing. With her bronzed and sultry exotic looks, she needed some sparkle to set herself off. She compromised with a Tiffany choker and the lucky earrings she'd had from Cal to celebrate their first six months together.

11

As she hooked the wires through her delicate lobes and watched the effect against her tawny streaked hair, she thought back to that time long ago and tears sprang into her eyes.

'Madame, is there something wrong?' asked Yvette, as she skilfully teased Cristina's mane, brushing and lacquering it into a tousled birds' nest. The raucous diktats had suddenly ceased; what the maid observed in the glass was wistful and sad.

'No,' snapped Cristina, herself again, shaking her head to improve the effect and applying another shimmering coat of lipstick. 'Dépêche-toi and get me a cab toot-sweet.' Mustn't risk keeping him waiting.

They laughed at her, the household staff, sick of her posturing and fancy airs; they considered her third world trash. The way she ordered them all around as though they were of a lesser class and had no feelings nor standards of their own. They only stayed on because of Claude, who always treated them courteously and wasn't averse to putting his hand in his pocket. Not so Cristina, with her chronic meanness, who siphoned money off the elderly fool but hated to part with any of it herself. Yvette gazed sourly at the wreckage of the bedroom – the coffee-stained sheets that would have to be changed, the couture clothing abandoned on the floor, and she hadn't even yet dared to check the bathroom. She vowed, as she regularly did, to leave forthwith. This pig of a woman was not worthy of her care; she would sooner sweep the floors or empty the bins.

Yvette, however, had burdens of her own: an ailing mother, a sickly child, a husband with a taste for too much Pernod. She lacked the security to throw in the job and it did have occasional bonuses. Clothing Cristina had grown tired of or too big for, soiled or torn but redeemable by a patient seamstress who valued the cut and the cloth. A bottle of perfume she no longer liked or a handbag now last year's fashion; even, once, a pair of uncomfortable shoes. Though usually shrewish, Cristina had moments when something unexpectedly cheered her and the sulks and petulance fleetingly changed to laughter. Only then did she show her true beauty, the mixed blood siren who had lived all her life on her wits.

And now she declared herself in love. Yvette decided to stick around, at least until she saw how the future panned out. The Brazilian lover, Madame's latest craze, should provide, at least, a little diversion. He was all Cristina could talk of these days. Yvette was curious to know how Monsieur would react.

Cristina slumped limply into the cab, fighting to hold back her tears. Lunch with Claude had not been a success; things were not going well for her today. To start with, he had been furious she was late, equated unpunctuality with bad manners. He had a meeting at three with his bank so could only manage two courses. His admiration was losing its lustre; there had been a time when, in his eyes, Cristina could do nothing wrong. Then they never met for lunch without his producing some elegant love-gift: a piece of

13

exquisite jewellery, a sumptuous chinchilla scarf. He would fuss and fawn all over her, insist on arranging the bauble round her neck, which gave him a chance to caress her caramel skin. Those days, however, had slipped away. Now, whenever he looked at her, his eyes lacked approbation. He was growing bored; she recognised the signs. Soon, if she wasn't careful, he might even dump her.

Since Claude was testy and short of time, she hadn't dared bring up the subject of Rocco. She would simply have to wait and play it by ear. As the house was nominally hers, not his, and he wasn't there for three days every week, it was up to her how she spent her time and whom she entertained. The night that Rocco had mentioned marriage she had been too giddy for rational thought. All she'd seen were the stars and the phosphorescent waves, with a jaunty background of salsa music and Rocco toasting her with champagne while also surreptitiously fingering her crotch.

Put like that, it did seem crude. Cristina's misery deepened. The truth was she hadn't felt this strongly for a man since Cal Barnard, who had broken her heart by dropping out of her life and disappearing.

The gardener, Serge, was trimming the topiary when Cristina's cab pulled up outside. He watched her from the top of his ladder as she tossed a handful of euros to the driver, then stalked straight past him without so much as a nod. Not a good lunch; he could see that from her snarl and privately smiled to know that she didn't always win. M. Daumier was a good employer; Serge had worked for him for fifteen years which was longer than that trollop had been installed here. And he intended to outlast her too, had seen the discontent in the master's eyes. That luscious body might be seductive but she lacked the grace of a true Parisian, besides being rude and coarse. It was hard to see now what had attracted Monsieur, apart from the obvious factor of raunchy sex.

Cristina slammed the heavy front door and Serge smiled with satisfaction. From his vantage point he could see into her bedroom, enjoyed the way that she flounced inside then threw her Hermès purse across the room. She bounced around on each four-inch heel as she tried to unbuckle her sandals, then ripped off her little couturier outfit, angrily scrunched it into a ball and hurled it against the wall. Serge laid down his shears and lit a cigarette while he studied her voluptuous naked body, for she rarely wore anything underneath her clothes. Soon, he sensed, he would get what he was after; she was clearly very much out of sorts and that, as any true Frenchman knew, was because she was not getting laid.

Though they said in the kitchen there was someone new, someone she seriously hoped to marry. Serge stubbed out his cigarette and resumed his desultory clipping. She had pulled the shutters to, presumably for her afternoon nap, so the show was over for another day and he could get back to his work.

No, there weren't any messages, said Yvette when she came up later to run Cristina's bath and lay out her clothes for the opera. Wagner tonight; she hated the music which made her positively gag with boredom but the opera house was an absolute must for any upwardly mobile socialite whose principal purpose in life was to be seen. Claude, still grumpy and unrelenting, had set off early for his country estate, leaving Cristina with an extra ticket for the second row of the stalls. She had rung round her coterie of hangers-on, mainly men of the gay persuasion, who were usually all too keen to help squander Claude's money. She rarely had difficulty finding a date; she was still well known and scrubbed up well, but tonight, for whatever reason, she had no takers. So she ended up doing that most mortifying thing, falling back on the company of a female friend, the Countess de Bourgrave, a good-time girl currently in the throes of her fifth divorce.

Which certainly didn't improve Cristina's mood, especially since she had no idea where in the world Rocco could possibly be. Throughout the evening she tried his number but his mobile appeared to be permanently off. She could only hope it meant he was on his way.

3

Cabbage soup was all very well but, after all these dreary months, definitely starting to pall. The Belgians cooked it with caraway and dumplings which, combined with the coarse black bread, made Frankie feel like a peasant herself, bloggy and overstuffed. Not that there was much wrong in that; she certainly wouldn't dare say so in the commune. She stood at the window, watching the weather, an incessant downpour that streaked the panes. Soup tonight, oxtail stew tomorrow; their diet was basic as well as relentlessly dull. She made a note to lay down more potatoes. After the harsh winter they'd had, supplies were perilously low. At least, with all the hard work she did, there was little chance of her gaining weight. She still had the lean, rangy figure of her youth with narrow hips, a flat stomach and enviable legs. Not that anyone noticed or even cared. Sometimes she felt as much a prisoner here as she had in jail.

Magda, quietly stitching by the stove, was used to these flashes of malaise. She could tell from the tension in Frankie's shoulders that her jaw would be set and her eyes hazed over with grief. There was nothing, Magda had learnt, she could do except wait for the storm clouds to pass. Frankie's outlook still remained bleak, her heart and mind consumed by a hollow ache.

'Well, you're the boss,' tried Magda brightly. 'So why not go wild and come up with something new? If you plant it we'll have to eat it, so go ahead and surprise us. Artichokes, perhaps, or aubergines. Allow yourself some artistic licence. That, after all, is why we're here. To work but also to create.'

'As long as you don't ask for Brussels sprouts.' Slowly Frankie turned her head, her expression softening into a foxy grin. When she smiled, which she did all too seldom, she was still a striking woman, good for her age. 'It's okay, you don't have to humour me. I just wish this beastly rain would slack off a bit.'

Communal living was all very well, and the other women were nice enough, but there were times when Frankie felt she needed privacy to stop her losing her mind. Magda, all too aware of this, humoured her by discreetly withdrawing whenever she thought she should. Most meals and meetings were held in the barn; they only came back here to sleep or relax on the rare occasions they were not actually working. Since Frankie spent most of her time outdoors, she'd developed an all-year-round weathered look which tempered the sallowness of her skin and gave her a glow that became her. She kept her straight dark hair cut short and never ever used makeup, yet when fleeting laughter lit her face, a hint of her vanished beauty could still be seen.

Magda, older, was solid and square-built, an inheritance from her ancestry, and her once fair hair had turned to iron grey. They rubbed along companionably enough, careful of each other's space and needs. After twenty-three years of sharing together, there was little about each other they didn't know. And before that had been the prison years. It was still a source of pride to Magda that she'd managed to gain the tortured young woman's trust.

'Do you know what I'd really like?' said Frankie, still with a hint of a smile. 'Pheasant, casseroled in red wine with bacon, mushrooms and shallots.' She smacked her lips. 'With just a soupçon of brandy in the sauce.'

'Wow!' said Magda, pausing mid-stitch. 'When in the world did you ever eat like that?' Frankie had been locked up since her middle teens.

'In my childhood,' said Frankie airily. 'There is still a lot you don't know about my life.'

The colonel, Frankie's stepfather, had been an excellent shot. And there had been a time, when the marriage was new, when he treated her as he might have done the son he had never had. Which included taking her out to follow the guns.

'Be careful,' her mother had warned, alarmed, aware of her daughter's capriciousness, but Humphrey had waved her protest aside in his customary autocratic manner. Women and animals: he lumped them together, though then, in the aftermath of new lust, he treated the little filly with more care. She was a sprightly child, good-looking too. It fed his vanity having her around. That was where the pony came in; anything Frankie wanted she could have. Skinny and agile, a natural athlete, she had entered womanhood unenlightened. For the first two years they were the best of pals, the gawky child and the overbearing man. But as she grew, she got prettier too and soon had more on her hands than she'd bargained for.

'Dirty old bastard,' she would later say. 'Whatever he got, believe me, he richly deserved.'

None of this had she shared with Magda; her lips concerning the original crime remained sealed. At the hearing she had been stoically defiant, which was how she had come, at just fifteen, to find herself locked up. There was no support from the colonel now; as far as he was concerned she could rot in hell. A damaged child, Magda's colleagues had assessed. Even after what happened next, they never found out quite how much.

Most evenings, after they'd had their meal, everyone reconvened in the barn and gathered around the hearth. Some of them sewed by candlelight; the rest preferred to relax. They all worked hard at their various chores and this was the time they liked the best, when the spirit of the community came to the fore. Frankie, who had worked eight hours straight, stretched out on a beanbag and nodded off. Occasionally somebody told a story in the fine tradition of oral folklore or else they broke into groups to catch up on the chat. Tonight they felt in a party mood, so Sister Breeda brought out her fiddle and soon had them dancing Irish jigs and clapping along to the tune. Even Frankie opened her eyes and propped herself up to watch. She had laboured so long in the biting cold that her fingers were swollen and starting to throb but the hearty soup had done its job; she felt calm and soporific.

Inspired by the dancing, they wanted to sing, so Sylvia, with the seraphic voice, took her place next to Sister Breeda to lead them all in a folk song. Frankie watched the firelight flickering, which brought back memories she'd sooner forget. She liked it here: it was womblike and safe, away from the terrors of everyday life. The lack of male company didn't bother her at all; within the closeness of the sisterhood, she had finally found a kind of peace.

But then Sylvia swung into 'Blow the Wind Southerly' and, all of a sudden, it became too much. The melancholy sadness of the beautiful song struck a chord in Frankie's heart and she stumbled to her feet and out of the barn. She ran the few yards through the driving rain then up the stairs of the cottage she shared and threw herself down on her narrow bed in anguish. Whenever she thought she was coming to terms with the past, the whole thing persisted in flooding back. After all this time, she could still not erase the memories of that terrible day when her life had effectively ended.

4

The woman alone in the Danieli bar was stylishly dressed but looked lonely and sad. She was fiddling with the stem of her glass; the waiter crossed and politely inquired if she'd like another bellini. She looked up, startled and ill at ease, checked the time – it was 7.15 – then shyly told him she would. English; he had guessed that from the quality of her clothes but the fluency of her Italian surprised him.

'You are staying here, signora?' he asked, picking up her glass.

'I am,' she said. 'I arrived today.' Then, giving him a tentative smile, she ducked quickly back into her book.

Fine eyes, he thought as he walked away. A woman like that should not have to drink alone.

Cassandra Buchanan, here on impulse, could still not quite believe what she had done. The first time she'd been here was on her first honeymoon, an unbelievable thirty-eight years ago. She wondered now where the time had gone and wished she could relive those happier days. As a bride of eighteen she had loved the Danieli, awed by the dignified splendour of its rooms. She smiled to remember how gauche she had been, but Edwin could not have been a better guide for a wide-eyed teenager, just out of school, who had never before left Cornwall. They had walked every inch of the magical city and he'd introduced her to its finer sights, telling her just enough not to lose her interest. It was he who had sown the seeds in her of a lifelong passion for things Venetian. She had studied its art and absorbed its culture; strange, therefore, that she hadn't been back for so long.

The fleeting smile faded, replaced by a frown. She was here to escape the shocking events that had blown apart the calm of her family life. When Charles had lobbed his grenade at her, she had not remotely seen it coming. She had truly believed that her second marriage was even more successful than the first. Her feelings for Edwin had been dutiful and fond and had not prepared her for the turbulent ride of twenty-two years with the highly unorthodox Charles. True, some of the passion had lately faded, for no one could maintain such a high-octane love. But to have it suddenly fall to ashes was still almost more than she could believe. For the advent of Charles in her life had been a genuine *coup de foudre*.

She was up from the country, a recent widow, overwhelmed by the bustle of the London streets to which she was so unaccustomed. Cornwall had always been her home; she had never felt any particular urge to stray. She had been content, as a dutiful wife, to remain at home and raise her girls with her husband always at her side, running his sprawling estate. Darby and Joan, he had fondly described them, reflecting the humdrum nature of their lives. All Cassie did was run the house, walk the dogs and weed the garden and, twice a week, take coffee with her mother. Old before her time, she had realised, when the heart attack had suddenly carried him off. She had studied her face and regretted the crows' feet, stroked the skin of her crêping neck and wondered if she would ever know happiness again. Thirty-three and already bereft, with two adolescent daughters just reaching the difficult stage. Cassie had been desolate, resigned to the fact that her life was over before it had properly begun.

How wrong she had been; again, that smile as her mind went back to the giddy events that morning at the Basil Street Hotel. If it happened once, why not again? She did not believe in conceding defeat. She drained her glass and caught the waiter's eye, which had never really left her. Three bellinis might be one too many but she was no longer a country mouse nor answerable to anyone any more.

What with their uneventful life and Edwin's slowly declining health, Cassie had rather neglected her household chores. With two lively children, two cats and three dogs, and Edwin clumping around in his boots, she had started just to sluice down floors and turn a blind eye to the animals' ruining the furniture. It had never been smart but was certainly comfortable; most nights, year round, they lit a big fire, a focal point around which the family clustered. Instead of watching television, they talked and read books or did a huge jigsaw together. Country living might be remote, but it provided a solid base from which they taught the children the true fundamentals of life.

The day that followed Edwin's funeral was bleak and Cassie, for the first time ever, found herself with very little to do. The mourners had left, the girls were back at school; everyone had agreed that was for the best. Cassie, alone in the great rambling house with only cats and dogs to talk to, found that time weighed heavily on her hands. The estate, overseen by a competent manager, more or less ran itself these days and, now that she had no meals to prepare, she didn't know what to do. So she looked around, took stock of the place and saw how rundown it had become. For fifteen years it had been her home, since she first moved in as an ingénue bride, and now she was a widow.

The curtains needed cleaning, if not replacing, and the rugs and armchairs were strewn with hairs and mysterious stains that did not bear too close inspection. Fuelled by manic energy, brought on by grief, she made lists of everything that needed to be done; then she and the cleaner did what they could, which wasn't nearly enough. So Cassie did something she had never done before: went up to London on her own.

The Hawksmoor family, for generations, had always stayed at the Basil Street Hotel, which was close to Harrods where Edwin had an account. The fabrics department was warm and soporific and did wonders for Cassie's shattered nerves. She reminded herself that she wasn't short of cash and the poor old house was long overdue for a facelift. With the help of a sympathetic sales assistant, she chose heavy brocade for the downstairs rooms and flowery prints for both the girls' bedrooms to replace the nursery fabrics. Then she threw in a whole pile of cushions as well until she was laden down.

'Would Madam like it delivered?' asked the salesman, checking delivery days for Tintagel.

'No, no,' said Cassie, suddenly inspired and eager to get down to work. 'I am staying nearby, just round the corner, and should be able to carry it there myself.'

A dark-haired young man in a well-cut suit had been listening quietly and looking on. He now stepped forward and offered her his help. Taking him for another sales assistant, Cassie admitted she might, after all, need a hand. 'Just as far as the door,' she said. 'After that, I am sure I can manage.'

'I can do better than that,' he said, grabbing her parcels and leading the way. 'I am, as it happens, just cooling my heels till it's time for lunch at my club.'

Overriding Cassie's protests, he insisted on walking her to the hotel and explained on the way that he had just returned from abroad. He was, he told her when she asked, in pictures.

'Pictures?' said Cassie, for a moment confused. He certainly had the looks and charm.

'Works of art,' said Charles Buchanan. 'I dabble a bit on the side.'

*   *   *

After the third bellini, she strolled past the Doge's Palace and on into St Mark's Square. The night was balmy; the square was packed so she settled down with a glass of wine to listen to the music outside Florian's. Later she'd look for a quiet trattoria. She was not yet ready to face the fancy hotel dining room. Venice, for all its crowds, was benign. Even without a male protector, she felt quite safe in the streets. She needed to spend some time on her own, which was partly why she had come here. So much had happened in the past few months, she had to be able to think things through without interference or comment from her children.

From this point on, she was on her own; they no longer really needed her and the last thing they would want was a clinging mother. Rose and Daisy had lives of their own and Aidan would soon be gone too. It was time to start thinking for herself, to do, for a change, what she wanted to instead of always putting the family first.

She found a restaurant on the corner of a square that was just what she'd had in mind, neither too lively nor too smart, with muted lights and tables outside, round the corner from the Accademia Bridge. Over a plate of excellent pasta, Cassie found herself starting to relax. It was spring, it was Venice; she had plenty of money and no one waiting up for her at home. The night was young, she would enjoy herself. Then figure out what to do with the rest of her life.

5

Meeting Chad was like a ray of sunshine penetrating the murk of Frankie's existence. For months she had been in such a state of disgrace that no one, not even her docile mother, had anything to say to her. First the police, then the social workers, had turned it into a major event, yet no one appeared to have even considered what might make a normally biddable child act the way she had. These days, it could no longer happen. The system had gradually grown in compassion and insight.

For months she had lingered in a halfway house while they debated what to do with her and, when she eventually ended up in Middlesbrough, the very first of the inmates she met was Chad. It was in the refectory the day she arrived, to which she was brusquely led by a member of staff.

'Help yourself,' the warder said, handing her a tray. 'You may sit wherever you like.'

With her meagre supper – there was very little left – and a glass of milk to wash it down, Frankie chose a corner table where she could mope in peace. At the far end of the almost empty room – her arrival had been delayed by traffic – a group of boisterous lads were crowded around their obvious leader. Frankie clammed up in her usual way. Though tall for her age and not easily scared, she was not yet prepared for a head-on confrontation. She was quite confused enough as it was, not to mention mentally bruised.

It took him all of fifteen minutes and then she shrank from the sound of approaching feet.

'Hi,' he said, looming over her. 'I'm Chad. Who are you? Come and join us.'

Mumbling something he couldn't quite catch, Frankie shook her head. Then, when he didn't go away, she raised it defiantly to meet his gaze full on. He was not the thug she had taken him for, though she wouldn't have wanted to meet the others late at night. He was even taller than she was herself, with cropped black curls, an inviting smile and eyes of a startling blue.

'Come along,' he said, reaching for her hand. 'You'll have to learn to put up with us. Nowhere else you can go to. We don't bite.' Then he swooped and carried her tray away so that Frankie, unwilling to be seen to lose face, had no alternative but to follow him. This wasn't the moment to make a stand; she had never felt more alone. They listened wordlessly to his introductions, then slid apart to allow her space to sit. That, she was later to realise, was a piece of incredible luck. For Chad, indisputably, was leader of the pack and where he went, the others compliantly followed. By offering Frankie his hand in friendship, he had also established his rights.

It was true that, when she gradually got to know them, they were not as bad as she had thought, mainly under-privileged kids who had ended up in remand for petty crimes. Chad and Frankie stood out because of their height, their striking looks and the fact that they both had educated accents. The other girls there were a paltry crew, habitual shoplifters, a baby-snatcher, teenagers caught on the game. They resented Frankie but dared not show it. A single glance from her scornful eyes was enough to make them cringe and slink away. Likewise the boys who were nowhere near her equal, though some made lewd remarks until Chad intervened. The two of them were an impressive pair, matched in almost every way although Chad, at seven-teen, was two years older.

They both had a sense of humour, too. The first time he managed to make her laugh lifted a weight from Frankie's soul. Their shared perception of the other inmates and anarchic attitudes to the screws turned them into the Bonnie and Clyde of their set. Why was she in there, he wanted to know, and when, at last, she reluctantly told him, he roared with approving laughter. To set fire to anything took guts and daring; to have burnt down her family home earned his full respect.

'Are you a pyromaniac?' he inquired. 'Or was it simply a chilly night?' And grinned when he saw her finally starting to thaw.

An arsonist, they had called her in court. There was nothing sick about her act; she had done it quite deliberately, in cold blood. For which she was going to have to pay: no wriggling out on the grounds of juvenile psychosis. She should have known better, had had all the benefits; it was up to the court to decide. Her mother couldn't face attending the session but the colonel was there, at his most self-righteous. The sole consolation Frankie had was that he had lost, along with everything else, his prized collection of guns.

The spark between them was instantaneous; it seemed to Chad that the natural next step should be sex. Frankie, however, seemed oddly unsure, which puzzled him. It made no sense that a girl with her sort of fire should be such a prude.

'What is it?' he asked as he felt her recoil. 'You know you are safe with me.' But she still continued to hold him at arm's length. Even the thought of physical contact made her feel positively sick, which wasn't something she cared to explain.

Chad, however, was not easily deterred; at seventeen, he was almost a man, with more than his share of sexual conquests behind him. With patient handling and much finesse, he slowly won her over and gained her trust. And when they lay in each other's arms and Frankie asked if he loved her, he said he did.

6

Bath, all year round, was a tourist trap. By the early spring, it was heaving. An excellent thing for the catering trade if only it weren't such back-breaking work. But Jenny had nobody else she could blame, had signed the lease with wide-open eyes. As she told her friends, the realisation of a long-time dream. Already into her thirties with a baby on the way, if she didn't do it now, she never would.

'But you've no experience of running a pub.' Or any business, come to that; since leaving school she had earned her living exclusively with her pen.

'I can learn.' It surely couldn't be that hard. Over the years she had done much research by writing reviews of new restaurants, hence the dream.

'Propping up bars is hardly the same as working long shifts in a seven-day week while remaining polite and amenable to the punters.' Plus heaving crates and changing barrels and throwing out drunks at closing time, the strenuous stuff that really required a man. Which, at that time, was not something she had. In her working life she had always done well; she was just not so hot on relationships.

All her friends were suddenly experts though she sensed a hint of envy there too, that she had the courage to risk such a gamble while they remained stuck in their soulless jobs. With pension plans and equity, though mortgaged up to the hilt. What few realised was that she had had no choice. When she told Douglas she was pregnant, things had fallen apart so fast she could scarcely believe what had happened. Six years it had been and he'd sworn that one day he would leave; his wife was going through the menopause and he dared not walk out on her now. Jenny, aware that she really shouldn't, put up with it and accepted his evasions. It suited her lifestyle, she kidded herself, not to have to cook and clean or tie herself down to just one man while she was still young and sexy. That, at least, was the line she took; the truth, late at night, was quite different. The clock was ticking, she wanted a child. With every year that Douglas stalled, that dream grew steadily fainter.

'Leave him,' her closest friends all urged, but Jenny always came up with excuses. They were genuine soulmates and she had no doubt that he really loved her, but a man with so many pressures upon him could not simply follow his heart and get out. One of the things she admired him for was his loyalty to his wife. Her friends despaired; she was feisty and bright and hugely attractive to men. She had played the field for years, could do so again if only she would wake up and see what a cul-de-sac she was in. She had come-hither eyes and a cheeky grin and was still an enviable size eight. They made introductions, found her blind dates, yet Jenny continued impervious. Until her pregnancy was confirmed and she joyfully broke the news to her lover. And he sacked her.

The brewery weren't too keen at first on a single woman as licensee, but Jenny exerted her charm to win them over. These days, she reasonably pointed out, it was no longer p.c. to exclude anyone at all because of their race or sex or marital status. She was fit and strong and self-supporting, owned her own home and had always been in paid work. And that income, she hoped, would continue to flow since she'd had her own column in a glossy magazine as well as being a restaurant assessor for Zagat. She suspected that last bit had proved the clincher, that or her irresistible charm or the fear of trouble from the powers that be if she played the political card. Whatever it was, they reluctantly gave way so she set about finding more freelance work and daringly put her South London house on the market. From Brixton to Bath, she'd be daft not to do it. A change of scene as well as a change of profession.

'You are totally crazy,' said her friends. 'What if it doesn't work? Talk about throwing the baby out with the bathwater.'

But for Jenny there could be no going back. The man she had loved so deeply for so long had now become public enemy number one.

* * *

That wasn't precisely how he'd put it, of course.

'Me or the baby,' were his actual words but his eyes had turned red with hostility and she sensed from the way he was clenching his fists that he felt a strong urge to hit her. Despite the years she had dragged her feet, Jenny could make fast decisions. Without a word, she spun on her heel, went back to her office to clear her desk and was out of there that same afternoon, without even pausing to hand in her resignation.

'What,' they all asked, 'are you going to do?' Jobs like hers were not easy to find and her lifestyle would be hard to recreate. But that was no longer a priority with Jenny; the house provided some sort of security, plus she had many contacts. Until she worked something out, she would just go freelance. She had lived on her wits since she left South Wales and achieved a lot in a tough profession. Whatever happened, it wasn't likely she would starve. The object of prime importance now was to save this precious embryo from extinction.

So since she urgently needed to leave town, she got in her car and went to ground in her friend Vanessa's beautiful house outside Bath.

She had never wholly understood how Vanessa could leave a well-paid job and withdraw to the country in order to do up a ruin. They had worked together for many years, side by side on the same magazine, and become the closest of friends. Vanessa, who was arty and an expert on design, had worked her way through a series of men, collecting children and pets along the way. None of them ever meant much to her – the men, that was, not the children or the pets – but when she first saw the house she had fallen in love.

'It's the real thing. I have to have it,' she said when she brought in the agent's brochure for Jenny to check out. She'd been down in the West Country visiting friends, taken an accidental wrong turning and come upon it by chance. It stood alone on the top of a hill, and despite its obvious decrepitude something about it spoke to her and that was all it took. For too many years she'd been something of a gypsy, moving camp when her love-life dictated, never putting down permanent roots. The kids were okay but needed a base. She was weary of constantly living in temporary digs.

The brochure was certainly optimistic; in truth, the house was virtually a ruin. When Jenny drove down there to take a look and saw it first in a thunderstorm, it didn't even have a roof but was sealed by a flapping tarpaulin. They sat, huddled together in her car, while lightning dramatically split the sky and the house just stood there and glowered at them in contempt. It had lasted for three hundred years, it proclaimed, and was not going to crumble now.

Jenny could see that Vanessa was right. With her specialist knowledge and artistic flair, the house cried out for the kind of love she could give it. They ran through the rain and stood shivering in the porch. The studded front door was heavily padlocked; all the windows were firmly closed though some of the panes had been smashed.

'Vandals,' said Vanessa. 'It's been empty too long. I must raise the cash before more damage is done.'

The property developer was reluctant to sell and kept her hanging around for months. It had taken all the money she could raise – her post office savings that were meant for her children, her life insurance and her jade collection, plus loans from a few trusted friends. As well as her car. Jenny helped out with a piece about the house which landed Vanessa a real stroke of luck: a publisher offered her a fat commission for a detailed history of the place, which had both literary and artistic connections.

'You are going to have to work hard,' said Jenny, not envying her friend a bit except that her heart was set upon it and dreams were meant to be fulfilled. After three failed marriages and as many children, the house represented a stability Vanessa had never known. No man she'd ever met in her roller-coaster love-life – and, unlike Jenny, she married them all – had provided the visceral tug she got just from looking at its solid walls and sensing the cosmic vibrations of earlier owners.

'Don't you find it thrilling,' she said, when the property man ceased prevaricating and the deal was allowed to go through, 'that in this room Dr Johnson held court? I wonder if his spirit is still around.'

'It's a friendly feeling,' said Jenny, and it was. Nothing spooky in this generous house; it was simply waiting to be brought back to life by someone able to give it the love it deserved.

For the months it took to repair the roof, Vanessa's

ménage moved into the gatehouse which later, when the work was done, she hoped to be able to let. Jenny, who popped down several times, began to see the house's potential. As the reconstruction got under way, its original splendour was gradually revealed.

'I may even come to live here myself,' she said, only half joking.

Now that things had radically changed, she had nowhere else to go and Vanessa's current partner was working abroad and would be gone for several weeks. It worked out well; Jenny had her laptop and several commissioned articles to write and, from her room in the tiny gatehouse, could oversee the builders at work, while supplying them with occasional cups of tea. As spring arrived and foliage burgeoned, the countryside slowly revealed itself and Jenny, whose life had been totally urban, began to understand Vanessa's compulsion. And then she found the Coot and Hern, and everything slotted into place.

'The coot and *what*?'

'Tennyson,' said Jenny. God, what a load of philistines they were. It was by a brook. With a waterwheel. Grey stone walls with weeping willows, steep stairways and rooms to let. It would need a bit of work but so what? If Vanessa could make a go of it, so could she. She was five months pregnant and needed a job. The pub might prove the answer to her prayers.

7

Unlike Frankie, whose family had proved her ultimate undoing, Chad had nothing at all to say about his. He had been a foundling, the first she had known, left in the porch of a Yorkshire church without so much as a note pinned to his shawl. He only knew it had been midsummer and that his crying had alerted the gardener's boy.

'The church was St Chad's and the boy's name Barnaby. Voilà! A ready-made identity. The vicar announced my existence from the pulpit, and went on doing so for several weeks, but no one ever came forward to claim me. Why doesn't that surprise me?'

His eyes, of that startling electric blue, crinkled at the corners when he smiled. His teeth were good and his hair was coal-black. Frankie wondered how any mother could have turned her back on such a ravishing baby. She guessed he might be of Irish stock; 'black' Irish was what they called them. He certainly possessed the necessary blarney.

*　　*　　*

Once over the shock of being locked up, she adapted, more or less, to the rigid regime. It was not quite a prison but she wasn't free to leave; since the fire, there had been a frozen silence from home. The colonel had washed his hands of her and forbidden her mother to be in touch, despite the fact that Frankie was still her only child. Frankie had realised long ago how frail a reed her mother must be; how else could she have married that terrible man? But it wasn't till now that she'd understood the full measure of his control. If her real father were still around, things would never have come to this. But, then, her mother would not have married the colonel.

'She'll come round,' Chad assured her. 'And if she doesn't, she's rubbish.'

Frankie grinned. He was always like that: eternally optimistic. The fact that they were both on the wrong side of the law appeared not to faze him at all. But he'd been in trouble most of his life and was not ashamed to discuss it. They spent all the time they could together, though mainly supervised. His band of heavies slunk away whenever Frankie appeared. Now she'd discovered the joys of sex, she couldn't get enough of it and much of their time was spent finding ways to be alone together.

'You have the cheek of the devil,' she said, watching him use his formidable charm to get whatever he wanted from authority. The eyes, the smile, the dazzling looks worked wonders even here, on this bunch of dull screws. Something that she thought had died in her when she struck that fatal match reignited.

She had fallen completely under his spell. There was nothing she wouldn't have done for him. And yet he had casually murdered someone. It simply didn't add up.

'He was just a playground thug,' he said. 'No one of any note. One day he pushed things a little too far and – bingo!' The dazzling smile didn't flicker as he drew his finger across his throat. 'These things happen,' he said casually. 'Just one of life's little accidents.'

Before that they'd sent him to public school, the well-heeled family who had taken him in and fostered him for a while, which explained his polish and lofty air. He acted like a democratic lord of the manor, and took it for granted that everybody liked him.

'So what went wrong?'

'Expelled,' he said, with his little boy air of false contrition. 'They caught me smoking and kicked me out.'

'Smoking?' she said. It did sound harsh even for somewhere like Repton.

'Hashish. They said I was a bad example.' He laughed. 'I was only fifteen.'

So they'd sent him back to Barnardo's in disgrace and totally washed their hands of him. The Tewson-Finches, Miles and Yolande; even their names made him smile. Having been through something similar herself, Frankie totally empathised. Families who gave up on you were not worthy of the name. A parent's duty was to back you up, to love you unconditionally.

'So they simply threw you out?' she asked.

'Yup,' said Chad, who had then gone on to murder a boy in cold blood.

'Will we always be together?' she asked as they lay entwined. It was cramped behind the water tank but at least they had some space to themselves and no one knew where they were.

'Always,' he promised. She was such a child. Though tall for her age and as brave as a boy, in fact she was barely fifteen, whereas Chad, almost eighteen by now, would soon be able to vote. With his heavy beard, he'd been shaving for years and might easily have passed for twenty-two.

'When you leave here, will you take me with you?' By now she knew he was all she wanted in life.

'I will,' he said. 'You can count on that. And once we're free, who knows, we may even get married.'

8

Pippa stood ankle-deep in rubble, trying to heat the babies' milk in an improvised bottle-warmer on the stove because the power was off. All around her was builders' rubbish and a strong smell of turps pervaded the air. From somewhere in another room she could hear the distant sound of mewling. The twins were on the verge of waking; hostilities would shortly be resumed.

'Once you've stopped messing around with that milk,' said Ernie sternly from the top of his ladder, 'you might boil some water for our tea.'

'Right you are, boss,' said Pippa placidly, grinning as she tested the milk by dabbing it on the inside of her wrist. The way these workmen pushed her around, no one would guess who was paying their bills. But she loved being there in the thick of things, despite the inconvenience. Normally she would have done it herself – she'd been apprenticed to a decorating firm – but Charles had put his foot down and that was that.

'I won't have you risking it up that ladder,' he'd

said and, perhaps for the first time ever, Pippa had actually done as he'd said.

Things had happened at a dizzying pace since she had found she was pregnant. To start with, she had been petrified by the thought of how he was likely to react, feared she had scuppered their illicit relationship with this unforeseen complication. She must have been careless; it ought not have happened. She cursed herself for the slip. But when the test had proved positive and, furthermore, shown that it was twins, she'd had no other option but to tell him. It could not have been a less opportune time; her career was very much in the ascendant. But nor had she wanted to face an abortion alone. Charles, when she finally spilled the beans, at first said very little. Had gone, grim-faced, to the country to think it over.

Which meant they were almost certainly doomed; she could have kicked herself. Her mother had always said she was too impulsive. Well, this time she had majorly screwed up. Pippa, facing the future alone, at twenty-seven had huge decisions to make. If it came to it, as she knew it would, even without his support she would keep the babies. She had never been drawn to motherhood; was still too young, she felt, to settle down. But faced, as she was, with a fait accompli, she had no other choice. Charles had Cassie and their solid marriage which was, she knew, unassailable. And there were the kids to consider. Cassie's daughters were not his own but he'd supported them through their teenage years and loved them as much as he did his son Aidan. Something Pippa had always envied was his close and happy family life. She was sure he would have no love to spare for her own unwanted twins.

But now was not the time for self-pity. She needed to start making plans.

The first priority was to move. The five-floor walk-up off the Fulham Road was all very well for a fit twenty-something who rode a bike and went to the gym, but out of the question for a mum with a double buggy. So while Charles was in Cornwall she settled down at the kitchen table to draw up one of her lists. She had always been very well organised, part of the secret of her success. She ran her business almost single-handed and lived only two blocks from the shop, which meant she was nearly always there.

She'd first met Charles five years before when, a bubbly twenty-two, she was temping in Liberty's fabric department while looking around for something in design. He'd been after a chintz of a certain colour for Iranian clients in Wilton Place and had been impressed by Pippa's knowledge and the trouble she'd taken to find him just the right thing. The mutual attraction had been instantaneous. In less than a week he had got her into bed.

'Be careful you don't end up as his nurse,' her mother had warned her when she knew. 'Twenty years is too large a gap. You still have most of your life ahead while he must be almost my age.' Gorgeous with it, she had to concede but only to herself.

Endorsing a daughter's adultery was something no mother should ever do. She had played around herself, so knew the score.

The shop, which had started as Charles's idea, into which he had sunk substantial funds, had taken off with surprising speed so that now she had a mail order business too. Even apart from financially, Charles had been a tremendous support by introducing her to his clients and throwing business her way. Another good reason for Pippa to love him; she never could resist a successful man.

But now she would have to manage alone and she steeled herself to the fact. Her mother was right: he was much too old. Whatever his energies in the sack, as a future father he was a less good bet. By the time the babies turned eighteen, he would already be drawing his pension, leaving Pippa to support them all. It wouldn't be fair to any of them. She would have to face up to life as a single parent.

But Charles, as he did so often, surprised her by turning up late on the Monday night, arms overflowing with full-blown roses and a diamond brooch in a velvet box which, although too formal for her, was a generous gift.

'Twins!' he said, embracing her hard. 'If I really luck out, they'll be girls.'

Dearest Charles. As she fed the twins, Pippa was practically purring. It's a well-known fact that married lovers never ever leave their wives, but at the end of the following week, before he departed

46

for Cornwall again, he held her close and told her his decision.

'I am going to ask Cassie for a divorce. We ought to get married as soon as we can. We don't want them born on the wrong side of the blanket.' Till now the M-word had never been mentioned and Pippa had not expected it. But he, so much older, was taking charge and wasn't going to let anything stand in his way. It was all part of the compelling charm which had landed her where she was now: in this beautiful house he had bought her in Barnes, which was in the process of being fully restored. The Pont Street flat he would keep for business and the use of the kids when they came into town. And he seemed to be genuinely chuffed by the fact that they'd soon have two more half-siblings.

If Charles had surprised her, Cassie did too by meekly refusing to stand in their way.

'Go,' she had said, 'if you feel you must.' And had taken the dogs for a walk.

Pippa was really consumed by guilt at the thought of what she was doing to Cassie, but Charles assured her it had just been a matter of time.

'She's got plenty to fill her days,' he said. 'And she loves Tintagel more than me. Now that she's got her grandchildren, she'll be fine.'

He displayed no feelings either way at walking out after twenty-one years and Pippa, despite her relief, was secretly shocked. She had only really met Cassie once, and had been very much taken by the older woman's dignity and calm. But now was no time for regrets. The die was cast; there could be no looking back.

9

It seemed to Frankie, the closer they got, that beneath the banter Chad minded not having real roots. He occasionally made a joke of it, the way he had entered the world unannounced, but sometimes she caught him unawares with a wistful look on his face. At least she knew where she had come from, despite the way it had later turned out. Her childhood, when her dad was alive, had been full of happy memories, which was also true of the early days on the Wirral. She still hadn't talked much about it to Chad but he was an expert at picking things up. He held her tight when she cried in her sleep or woke in sudden terror. These days they slept outside the main complex, in a hostel in a neighbouring street, where they managed to share a bed most of the time. The female warden, bewitched by Chad, obligingly looked the other way and, provided they behaved themselves, they could more or less do as they liked.

'I won't let anyone harm you, babe,' he said when Frankie clung on to him. Whatever it was apparently went very deep.

He liked to listen to her childhood stories of riding her pony and following the guns; the countryside was what she missed most of all. The breeze, the sunshine, the scent of damp earth, the freedom to ride all day on her own and only come home when the pony was tired; the memories lit up her face. Confined within this grim institution was no way to be spending their teenage years.

'He stole my childhood, that thieving bastard.' It was why she'd set fire to his house.

Things would have been far worse if it hadn't been for Chad. He had brought new life and hope into Frankie's life. Her parents had given up on her but Chad had taken their place. He was more than a lover, he was her protector too; even the warders respected that and it gave her a whole new confidence, along with a dawning beauty. He liked to ask about the fire and how she had managed to carry it off.

'Did it burn down completely?' he wanted to know.

'Enough,' she said. 'They knocked down the rest because it was no longer safe.' A Grade Two listed manor house set in extensive grounds, it had gone up like a tinderbox when she lit it.

'It must have been spectacular.'

'It was.' She had stood there, transfixed by the blaze, overwhelmed by a sudden manic excitement. And not until the fire was well under way had she thought to wonder if anyone could be inside. Her mother and the colonel were safely in London but there might have been others she'd overlooked. She simply hadn't thought. Which had gone very much against her at the hearing.

'Servants, you mean?' He was curious. His interest in her earlier life was intense.

'Well, hardly that. We weren't that rich. A cleaning woman, the guy who cut the grass and fed the colonel's dogs. A number of people had easy access – it wasn't exactly Fort Knox.'

'So how did they figure out it was you?'

'Apart from the fact I hated him? I stuck around, like a fool, until they caught me.'

The blaze had been totally wonderful; to this day she couldn't forget it. November the Fifth, though without the seasonal drizzle. That summer had been unusually dry; the timber was highly combustible. Especially when assisted by the paraffin Frankie had used.

'But how did you know how to do it?' he asked, not sure he'd have had the guts himself. His admiration for her grew with every extra detail.

'Intuition,' said Frankie modestly. 'I figured it out for myself. Different people have different talents. Someone worked out how to split the atom. Someone else developed lateral thinking. I just know how to set a really great fire.'

She knew it was love, had never felt this way. The only boys she had known had been kids and she'd never even been on a proper date. She worshipped Chad, was obsessed with him and clung to his every word. She dreamed of the day they would one day be

51

free to spend their lives together. His future, however, was bleaker than hers since he was in on a murder charge whereas she, all going well, would soon be out. Arson was serious but she was underage. Despite her stepfather's obdurate stand, the social workers were busy on her behalf.

'He's the one who should be inside,' said Chád, who only knew part of the truth. 'Wait till I get out and I'll fix the bastard.'

'He isn't worth it,' said Frankie wisely. 'And you're in enough trouble as it is.'

10

There hadn't been a word from Rocco; Cristina was growing frantic. By the time she got home from the opera that night, there still wasn't any news. And Claude was only gone for three nights. Unless she acted extremely fast, it could be that she'd find herself back on the streets.

Even in her middle twenties, she was still at the top of her catwalk fame, despite the fact, it was popularly rumoured, that her cocaine habit was spiralling out of control. At nineteen she'd been at her most spectacular, featured on lists of the world's most beautiful women, and had made a couple of 'art-house' movies, though under another name. It was at that age she had first met Cal, in Ipanema at the height of the season, with her credit card tucked into her minuscule bikini and her door key round her neck on a leather thong. The bare necessities of a pampered life; it was instant lust, he had told her later. They halted only yards apart, these two exotic strangers, locking eyes, before falling recklessly into each other's arms.

Brazil in the seventies was decadent and lavish, its

beaches strewn with naked flesh, its nightspots with the rich and famous, its casinos overflowing. Cristina's picture, sixty feet high, dominated hoardings all over Rio so that Cal encountered her aggrandised image virtually everywhere he looked. It meant no privacy but what did she care; adulation had become her very lifeblood. Nor could she get enough of him; he was new in the city, in his early twenties, with a natural beauty almost as striking as hers. Together they made a dynamic pair and were quickly the toast of the town. Within days he had moved into her apartment, with its penthouse terrace and ocean views, and shortly after that he mentioned love.

Since they both had money (she was very rich) they devoted most of their waking hours to prodigal spending and having fun, except when she had to work, which wasn't often at that time of year. The heat was far too great, she complained, to stand around for hours just changing her clothes. Her sponsors, who loved her, put up with it. Her sultry beauty was in such demand that if she frowned, as she often did, instant alarm bells rang and someone would be dispatched to calm her down. On the few occasions when she did a show, Cal would sit loyally in the front row, enjoying the prestige of escorting her as well as the way he knew he too was turning heads.

'Have you ever thought of modelling yourself?' The question was frequently asked. But Cal was far too fly for that. He liked the clothes and the lifestyle they paid for but considered the fashion world a tad too sleazy. Also he was basically idle, preferring to stay out late at night and sleep through most of the morning, rising at noon to mix his first drink and carry one back to Cristina in her boudoir. They were mirror images of each other: their looks, their vanity, their basic avarice. It was only a matter of time before she started dropping hints about commitment.

From the start, she encountered an odd resistance, though Cal declared he adored her. And the sex was out of this world, so what was his problem? There were few red-blooded men in the world who would not have killed to have taken his place. Cristina, accustomed to having her own way, stamped her foot and sulked. She thought he was playing hard to get so tested him by being unfaithful. She brazenly checked out an old flame who took her for the weekend to Copacabana.

That was nearly the end of them. Cal immediately packed his bags and left without leaving a contact number. It reduced her to an emotional wreck; unused to being treated like that, she expected to do whatever she damn well pleased. Five weeks later, when she'd lost seven pounds, been to a shrink, developed a drinking problem and sent out spies all over the city, desperate to find out where he was, he strolled back in with a friendly grin and asked if she would consent to be his wife.

In later years she often looked back on the man who had rocked her life then disappeared as mysteriously as he had arrived. But long before it came to that, most of her money had been spent and her adoration had changed to bitter resentment. He always remained quite a shadowy figure; she had never even been clear about his country of birth. His accent was resolutely cut-glass and he claimed connections in Hollywood, though his knowledge of London, too, seemed pretty extensive. She never found out where his money came from; he was twenty-two when they met. But he looked and dressed and acted the part of a playboy born to a life of ease, who was never socially out of his depth and always had the readies in his pocket.

'I'm a traveller of the world,' he said, when asked how he had lived before Rio, and seemed to have no profession at all apart from being a great lay. Once they were married, he moved back in and extended his personal space by one room to accommodate his rapidly growing wardrobe. They continued to party most of the time and it was he who first introduced her to coke, to the fierce disapproval of the corporate sponsors who indulged her every other whim. It would damage her beauty and reputation but at least, as Cristina pointed out, it also kept her satisfyingly thin.

Waiting in a bar for her friends, she thought back to those headier times when the world still lay at her feet. She was twenty-four now, and the drug had started its pervasive damage; these days she couldn't get out of bed without it. She spat her chewing gum into an ashtray and scrabbled in her purse for a ciga-rette. The others were already forty minutes late; she had started drinking without them.

Izabel, Alicia and Marie-Hélène were party girls with a vengeance. The first two, by their own reckoning, were 'starlets'; Marie-Hélène, who was far more astute, was an international adventuress. Cristina was into her second Bacardi by the time the trio burst through the door, screaming their heads off and tossing their hair, causing enough disruption to silence the bar.

'You're late,' snapped Cristina, not well pleased, furious at being excluded. It was clear all three were at least one party ahead.

'We ran into Raoul,' said Alicia, smirking, 'and he took us up to his pad for a couple of joints.'

'In any case,' said Marie-Hélène, expertly glancing around the room, 'it's not yet eleven. The night is young. The party won't liven up until after two.'

This was how they lived in Rio, hitting the high spots every night. There were times Cristina would have liked to sleep instead but she was far too imperious to say so. She and her acolytes were ever on display, strutting their stuff in the fanciest joints. She constantly craved an audience and wouldn't go hunting on her own, although the instant she made a hit she expected the others to get lost.

But this riotous living was taking its toll, on both her looks and her career. No longer rich, she could barely scrape by with the fewer catwalk bookings she was getting and the hugely inflated expenses she had to shell out. Living the high life was all very well when you were still the most celebrated beauty in town and someone else would always pick up the tab. Since she stopped being half of a beautiful couple, her notoriety had taken a dip while her unreliable reputation had decimated her income. In addition, her expensive habit was relentlessly bleeding her dry.

Now, however, was not the time for taking stock of her life. Her cohorts were restless and ready to go, so Cristina slipped off to the powder-room and returned with brighter eyes and her humour restored. She wore a shimmering satin shift, daringly slashed to the base of her spine, and as she undulated through the crowd there wasn't an eye in the place that wasn't on her.

The noise was so great as they entered the club that all they could do was gesticulate and edge their way through the heaving masses to the bar. There were flashing lights, enough to bring on a migraine, and the heat was so intense bodies glistened with sweat. The Beautiful People were out in force and, when they saw Cristina enter, they parted to allow the four of them through. Hands reached out and kisses were blown. In the popularity stakes she was still hot.

'Let's get out of here,' she said. In this light she couldn't be seen to her best advantage.

The next club was right on the waterfront, with windows flung wide and a welcome breeze that cooled and caressed her skin. Here she spotted a number of faces that, in her shifting world, she thought of as friends. When Cal was around it had all been different. He would grab her hand and lead her through and make them the focal point of any group. She missed his reassuring smile and the hand-squeeze that confirmed he was there for her. When he disappeared, she had thought she might die though by then she was hurling plates and creating scenes. She knew now that she had been too hasty. The years since Cal disappeared had been really tough.

But people embraced her and the music turned her on. In seconds Cristina was out on the floor, salsa-ing on her own to much applause. With her caramel skin and abundance of hair and a body that moved like liquid silk, she achieved the attention she always yearned for and was happy, at least for the moment. Marie-Hélène was off in a corner, schmoozing with a former beau, while the starlets had settled themselves at the bar and were competing for what they could pull. Neither could ever face going home alone; it would mean losing too much face.

Exhausted, Cristina took a breather and went to freshen up. She brushed her hair, which fell halfway down her back, and spritzed the sheen of perspiration from her face. Her feet were aching so she kicked off her sandals and massaged her throbbing toes with expensive cream. Soon she'd be ready to return to the fray, but there was one more thing she needed to do. Checking that she wasn't observed, she removed the small white sachet from her purse. In a matter of seconds her eyes were brighter and her glossy lips parted with elation.

The girls had gone but she didn't care. She was perfectly happy dancing alone with the eyes of the room upon her. She danced all night, till she almost dropped and her famous boobs were hanging right out of her dress. And just when they thought she was finally spent, she would pop back into the powder-room and revitalise herself with the magic white powder. She never knew who went home with her; by then the room had started to spin and she had virtually blanked out. She smelt his cologne and endured his groping and registered only the click of the door when he left.

She awoke next morning in crumpled sheets with a head that thundered so painfully she dared not even attempt to open her eyes. She dragged a pillow over her face to protect them from the morning glare, then sank back into oblivion for two more hours. When she woke again, it was almost noon and she'd missed her early call. The Prada people would not be bothering her again. So what? There were plenty more fashion houses. Right now all she cared about was ridding herself of this blinding pain in her head. She woke again at four with a raging thirst and an urgent need to empty her bladder but, when she attempted to get out of bed, the room swung round and she lost her balance, crashed to the floor and knocked herself out on the edge of the bedside table.

Two hours later she finally came to, sprawled in a pool of urine and blood. A gash on her temple hurt like hell, and her designer shift was all rumpled up, revealing to anyone entering the room everything she had got. She prayed the maid had not been in, looked nervously round for her morning tray but, to her relief, could see no evidence of intrusion. She raised herself, which made her throw up, then sank back into a dreamless sleep. It was almost midnight before she woke again.

Cristina staggered into the bathroom and threw up again all over the floor, then crawled on her hands and knees into the kitchen. She was now so parched she could barely swallow and desperate for a drink. Coffee wouldn't do it and she had no milk so she pulled the top off the vodka bottle and glugged down a mouthful which made her vomit again. She groped her way to the bathroom mirror, avoiding the mess on the floor, and groaned when she managed to open her eyes and saw the ravages of the night. A face all bloated with drink and drugs, with a bruise the size of a ping-pong ball and a smear of dried blood on her cheek. A whole day wasted and she'd had no food. It appeared that no one had called to find out how she was.

With the utmost effort, she rinsed her face, then tied back her matted hair. She had to get out of this stinking place and eat something fast before she fainted again. Wearing her trench coat but nothing else except for a pair of feathered mules, she ventured into the elevator, hoping not to be seen.

The porter on duty was the young, handsome one who had several times seen her the worse for wear.

'Good evening,' he said, jumping swiftly to attention, and she sensed from the way that he looked at her that he knew what her trench coat concealed. Any other time she might have been tempted; she liked his insolent stare and the cut of his pants. The way she felt now, though, it was out of the question. If she didn't get out of there fast she would throw up again.

There had, she dimly remembered now, been another wife before they met, though Cal had never been willing to talk about it. It seemed scarcely possible – he was still such a boy – but would make sense of his reluctance to tie himself down without a struggle. And it might explain where he'd got his money. Though he'd been through hers with alacrity, he had seemed to have no shortage of it when they met. He'd been staying in one of the grand hotels when he'd picked her up on the beach, and his luggage, when he moved it in, had been of the very best quality, as had his clothes.

She had loved to lie and watch him dress, preening and posing in front of the glass, patting his freshly shaven chin, as sexually confident as she was herself. No wonder they'd been such a social hit; society had adored them for their blatant narcissism. She sighed for those days which were careless and free, when the only thing on the agenda was making love. The money she'd made, plus his own private income, left them free to do as they liked. The first thing he'd bought was a red Ferrari in which they had cruised the crowded streets, hailing friends and stopping at intervals to drink. She could see him still, with his joie de vivre and eyes alight with mischief. Cal Barnard, still the love of her life, the mystery man who had had no past and now, it seemed, no future.

When he disappeared it had been without trace; she came home one day and he had gone. He had taken his luggage and all his possessions, leaving her nothing but an empty fridge and a cellophane packet containing her poison of choice. Beside it lay a single red rose and a note that just said: 'Je regrette.'

11

It would take a lot of working out. It was crucial that he anticipate possible hitches. Since the moment he had been apprehended, Chad had been planning the perfect escape and now, since knowing Frankie, favoured fire. If she had done it, so could he. She'd have got clean away if she hadn't hung around. The trick was to do it, then get the hell out without wasting any precious time or involving another person. Chad believed in travelling light; at heart he was still a loner.

He grilled her over and over again until he had every detail by heart. He knew she hadn't yet cottoned on, which made things easier for him. The basic combustibles were relatively simple; there was paraffin stored in the gardener's shed, matches in the kitchen. Frankie's device of making a long wick had been a stroke of genius, had meant she'd been able to light the fire without much risk to herself.

Chad's idea was to set fire to the hostel when none of the other residents were there, then slip away in the ensuing furore. His biggest problem was finding a way to be alone on the premises, something expressly forbidden by the governing board. The hostel was simply a dormitory, an annexe of the main reform school though situated outside the locked iron gates. Only a handful of inmates at one time were allowed the privilege of sleeping there, a sign from above that they were now worthy of trust. Frankie and the others were bona fide; only Chad had wheedled himself in through charm.

Meals were served in the main building, where they also spent the rest of the day. They were not allowed to return to the hostel unless it was an emergency. Which, he now reasoned, should include being suddenly taken ill. If he used his lethal charm again on the highly susceptible female warden, he was confident she would turn a blind eye and allow him to stay in bed. Though he must be careful not to overplay it and end up in the sickbay. Everything seemed to fit into place. There were just a couple more things he had to do.

Frankie was woken in the early hours by a sudden icy blast. The window was open and someone was climbing in. Before she could even make a sound, a hand was clamped firmly over her mouth as Chad threw himself headlong across her bed. He wore thick gloves that smelt of petrol and was clad from head to toe in black like a member of the SAS.

'What on earth are you doing?' she asked, once she had shaken him off. He would persist in taking these crazy risks. If anyone else had happened to see him, all privileges would have been removed and, before he knew it, he'd be back behind locked doors. Yet she had to admire his style; nothing seemed to scare him.

'Move over,' he said, wriggling out of his clothes and sliding in beside her. His face was cold but his pulse was fast. He was also in a state of sexual arousal.

'What have you been up to?' she asked later, when he lay exhausted in her arms.

'Never you mind,' he said. 'It's none of your business.'

In the end, however, he had to tell her because he needed her help. He was only going to get one shot and wanted her as a decoy.

'But you have to do exactly as I say,' he insisted before he told her. 'It's essential that everything goes according to plan.'

Frankie, at first, was apprehensive and keen not to get involved. She was scared his actions might jeopardise both their futures. But when he explained what she already knew, that he could not endure one more day in the place, and she heard the anguish in his voice, she saw his point of view. Soon she'd be walking out of there with the rest of her life before her while he would remain locked up, perhaps for years.

'The truth is,' he said, with his lips on her throat, 'I cannot live without you. And will kill myself if they let you go and I am left here to rot.'

12

Next morning the weather was brilliantly sunny so Cassie took a boat to the Lido and treated herself to lunch at the Hotel des Bains. The only other people there were a party of grey-suited businessmen who stayed at the far end of the terrace and kept right out of her way. It was early spring so the swarming crowds had not yet made an appearance. She sat and sipped a glass of champagne and remembered the scenes from *Death in Venice*, filmed on this same stretch of beach. Poor Dirk Bogarde, brought down by love. The way she was feeling now, she empathised.

Cassandra Elwes had been a war baby, conceived on her father's final leave and born in May, just a few days after the war in Europe ended. Her older brothers were already at Eton when her mother brought the new baby home and Cassie became their beloved plaything, petted and cherished and always indulged, including being allowed to tag along. Cornwall, even in those days of strict rationing, lived off the fat of the land, so she was well provided for and, due to the gap between the siblings, more than able to hold her own in company of all ages. She grew up tall and naturally graceful, with solemn eyes that always seemed to be searching for the truth, and wore her thick brown hair in a single plait. Edwin Hawksmoor, who had known her from her childhood, watched her growth with a deepening affection and, as soon as she turned eighteen, astonished her father by asking for her hand. Her parents initially were taken aback; Cassie was only just out of school and still, in their eyes at least, very much a child. But Cassie herself was immensely flattered at being taken so seriously by a man on whom she'd had a crush since adolescence. So, because she invariably got her way, within the year she became his bride and moved a few miles along the coast to become mistress of his manor.

Despite the fact that he was more than twice her age, Edwin had tutored Cassie well, widening her interests and encouraging her to study so that, by the time they were man and wife, they had more in common of a cerebral nature than most new couples closer to each other in age. Having older brothers helped, of course, and she had grown up with a bright and inquiring mind. Edwin's first fiancée had perished in the Blitz; rumour had it he'd been mourning her ever since. But thrown, as he was, into almost daily contact with this pretty and impressionable child, he had found it all too easy to love again. The knowledge he'd garnered in his solitary years he now had the utmost joy in sharing with her. Their bond was founded on a master/pupil basis that gradually grew into deep and lasting love. She looked up to and respected him as a man she could revere and trust.

At the time of their marriage her father was Lord Lieutenant of Cornwall, with extensive land that bordered on Edwin's estate. Thus Cassie had little uprooting to do, and most mornings she would walk the dogs along the rambling coastal path and drop into her mother's kitchen for coffee and a chat. And when the babies, Rose and Daisy, arrived her extended family was complete, with doting grandparents on the scene to help raise the little girls.

It was a tranquil existence and Cassie loved it, content as she was to cook and potter, play the piano by candlelight or read in front of a blazing fire, her husband dozing at her side. Edwin had ten thousand acres to farm and, although he employed a capable manager, was out in all weathers from dawn till dusk, a strenuous life for a man his age who had never really been strong. Sometimes his sister, Sybil, would visit from her busy studio in St Ives where she worked, year round, as a brilliant, innovative sculptor. Three years older even than Edwin, she was inclined to be critical of the young bride. The only things she cared for were her art and the Hawksmoor land, handed down through many generations.

She still kept rooms at the rear of the house, with a view of the sea at the end of the lawn, which no one ever entered without permission. She usually came between sculptural projects, when she needed time to relax and recharge before starting something new. She was quite celebrated in her field and could choose the commissions she wanted. Her work, like her, was simplistic and stark, recognisable to the masses so that visitors flocked to her studio all year round. While she was staying with Edwin and Cassie she would work energetically in the garden, or spend long hours in the library browsing through Edwin's collection of art books.

The girls were slightly in awe of her; her speech was forthright and her manner gruff and she had very little patience with small children. But as they grew older, she softened towards them and started teaching them both to draw, displaying a kindness she usually chose to hide.

'Would Sybil ever have liked to marry?' She'd been twenty-three at the outbreak of war and had worked in a munitions factory, risking her life every night.

'No,' said Edwin. 'I am pretty sure not. All she has ever really cared about is art and her independence.'

Cassie, intimidated, secretly hoped that some of her sister-in-law's formidable talent might, in due course, be handed down to the children.

The idyll, alas, was not destined to last. When the heart attack carried Edwin off, Cassie found herself widowed at thirty-three. What had once been a haven of peaceful content became just a shuddering hulk of a house, especially when the weather at sea was bad. She would huddle with the dogs in front of the fire, listening to the booming breakers, and agonise as to how she could manage alone. Ten thousand acres was a lot to oversee, but she knew she could depend on

William Tremayne. The farm manager was a man in his forties, weather-beaten and taciturn, who had lived on the Hawksmoor estate for most of his life. His job continued without interruption; he came to the house to offer condolences but seemed to take it for granted that nothing would change. Cassie could also have turned to Sybil, but she wasn't keen to. The ingenuous child who had married so young, and always looked up to her husband for guidance, was now an adult with daughters of her own. It was up to her what she made of her life.

Talk about funeral meats furnishing the marriage feast; that rapturous morning in the Knightsbridge hotel changed for ever Cassie's perception of life. When the nice young man had come to her aid by carrying her parcels back for her, nothing had prepared her for what happened next. While she was nervously wondering whether to tip him, he tossed her packages on to the bed and kissed her.

'Sorry,' he said. 'I shouldn't have done that. I just couldn't help myself.' Then he gave her a dazzling smile and did it again.

Cassie, offended to her core, stared at him, rigid with indignation, uncertain whether to scream or faint or call for assistance from the desk. 'I have recently lost my husband,' she said, then spoiled the impact of the reprimand by bursting into tears. At which he put his arms round her and patted her comfortingly on the back, offering his handkerchief to mop her eyes. His own eyes were blue and filled with compassion; she saw he meant no disrespect. And though he was clearly much younger than her, she felt instinctively that she could trust him.

Before she knew it, they were on the bed and he had taken his jacket off and, once again, was smothering her with kisses. And Cassie, after her first rebuff, found herself entering into things and behaving, she later thought, like a shameless hussy.

The deep affection she had felt for Edwin had always been more on a spiritual plane, whereas Charles was keen to make love to her all the time. Edwin had been a father figure to whom she had always looked up; he had handled her like porcelain, and she, in her innocence, had not known what she was missing. Charles Buchanan was a total contrast; lusty, sensual and twenty-three. If he'd had his way, they'd have stayed in bed all day, but Cassie was older and more restrained. With other pressing matters to worry about.

'You're insane,' she said when he told her how he felt. 'I am far too old and you hardly know me.'

'I know enough,' he said, kissing her palm, 'to want to devote my life to you and try to make you happy.'

At first she didn't mention the children, just that her husband had been much older and that she had loved him very deeply and had not yet recovered from the shock. But Charles had been there when she paid her bill and knew approximately where she lived. And that she was renovating her house so soon after Edwin's death. Embarrassed, she went on to the defensive. Her husband had been ailing for years. She was doing it mainly in memory of him.

'I'd love to come and see it some day.' The house she so clearly loved. But now would not be appropriate. She had lingered in London too long as it was, and dared not imagine what the village would say should she return with a handsome young man in tow.

'I must go home first thing,' she said.

'May I help you with your luggage?'

His eyes were bright as he stroked her cheek and Cassie felt a great wave of passion engulf her in a way she'd not known before.

'Wait,' she told him, after some thought. 'First there are things that have to be taken care of.'

'Remember my profession,' he said, holding her close against his heart. 'If your home comes first, which I understand, allow me to offer my services.'

Put like that, she found it hard to resist. In addition to pictures, he now explained, he also dabbled a bit in interior design. Cassie laughed at his self-assurance. 'Wait,' she told him again, 'until I call you.'

On the journey home her thoughts were spinning. She could scarcely credit what she had done. She studied her face in the carriage window, searching for signs of debauchery. She had acted quite out of character, behaved like a pathetic fool. Hindu widows committed suttee, while she had fooled around with a total stranger, much younger than herself. There was nobody she could possibly tell; no one who wouldn't condemn her. Because her marriage had been so close, she had felt no need of female friends. Now, for the first time ever, she realised their lack. The girls were too young to understand, which would not only apply to Charles. Both of them had always worshipped their father.

She sent Charles a telegram, asking him to wait and promising to be in touch when she felt it was time. She dared not risk public disapprobation by taking up with another man quite so soon. But she couldn't forget his expressive eyes, which started to haunt her dreams, nor the way she'd felt when he held her close and covered her face with kisses.

Charles was able to curb his impatience and when the reunion did finally take place, it all went very well. The girls both took to him on sight, put aside any rebellious thoughts, and treated him like an elder brother which, indeed, he could almost have been. He was tall and lithe, in T-shirt and jeans, and he vaulted out of his open car and greeted them with an infectious grin, his eyes concealed by dark glasses. Cassie made the introductions and Charles shook hands with them each in turn, then swept her into a passionate hug that instantly killed off any pretence that he was nothing more than a casual friend. Rose and Daisy exchanged a look but entered into the spirit of things when they saw the effect this dashing young man was having on their mother. They had not seen her so skittish in years. Being in love became her. All of a sudden she looked her age, which was young.

'It's going to be all right,' she said, after the girls had gone to their rooms.

'Naturally,' said Charles. It was what he'd expected.

It went so well that, in just a few months, he persuaded Cassie to marry him. And when she mentioned it to the girls, she was thrilled by their positive reaction. Because he treated them both as equals, they were more than a little in love with him themselves. He brought new vitality into their lives; after a father who was ailing and withdrawn, this vigorous newcomer in his early twenties was like a breath of fresh air. Cassie found herself relaxing. She still had to face the neighbours, of course, but Charles pointed out that it was none of their business. All her life she'd put others first; now, at last, she had come into her own. She'd been given a second chance of a happy marriage.

The wedding was to be small and low-key but first she had to tell the rest of the family. She was apprehensive about her brothers but more so about Edwin's sister. Sybil could scarcely believe her eyes the day she first caught sight of Charles, seated astride one of Edwin's hunters, in conversation with her nieces. For a while she sat in her car and watched, at first suspicious of the scene, then remembering that her brother's children had not, until now, had very much fun in their lives. Surprising herself, she got out of the car and walked across to greet him, knowing at almost first glance that she would like to sculpt him.

She did, however, question his motives in marrying a widow ten years older than himself,

75

already encumbered with children. The estate was a considerable prize, not least because she'd never have children herself. Charles, however, responded to her queries with answers that were both frank and sincere. He would do his best to make Cassie happy, had simply taken one look and fallen in love. The difference in age, as the years went by, would cease to matter at all, certainly as far as he was concerned.

Cassie's brothers were similarly suspicious. If anything went against Charles, it was mainly his looks. He had the air of a young adventurer, but his charm and manners could not be faulted and there wasn't the slightest doubt that Cassie was smitten. After all she'd been through, she deserved a break. Their inquiries about his earlier life he answered with absolute candour. He'd been raised in India, sent home to public school, then furthered his education with overseas travel.

'And what exactly is your line of business?' Richard Elwes wanted to know.

'Fine art,' said Charles. 'I act for private clients, locating paintings to specific needs to fill a gap in a collection.'

'Sounds fascinating.' Richard was quite impressed. Charles had the air of a man on an upward curve.

But Edwin's lawyer was less sanguine and produced a list of questions that needed answers. The Hawksmoor inheritance was worth a lot; it was up to him to secure the children's future. 'You're sure he's not after your money?' he said, but Cassie refused to discuss it. She could take care of herself and wouldn't let anyone stand in her way when it came to following her heart.

They were married quietly in the village church and the few who attended all agreed that they'd rarely seen a more radiant bride.

And yet, after twenty-two tranquil years, without warning things had fallen apart. Charles was in love with somebody else and had once again rushed into marriage. Cassie was still in a total daze and had not properly taken it in. The love she'd depended upon for so long belonged now to somebody else. She had met the new wife on several occasions and always rather liked her. She was blonde, vivacious, a product of her age, with the confidence of the archetypal Sloane, able to cope with anything, quite unfazed. Cassie, of course, had been unaware of the true relationship between her and Charles until he'd broken the news that Pippa was pregnant. By which time, of course, it had been too late. She had done the only decent thing and offered him a divorce.

Feeling suddenly rather fragile, Cassie returned to the trattoria and was touched to be greeted like a familiar friend. She had fluent Italian and plenty of money; was no longer just an abandoned wife but a single woman of independent means. She was thoroughly through with domestic life and now had an urge to spread her wings. For one more night she would savour just being in Venice. Tomorrow she would embark on a brand new life.

13

Frankie was simply to do as he told her, act as decoy and stay right out of the way. Chad had decided the best time to move would be while they were all at their evening meal, in order to escape under cover of darkness. Frankie's job was to make quite sure that none of their housemates returned before time, until after the fire was lit and well under way.

'How do you suggest I do that?'

'Use your brain. Start an argument or even a Scrabble game. You are first rate at causing diversions. Up to you.'

'And you promise you won't leave without me?'

'I do.' He gave her his ID photograph as a pledge.

Frankie was touched. The gesture was not at all like him; he normally didn't hold with sentiment. She fitted it into her grandmother's locket, the one piece of jewellery she possessed, and hung it round her neck. 'I will never take it off,' she vowed. 'Whatever happens, I'll always have something of yours.'

In case they should miss each other in the chaos that was bound to follow the conflagration, she suggested they fix a meeting place where neither of them would be known. The railway station was far too obvious; besides, Chad was planning to hitch.

'Why not outside the church?' said Frankie. It seemed an apt way for him to depart, mirroring his entry into the world.

'Great idea.' He kissed her hard. Tomorrow was the chosen day. There was no guarantee that they'd meet again, though he didn't tell her that.

Setting a fire was a tricky business. Correct preparation was the crucial part.

'Don't use paraffin,' Frankie warned. Hers had been a malicious statement but this one had to appear to be accidental.

'Why not?' asked Chad, only partly listening since he already had it safely stowed.

'Too dangerous,' she said. 'It ignites too fast. Weren't you ever a Boy Scout?'

'You have to be kidding.' She seemed to forget that he'd been in Barnardo's and later at public school.

'Well, I was a Guide and we learnt these things.' And careful planning and building were essential. She'd provided him with a ball of rough twine which they'd soaked in candle wax, then allowed to dry. That was the secret of Frankie's success. She had stretched her wick right across the lawn and hidden in the bushes while she struck the match.

'You are sure it will work?'

'It did for me.'

But he'd keep the paraffin handy just in case.

'Do you still love me?'

'Of course,' he said. Then checked his watch; it would soon be time to put into action the first part of the plan.

The warder, predictably, was sympathetic when Chad, in a barely audible croak, told her that his throat was really bad. She peered in his mouth, which looked normal to her, but since he was not one to make a fuss, she agreed he could miss his classes that day, provided he stayed in bed.

'I will catch up on my studies,' he promised. 'I just don't want to go spreading germs around.'

Once he was sure she was out of the house and the others had gone up the road for breakfast, Chad quickly put the final touches in place. Both their rucksacks were in the gardener's shed, beneath a tangle of tennis nets, stowed away for the winter. The ball of twine, matches and a bundle of kindling were hidden in the basement. He carried them stealthily up to his room and, after a moment's contemplation, went back for the paraffin too. Despite Frankie's warning it was, he decided, always better to be on the safe side and the weather was not looking good. He studied the sky, which was bruised and angry, and hoped they weren't in for a sudden shower. But since there was nothing he could do about that, instead he checked inside every room to ensure that no one had stayed behind unnoticed. After that, there remained just one more detail before he could relax.

*   *   *

Frankie's part in the plan went off smoothly. She got the whole group telling spooky stories, a ploy which invariably worked. As, one by one, they rose to the challenge, she kept an eye on the dimming light and, as soon as darkness began to set in, announced that she was worn out and needed her bed. Her group strolled back to the gates together and the guard on duty let them out. A gentle rain was just starting to fall; Frankie worried about the fire. All that was left for her to do was raise the alarm when she saw the first flames and then fade away, unobserved.

But suddenly, from beyond the trees, they heard the sound of a muffled roar.

'Fire!' someone screamed and everyone pointed as a finger of flame erupted into the sky.

He's used the paraffin, thought Frankie dully. After she'd told him not to, the fool. How could he imagine he would get away with that?

As Chad had predicted, pandemonium reigned and Frankie's companions rushed around wildly, watching the billowing smoke engulfing their home. The rain seemed not to be making much difference; the house had gone up like a bomb. Despite her anxiety, she was proud of what he'd done. There was no need now to summon help. Within minutes the police and fire brigade had arrived.

'Everyone please stand back,' they ordered and Frankie realised the moment had come. She had no trouble slipping away for everyone's eyes were on the blaze and she had to force herself not to stay and watch. But this was the turning point of her life. A bright new future lay ahead.

Five hours she waited on the steps of the church, drenched to the skin and increasingly worried, but when, by two a.m., he hadn't come, she finally gave up hope. Since she had no money and nowhere to go, she had no option but to turn herself in.

14

They were right when they said it wouldn't be easy, especially now her pregnancy was so advanced. The worst thing about it was the very long hours. To start with, there were no overnight guests but that would change when word got around that the pub was open again. And then she'd be faced with the problem of breakfast, for paying customers had to be fed and she couldn't expect the part-time staff to help. Because of the recent upheaval in her life, she had lost the habit of cooking. Now was the time for her to start polishing her skills.

Jenny couldn't remember how or when she learnt to cook. It was certainly nothing her mother ever taught her. She grew up in Neath in a terraced house that overlooked the railway line. Her father, until they laid him off, had worked as cashier for the Metal Box while her mother, in order to supplement his income, had done regular shifts at the Co-op. Meals were basic and overcooked; tasteless roasts with soggy veg were what she mainly remembered. Jenny herself had done well at school, got five Os and left at sixteen to become a trainee reporter on the *Western Mail*.

'There's nice,' her aunties had all agreed. 'Who knows, one day we may see your name in the paper.'

And it hadn't been long before they did. From the *Western Mail*, covering weddings and flower shows, she had shot straight up the journalism ladder, moving to Reading and then to Wapping by the age of twenty-one. From the *Hardware Trade Journal,* where she worked for a year, she took a great leap to *Good Housekeeping*, learnt all she could about magazine publishing and landed a much-prized job with Condé Nast. Which was where she encountered Douglas Fairweather who, albeit inadvertently, would be responsible for altering the course of her life.

She moved around and did many jobs until she was given her own column. In addition to writing about food for the glossies, she had a practical cookery slot, and that was when she realised she urgently needed to learn the nuts and bolts. She'd lived alone since leaving home and had grown accustomed to knocking up meals, which she liked to do in the odd hours she wasn't working. Much of the time she ate out, of course, vetting new restaurants all over the south and giving them marks out of ten. Often Douglas was her dining companion. It was how things had really got going between them and provided excellent cover for their alliance.

He was forty-two and her overall boss, publisher of the magazine division, and she'd found his greying good looks an immediate turn-on. To begin with they had very little contact but he, it turned out, had an eye for the girls and Jenny, at twenty-seven, overflowed with pizzazz. She was small and trim with alert brown eyes framed by a silky fringe of dark brown hair. Like a little Welsh mountain pony, he said, and it fitted. They began by having working lunches, sometimes in the company canteen; later – when he wished to be more discreet – in chic and fashionable restaurants. That was how she got the restaurant slot; not only did it fit into his plans but he respected her knowing assessment of food as well as her slick turn of phrase.

Which was all very nice but she wasn't an expert and it soon became clear that, to do the job well, she needed the sort of basic knowledge other food writers had.

'What I'd really like,' she sometimes said, 'is to train full-time as a master chef' – if that would not mean the end of the job and be thus self-defeating.

But it underlined her interest in food so that, rather than taking time off to do courses, she ordered a load of cookery books and began to experiment at home. By then she had bought the Brixton house and the first thing she did before even moving in was have a brand new kitchen installed with all the professional implements she could afford. She cooked for her friends and, occasionally, Douglas, and found the whole process immensely relaxing as well as rather fun. No more overcooked Sunday lunches; since that was the one day she didn't work, she made it a feature of her social life. Eight for lunch became a regular fixture and her friends learnt to cancel existing plans in order to sample and wonder at Jenny's feasts.

'I don't understand how you don't put on weight,' people often remarked.

'It's the quality not the quantity that counts.' So that, even when she was eating alone or came home late and exhausted from work, she would always bother to cook from scratch and ensure that she ate well.

Which was how she now came to be living in Bath, alone, five months pregnant and without a job, with an overdraft and an outsize mortgage, gazing around a dark panelled room that reeked of smoke and stale beer.

It was good old Vanessa who had rushed to her aid, first by helping her out in the bar, then by finding a part-time cook who would also give a hand with the clearing up.

'I had never imagined it would be such a grind.' Not even press nights and last-minute schedules had prepared Jenny for this.

'It won't be so bad once you've had the baby.' Vanessa was expert at such things. And Joyce, the cook, was a practical soul who could be relied on to turn up on time and deal with any random chores that might unexpectedly need doing. They only served the most basic pub food, ploughman's lunches, Scotch eggs and crisps, sandwiches freshly made by Joyce every morning. The pub had a regular clientele, plus a dribble of drinkers who came and went, curious to see the new management and wonder if she was going to make it work. The previous landlords had been a married couple who had taken early retirement in their fifties and moved to Tenerife. Jenny never even got to meet them; the place had been closed for a couple of months.

'Just as well,' said practical Vanessa. It might have dampened Jenny's spirits to be told the true reasons they had quit. And she needed as much buoying up as she could get, faced with the daunting task that lay ahead.

There were six double guest rooms and a couple of singles up the twisting oak-panelled stairs, and the fourteenth-century beams were so low that taller people had to duck their heads. Jenny had her own separate quarters in a private section above the kitchen, without any access from the public rooms. Here she had a fair-sized bedroom, with a smaller one for the baby; a bathroom and a cosy sitting room. Her rooms overlooked the tiny yard where the drayman unloaded the barrels. It was noisy at times but that couldn't be helped. The better rooms, with the pictur-esque views, had to be reserved for paying guests.

Outside, the garden was spectacular. She would need some help with that too. The lawn stretched smoothly down to the brook where the waterwheel at present stood motionless, though Jenny already had plans to have it repaired. She would have to make certain the baby was safe. All sorts of bad things could happen to a child living in close proximity to water. There was no way the brook could be fenced off; it was part of the charm of the place. And the waterbirds that had made it their home were an equal part of the pub's attraction, in fact had given it its name.

With the season already under way, she had several advance bookings, though luckily no one was due for a couple of weeks. At the end of each day, when she trudged up the stairs, her legs ached and her back was bad from standing so long while carrying the extra weight. At this time of day she felt most lonely, homesick for London and her friends. She would lie and listen to the rushing stream and feel the baby moving inside her and wonder, for the hundredth time, if she had done the right thing.

Toby was born on the first of May, a tiny sprite with thistledown hair and a smile that, even though she knew it was wind, broke her heart. Vanessa, who'd acted as her birthing partner, was there to see him emerge.

'Hey, little fellow,' she said tenderly. Then: 'When are you planning to let your parents know?'

'Don't,' said Jenny, wincing at the thought. Having to face them, especially her dad, was something she hadn't the strength to contemplate now. They had never even known about Douglas. The fact of their daughter with a married man would have been too shameful; they would not have been able to hold up their heads again.

'So how are you going to explain a baby?'

'I have no idea. Don't ask.'

She was, however, now thirty-two, well able to make her own decisions. And sooner or later she would have to face up to them both. As it was, she had scarcely dared mention the pub. Women who even set foot in a bar were, in South Wales, considered loose.

'They'll be thrilled,' said Vanessa, who hadn't met them.

'Once they are over the shock.' Imagine what all the aunties would say when they heard she had been a dirty girl and gone with a man out of wedlock. Well, that was another problem to be shelved until she felt up to it. For the moment all Jenny wanted to do was cuddle her baby and shout for joy at having achieved her most cherished dream on her own.

She was back on her feet much sooner than she'd thought and working behind the bar. Toby became the focus of attention. She would place his pram in a shady spot so that he didn't get too much sun, where the outside drinkers could coo around him and check that he was all right. It was a friendly place, the Coot and Hern. Now that her face had begun to fit, the regulars soon came back.

And when she finally grasped the nettle and invited her parents for the weekend, things went off better than she had ever dared hope. At first, of course, they were taken aback, her father openly outraged. But once they had seen the setup she had created and held their first grandchild in their arms, their indignation was mollified. These were, after all, her mother conceded, far more permissive times. And London was a far cry from the valleys. At least she had now had the sense to get out and settle in elegant Bath.

Vanessa invited them over for tea and Jenny's father was stupefied when he saw the size and splendour of her house. How had she achieved it, he wanted to know. Was there, perhaps, a rich husband in the offing? A working man with basic values, he still couldn't grasp that women could manage on their own.

'He isn't my husband,' said Vanessa gaily. 'And most definitely not rich.' Nor even the father of any of the children, though she didn't intend to go into that. Couldn't have old man Matthias believing his daughter was mixing with such disreputable folk. It was clear enough from the things he said that he still hadn't quite come to terms with her owning a pub.

Vanessa offered them all more tea but a beer was more to his taste.

'*Dew*,' he said in bewilderment. 'I don't know what things are coming to these days. All this fornication. It just isn't right.'

As the months rolled by and the baby grew, Jenny got used to her brand new life. It was stressful, though in a different way from having to meet a regular dead-line or keep coming up with bright ideas to help raise the circulation. She didn't miss Douglas, was still far too cross, but occasionally yearned for a man's warm body pressed against hers in the night. There was plenty of scope for flirtation here; she was young and attractive with a sparky manner and the bar was invariably packed with attentive men.

She had two male students doing shift-work at the

bar, plus Joyce in the kitchen preparing the food, and Vanessa often lent a hand when she could get away. At night Jenny went to bed worn out yet feeling at peace with herself. It was hard work, but she had anticipated that, and what she was throwing her energies into represented her financial future and her son's. It was far too soon to be dreaming of commitment but she half kept an eye out, as the customers flowed in, for that extra special someone she still hoped to meet.

When he did arrive, she almost missed him. She was down in the cellar, changing barrels, and only popped back for a second to tell the barman she was going upstairs for a shower. The stranger was standing alone at the bar, gazing around with appreciation, and when she entered he turned and smiled and something inside Jenny knew. He was tall with dark hair lightly touched with grey and the kindest, bluest eyes that drew her straight in.

'Nice place you've got here,' he said with approval. 'Mind if I look round?'

Jenny, aware of her scruffy appearance, told him to make himself at home. In the meantime the barman would fetch him a drink. He picked a spider's web out of her hair and wiped a smudge from her nose.

'A working landlady. I like that,' he said. Then casually strolled through the open door and out into the garden.

Instead of just showering and changing her shirt, she slapped on makeup and brushed her hair, then sprayed herself liberally with fragrance. Downstairs she found him back in the bar, chatting chummily with the barman and teaching him to mix a dry martini.

'The merest hint of vermouth,' he was saying. 'With a twist of lime, if you have one.'

'Transformed,' he said when Jenny appeared, looking her up and down with approval. 'Have you the time to join me in a drink?'

It was almost seven and the end of a long day. He had been on the road since mid-afternoon and needed a break and a couple of drinks before he headed on. She led him to a corner table and the barman carried their drinks across. It was Thursday night, which was usually quiet. Even Toby, for once, was already asleep.

He asked her questions about the pub and said he occasionally came this way. In future, he promised to make it a regular pit-stop.

'Have you thought of serving proper meals?' he asked. 'In a place like this, on the outskirts of Bath, there's no way you wouldn't clean up.'

Jenny explained she was new to the game, was taking things cautiously, stage by stage. At present her hands were full with the carriage trade. The stranger appeared to be thinking hard; she was not even sure he was listening.

'You would need to hire a first-rate chef, the main ingredient of that sort of venture. But you have the premises and, certainly, the location.'

Jenny's heart was beating faster; she had never been one to resist a challenge and the man's engrossed attention flattered her. She liked his style and the way he looked, as well as his obvious expertise. After a while she had to get on; it was her turn to take her place at the bar and he, having seen the time, said he must be off.

'I'll be back again very soon,' he said. 'Meanwhile, think about my suggestion. I really think you could have a money-spinner here.'

'Do you have a card?' She liked the idea and was fired with a new ambition. After all the restaurants she had written up, there was little about the business she didn't know, at least in theory.

'Sorry,' he said, patting his pockets. 'I don't seem to have any on me today. But the name, for future reference, is Clive Barclay.'

She woke very early and lay there, content, thinking about the attractive stranger. Something about him, not just his looks, had touched her profoundly. Then Toby stirred and began to wail so she dragged herself wearily out of bed and went to sort him out. Another gruelling day. But her heart was light as she set about her chores and she couldn't stop thinking about the man, with his easy charm and warm, expressive eyes.

As she changed the barrels and drained the pipes, then swept the ashes from the empty grate, she found herself giving serious thought to his suggestion. It did make sense though would mean more work and, almost certainly, huge financial investment. She knew enough from her magazine days not to underestimate the potential pitfalls. First she would need a much larger kitchen, updated to meet the stringent regulations imposed by the EU. Luckily, she had the space and could glass in part of the terrace at the side so that diners could sit overlooking the brook, next to the waterwheel. Once she got the latter working again, it would make a truly magical spot; there surely wouldn't be any shortage of patrons. But where she would find the finance, she had no idea. She was stretched, as it was, with existing costs and not yet breaking even. Unless she took over the cooking herself and brought in someone to supervise the bar.

Clive had certainly got her thinking and she started thumbing through catering magazines, seeking tips as to how to make things work. The city of Bath was awash with fine restaurants, all of them doing a roaring trade yet few with the picturesque setting that she could provide. She longed to talk it over with him, found herself constantly watching the door, wondering how often he made the journey from London. He also started appearing in her dreams; she simply couldn't get him out of her mind. The days and then the weeks went by and still there was no sign of him. Jenny started to curse herself for having been taken in.

'Men, they're all the same,' she said. 'I can't believe I was such a fool as to take him at his word.'

And then one day, perhaps three weeks later, she looked up from pulling a pint and there he was. Politely waiting to catch her eye with the same incandescent smile.

'Hi!' she said, more friendly than she should be,

ducking behind the barman to serve him herself. She mixed him a very dry martini and was pleased when he said it was perfect.

'You certainly know your stuff,' he said. 'Where did you learn to mix cocktails?'

'Well, not where I grew up,' she said. 'You can take my word for that.'

He asked if she'd given any thought to what he'd said and she told him she'd like to discuss it further, if he had the time and could stick around for a while. She was pleased when he said he would stay overnight. He'd been driving all day and was ready for a break now. Jenny was thrilled but tried hard not to show it. He was too attractive not to be married and nothing would ever induce her to go there again.

At closing time they took their drinks upstairs to Jenny's cosy sitting room and talked long after the rest of the staff had gone home. His take on what she could do with the place was well informed and reasonable. And would not necessarily need a prohibitive investment.

'What exactly is it you do?' she asked, not wishing to sound intrusive.

'I travel for a wallpaper firm. Very upmarket. Osborne and Cole. I'm sure you know them by name.'

She didn't; design was not her thing. The finishing touches to the visitors' rooms were Vanessa's. Her own expertise lay strictly in the kitchen, though she planned to learn more about bankrolling. Clive promised to rough out a business plan for discussion next time they met.

Toby woke a couple of times and called out to Mummy for a comforting hug. Clive insisted on holding him too and stroked his hair until he nodded off.

'Do you have children of your own?' asked Jenny, mightily impressed yet also apprehensive of his answer.

'Sadly not,' he said with a shrug. 'I guess I just haven't met the right woman yet.'

The second he left, Jenny called Vanessa. He'd be coming back, he hoped, in a couple of weeks.

'I can't believe he's not married,' she shrieked. 'And he's really great with Toby.'

'Watch out,' said Vanessa, pleased for her friend yet wary where men were concerned. 'You still know hardly anything about him.'

'Enough,' said Jenny with confidence. He really seemed committed to helping her out. 'I just can't quite believe that it's true. After all the shit I've been through, at last I appear to have met a decent man.'

15

Frankie was hauled before the beak and severely reprimanded. They wanted to know her involvement in the fire. They asked why she'd tried to run away and, even more to the point, what had happened to Chad. Since she didn't know the answer to that, she felt it best to stay silent. She couldn't believe he had gone without her after all the promises he had made; how he'd vowed that he would kill himself if obliged to remain there on his own.

The fire brigade, aided by the rain, had finally managed to douse the flames and would soon be able to pick through the embers and establish the cause of the fire. A band of gypsy travellers had been reported in the neighbourhood. The thinking was that they'd started the fire in order to do some petty looting. Whatever the facts, they had now moved on and seemed to be no longer germane to the current investigation.

Frankie remained the one under pressure; they wouldn't leave her alone. Or believe that Chad could have got away without her being involved. Everyone knew how close they had been, they were hardly ever apart.

'You will do yourself no favours,' said the beak, 'if you cover up for your boyfriend. Your record is good. In the normal way we would shortly be discharging you. But,' she added with eyes of flint, 'if it should transpire that you helped him escape, it will go against you in court.'

Frankie, however, remained silent. There wasn't anything she could say that could possibly make any difference at this stage.

In the course of the investigation, the grounds were searched and both their rucksacks found. Still underneath the tennis nets; Frankie was suddenly alarmed. Again she was summoned before the beak and bombarded with further questions. A lot less confident, she still said nothing, praying only that he was safe. He must have had to make a quick exit and would return later to fetch her.

At lunchtime, though, there was a commotion outside as a fleet of squad cars arrived. Everyone crowded to the windows to watch as a bunch of stony-faced policemen emerged and banged on the main door. They were ushered inside and the door was closed. Frankie's heart was beating fast. The good thing was there had been no sign of Chad.

It didn't take long for the rumour to spread. A body had been found among the ashes, too charred for instant identification. They would have to wait for the inquest. When they summoned Frankie and confirmed it was true, her heart stopped dead and she fainted. And when she'd recovered enough to talk and they plied her more kindly with cups of tea, she faced the policemen defiantly and confessed.

'I did it,' she said. 'I set the fire. He must have somehow got trapped inside. It is all my fault. Arrest me, please. I am guilty of his murder.'

If Chad were dead, there was nothing to live for. She might as well carry the can.

16

The best thing about Pippa's shop was its handy location. A stone's throw away from Brompton Cross, within walking distance of Peter Jones and only twenty minutes by car from Barnes. Each morning, when he wasn't away, they would load the baby-seats into the car and Charles would drop them all off at the shop on his way through to Walton Street. The days when he was away on business, Pippa would use her own car. Considering the vast upheaval in her life, she had taken to marriage unexpectedly well, enjoying the cosseting she received from her husband. There were things to be said for an older man. He lacked the unthinking boorishness of some of her own generation.

They had made it to the altar just in time; two weeks later the twins, Jack and Tom, had arrived. Identical boys, with their father's looks, they were miniature versions of Charles's first son, Aidan. Aidan, now twenty-one and at Oxford, was already acting the doting half-brother and would drop in to see them when he came into town, staying at his father's

Knightsbridge flat. Cassie had allowed Charles to keep the flat; she no longer had any interest, she said, in making excursions to London. Since the divorce, she had been in Venice which made the situation easier all round.

Pippa found it decidedly odd having a stepson only six years younger than herself, as tall and strikingly handsome as his dad.

'You ought to have gone for the younger model,' her mother had caustically pointed out. He would probably prove, in the long run, a sounder investment. But the opulence of Pippa's new lifestyle could not be denied. She no longer worked because she had to but simply because she refused to give up. The shop was hers and doing well, though Charles now acted as co-director and kept an eye on the financial side of things. Their allied professions worked neatly in tandem. He, the distinguished interior designer, used her shop as one of his main suppliers.

The mail order business, which was his idea too, was also up and running and Pippa had hired a couple of part-time helpers. Every morning, when she got to work, she would carry in the babies, still in their car-seats, and plonk them into the playpen she kept in the back. They were so sweet-natured they were very little trouble and hardly made any noise at all unless they were hungry or wet. If she had to go out, she would leave them with her mother who, handily, lived in Richmond, within easy reach. They were so much alike, she colour-coded their clothes as even she, at times, couldn't tell them apart.

The shop was a cornucopia of silks, brocades and other fine fabrics where customers came to browse and fulfil their dreams. Pippa was grateful to her mother for making her do an apprenticeship after she had finished at the Courtauld. She had learnt to paint and grout and tile as well as do basic carpentry but her leaning had always been more towards fabrics, a relic from the days when she'd made her own clothes.

At night she would drive the babies home or wait for Charles to pick them up and take them back to the house in Barnes, now a veritable showplace. As well as Pont Street, which he kept for entertaining, Charles would sometimes bring clients to the house. They had knocked down walls and done major reconstruction work and the handsome turn-of-the-century villa had properly come into its own. She had sold the flat in Elm Park Gardens and reinvested the money in the shop. In their separate fields they were both doing well and Charles's lifestyle, since leaving Cassie, had not visibly altered very much.

The difference was he no longer went to Cornwall, though he still spent much of his time away, visiting his clients.

'If I'd had a twin, she could have been called Aïda.' Aidan was lounging in a basketwork chair, watching the babies being bathed.

'Lucky for her, then, that you didn't.' Pippa, crouched beside the tub, was carefully sponging their hair. She had no idea where the twin gene had come from; there were none she knew of in her own family

102

tree and Charles had always been vague about his background. There was no denying Aidan's provenance, though; he was unmistakably a chip off the old block. They were like a set of Russian dolls, a big one and two identical miniatures. The apple, as the saying goes, never falls far from the tree.

Aidan was almost the age Charles had been when he swept Cassandra off her feet. Occasionally Pippa secretly regretted that she hadn't known him then. Aidan's springy curls were coal-black while his father's hair was now frosted with grey. But their eyes remained identical, cornflower blue, intense and unnervingly bright. And they shared the same dazzling smile and larkish sense of fun. She bet he set hearts fluttering back in Oxford.

'What do you plan to do when you come down? Have you made any decisions?' Aidan was bright and a competent student though he never appeared to do much work. He seemed to spend most of his time away from the college.

'Travel,' he said. 'For at least a year. I intend to do some serious living before I have to join the daily grind.'

'Do you still have your mind set on becoming a lawyer?' A barrister might be just his thing; he would certainly look very dashing in wig and gown.

'Whatever enables me to get rich quick.' Again, that bewitching smile. 'Preferably with the least amount of effort. Only a mug works hard these days. There are easier ways of making a lot of money.' He rose and stretched then kissed the boys and said he

103

should make a move. He was going into Soho to meet a friend.

'Male or female?'

'What do you think?' He winked and was gone, leaving Pippa feeling frumpy and, for some obscure reason, slightly put out.

Charles hardly ever mentioned Cassie though Pippa was always angling to know more about her. She was fascinated by the older woman, had always admired her looks and style and still felt guilty at having destroyed her marriage. The irony was, it had not been intended; she had entered into an adulterous fling, never expecting it to be anything more. She'd been young and pretty and utterly thoughtless, snared by Charles's roving eye, and had gone along with it just for a bit of fun. That and the fact that she fancied him rotten and liked the kudos that knowing him brought to her own sky-rocketing career.

She was just starting out when they'd first met and he'd swept her off her feet with his glamour and charm. She'd given him a lot of her time because she found him irresistible and didn't want him to leave. The next night he had taken her out to dinner.

'You know,' he'd said as they'd dined at Aubergine, 'you should think about making a speciality of providing rare and unusual fabrics to rich and discerning clients.'

Pippa had stared at him in surprise; she was only temping at Liberty's while she looked for something permanent that really turned her on.

'You mean like the Designer's Guild?' She was passionate about the King's Road shop and always popped in when passing. Fabrics, paint and fantastic wallpaper; how clever he was to know so precisely where her true interests lay.

'Something like that.' He grinned at her expression, seeing he'd scored a direct hit. 'Only maybe restrict it to fabrics alone. Sometimes the boutique approach works better.'

'I don't think I could do that,' she said. She earned very little and had only recently finished her stint as a decorator's gofer.

'With a little help you might be surprised. Even Tricia Guild had to start at the bottom.'

Pippa sat and thought about it, stunned but excited too. This gorgeous stranger who had swept into her life was putting all sorts of ideas in her head she would never have dared to dream up on her own. She wondered what her mother would say and where she could possibly raise the finance. Her father had left them a long time ago so her mother was a single working parent.

'Think about it and we'll talk again.' He paid the bill and then walked her home. The next night he took her straight to bed where they had the most amazing sex. Cassie's existence had not been mentioned and would not be for a matter of weeks. But Pippa was level-headed enough to assume that there must be a wife in the background. And, at twenty-two, she had far too much ahead even to think about settling down at this stage.

*   *   *

The first time Pippa set eyes on Cassie was two years into the affair. The shop was already up and running; Charles had been as good as his word and even come through with a hefty financial loan. It was Friday lunchtime and business was slow so she'd turned the sign on the door to Closed and popped off to Knightsbridge to have her streaks redone. The gorgeous Emilion was, as usual, running late so she sat in the corner and flicked through *Hello!* while he finished perfecting the style of his current client. Having quickly exhausted the vapid magazine, Pippa closed it and watched the proceedings, smiling at her stylist's antics as he skipped around with a mirror to display the back of her head to the woman seated in his chair. She was slim and serene with quite beautiful hair, now softly swept into an elegant pleat which drew attention to her fine-boned face. She nodded and smiled and thanked him profusely and, when she left, tipped him substantially.

'Thanks, Mrs Buchanan. Have a safe journey home. I hope we'll see you again before too long.'

The name attracted Pippa's attention so she watched more curiously as the woman put on her coat. She was tall, about five foot ten, Pippa guessed, with thoughtful eyes and a shyish smile as Emilion rushed ahead and opened the door.

'Who was that?' asked Pippa, with interest, as she took her place in the chair. The face, she thought, seemed faintly familiar. Perhaps she was an actress or something. She certainly had the bone structure and the poise.

'Mrs Charles Buchanan,' said Emilion, running expert fingers through Pippa's hair. 'She lives in Cornwall but comes here to get her roots done. I've been doing her hair for years. Nice lady. Loads of class, if you know what I mean. Her husband's a well-known interior designer. You may have heard the name.'

Small world, thought Pippa, giving nothing away. She was slightly shaken by the encounter and would have to give it some thought. It was one thing to know that her lover was married, another to actually see the wife. Who looked, as Emilion had said, like a lady, classy, well dressed and refined.

She decided not to mention to Charles that she'd inadvertently seen his wife. He might not be happy with the thought that their paths could so easily cross. But her curiosity had been aroused and now she wanted to know a lot more. Charles rarely spoke of his family, seemed to think it was not the done thing, so the knowledge she had was still sketchy in the extreme. She did know Cassie lived mainly in Cornwall, in the house she'd shared with her daughters and previous husband. And came to London less and less, which was how Charles managed to spend so much time with Pippa. In the old days he'd gone home every Thursday but had started to find the driving too much so now he either flew or went less often, breaking his journey on the way. He talked, with obvious pride, of his son and the two stepdaughters he also considered his. But of Cassie, his wife for the past nineteen years, he said nothing.

*   *   *

The next time she saw her was two years later when she suddenly walked into the shop. Pippa, in the stockroom at the time, heard the clang of the bell and went rushing out, only to stop in her tracks when she saw who was standing there. Cassie, elegant in well-cut tweed, slightly preoccupied and clutching an envelope.

'Miss Harvey?' she asked and, when Pippa nodded, relaxed into a lovely smile. 'Oh, I'm so glad. My husband sent me. He suggests you're the person to help me with a problem.'

When her heart stopped racing, Pippa started to listen and the tension slowly flowed out of her when she heard what Cassie wanted.

'I am doing up our London pied-à-terre and need some fabrics to go with these.' She proffered samples of wallpaper and paint. 'For the main reception rooms.'

'Right,' said Pippa, limp with relief. She could tell that Cassie suspected nothing. 'If you'd care to come into the stockroom, I am sure we can find you something that will suit.'

As she pulled down rolls and brought out samples, it all came flooding back. An action replay of that very first meeting with Charles. Cassie now was beaming broadly, revealing her striking good looks. Her dove-grey blouse matched her eyes exactly; she was clearly a woman of exquisite taste.

'Bless you, you angel. He said you worked miracles. Another horrible chore I can strike off my list.' She left the shop with laden arms but paused when she reached the door. 'Perhaps you'll come over for cocktails one evening. I would love to show you the revamped flat. I'll get my husband to set something up very soon.'

'Why not?' said Charles with his customary calm, apparently unfazed by his wife's suggestion. 'I'd quite like to show you the flat myself. I think you'll agree she has done a brilliant job.'

There were times when Pippa just didn't get him, he sailed so close to the wind. How could he do this, to either of them? Having talked with Cassie and liked her a lot, she now felt an absolute bitch. But Charles, undeterred, took it all in his stride, flicked through his diary and suggested a day, then pencilled it in and told her he'd check it out.

'Wait till you see how the curtains look,' he said. 'I don't think you'll be disappointed.'

So Pippa found herself, a few weeks later, ringing the bell of the Pont Street flat and being admitted by a smiling maid in black. Having left her coat, she was shown into the drawing room where both the Buchanans were entertaining a group of assorted friends.

'Miss Harvey!' said Cassie, advancing to greet her.

'Please call me Pippa,' Pippa said.

'Pippa,' said Cassie, 'I'm so glad you came. Grab a drink and let me show you around.'

The flat, as Pippa had rather expected, was done in the most impeccable taste, understated like Cassie herself, but with a keen eye for detail. There were bowls of hydrangeas, brought up from Cornwall, which subtly picked out the colours of the newly made drapes. The bedroom was plain, pale wood and white linen, with piles of books on the bedside tables and fluffy white towels in the en suite bathroom, which smelt very faintly of grapefruit.

'I love it,' said Pippa, incredibly moved and increasingly feeling a duplicitous interloper.

'Thank you,' said Cassie. 'Your praise is praise indeed. I feel very guilty that I'm hardly ever here and leave my poor husband too much on his own, having to fend for himself.'

Does she know? thought Pippa but was certain she did not. Cassandra Buchanan was a very nice woman, with thoughts on too high a plane to stoop that low. Pippa felt rather grubby at being here at all and wondered if the burning letter A was evident on her forehead. She lingered behind to freshen up while Cassie returned to her guests, and wondered how long would be appropriate to stay. If she made her exit too soon it might be noticed.

She needn't have worried; on rejoining the group, she found that the focus of attention had swung to the charismatic son, who had only just arrived. Aidan, nineteen, had dropped in on a whim, planning to crash in his parents' flat, unaware that they were entertaining. From the guilty flush on his handsome face, Pippa could see that in some way he'd been caught out. Somewhere, probably in a nearby bar, an innocent girl was doubtless waiting while Aidan checked to see if the coast was clear. Or else he had other plans for the night and hadn't selected the victim yet. He was so much like the old man, it made Pippa smile.

But she was in no position to smirk. She felt totally treacherous at being there at all, so made her farewells as soon as she could and slipped off into the night.

When Charles came home he seemed preoccupied; Pippa put it down to overwork.

'I am sorry, my dear,' he said, after a while. 'But I have to go back to Bristol again. One of my clients there wants a consultation.'

'This weekend?' She'd been hoping to relax: lunch at Hurlingham, a game of tennis, and a video for after the twins were safely in bed.

''Fraid so,' he said. 'It's very short notice but the contract should be worth a great deal of dosh.'

In the old days Pippa would have wanted to go too, might well have proved an asset to him, but the boys had drained all her energy away. She would ask her mother to keep her company and perhaps fit in a couple of early nights.

'When do you think you'll be back?' she asked.

'Sunday morning should do it,' he said. 'They can't expect me to dance to their tune all weekend.'

'I tell you quite frankly,' said Pippa's mother, 'I never thought you'd hang on to him. No disrespect, but he does have a roving eye.'

'Had,' said Pippa, correcting her. 'These days he's got far too much on his plate ever to find the time to play around.'

'Well, I'll hand it to him, he's certainly done you proud.'

They were settled in the sunny breakfast room, the babies playing at their feet. The white-painted walls had been picked out in lemon, which enhanced the sunlight and brightened the whole place up. In its former existence it had been panelled and fusty, part of the scullery and pantry. It was amazing to see what could be achieved with a little imagination and adjustment. Plus, of course, a sufficient injection of cash.

Pippa, looking no more than fifteen in her sprigged cotton robe with her hair unbrushed, was sipping mint tea and leafing through the papers. Her mother, spellbound by the beautiful twins, had transmogrified from a bitter divorcee into an infatuated granny. Tom – or was it Jack, she was never sure – was reaching out with one tiny hand towards the pile of bright building blocks she had brought as her latest gift. He crawled towards them, happily gurgling, then swiftly demolished the precarious structure with one sweeping wave of his hand. Doting granny cried out in delight, then carefully reconstructed the pile and sat back, enchanted, to see if he'd do it again. Wham – a bull's eye. 'You know something,' she said. 'I think perhaps Tom is left-handed.'

'Jack,' said Pippa, barely glancing up, involved with the Sunday papers. Her mother was always noticing things about the twins. But she knew she was lucky to have her around, available at the shortest notice, willing to play and be bored and just love them to bits.

'In which case,' said her mother, rebuilding again, 'they are very probably mirror twins. Genetically identical but a mirror of each other.'

'Really?' said Pippa, still only half listening, deep in the details of the latest football scandal, glad to have someone to share the burden and let her relax for a change.

'Yes,' said her mother, watching them both now, two gorgeous babies with coal-black hair that she now observed swirled softly in opposite directions. 'So is Jack right-handed?'

'Tom,' said Pippa. And then, growing aware of her mother's impatience, 'I can't say I've ever noticed. Does it matter?'

'Of course not, my precious,' crooned her mother to the baby, picking up a struggling Jack who was still fixated on the bricks. She nuzzled her face against his neck but he arched his back and drummed his tiny heels until she was forced to put him back on the rug. She thought, though did not say it aloud, that he seemed not to like too much physical contact, unusual in a baby so young and not at all like his brother.

So she moved to Tom who cooed in delight and held out his arms to be lifted.

'Who's my big boy then,' she said in delight. Wham went the blocks over the floor as Jack demolished them again.

Somewhere offstage a door clicked shut and Charles strode into the room. In his weekend clothes, he looked sporty and fit, the great charmer her daughter had married whom, privately, she still didn't trust at all.

He stood in the doorway, beaming down at them all, then crossed to give his wife a peck.

'What a lovely tranquil domestic scene after the weekend I have had.' It was heading towards the cocktail hour; the sun would soon be over the yardarm. Time for a gin and tonic.

Pippa, laying her paper down, rose and gave him a hug. He smelt of clean linen and cologne and his hair was immaculately cut.

'Have you had breakfast?'

'Two hours ago. I wanted to get back here in time for lunch.'

With her arms round him, she leaned against his chest and her mother was bound to admit that they made a striking couple. His eyes were tender as he looked at his small sons and her secret reservations ebbed away. Perhaps, after all, it would work out. She fervently prayed that it might.

17

The hearing was brief and to the point. 'Francesca Wilde,' said the presiding judge. 'You are hereby accused of the manslaughter of Chad Barnaby.'

Since she had already confessed and taken full blame for starting the fire, the accident that had caused Chad's death was due entirely to her, which she didn't dispute. He, as far as the inquiry went, had been asleep in the hostel.

'Murder,' she muttered in silent frenzy but nobody was listening. The evidence was conclusive; the case was wound up. Since Frankie had just passed her eighteenth birthday, she was sentenced to eight years in jail. The inquest, which she had asked to attend, had been equally succinct. A heavy door in the blazing building had fallen, pinning the victim to the floor. There was no way he could possibly have survived. Commiserations were offered to Frankie after which she was formally arrested.

Her mother had asked to attend the hearing but Frankie insisted it should not be allowed; she still had her civil rights. From this point on, she would be on her own and that was how it would stay. All she could wish for now was an early death.

'Don't be too hard on yourself,' said the judge. 'You have done great wrong but are still little more than a child. Playing with fire does not make you bad. Prison will teach you many lessons from which I hope you will learn.'

'Chad Barnaby's death was entirely my fault,' said Frankie, stubbornly resisting help. 'I neither want nor deserve any kind of reprieve.'

She was sent to a prison on the Isle of Man where she would stay for the whole eight years unless she was granted remission for good behaviour. She no longer cared where she was or for how long; her life was effectively over. She still had Chad's picture in her locket but found it too painful to look at now. But she thought about him all the time, still unable to come to terms with the fact that he was dead.

Before leaving Middlesbrough to start her sentence, she was allowed to visit his grave, a patch of dug earth in the prison yard, with only a wooden marker on it, bearing his ID number but not his name. A pauper's grave for an unwanted foundling. His death ironically mirrored his inauspicious start.

The other prisoners were a varied bunch, some old lags whom she learnt to keep clear of, plus a bunch of misfits, in mainly for drug-related crimes. Sunk as she was in deep desolation, she didn't even look for a kindred spirit but kept herself to herself as much as she could. Word went round that her man had died so they mainly left her alone.

Around that time Frankie first met Magda who was to have such a lasting effect on her life. A social worker with a psychology degree, the older woman was on the prison staff to liaise with and counsel prisoners with emotional problems. Against Frankie's will, Magda arranged sessions in a vain attempt to get her to talk and unburden herself of her grief. Magda had read the case notes and sympathised.

'You must try to come to terms with it. It wasn't your fault, just an accident.' She hadn't even been there when the fire broke out.

'It was my fault,' said Frankie stubbornly. 'I had done it before and told him how. If it weren't for that, he would still be alive. In effect, therefore, I killed him.'

'Only by default,' said Magda. 'You must stop beating up on yourself.'

But Frankie stubbornly closed her ears, turned her face to the wall and wanted to die.

Only weeks into her sentence, Frankie heard of another death. The colonel, her stepfather, out with the guns, had been involved in a fatal shooting. No one had actually witnessed what happened; she was only told he was dead. Her mother was asking for Frankie's release to be at the funeral. The authorities were prepared to allow it but Frankie flatly refused to go.

'You ought to be there to comfort your mother,' said Magda, 'at the very least.'

'I hated him,' said Frankie, 'and am glad he is dead.'

'But he was your mother's husband.'

'I don't care.'

She was clearly more damaged than Magda had thought. She made it her top priority to help to sort her out.

18

Cristina first burst upon a startled fashion world at the tender age of sixteen. Her father, a mixed blood itinerant worker, who had raised eleven children in the Amazon basin, left them all to fend for themselves and she, without any contest, was the one who came out on top of the pile. At thirteen she was living off the streets in a steamy quarter of the Rio slums when a scout for an international model agency spotted her scavenging in rubbish bins and, struck by the child's quite astonishing beauty, signed her up on the spot. Bewildered and not quite comprehending, she went along with what he said and, in only a matter of months, advanced from dire poverty to being the latest fashion find. The agency, World Models, seeing her potential, invested shrewdly by sending her to school. They predicted that, once she was properly trained, her face would become internationally known. Even then they were the front-runners in the field; their judgement was rarely proved wrong.

She had no need of parental approval, had lost all contact with them when they threw her out. In later years she had little recall of how she had managed to survive on her own, only that, occasionally for weeks at a time, she'd had almost nothing to eat. Now, while they groomed her at model school, they stuck her in a hostel with a bunch of other hopefuls, overseen by a draconian older woman who taught them manners and stopped them stepping out of line. It was, Cristina supposed, looking back, her version of being at boarding school. She learnt about hygiene and diet and nutrition, to handle a knife and fork, to improve her posture by standing up straight, and basic yoga. They also gave her makeup lessons and stopped her chewing her cuticles. Despite her wild and exotic beauty, she was still just a child who had grown up rough, whose only preparation for life was what she picked up on the streets. They paid her peanuts but provided all her meals as well as somewhere safe and warm to sleep. After the years of fending for herself, the scratchy sheets and basic amenities seemed to her the utmost luxury.

Once a year there was a fashion show, plus the occasional newspaper ad, for which they taught her to pose and do runway and stand still for endless interminable hours while the photographers did their work. She came out well: magnificent cheekbones, provocative eyes and skin like caramel velvet. Her body, though still skinny and under-developed, already showed promise of what was to come. Apart from that, there was little to do, except for some rudimentary education, so Cristina, boiling with impatience, started to look around. And quickly found, in a tobacco kiosk, the answer to her terminal boredom: an ad for a life-class model, urgently required.

She got the job (well, of course she did) and started spending her Wednesday evenings posing nude for a motley group of lecherous, untalented men. But this exposure was the making of her; she had no problems with stripping off. And the more they ogled, the more she preened, their open-mouthed lust defining the person she was. She told the school she was taking tango lessons and no one thought or cared enough to check. It was all part of her learning curve, flaunting her naked body for easy cash.

One thing rapidly led to another and Cristina grew more ambitious; more ambitious and also much more venal. What she'd achieved by this stage of her development she had done entirely by herself. She was greedy now for all she could grab from life. The art class was one thing but the men were old and the pittance they paid her not worth the strain of having to hold one position for such a long time. She looked around and found another ad, this time for a dancer in a strip club.

The dancing was easy once she'd mastered the rhythm, a slow gyration to a pounding beat without ever moving from the spot. All she wore was a tasselled G-string beneath which men often stuck money bills (though forbidden by law from actually touching her flesh). Cristina revelled in their admiration as she writhed and cavorted beneath a spotlight, and had no shortage of hangers-on, each one jostling for a chance to walk her home. At first she didn't give in to this, since the school locked its doors at eleven p.m., until it dawned that their sole concern was that she should be there in time for early classes. So she took her pick of the drooling punters, and found it a nice little earner on the side.

They weren't all disgusting, mainly out-of-town businessmen, lonely, bored and invariably vapid, simply in search of something to brighten their nights. Cristina, discovering a natural talent, preferred the physical side of things to the tedious hours she spent practising for the catwalk. The men were grateful and often brought her gifts and made her feel like the star she wanted to be. Her savings grew and she bought nicer clothes so that some of them even took her out on the town, where she quickly learnt about menus and fancy food. Bit by bit her confidence grew and with it a streak of pure avarice, destined to stay with her for the rest of her life.

The movie approach came out of this sideline and Cristina was far too flattered to turn it down. A fat man with a large cigar slipped her his card as he left the club, muttering something about a screen test. Not mentioning it to the agency, with which she had signed an exclusive contract, she fixed a date for a free afternoon and turned up, for once on time, at a seedy-looking warehouse. All the windows were boarded up and she found herself in a large bare room with a bed in the middle of a white-painted stage, covered with synthetic fur. A man in an eyeshade, clearly the director, was giving instructions to the camera crew while a handful of others just stood around and watched. The lights were so bright, she could make little out and shielded her eyes as the director called her over and introduced her to the man who would act as her co-star. He was powerfully muscled and wearing just tight jeans; she could hardly keep her eyes from his bulging crotch.

Even her antics in the sleazy club had not prepared her for this. She was asked to strip while they all looked on and then to revolve while they studied her from every angle. Cristina, hearing their murmurs of approval, proudly strutted as though on the catwalk, regarding them haughtily down her imperious nose. Someone handed her a pair of spike-heeled boots and asked her to slip them on, then bestraddle the man who was now on the bed, in the process of peeling off his jeans.

'Action!' called the director and the cameras rolled.

There was neither script nor dialogue; all she did for the next forty minutes was obey the barked-out instructions from the director. Unspeakable things were done to her while the lights blazed down and the crew looked on and the man on the bed, who was hung like a bull, invaded her body with such extreme force that she thought he might split her in half. It was violent and painful yet also exciting and Cristina, panting and slicked with sweat, was disappointed when the director at last called out: 'Cut!'

A movie star, that was what she was going to be. They rinsed her down and touched up her makeup then asked her to go through the whole performance again.

'Good,' said the director, when the cameras finally stopped rolling and the crew began packing up. 'You're an absolute natural. We'll be using you again. Leave a contact number when you go and please close the door behind you.'

They did ask her back and she did it all again, though this time with a couple of extra leading men. A career as a skin-flick actress quite appealed to her, as long as they didn't use her name. And there was no telling where it might all lead; there were Hollywood stars, she had read, who had started from less. But, as it so happened, her luck was on the turn. The agency told her they had found her an opening to model clothes for a mail order catalogue. Not especially well paid at this stage but steady work that would mean wide exposure that could, in the long run, lead to better things. Cristina would have liked to think it through but the catalogue needed a speedy reply. Or so the agency said. So she turned her back on her movie career, moved out of her lodgings and into a hotel in a slightly more salubrious area of town. She had made no friends so had none to leave. Her modelling career was about to take off and she still wasn't quite seventeen.

The work was easy, though hardly inspiring, and Cristina hated the clothes. But she liked the money, which bought independence: the luxury of finally having her own place with a door she could lock

124

behind her when she went out. Or, indeed, when she stayed at home. Something that, other than a cardboard box in a smelly doorway beneath a railway arch, she had never in her life experienced before. The hours were regular, nine till four, but having to stand and keep changing her clothes was far more tiring than she had ever expected. Also she found the arc lights draining; by the time they broke for lunch she was often a wreck. The building had its own canteen but Cristina rarely went up there. Instead she would hang around in the studio, smoking and watching the photographer's assistants rearranging the props. The minute the boss had left the room, illicit bottles would materialise and Cristina would graciously join the boys in a tot, until one day the boss caught them at it and warned her that it would ruin her complexion, her figure, her liver and, unless she was lucky, her life. She pouted and sulked; she answered to no one and would bloody well do as she liked, it was only a job. But when her tantrum made no visible impact and she felt his indifference to her charms, mortified, and secretly piqued, she stopped. But it never ceased to rankle.

The work might be tedious and grindingly dull but when she saw the results, she was staggered. The man was truly a creative genius who could take the most mundane of garments and, with his magic camera, transform them from high street tat to international couture.

'It's all to do with the lighting,' they explained. 'And the love affair he has with the lens. He lives and breathes photography and it shows.'

Jorg Schreiber, a German, was in his mid-thirties and already quite a star of the fashion world. He was here, in Rio, on retainer to *Vogue* and doing a bit of catalogue work on the side. He was so preoccupied with his craft that he could go whole mornings with scarcely a word, just curt instructions for her to alter her pose. The results, however, were more than worth it. With her nostrils flaring like an Arab stallion's and tossing back her great mane of hair, she strutted and posed like the best of them on the catwalk. He wore black leather and a single gold earring and often went days on end without bothering to shave. Cristina, who was still very much a child, had never met anyone like him. She was awestruck right from the moment they met because of his prodigious talent.

He might not be turned on by her but his camera certainly loved her and when he studied the roughs he was obviously pleased. He asked if she'd do a private session to add to his fashion portfolio and Cristina, thrilled, was only too pleased to oblige. She thought that, apart from anything else, it might help to bring them closer together. She was used to men coming on to her, could not understand why Jorg still kept his distance.

'Sweetheart, you don't stand a snowball's chance in hell,' said one of the cheeky (now snotty) assistants, bored with her attitude. 'Can't you see that he bats for the other side?'

But Cristina, having no idea what he meant, simply turned her back.

* * *

Dreams, as Cristina was soon to discover, occasionally do come true. World Models, impressed by his skill and reputation, permitted Jorg to sign her up so that, shortly after, she flew with him to New York. Since he was already retained by *Vogue*, there seemed no shortage of fashion assignments and *Harper's Bazaar* were also keen to get in on the act. 'The face of the future,' the headlines proclaimed so that very soon, wherever she looked, Cristina saw herself on buses and hoardings. She looked phenomenal in the latest fashions, with her dusky skin, her sultry smile, her sinuous figure, which had now developed curves, and the scornful light in her eyes. There was nothing and no one she couldn't now afford. Except, as she was yet to find out, the one thing she truly desired.

Jorg's studio, on the Upper West Side, was part of his penthouse apartment, high up and with sweeping views across Central Park. Cristina assumed she would stay there too, as there was bags of space and he lived alone, but, without attempting an explanation, he booked her into the Sherry-Netherland Hotel. Only a cab-ride away, he told her, unless she felt like stretching her legs. Cristina, mortified, was very angry. New York was even more dangerous than Rio, which at least she knew and where she spoke the language. He had dared uproot her and bring her here, yet remained indifferent to her happiness or comfort, leaving her alone most nights to sulk in her hotel room. Movies and room service were all very well, especially in a luxury hotel, but what she craved was company and somebody to adore her.

Things started to change as her face became known and the world began to beat a path to her door. When the photographs hit the media, she became a celebrity overnight and the invitations started pouring in. From that point on she was rarely alone, nor did her telephone cease to ring. Cristina Calvão, in a matter of weeks, became the star of the fashion world because of the German's fantastic vision, though, of course, she never knew that. She accepted it all and became a star but it did not make her happy. Although she was barely aware of it, there still remained a yawning hole in her heart.

It was Tuesday night and, on West 54th Street, the rain was sluicing down making little difference to the crowd of fans clustered outside the new hot venue where a bunch of heavies were restraining them from breaking through the cordon.

'You and you,' said the man at the door, picking at random the prettiest girls and allowing them into the club, which had only just opened.

A limousine with darkened windows purred to a halt at the kerb and two dusky beauties in shimmering gowns stepped delicately over the swirling gutter while their driver, carrying a huge umbrella, ushered them safely inside.

'Diana Ross!' cried a voice from the crowd. 'And with her Cristina Calvão!' They had just seen Brooke Shields and Michael Jackson, while Truman Capote had also been glimpsed with, it was rumoured, Andy Warhol. They were all in a mega party mood, despite the fact that they were soaked to the skin and stood little chance of gaining admittance to the newest, coolest club in town: Studio 54.

Inside, all was dark and the music deafening as the girls dropped their wraps with the hat-check girl and joined the party of celebrities gathered there on the personal invitation of their host, Steve Rubell, who was waiting at the bar.

'Darling,' said a movie star, as she kissed Cristina. 'I simply adore your dress. Is it Versace and would it fit me?'

'No,' said Cristina, affecting boredom. 'Armani.'

Beneath her studied nonchalance, Cristina was thrilled to be there, part of the in-crowd and on the guest list of every cool function in town. The gown was exquisite and understated, a gleam of pale satin beneath the strobe lights, and round her neck she wore fifty thousand dollars' worth of diamonds from Harry Winston, lent her for the night. It was like Oscars night in L.A. but better. Here, only people hand-picked by the host were welcome. Champagne was passed as the crowd air-kissed and some of them slipped off into corners to indulge in the drugs which were also freely available. By nineteen, Cristina had really grown up and maintained the slightly petulant expression that now summed up her attitude to life. Keen not to show how excited she was, she maintained a mask of weary boredom that quickly became a snarl.

As the crowd undulated and Cristina glanced

around, careful not to lose her indifferent air, she suddenly saw him, there at the bar, deep in conversation with Calvin Klein. The only man in New York who turned her on: Jorg Schreiber, as always in head-to-toe black, the lights gleaming dully off his hair. A jolt of electricity shot right through her and Cristina hurriedly broke away, leaving the movie star standing there in mid-sentence, totally forgotten.

'Jorg,' she said a moment later, having forced her way through the crowd.

'Cristina,' he said, with no sign of emotion. 'I hope you are enjoying yourself.' He introduced her to Calvin Klein, then made his excuses and left.

There was no one in New York she could talk to. In the time she had been there she had made no real friends, but she badly needed to unburden herself about Jorg. She could not understand his continuing indifference when *Women's Wear Daily* and the glossy magazines were calling her the face of the year, one of the most beautiful women in the world. Because of the bitchiness of the business, the thing she lacked most was a confidante; while the men were throwing themselves at her, the women stayed firmly away.

Back in her room, she broke into hysterics and hurled her hairbrush at the bathroom mirror, which broke with a satisfying crash. Well, all to the good; they could charge it to him. It was his tab, anyway, since he'd made the booking, so the more expenses she could run up, the better. She ripped off the dress, which had been a freebie, and wrapped herself in a towelling robe, retaining Harry Winston's gems because of the way they looked against her skin. She might try modelling for De Beers; she would get the agency to fix it.

She pulled out the pins and let her hair cascade, then stood in front of the full-length mirror and asked herself, as she had so often, why she could not make him want her. Over and over she saw the way his eyes caressed her from behind the lens, but as soon as the session was over he seemed to switch off. Yet she had never seen him with anyone else nor heard any gossip about his private life, which, in a bitchy profession like this, was unheard of. She'd done everything possible to get his attention – rages, tantrums, once getting drunk and tearing off her clothes in front of him. It was in the studio when the back-up team had left and she'd stood there, swaying, in the blazing light, wearing nothing but her four-inch heels and a seductive smile.

But the body that most men lusted after and would give all they'd got to possess left the only one she wanted unmoved. He barely looked up from polishing his lenses before laying them reverently into their case.

'Put on your clothes,' was all he said. 'We can't have you catching a chill at this stage.' And then he asked her to stay and lock up because he was running late.

Homesick and bitterly disappointed, Cristina returned to Rio for Carnaval. The contract she'd signed with Jorg was almost up; she doubted he'd want to renew it. In any case, the sunshine beckoned; the New York winter was severe and Cristina's spirit shrivelled in the cold. World Models were thrilled by her huge success and would line her up work wherever she wanted. There was also talk of Los Angeles and a screen test. No one knew about her skin-flick days and she would ensure that they never did. It was part of the childhood she preferred to forget, along with her dicey antecedents.

She left without saying goodbye to Jorg; if he cared, then let the bastard sue. When it came to the crunch, all he did was take snaps whereas she had become an international star, famous throughout the world and now earning millions. The agency sent a stretch limousine to meet her off the flight and had booked her into a five-star hotel right on the beachfront at Ipanema, where she planned to chill out for a while before doing any work. She was more than worth it so the agency could pay. She had entered this city as a starving beggar but returned like a conquering queen.

Back in her homeland, at the height of the season, Cristina's dreams about Jorg quickly faded away. She was now a world-class celebrity and, accordingly, much-feted. Doors that once had been slammed in her face were now thrown open in ardent welcome and there wasn't an A-list occasion to which she was not automatically invited. There was also masses of work when she deigned to do it and her modelling fees had gone right through the roof; she could ask for whatever she wanted. The agency found her a penthouse apartment in a portered block, with a maid. They supplied a P.A. as well as a driver whom she kept on call night and day. It was an easy life, being flattered and spoilt, though the new Cristina failed to see it that way.

And then, one morning, as she walked along the beach, she came face to face with a blue-eyed stranger and suddenly understood what was wrong with Jorg.

19

Magda Kaplinsky, at twenty-nine, was ten years older than Frankie. Having trained originally as a clinical psychologist, she had later entered the prison service where her chief responsibility lay in trying to fathom the underlying causes of crime. In Frankie she found a strong-willed young woman, highly intelligent though hard to control, whose battle against authority stemmed from a deep-seated sense of inner grievance. Exactly what that grievance was, she stubbornly refused to discuss. At the age of fifteen, from an affluent background, she had burnt her parents' home to the ground and, when questioned about her motivation, had persistently clammed up. The later tragedy of her boyfriend's death, which had destroyed her will to live, was more easily understood. She had helped set the fire for altruistic reasons, to enable him to escape from the institution. It had taken Magda months to break through, though lately Frankie had been showing signs of gradually opening up.

In their regular sessions Magda just listened, allowing the girl to talk or not as she chose. Sometimes

134

Frankie just sat and stared, twisting a tissue between nervous fingers of which the nails had been chewed right down to the quick. At other times, when her mood was more buoyant, they would chat about ordinary things. Magda attempted to draw her out, keen to discover what made her tick; inevitably, the conversation always returned to Chad. She believed she was responsible for his death; by telling him how to set a fire, she had effectively murdered him. She felt her sentence was, if anything, too short.

'You couldn't have known what would happen. It wasn't your fault.'

'I knew enough to have tried to stop him. He used the paraffin though I warned him not to. He was just so frantic to get out.' Her face had crumpled; there were tears in her eyes. Whenever she spoke of Chad she visibly shook.

Magda repeated: 'It wasn't your fault.' She reached across and touched the girl's hand. 'You must learn not to blame yourself and come to terms with what happened.'

When Frankie had been in prison a year, her mother applied for a visitor's pass but Frankie refused to see her, though wouldn't say why. Her hands tensed up and her mouth was tight; her eyes were like chips of ice. Yet her mother had recently lost her husband; surely the time had come, Magda said, for them to be making their peace. Whatever had happened in the past was over now that the colonel was dead. And she'd still need somewhere to live when they let her out.

'No,' said Frankie, implacably. 'I never intend to see her again. She blew it when she married that man and turned a blind eye to what was going on.' Which was as far as she'd ever go, no matter how hard Magda pressed her. The past was closed, she would not discuss it. Magda couldn't get her to say any more.

When she spoke of Chad, as she frequently did, Frankie's ravaged features instantly softened. And, between the bouts of anguished weeping, she built up a picture of the boy she still loved, without whom she felt she could not have any future. He was tall and handsome, funny and bright, and had always acted as her protector. She opened the locket she constantly wore and shyly showed Magda his picture. An intelligent face with a cocky grin stared from the silver frame and Magda's heart went out to the grieving girl.

'He looks a great guy,' was all she could say, a lame response to a person so patently suffering. But when she reached over and touched Frankie's hand, it was not immediately withdrawn.

'Sexy, too,' she said, with a rare smile. 'He said that he couldn't live without me. He talked about marriage and settling down. He badly wanted children.'

He had killed a boy quite unprovoked and later burnt the hostel down. Hardly the actions of a sensitive soul but it wasn't for Magda to point that out. She hoped that, in time, Frankie's suffering would cease and that she would one day forget him.

20

Charles surprised Cassie early on by saying how much he longed for a son. He loved her daughters, both of them, and pandered to them right from the start but she felt in her heart he was still too young to think about babies of his own. She, on the other hand, was ten years older; if she left it too long she would find it much harder to conceive. So when, within the first year of their marriage, she found herself pregnant, both were thrilled.

'Now our union is truly complete,' said Charles, embracing her tenderly.

Cassie beamed; she had never been happier. After the sadness of losing Edwin and the guilt she had felt at remarrying so soon, at last she felt absolved. Her daughters had acquired a loving stepfather, and they greeted the news of the baby with genuine joy.

'I hope it's a boy,' said Daisy to Charles as they groomed the horses in the stable yard. Since coming to live on the Hawksmoor estate, Charles had become an accomplished rider and exercised Edwin's big hunter daily, with a little tuition from the girls.

'Either would make me equally happy,' said Charles with his usual diplomacy, though in his heart he fervently hoped for a son.

'Better than a nasty snivelling little girl,' said Rose, at sixteen as acerbic as Aunt Sybil, taking after the Hawksmoor side more than her mother's.

'By the time she reaches the snivelling stage, you'll be away at college,' said Charles. Rose was bright and planned to train as a lawyer.

'But I'll be here to look after her,' said Daisy, who still liked playing with dolls. A baby sister would be nice, more interesting than a puppy or a kitten. She loved the new family setup they had with her handsome stepfather who treated them like pals and on whom she had something of a secret crush, though she'd die if he ever found out.

'Whatever,' said Charles, as he finished his grooming and slapped the horse lightly on the rump. 'You two will still be my precious girls. You know I will love you however it turns out. This baby won't come between us. I promise you that.'

Sybil still had her own rooms in the house, though since the marriage she visited less often. Cassie put it down to natural tact, something she didn't associate with Sybil. Perhaps her sister-in-law was mellowing with age.

'You know you're always welcome,' she said. 'This house is as much yours as ours.'

Sybil, frenetically pulling up weeds, paused and regarded her levelly for a second. 'Thanks,' she said, continuing her work without any further comment.

She hadn't yet made up her mind about Charles; the jury was still out. Although he was always impeccably civil and greeted her as a much-valued friend, she could not entirely understand why he'd fallen for Cassie. The obvious answer was money and cachet; the Hawksmoor estate was worth a great deal and Cassie was socially well connected not least, if Sybil were honest with herself, because of her own not negligible fame. Yet, to be fair, he appeared to adore her, followed her with his eyes wherever she went. And both the girls were crazy about him, talked about little else. To their teenage perception, he was rock-star glamorous, lights years away from the elderly father who had always been slightly remote, however well meaning.

'What do you think?' Sybil asked Tremayne as they sat together in the local pub, over a neighbourly beer. They had few secrets, this misogamic pair, who had known each other for many decades and shared a brotherly kind of taciturn friendship. The farm manager stared silently into his glass while rehearsing his own reservations.

'I don't think I trust him,' he finally said, unable to explain quite why.

'Could it be because of his charm? Slightly too good to be true, would you say?' Sybil, the sculptor, with her sharp eye for character, was usually well on the mark. Yet she liked the man, could not deny that, found his congenial presence life-affirming. It was good to have youth and exuberance around after the stagnant years.

'Could be. Don't know. We will just have to watch him.' He secretly nurtured warm feelings for Cassie himself.

'But he makes her happy.'

'Apparently so.' The pair sat on in comfortable silence, pursuing their separate trains of thought.

Aidan Christopher Buchanan was born on the night of a full moon. The light lay silvery on the grass as the midwife cut the umbilical cord and handed the tiny bundle to his father. Charles, delighted, took him in his arms and rocked him gently to stop his crying.

'My son,' he said proudly while Cassie lay and watched. 'Don't you think he looks exactly like me?'

He most certainly did, with the same blue eyes and, later, the same lustrous curls. 'Peas in a pod,' the guests all agreed when they met together at the Hawksmoor house to welcome him formally into the world, a much-wanted baby who would always be very well loved.

His half-sisters hovered beside his cot, jealously guarding their precious new toy, taking it in turns to cuddle and wind him, perfect little mothers in the making.

'It has all worked out so well,' Cassie whispered. 'Who would have thought it, a year ago?'

'The instant I saw you, I knew it was destined,' Charles murmured softly as he kissed her.

The Elwes family was there in force, keen to get to know Charles better and to welcome aboard his son. These days Richard was running the estate, his father having retired, so the two new landowners had much in common. As well as the bond of relationship in law, their land abutted so they often met. Henry, the brother who lived in the States, was keen to know what Richard thought.

'He's a nice enough chap, though a tad on the brash side. Doing his best to learn the ropes and keep our Cassie happy.'

'He always seems to be smiling,' said Henry, distrusting Charles on sight. 'What do we know about his background?'

'Not a lot so far,' said Richard. 'Try asking him yourself.'

Charles responded with charm and grace and took Henry's probing in good part. He gave the same answers: he'd been raised in India and later sent home to public school. His parents, sadly no longer alive, had spent most of their marriage abroad.

'Have you no siblings?'

'Alas, no,' he said. 'Becoming a part of the Elwes clan has helped me fulfil a cherished dream.'

'I think he's cute,' declared Henry's wife, and there the matter rested.

Life in Cornwall resumed its even tenor, with Charles as nominal head of the house. While Cassie continued her daily routine – cooking, gardening, walking the dogs, dropping in on her mother for coffee – Charles boned up on managing the estate and did his best to stay on top of things. His brother-in-law was extremely helpful and he also relied a lot on Tremayne, who had started off guarded and openly resentful but now appeared to be coming round. Most of their meetings took place in the village pub.

'I think he's starting to like me,' said Charles. 'Perhaps because I treat him as a mate.'

Now he felt confident on a horse, he also started to ride to hounds and looked very dashing in his hunting kit, which he wore whenever he had the chance.

'A bit of a showman but none the worse for that.' Even Sybil was starting to come round.

The house, since Cassie refurbished it, was back to its earlier splendour. Charles, with his specialist knowledge of art, persuaded her to shift to the attic some of the darker family portraits and insipid Victorian landscapes. In their place he hung some vibrant new paintings which he brought back from one of his London trips and displayed in salient positions throughout the house.

'Where did you get them?' asked Cassie, delighted. They certainly made a difference.

'They're on loan,' said Charles, 'for as long as it takes for us to decide if we want to buy them. It's up to you but I don't think we can go far wrong.'

It made good sense. She had plenty of money and now it was his home too. As he pointed out, she was simply looking to the future. The artists he had carefully chosen would, in due course, appreciate. She spoke to her broker, then told Charles to proceed. It was quite an investment but, apparently, a sound one and this way they could enjoy the spoils.

Aidan, from an early age, displayed his father's restless spirit as well as his sharp intelligence. Gazing down at him in his cot, Cassie, overflowing with love, was occasionally disconcerted by the look in his knowing blue eyes. At moments she almost expected to hear the familiar worldly chuckle, with its innuendoes of a misspent youth and slightly risqué humour. How alike they were, father and son; one a clone of the other.

'Why, there's an old soul if ever I saw one,' was Tremayne's instant comment on first meeting Aidan. He had dropped by with papers for Cassie to sign and was bound to admit, though reluctantly, that this odd new marriage appeared to be suiting her well. He had rarely seen her more radiant; she looked a good ten years younger. Post pregnancy she had put on weight which suited her height and her sculptured bones. Her skin was as clear and unflawed as her daughters'; her eyes shone with happiness. She had taken to twisting her heavy hair into a careless knot, which became her. As she stood in the doorway, waving him off, her son clasped protectively in her arms, a shaft of envy punctured Tremayne's wintry heart. He wished her only the best out of life but sometimes found it hard that she seemed to love this cocky new husband even more than the first one. If only he'd had the courage to speak out in those first lonely days of her widowhood. But Tremayne had never been a man of impulse, which was why he was still on his own.

It gave him pleasure to watch Aidan grow and take his first staggering steps. The child, it seemed, was entirely fearless so that, from the moment he could walk unaided, his endless curiosity led him into all kinds of scrapes. Sometimes, in order to help Cassie out, Tremayne would take him off her hands and drive around with him in the truck as he went about his business. All the workers on the estate would stop what they were doing to greet him and Aidan, right from the start, became a favourite with them all.

'You'd better watch out that he doesn't get spoilt.' Charles seemed doubtful about the friendship though Cassie suspected that he was simply jealous. She had known Tremayne for most of her life and it touched her to see him with her son, gravely explaining country matters in words he could understand. He'd have made a wonderful father, she thought; perhaps it was still not too late. Aidan came home from these expeditions carrying trophies that they had found: a kestrel's feather, a plover's egg, a tiny quivering field mouse.

'In the spring we are going to grow baby frogs,' he told his parents importantly.

'Well, mind you don't fall in,' said Cassie, though she did oblige with a suitable net, left over from when the girls had gone through this phase.

In time a jam jar of frogspawn appeared which Cassie put on the windowsill so that Aidan could watch it slowly hatch into tadpoles.

'Do we really need this muck near our food?' Charles was less than impressed.

'It's educational,' Cassie explained. 'He will learn a lot about nature just from watching.'

Charles, it appeared, was growing fidgety. He no longer found running the Hawksmoor estate enough to satisfy his agile brain. With Rose at Oxford and Daisy working, the house seemed suddenly empty and, although still fascinated by his young son, he felt the need of a larger challenge in his life. They enjoyed a limited social round, within the boundaries of a tight little circle. The neighbouring properties were huge and rambling; Charles began to show a marked interest in their contents.

'Did you see what was hanging over the fireplace?' he said one night as they drove home.

'That flat-looking painting of sailing boats?' Over the years, she had seen it many times yet never really looked at it, assuming it to be an amateur work.

'It's a genuine Alfred Wallis,' said Charles. 'Circa 1930, I'd guess. My God, these houses are loaded with stuff that people don't even know they've got.'

'Worth a lot? It doesn't look it.' As always, she was impressed by his expert eye.

'Could go as high as a hundred thousand bucks. He's in the Tate and the Museum of Modern Art. An interesting primitive painter from these parts. Started off as a fisherman.'

'Well, whatever you do,' said Cassie, amused, 'please don't go offering to buy it. We certainly don't have

145

money like that for picking up every picture you like. Besides, in these parts things like that just aren't done.'

'But it oughtn't to stay where it is,' said Charles. 'The fire is drying it out. Wallis painted on pieces of driftwood. Take a closer look next time we're there.'

'How come you know so much?' asked Cassie, never failing to be surprised. At times Charles came over as a bit of a bullshitter, yet he did seem to know his stuff. She sometimes wondered where he had got his knowledge.

'I don't really know. Just picked it up. I told you I used to deal in pictures.'

He started slipping up to London more often, returning, after a few days, seemingly revitalised and full of new energy. She knew he found the estate confining and started to worry in case he wandered off.

'I often wonder,' she confided to Daisy, 'if he misses the wheeler-dealing of the art world.'

More and more, as they visited neighbours, Charles unearthed hidden treasures. He saw Cassie's point about not being pushy, yet used his charm to winkle out if the owners properly understood what they had. More often than not they had no idea and were grateful to him when he told them. The owner of the Alfred Wallis agreed to allow him to get it valued and was very pleasantly surprised when he found a buyer.

'You're wasted here in the sticks,' said the man. 'You should be up there, in the smoke, doing what you do best.'

*   *   *

146

They settled into a new routine, congenial to them both. Charles spent most of the week away, either in London, making contacts, or travelling around the countryside, seeking out art. He soon had a lucrative power base of clients who used him specifically to track down paintings they wished to acquire for their private collections. He loved the work, found it energising, and was soon staying away for much longer periods, only coming home on alternate weekends.

'I miss you, of course I do,' said Cassie. 'But I am thrilled your career is taking off. I hated to think you were stagnating down here.'

The management of the estate was now back in the capable hands of Tremayne, which meant that all concerned had got what they wanted. Cassie had her work cut out just looking after her boisterous son and helping Daisy, recently married, furnish her new house. At the end of the weeks when Charles was due home, she would put her mind to looking her best and cooking his favourite dishes in order to spoil him. Daisy would often take Aidan in order to give them some time to themselves and, as a result, their sex life improved immeasurably. Daisy, hoping for a family herself, was devoted to her younger brother so, in the end, it all worked out to everyone's satisfaction.

'You know,' said Cassie as they lay together. 'You ought not to have to live in a hotel. You work so hard, it just isn't fair on you. It would probably work out cheaper in the end if we bought our own place in London.'

Charles, who had already worked it out, silently

exulted. There were times when having a richer wife got him down.

'Do you think we can spare the capital?' he asked, running his fingers over her breasts and smiling as she arched her back in response. Foreplay was something he had always excelled at. He had certainly had enough practice.

'It depends where it is and how big,' she said, her eyes still closed and her mind unfocused. 'I hear that Battersea's coming up. The kids could use it when they go to London. And even I, on my shopping excursions, would prefer it to that hotel.'

They smiled at the long-standing private joke, but having a place of their own made sense. Charles was now earning substantial commissions; it would pay to have somewhere where he could entertain.

'Battersea's great but a little far out. I was thinking of somewhere more central.' Like Knightsbridge or Chelsea; in the end he'd get his way. The trick was to keep her believing she'd thought of it first.

It was late afternoon and Cassie was weeding; Charles would shortly be home. Supper was slowly cooking in the Aga and Aidan was quietly engrossed by the pond, fishing net in hand.

'Don't get too close,' Cassie called to him. He'd been told many times to stay away from the water but, with Aidan, she could never be certain. And he'd been unusually quiet for so long; in a moment she'd go and see what he was up to. Charles had wanted the pond filled in but it made a lovely wildlife feature; deer and foxes drank from it and the herons came down to try to catch the fishes.

Aidan was trying to find his frogs. A few weeks earlier, he and Tremayne had ceremoniously emptied the tadpoles into their natural environment. Aidan had cried when the last disappeared; he wanted to keep one as a pet. But Tremayne, backed by Cassie, had quietly explained that, as frogs, they'd be happier in the pond.

'It is nature's way of doing things,' he said. 'They'll be here whenever you want them.'

At the time Aidan seemed to have understood, though Cassie suspected he was moping. Without any siblings close to his age and too many fawning adults around, plus the fact that his father was often absent, he showed signs of turning into a little monster. Now he was sitting quietly on the lawn, playing with something in the grass. Cassie, relieved, went back to what she was doing.

From somewhere close came the sound of mowing; the gardener was working overtime because the lord of the manor would soon be home. She smiled and reflected how much she loved them, her husband and their maverick child. Who would have thought eight years ago that things could have turned out so well.

'Aidan,' she called, as the mower drew closer. It was one of those great big industrial things, lent by Tremayne from the main estate to keep the garden in good shape. She turned to check that her son was safe but he was still deeply engrossed with something in the grass.

'Move,' she said, 'or the mower will get you.' And, although he took no notice of her, he did roll out of the way.

'What the fuck!' suddenly screamed the gardener, grinding to a precipitate halt, and when Cassie ran over to see what was wrong, his face and shirt were splattered all over with blood.

'Frogs,' said the man, when he'd wiped himself down and inspected the carnage in the grass. 'I swear I never even saw them.'

21

It was due to Magda that Frankie got to work in the vegetable garden. She needed taking out of herself and the fresh air would be good for her. She spent too much of her time alone, brooding in her cell, refusing to mix with the other prisoners, and the daily circuit of the prison yard was, at its best, entirely soul-destroying. The strenuous effort of digging the soil was bound to prove beneficial and might help take her mind off her endless grieving. It would also provide a valuable lesson in basic survival skills. One day she would have to fend for herself so the more she learnt now, the better. Frankie was reluctant but could not refuse. When the prison officials approved the plan, she was set to work on a regular basis, under the supervision of the head gardener.

'Now don't go getting ideas,' said Magda, remembering Chad's ill-fated plan, but Frankie's spirit was far too crushed ever to contemplate anything like that. She seemed resentful of this change of routine, would rather have been left alone in her cell to rot.

'Well, I guess it beats sewing mailbags,' said Magda but failed to raise a smile.

Slowly, however, as time passed by, Frankie grew less morose. The physical effort was having an effect and not only did she start looking better but her appetite and her mood improved until she was almost civil again and no longer snapped at Magda. She stopped referring to Chad quite so much and occasionally talked about other things. Magda hoped that she might, in time, even come to terms with his death.

Once she had finished preparing the ground, uprooting weeds and tilling the soil, the next stage of the operation was far less concentrated work. Under the watchful eye of the gardener, Frankie was allowed to do much of the planting herself. She recalled a lot from her country childhood and settled contentedly back on her heels to make regular holes in the newly mulched soil with her dibber. Once the boss had approved what she had done, then came the more interesting matter of the seeds. She opened the packets and dribbled them in, in meticulously straight rows.

'I think you may have cracked it,' said the governor, watching from her office window. 'If so, you have done an excellent job, my dear.'

Magda was pleased; she hoped so but wasn't expecting miracles. These things took time. The girl was very damaged and pain like hers could not just be driven away. But it was a start. She would build on that and pray there would be no backsliding.

* * *

As Frankie grew fitter, she got prettier too and Magda started to see how she once must have looked: tall and graceful with glossy dark hair and classic features that came alive when she smiled, which she still seldom did. They must have made a striking pair, she thought, recalling the photograph, and once again her heart was stirred by the terrible sadness of it all. Whatever Frankie might be guilty of, she did not deserve to have lost her great love in such horrific circumstances. No wonder she couldn't stop blaming herself; the terrible image of his death was enough to drive anyone crazy. Magda resolved to do what she could to improve the quality of Frankie's life and help to lead her back to a more normal existence.

Since Frankie had taken so well to gardening, enjoyed the outdoor life and the back-breaking work, a plan was evolving in Magda's head which she'd keep to herself till a more appropriate time. Now that she had disowned her mother, Frankie had nobody left in the world to whom she could go when they finally let her out. Even if she had to serve the whole sentence, without remission for good behaviour, she'd be only twenty-six when she was released. Far too young to fend for herself when she'd been locked up since her middle teens and had no experience whatever of life outside.

Magda's plan, which she didn't divulge, was to stick around until Frankie got out then do whatever she could to help her adjust. It wasn't part of her job description; her official duties would end at that time. But, over the years, she'd grown fond of the girl and now couldn't bear the prospect of letting her go. She thought of discussing her thoughts with the governor but knew she would probably not approve. Instead she decided to wait to see how things eventually worked out.

22

Clive was the most considerate of lovers, making every meeting a special event, with flowers, chocolates or a bottle of vintage champagne. It was weeks before he made a move, by which time Jenny was starting to lose her cool. She had flipped for him from the very start, knew it would break her heart if he went away. She couldn't face up to another disappointment, truly believed he had feelings for her if only he would let them show and not keep her constantly guessing. Then one starlit night, as they stood by the brook having a final drink before bed, he placed both their glasses on a nearby table, drew her to him and kissed her. Jenny practically fainted on the spot, overwhelmed with relief.

'I've been wanting to do that since the first time we met,' he murmured as they stood entwined, her head against his chest, eyes closed, all of a sudden in heaven. 'I was careful not to move too fast for fear of scaring you off.'

That night they went upstairs together, to her private quarters and not his rented room, and from then on he stayed in the pub as her guest. He tried to arrive before opening time and drag her upstairs for a personal moment before showering and coming downstairs to the bar. This routine suited both of them; he made an excellent host. She asked if he'd ever done bar work before and he laughed and said for a while in his youth while he was still sorting out who he was and making up his mind about his future. Where had he worked? she asked and he told her Mayfair. In those days he'd been a bit of a lad. I'll bet, said Jenny, but couldn't fault him. He knew how to mix almost any cocktail and could flip a glass high from behind his back and catch it in front in one hand. That was the trick that kept Toby amused. He made Clive do it again and again until he pleaded exhaustion and begged to stop. He'd been driving all day, he reminded them both, and was not as young as he had been.

'He's really great with the kid,' said Vanessa, who judged men on that kind of thing. Skill with a child came high on her list; he was certainly earning brownie points with her. 'And you say he doesn't have kids of his own?'

'No,' said Jenny. 'Which does seem a waste. Since he is such a natural.'

Toby adored him and would not go to sleep until Clive had been up and read to him, then stayed to tuck him in and switch off the light.

'What's his family background?' asked Vanessa. 'Does he have brothers and sisters with kids?'

'Don't know,' said Jenny. 'I don't think so.' The truth

was she knew very little about him. Their meetings, only every second week, were so high-octane on the sexual front there was little time left for anything else, least of all conversation.

After two years under Jenny's rule, the pub was starting to flourish. It had always been popular with the locals but now was drawing in tourists as well, a younger and more adventurous crowd than before. The village was two miles from the centre of Bath and attractive because of its river location. The waterwheel was now working again and, on sunny evenings and weekday lunchtimes, the crowd would carry their drinks outside and sit at the wooden tables by the brook, watching the waterbirds. On wintry nights, they'd squash into the bar and warm themselves by the blazing fire which Jenny kept going throughout the year, except at the height of summer. Logs were delivered from a timberyard but she still had to lug them in every day, heavy work that damaged her hands.

Joyce was still valiantly running the kitchen but Jenny was taken with Clive's idea that she should be offering more upmarket food. As it was, the workload was as much as she could cope with, what with having to look after Toby, but the longer she stayed there, the more she saw the Coot and Hern's ultimate potential. Jenny had always been highly ambitious; walking out of her job was just an unfortunate blip. She was still only in her early thirties, and her expectations were high; she liked the idea of a gastropub that could, if she really worked at it, eventually perhaps become nationally known. Clive worked out a rudimentary business plan which, at night, they both pored over, juggling with numbers which were, to Jenny, alarmingly high yet seemed not to worry him at all.

'In a setup like this you cannot lose. Bath, according to all the guide books, is still the hottest tourist spot in the country.'

Since he spent so much time on the road, he knew a fair bit about such things and had a definite taste for indulgent living. He also spent much of his time in London and was well boned up on the restaurant front. Gastropubs were a fairly recent concept, only now coming into their own. The Coot and Hern had all the essentials to turn it into a top-notch venue, provided she did as he said and invested more money.

'It's spending money to make even more. You know it makes sense,' he said.

The stumbling block would be the finance. She had no savings left of her own, having sunk all she'd got into the down payment, and still had a massive overdraft. There was no point in talking to her parents; what savings they had were carefully invested against the time when her dad would no longer be working. Also she felt he still disapproved of his daughter's being a publican, would rather she'd taken the old-fashioned route and gone for conventional marriage. Which was out of the question, at least for now, though somewhere deep down she was cautiously starting to hope.

Clive solved the financial problem by saying he'd help her raise the funds.

'Are you sure?' asked Jenny, overwhelmed. 'Do you

really think you should risk it? They say opening a restaurant is the fastest way to go broke.'

'Don't worry,' he said. 'It won't be my money. These things can be arranged. Besides, I have absolute faith you will make it work.'

'What does he do when he's not in Bath?' Vanessa wanted to know. Handsome, urbane and obviously caring, Clive seemed almost too good to be true. Single, too; given half a chance, she'd have snapped him up herself. She had been with her current boyfriend too long; he wouldn't marry her and was starting to get on her nerves.

'He works in the wallpaper business,' said Jenny, 'for a highly prestigious London firm. His territory covers the whole of the southwest, which is why he is always on the road.' Except for the time he spent in London; he hadn't said much about that.

'Where is he based?'

'I'm not quite sure.' She realised it sounded pathetic. She imagined some kind of anonymous digs though he'd never actually said that. When he was here and she lay in his arms, or watched him keeping the punters happy, all she could think was how happy she was and how well things had turned out. She rarely thought about Douglas these days, except to compare him to Clive and be glad she'd moved on.

'He must have some sort of family,' said Vanessa. 'An adoring mum or an aged nanny. Nobody travels through life entirely alone.'

Clive had even met Jenny's parents, who had come

to vet him as soon as they could. She could see her father was hugely impressed though he tried hard not to show it. A man of few words, he was always suspicious of anyone he could describe as posh.

'I'll tell you something,' he said when Clive had gone. 'He won't be coming to visit us in Neath.'

Her mother, glad to see Jenny so happy, was already hearing wedding bells. He might be older but seemed besotted. And the way he played with Toby was really lovely.

'Now,' she said before they left. 'Don't you go driving him off with your independence.'

Apart from building a much larger kitchen, according to EU regulations, the place would require some general sprucing up for the sort of clientele they hoped to attract. Clive planned to do it all himself. He was, after all, an expert in this area, advising people what colours to choose, sometimes helping them rethink their whole décor.

'We won't be needing wallpaper, will we?' Most of the pub was wood and stone, apart from the bedrooms which had been recently done. Vanessa had overseen all that and every detail was perfect. She had even provided teddy bears to make the visitors feel at home, and magazines on the bedside tables in place of the Gideon Bibles.

'Wallpaper's only a part of what I do.' He had, he explained, a select group of clients to whom he offered a comprehensive service. These customers gave him a free hand to redesign their interiors within an agreed ballpark figure. As they talked, Jenny realised how little she knew about the rest of his life but, unlike Douglas, he seemed to be totally open.

'So where do you do all the office work?' she asked. 'You must have a permanent base.'

'In my car or at the clients' houses. It's a business I'm gradually building up while still on the road for the firm. A natural adjunct to what I'm paid for.' He grinned. 'The only office I need is my trusty laptop from which I am seldom parted.'

Which explained where he was when he wasn't with her. Driving for miles on the motorway or holed up in a service station, catching up on his paperwork. It didn't sound much of a life for him. How lucky for both of them that their paths had crossed.

'Why not suggest he moves in with you? He's handy to have around.' Vanessa changed partners on a whim; the chief priorities of her life were her children, her pets and her home.

'I can't,' said Jenny. 'It's much too soon.' Though she'd hung around all those years for Douglas and look what had happened there. She was determined never to raise the subject. It had to come from him.

Now and again he didn't show but, on those occasions, he always phoned. A business appointment, some unexpected meeting; occasionally a consultation with a client who could only manage weekends. He seemed to spend most of his time on the job which, as he was quick to point out, was also true of her. A disadvantage of living over the shop was that she could never be totally off duty. Something or other would always come up that only she could deal with. But he was still a paid employee; it seemed unfair when he worked such punishing hours.

'What does he do at Christmas?' asked Vanessa but Jenny didn't know. She fantasised about having him there, playing Santa in front of the fire, but when she raised the courage to ask, he said he usually went away.

'Skiing in Austria. I do it most years. With a bunch of my old army cronies. It's become a sort of sacred tradition. I couldn't let them down.'

His only other regular break was two weeks in August when he went on cricket tour. He had played with the team all his adult life; they were like a band of brothers.

'He certainly is a man's man,' said Vanessa. 'I wouldn't have had him down as that.'

Behind the bar he was in his element, very much the genial host. The women jostled for his attention and he treated them all with his dazzling charm but, mainly, it was the men with whom he clicked. They considered him a jolly good bloke and accepted him as Jenny's partner, despite the fact that he was hardly ever there.

'Tell him that you have needs too,' said Vanessa, who didn't entirely approve. She expected men to be in constant attendance.

'I don't want to crowd him,' Jenny explained. She had learnt that lesson the hard way, from Douglas. Even though she had always known about the wife, her life had been on perpetual hold because he always cancelled at the last minute. She had usually spent her birthday alone, as well as every Christmas. If only for that reason, she intended never to become dependent on Clive.

'In many ways it works perfectly,' she told Vanessa over lunch. 'Because we are so much apart, we don't get bored with each other. And he only gets to see me at my best.'

'What will you say if he pops the question?' Vanessa was pretty sure she knew. She had seen Jenny through the Douglas affair and prayed things would work out this time.

Jenny had no need to answer. It was written all over her face.

To avoid the expense of hiring a chef, Jenny decided to do all the cooking herself. In recent years she'd had lots of practice and would rather work in the kitchen than in the bar.

'What we are really after,' she explained, 'is elevated domestic cooking.' Precisely what she'd been doing all these years for her friends. 'None of that overrated fancy stuff. The pub is where people feel most at home. They come here to relax and eat comfort food.'

'You'll still have to show your face now and then so they don't forget who is boss.' Clive, who'd been reading up on the subject, was starting to sound like an expert.

'I'll stick my head round the door now and then, wearing my tall chef's hat.' She liked the idea of becoming a chef, the fulfilment of her long-held dream. If everything worked out, she could get her diploma, when she could find the time.

Joyce was content to become sous-chef, making sauces and keeping the dishwasher stacked. Since orders for food would be taken at the bar, all they needed now was some part-time help to serve the meals and clear away the plates. Then Clive came up with the backing and they were away.

'Smells divine. What is it?' he asked, planting a kiss on Jenny's neck as she slaved away at the stove.

'Beef and mushroom pie,' she said, passing him a forkful of filling. 'It's the Worcestershire sauce that gives it that extra kick.'

She turned to greet him; her face was red and shiny from the heat and her hair was tucked beneath her white gauze hat.

'How's my girl?'

'I'm great,' she said. It was four weeks since they'd last been together, though they'd talked almost every day. Something last minute had happened in his life that had caused him to cancel his last planned visit but Jenny had been so rushed off her feet, she'd scarcely had time to miss him.

'Pour yourself a whisky,' she said, 'and a glass of red wine, please, for me.' She needed to roll the pastry out and cut neat lids for the rows of pie dishes that Joyce would later place in the oven in batches.

'I don't suppose you have time for a quickie?'

'No chance,' she said, with an eye on the clock.

Twenty minutes to opening time and she still had to change her clothes. 'But you might stand in for me at the bar, then pop upstairs and read to Toby.' At times they felt like man and wife, a feeling she very much liked.

They made an effective team, though she hated it when he had to cancel without, it seemed, a very convincing story. She knew there were other pressures on his time but he could have made that extra effort, particularly as he now had a stake in the place. Still, here he was and he did look good. Whereas she was all sweaty from the stove, he was his usual immaculate self, casually leaning against the counter, sipping Glenmorangie. With his silvering hair and those bright blue eyes he looked more like an actor than a salesman.

'What else is on the menu tonight?' At least he showed interest in the food.

'Braised rabbit with cider, rosemary and cream. John Dory with anchovies and capers. Oh, and a wonderful new dessert. Wait until you taste it. Geranium-scented panna cotta, trimmed with red gooseberries.'

She varied the menu as much as she could, while also including the staple favourites, and was experimenting with a lot of new dishes. She gave him a spoon and made him taste it, was pleased when he rolled his eyes.

'You're a genius,' he said, embracing her. 'Meanwhile, it's practically zero hour so scoot.'

*　　*　　*

The investment money, he told her later, came from a private source who was also a friend. Someone he knew socially, with whom he played the odd game of golf.

'I did up his place in Somerset,' he said. 'He was so delighted with the result, he now trusts my judgement implicitly and is willing to take a punt.' Not so much money that Jenny need worry but enough, for now, to cover the planned improvements.

'Surely he wants to see for himself.' A chance, perhaps, to meet one of his friends.

'He's not really bothered. Some time in the future. Right now he's got a lot of stuff on his plate.'

The first thing they did was extend the kitchen, with a brand new cooker, twice the size of the old one, which involved some fairly major structural alterations, as well as a lot of noise and mess. While this was happening, Jenny worked out menus that involved as little cooking as possible; when necessary she could use the oven upstairs.

'It's a little like camping,' she told Vanessa, 'but should all be worth it in the end.'

Meanwhile, they ripped out the jukebox in the bar and hung some wooden-framed paintings to brighten the walls. Vanessa, who had an eye for these things, trawled the junk shops for copper jugs and horse brasses, which they also hung on the walls. They planted huge terracotta pots with trailing ivy and cyclamen and placed them around the bar and dining room. It was fun and Jenny enjoyed herself, watching her dream come alive. One day she'd invite her old team to come down and write it up for the magazine but not until she felt she had got it perfect.

Much of her time, outside opening hours, Jenny spent sourcing ingredients and forging links with small food producers who could match the quality she was after. Here the years spent writing her column really did pay off. Her name was known as an expert in the field so the butchers, cheesemakers and other local vendors were only too pleased to oblige her and went out of their way to help.

'I must say,' said Vanessa one day, as they lounged outside by the waterwheel. 'I wasn't convinced you would pull it off. But you've certainly done so in spades.'

By far the highlight of Jenny's life was the moment, on every second Thursday, when Clive arrived around opening time and joined her behind the bar. She would stay no longer than twenty minutes, enough to greet the early drinkers, then withdraw to the kitchen and take on her role as chef. Joyce would have been there a couple of hours, preparing vegetables and making sauces, contentedly doing the basics for Jenny to work with. As a team, they fitted very well together and the bar staff were excellent too. But the nights Clive was there, Jenny really came to life. By now the regulars were used to him and most of them knew him by name. With his jacket off and his sleeves rolled up, he epitomised the genial host and drew them to him with his lethal charm and irrepressible good humour. Now and again he'd pop down to the kitchen or up to the nursery to settle Toby. Everyone felt much happier with him around.

Only Vanessa still had reservations but she'd long been Jenny's best friend. 'You must work awfully hard,' she said, cautiously trying to find out more, still not convinced that this charming man was one hundred per cent bona fide.

'I do,' said Clive. 'As it happens. For my sins.'

'It's a shame you can't be around a little more.' Vanessa rarely pulled her punches. 'It is tough for Jenny too, you know. Running this place on her own.'

'I do know,' said Clive, 'and am really glad that she has such a good friend as you.'

Later that night, when the pub was closed and the last of the drinkers had finally gone, Clive poured two glasses of vintage brandy and they went outside to drink it under the stars.

'To us,' he said, raising a toast to them both. 'May it last for ever. I know it can't be easy at times but what we have is better than marriage. I am here because I love you. I think you know that.'

Jenny's eyes were shiny with tears. 'I love you too,' she said.

23

Life grew fractionally easier to bear, though a day never passed when Frankie didn't think about Chad. She found tending her vegetables quietly sustaining, liked the calm repetitiveness of it all. Slowly she made peace with herself, as far as she was able, and found the constant activity kept her from brooding. She even made a couple of friends which meant she was less cut off. They would sit and chat in the social hour, play cards together and sometimes darts and, bit by bit, exchange their personal stories. The other two, Bella and Sadie, were older, one a time-hardened prostitute, the other a failed con artist. But Frankie found them both entertaining, once she had dropped her defences a bit, and they, in turn, were surprised to find that beneath the morose exterior she did have a sense of humour.

'What's a kid like you doing in 'ere?' Bella, the prostitute, wanted to know and, when Frankie recounted her story, shook her head in disbelief. 'They oughtn't of locked you up for that,' she said. 'You was only defending your man.'

'And had surely been punished enough,' added Sadie. 'If they'd had any heart, they'd have let you go, if only for reasons of compassion.'

'Life isn't like that,' said Frankie calmly. 'Besides, it no longer matters. At the time I was so shattered by his death, I couldn't even think straight. And I needed somewhere to live, after all. At least they have given me bed and board.' And stopped her learning to fend for herself or think about a career.

She took up yoga, then meditation from which she learnt to face her own death, which made what happened to Chad that much easier to bear. Having been raised with no religion she wasn't expecting to meet him again, but if she did, there were questions to which she wanted answers.

Magda, observing, was pleased with her progress and slow emergence from her morbid trance. She made an appointment to see the governor. Frankie had now served five years of her sentence and would soon be up for parole.

Frankie was summoned to the governor's office. Her mother was asking to see her. 'No,' she said, without thinking twice. 'I won't see that woman again.'

'Not just a woman. Your mother,' said the governor. 'It isn't natural to turn your back. She really needs you, you are all she has left. Give her a chance and hear what she has to say.'

'No,' said Frankie flatly, refusing to budge.

But the next day Magda took her aside and explained it would be to her own advantage to do as the governor said. 'Soon you'll be due for parole,' she pointed out. 'Don't let pig-headedness stand in the way of your getting out early for good behaviour. If that happens, the colonel will have won.'

She offered to be there when her mother arrived but Frankie preferred to see her alone.

'Don't worry,' she said. 'I can handle this. Though don't expect the meeting to last very long.' All the sparkle had gone from her eyes. She looked as she had six years ago, bitter and deeply disturbed.

Her mother, when Frankie was ushered in, was seated nervously beyond the grille and seemed to have aged a lot since Frankie last saw her. She had lost some weight and it didn't become her. Her once pretty face, with its laughing eyes, was now haggard and pale. Her hair, which she'd always kept freshly tinted, was grey where it straggled from under her hat. She was dressed in beige and looked nervous and uneasy. For a nanosecond Frankie almost weakened. She took her seat and they stared at each other in silence.

'You look well, dear,' said her mother. 'Surprisingly so.'

'Hard labour,' said Frankie. 'They have got me hewing rocks. Well, as somebody pointed out, it beats sewing mailbags.'

An uncertain smile flickered on her mother's face. She had never been able to tell when Frankie was joking. 'I hope they're not treating you badly, dear,' she said in a loud stage whisper. She was wearing a dusting of pale blue eyeshadow which, on a woman

171

her age, looked grotesque. She had always been a girlie woman, the characteristic that had first attracted the colonel.

'What do you think?' asked Frankie baldly, staring at her with hostile eyes.

For a nervous few seconds her mother fluttered and rummaged in her bag for a tissue. 'I have missed you, dear,' she said falteringly. 'I would like to think we might one day be close again.'

'Close!' snorted Frankie. 'You have to be joking. You don't know the meaning of the word. All you ever did was fuss over that man, yet you never saw what was going on under your nose.'

'I don't know what you mean,' said her mother, dabbing at her eyes. 'I tried to be a good mother to you. I can't think where I went wrong.'

'Warder!' said Frankie, rising to her feet. 'I want to return to my cell.'

As she turned to go without saying goodbye, her mother attempted one final bid. 'Won't you come home when they let you out and see if we can't make a go of it? The house, without either of you, seems so empty.'

'Tough,' said Frankie, 'you should have thought of that before.' And left.

'How did it go?' asked Magda later.

'Badly,' said Frankie abruptly. All the old anger had boiled up again and the more relaxed Frankie they were getting to know had disappeared entirely. Instead of responding to Magda's concern, she stared blankly at the wall.

'The news from the governor is good,' said Magda, deftly changing the subject. 'All going well, within a few weeks you may get an early release.'

'So what?' Frankie shrugged, no longer caring. 'I have nowhere else to go.'

'As it happens,' said Magda, playing her trump card, 'I think you may find you are wrong.'

Her plan, which she'd worked on for several years, had been approved by the governor. After thirteen years in the prison service, she felt she had done all she usefully could and now was planning a major change in her life.

'I am joining a group of women in Belgium, in a spiritual commune. They live together and are self-supporting from working mainly with their hands. There are potters, weavers, all kinds, producing work which they later sell to support the commune.' She glanced at Frankie, who hadn't spoken. 'I was rather hoping you might join us. The community spirit is very uplifting and it isn't nearly as worthy as it sounds.'

Frankie was silent for several minutes. Then, just as Magda was losing hope, she turned and said shyly: 'Okay.'

'Terrific!' said Magda, embracing her tightly. 'I promise you won't regret it.'

24

'Come along, slowcoach, what's wrong with you today? At this rate, you'll never get fit.' Dino, tall and impossibly handsome, was bouncing backwards on the balls of his feet while Pippa put on an extra spurt and tried hard to catch him up.

'It isn't fair,' she panted, 'your legs are much longer.'

'Shouldn't make any difference,' he said, grabbing her wrist to check the watch that monitored her heart rate. 'Move!' he said. 'You're not giving it your best. What were you up to last night?'

'Taking care of my husband and children,' said Pippa, suddenly defensive. The truth was, the nanny had been with the twins while she and Charles were out on the town, trying out yet another trendy new restaurant.

Being a full-time wife and mother as well as running a business on her own was starting to take its toll on Pippa who, these days, seemed to be permanently tired. And yet her husband retained all his original bounce. Charles could sail through a heavy workday and still put back a whisky or two as well as a bottle or more of expensive wine. She had no idea where the stamina came from. By his age he ought to be slowing down.

Now that the twins were at the toddling stage, life had become that much harder. No longer could Pippa just dump them in the playpen and get on with the business of running the shop. These days they demanded too much of her attention; somewhat against her natural instincts, she'd been forced to place them both in nursery school.

'I feel so guilty,' she confessed to her mother.

'Don't,' said her mother. 'These are modern times.' Meaning, though without spelling it out, that she didn't want her grandsons left with her. Besides, she reasoned, the nursery was better, providing company and mental stimulus to two such intelligent, hyperactive boys. They were far too much of a handful for the nanny, who was only part-time in any case, as Pippa wouldn't have anyone living in. 'You are lucky to have a husband who's so rich.' Her mother had radically changed her tune since the relationship began.

'But he works for it. Hard,' Pippa reminded her. He had so many irons in so many fires, he sometimes didn't come home for nights on end.

She had moved her workouts to the early morning in order to fit them in before starting work. The nanny would give the children their breakfast while, twice a week, come hail or shine, Pippa would put on her tracksuit and trainers and pound round Barnes Common with Dino. The route he'd worked out took precisely one hour and he'd drop her back at her own front door in time to shower and change her clothes, then deposit the twins at the nursery school on her way to the Fulham Road. The days of her driving in with Charles were gone since his hours had become so erratic.

'I hardly get to see him these days,' she frequently moaned to Dino.

Still, she couldn't complain: it was what she had wanted and, at one time, thought she might never have. An attentive husband and two gorgeous babies – and all before she had reached the age of thirty.

Occasionally, when Charles was away and the nanny could be coerced into staying, Pippa took the evening off and went on the razzle with her friends. They met in a wine bar in the Fulham Road or across the river in Putney. They were mainly female, about her age, and all had jobs that they liked a lot. Only, unlike her, they were single and unattached.

'Don't you miss your freedom,' they asked, 'now that you're half of a couple?'

And Pippa admitted that, yes, she did. She missed the laughter and female chat, the vulgar jokes and sexual confidences; the general camaraderie they all shared.

'How are the twins?' they asked politely, making it clear that they couldn't care less, that their single lives were too engrossing for them to envy her.

Of course she put a good face on it: the twins were lovely, her husband a dear. Life was perfect, he spoiled her rotten and now, good heavens, she'd have to fly because the nanny would be fretting. She was pretty certain that, once she'd gone, the rest of them would sigh and relax and raise a glass to their single state before moving on to a club.

The nanny was waiting, a little distraught. Jack, she told Pippa, had been playing up. Not just in his usual naughty way: he'd been having what seemed like a fit. Pippa was up the stairs in a flash, rebellious thoughts entirely forgotten, and down on her knees by the lower bunk bed to see what was going on.

'Jack?' she whispered, stroking his hair, and he turned and stared at her with the eyes of a stranger.

'I think you are overreacting,' said Charles. 'The poor little blighter is only eighteen months old.' He had arrived home late from a very long drive, dreaming only of a good night's sleep, to find the house in a state of hysterical uproar. The doctor was there and so was Pippa's mother, all of them fussing around the child who was seated, unmoving, in the centre of the rug, staring blankly into space. Pippa was crouched beside him, rubbing his hands.

'He doesn't seem to know me,' she wailed, raising a tear-stained face to Charles. She was now consumed with guilt at having been out.

The nanny, pale-faced and shaken by it all, had not quite known what to do for the best and so had called Pippa's mother.

'You should have tried my mobile,' scolded Pippa

but the girl hadn't thought of that. She had badly needed some reassurance and the older woman was fortunately at home and had arrived in a cab within twenty minutes. Not sure what to do, they had gone ahead and summoned the doctor who had roused himself, grudgingly, from his fireside and come.

'I don't think it's anything serious,' he said, relieved that the head of the house was now home. 'I have checked his temperature and looked at his eyes and the wee lad seems perfectly sound.'

'Jack,' said Charles but the child didn't blink, just continued to stare into space.

'I think what he needs is a good night's sleep,' said Pippa's mother, taking over, calmer now that the doctor had checked Jack out. 'You know what they can be like at this age, running fevers without any warning. You were constantly giving me frights when you were a baby.'

Pippa gathered the child in her arms and took him upstairs to the nursery while Charles picked up his car keys again to drive the nanny home. 'It was good of you to come,' he told the doctor, melting the dour old Scot's ill humour with a blast of his lethal charm. 'It's a gross imposition to have called you out. I thank you most sincerely.'

'My pleasure,' said the doctor, mollified. 'It is always better to be safe than sorry where babies are concerned.'

'I'll wait till Charles gets back,' said Pippa's mother, flopping down on the couch, exhausted, when Pippa came downstairs and went immediately to the fridge for a bottle of wine.

'What do you really think?' she asked, still worried and guilty at having been out. 'Is that sort of thing really normal at this age?'

'Of course it is, darling. He is only a baby. It is probably just a phase he's going through.'

But later, in the privacy of the cab on the short journey home to Richmond, she faced up to a private fear she had had since the twins had started to crawl and she'd first become aware of Jack's behaviour. She silently prayed that her hunch was wrong. If not, her daughter – and that meant her, too – was in for considerable heartache.

'Just occasionally,' said Pippa to Dino, as they practised Pilates on the breakfast room floor, 'my husband makes me feel an incompetent fool.'

'How so?' asked the trainer, as she worked on her abs. He took great interest in Pippa's marriage which he still hadn't quite figured out. Charles Buchanan, though still in peak form, was, in Dino's private opinion, too old for his spirited wife. Charming, yes, and generous too. But there was something about him he didn't quite trust. Not that he knew him well at all; they only met in passing.

Pippa related the incident with Jack and Dino listened intently. Twice he had witnessed the child having tantrums when he hadn't been able to get his own way. But that was quite normal with kids that age; what he really needed was a slap. He kept that to himself, however, since Pippa was not in the mood for jokes. She blamed herself for having left him with the nanny, felt it was somehow her fault.

'You've got to have some sort of life of your own. You can't fuss over them all the time.'

'But it's my responsibility,' she said. For falling pregnant in the first place.

She still felt guilt about the break-up of his marriage, the more so since Cassie had taken it so well. The twice they had met she had seemed such a lady, calm and gracious and slightly withdrawn, with fine grey eyes and a thoughtful air as though her mind were set on higher things. Yet Pippa had ruthlessly snatched her husband at a time when her own youngest child was just leaving home. She couldn't believe she had been so restrained, had let Charles go without a murmur.

Cassie was hardly ever mentioned these days, except when Aidan came by. Pippa got a buzz out of seeing him with the twins, the likeness between them was so striking. She hoped her boys would grow up just like him, as tall and good-looking as their father with the same irrepressible laugh and magnetic blue eyes. When you saw the Buchanans all together, there was no mistaking the dominant gene. It made her mother laugh, it was so nearly absurd.

'There is not a trace of Cassie in Aidan, nor of me in the twins,' Pippa said. She wondered fleetingly if there'd be another wife, then quickly suppressed the thought as downright unhealthy. But Dino, who understood her well, had picked up her train of thought.

'Does he have any other families tucked away?' He would not put it past the crafty old bugger, who seemed to have been less and less home since the babies were born. But he kept his tone deliberately light, was far too fond of his client to want to upset her.

'Are you kidding?' said Pippa, with a slightly forced smile. 'Don't you think two is enough?'

Hakkasan was pulsating with life; Pippa couldn't catch what Charles was saying as the suave black waiter led them to their table. It was the newest hot restaurant to open in London and everyone who was anyone was there. Starlets and B-listers out in force; it took him back to his earlier life, before he had been encumbered.

'What?' yelled Pippa, as Charles mimed a question then, getting the gist, yelled: 'White wine.'

'Won't you have something more exotic?' But since she still couldn't hear, he let it go. He was getting too old for this type of trendy joint, yet couldn't bear not to keep up. He raised a finger and summoned the waiter and ordered a bottle of Cristal.

'What's this in aid of?' asked Pippa suspiciously.

'Aren't I allowed to spoil the girl of my dreams?'

Pippa smiled; she could hear him now. That was Charles all over. Whenever he sensed she was slightly fed up, in he came with this sort of grand gesture which always won her over. He certainly knew which buttons to press. She remembered the diamond brooch he had bought her, which she hardly ever wore. It was still too old and formal for her but either she would grow into it or she would pass it on to the wife of one of her sons. Or perhaps they would still have a daughter of their own; she hadn't entirely ruled that out. She was just too tired with the shop and the twins to contemplate it now.

The food was delicious, she handed them that, and, once she grew used to the volume of sound, she relaxed and began to enjoy herself. The champagne certainly helped.

'You are looking especially pretty tonight.' Charles leaned forward and kissed her hand and, just for a second, she wondered what he was after.

'You don't look so bad yourself,' she said, proud as ever to be seen with him, grateful that they had stayed together even after she'd thought she couldn't win. She just wished he wasn't away so much. These days he seemed to be travelling most of the time. She knew it was because of his career but wished that sometimes he'd just stay home and spend more time with her and the boys before they were too much older. He was missing their childhood and that was a shame. Before he knew it, they'd be off to school and only home for the holidays, if Charles had the final word, as he usually did.

'Do you still love me?' she found herself asking before she could bite back the words. How grotesque; she was acting like a loser after he'd spent all this money to bring her here.

'Of course I love you and I always will.' His grip on her fingers grew tighter. His eyes, of that eerie electric blue, locked into hers and left her limp. 'Whatever else happens, remember this. I won't ever let you down.'

Part Two

25

'Calm down,' said Magda, when Frankie called, incoherently gabbling. 'You know it can't have been him. You saw him die.'

'It was him,' said Frankie. 'Though God knows how. I am telling you the evidence of my eyes. He was only feet away from me, though I don't believe he saw me.' If only she'd managed to yank the window down.

'It isn't possible,' said Magda firmly. 'Please calm down and get a grip on yourself.' She had long feared something like this could happen, that Frankie might suffer a total breakdown after all the years spent bottling up her grief. It was one of the reasons she'd invited her to Lier; she hadn't thought Frankie strong enough then to be able to cope on her own. But nearly thirty years had passed and she hardly mentioned his name any more. Perhaps she'd been wrong about the vegetable market but she had thought the responsibility would do her good. These monthly excursions into the real world had been designed to take Frankie out of herself. If only the fan-belt on the truck hadn't broken so she'd had to start taking the train.

'Come home,' she said, 'and we'll talk it through.' What she needed was a course of intensive treatment. Magda had been wrong to imagine she could sort her out without professional backup.

'I have to find him.' She was practically screaming and clearly not listening at all. 'I have checked the trains. He was headed for Bruges. There's another due in just a few minutes. If I don't get home tonight, don't worry. I'll call and let you know what's going on.'

She was starting to sound completely off her head, like a teenager high on speed.

'Wait,' said Magda. 'Don't ring off. At least let me go there with you.' Too late, for Frankie had ended the call. And when Magda attempted to reconnect, she found she had switched off her phone.

There was nothing she could do except wait for Frankie to call again. Perhaps, after all, it was no bad thing; might help her finally get him out of her system. If only she could exorcise Chad's ghost, she might at last be able to move on.

26

The puppy had been a gift from Claude, in the days when he pandered to her every whim and Cristina complained that he left her too much on her own. A cream chihuahua with great soulful eyes, Fifi arrived in a scarlet hatbox, wearing a diamond bracelet round her throat. Cristina had fallen upon her with glee, transferred the collar to the safety of her wrist, then spent a few weeks, until she grew bored, smothering the animal with love. She bought her all sorts of unnecessary things: a mink-trimmed coat, a sheepskin bed and a travelling case disguised as a handbag in which to carry her around. The Paris restaurants were lenient about dogs so Fifi accompanied her everywhere, except when she dined alone with Claude, who simply wouldn't allow it. On the occasions Fifi was left at home, it fell to Yvette to take care of her, to walk her twice round the garden daily and ensure that she did her business only outside. Even so, Fifi had become so spoilt that she frequently piddled on the marble floors, causing Yvette to scream in rage and threaten to wring her scrawny neck.

Except when Cristina was in the mood, Fifi lived in the servants' quarters where she grew adept at begging for food and nimbly avoiding the gardener's vicious boot.

'I can't imagine why she wanted her.' Yvette could never find much to praise in her self-indulgent mistress. 'She treats her like an unwanted toy. It's a shame. She should really be put down.'

'The dog or Cristina?' Serge asked languidly, lighting another cigarette.

His question didn't merit an answer but Yvette flashed him a conspiratorial grin. Though the pair were often at loggerheads, on the subject of Cristina they always agreed. Monsieur was a gentleman through and through whereas she was just mixed blood trash.

But when Cristina went out on the town, the dog became an accessory, with a great satin bow attached to her collar to tone with whatever her mistress was wearing. The servants might continue to sneer, yet it did seem that they were stuck with Cristina unless, of course, Monsieur should get wind of her much discussed marriage plans. Considering she owed her lifestyle to him, she was wildly indiscreet in the house, a clear indication of her contempt for the staff. She screamed at them and pushed them around, yet never apparently stopped to think that they might tell tales out of school if she wasn't careful.

'You owe it to him to let him know,' said Serge, who was strongly on the master's side, but Yvette didn't dare to interfere and risk possibly losing her job. Let things take their own course, she said. Though the arrogant cow had certainly got it coming.

There was still no word from Rocco and Cristina was frantic. Perhaps he had mislaid his phone. She had no other means of contacting him, since he constantly moved around. And to make matters worse, today was Monday and Claude would return from the country later, expecting her to be looking her best and to entertain him tonight. She sat and scowled in the beauty parlour, the dog on her lap and her phone in her hand, making endless unnecessary calls while the pedicurist silently worked on her feet. Every few minutes she barked out an order: she needed a tissue, a magazine, another *tasse du thé*. And a bowl of water for her panting dog who looked bedraggled, her ribbon drooping, as though in need of a beauty treatment herself.

Several more times she tried Rocco's number but his phone still appeared not to be switched on. So, once again, she called the house to check with Yvette if he'd left her a message.

'No, madame,' said Yvette again, biting back her irritation at these constant, meaningless interruptions which kept her from doing her job.

'If he does, please give him my mobile number and tell him I need to talk to him. I'll be home by one, so tell him that too, and warn Monsieur, if he gets home first, that I'm not feeling terribly well today and would like an early night.'

Yvette rolled her eyes despairingly at Serge, still

lolling around in the kitchen, watching her iron. 'Madame is a nasty piece of work,' she said. 'Monsieur deserves a lot better.'

'I wouldn't mind taking her off his hands, provided I didn't have to listen to her moan. It seems all she ever does is complain. Yet look how pampered she is.'

'She should try changing places with me,' said Yvette. 'Then she would find out what hardship really is.'

The pedicurist had finished her job and was now applying a final coat before standing back to admire her work, which had taken the best part of an hour. Her next appointment was already waiting; Cristina's constant demands slowed everyone down.

'*Voilà!*' she said as Cristina stopped talking, indicating with her hand the immaculate job she had done.

Cristina, with a pointed lack of enthusiasm, paused before making another call, and studied her toes for a long and critical moment.

'No,' she pronounced. 'I don't like the colour. Take it off and start all over again.'

After Cal had left and she'd screamed and cried, drunk too much and bent the ear of every passing acquaintance she had in Rio, Cristina, with the help of the magic white powder, had managed to reconstruct herself and crawl back into the semblance of a career. Her reputation went before her: unreliable, the fashion houses said. Also no longer quite the beauty she had been. Her life's excesses had taken their toll so that, by her late twenties, by the stretch of no one's imagination could she be styled this year's face or even the year before's. As her life went into a downward spiral and the important bookings started drying up, her friend, the adventuress, Marie-Hélène, belatedly came to her aid.

'Chérie,' she said, rapidly scribbling down a number. 'Call this woman and mention my name.'

'Why?' asked Cristina.

'Never mind,' said her friend. 'Let's just say that I owe you.'

Madame Zarco was a slim, discreet widow of indeterminate age, with jet-black hair drawn back sleekly into a knot and lips of a glossy ruby red, the only clue to her hidden sexuality. Her role in Brazilian society was simple: she organised dinners and villa parties in order to introduce beautiful women to out of town visitors, passing through. Her fees were steep but the women didn't pay; the entire financial burden was borne by the men.

'I suppose it might fill in an evening or two.' Cristina was doubtful but growing short of cash, since these days her habit cost more than she could afford. And, whatever her shortcomings on the catwalk, she was still a sensationally beautiful woman who turned heads wherever she went. Madame Zarco was delighted to add her name to her list and introduce her to a shady social world consisting mainly of C-list footballers and starlets on the make. The villa parties turned out to be fun and gave Cristina a chance to display her still voluptuous charms. She was putting on weight but it

193

suited her style and the men couldn't get enough of her. At almost every function, she was the star prize.

Over the years one thing led to another which was how Cristina found herself in Paris, courtesy of Madame Zarco's social list. It was early spring and the fashion shows were on. Each day she took her place in the front row, idly flicking through the glossy brochures while the cameras clicked around her. The designers lent her clothes for each occasion, as Cristina's face was still widely known, and her days were crammed with parties and receptions at which she was well received. A lot of the time she was bored and ungrateful yet her socialising did fulfil a function of sorts by introducing her to a much wider circle. And it was better than rotting at home in Rio where the phone rang less and less.

Claude Daumier styled himself an entrepreneur though Cristina was never entirely sure what that implied. It seemed to mean he had loads of money as well as an aristocratic background and a town-house close to the Bois de Boulogne, though his main abode, where his wife resided, was his château outside Neuilly. They met at one of the endless receptions that filled Cristina's aimless days, and his invitation to lunch lit a spark in her addled brain that told her that at last her luck might be changing. Cristina, by then, was thirty-four and Claude at least thirty years older but he kept himself in excellent shape, dressed in a chic though conservative style and possessed a kind of insouciance that she found immensely attractive. A

Parisian to his fingertips, he moved in the social circles she admired and had long aspired to be part of. Also, somewhat to her surprise, he was competent in bed.

They fell into a relationship that admirably suited them both. He persuaded her to remain in Paris and set up home in his elegant house, whilst also making it clear that they'd never marry. His wife and children were sacred to him, in a different compartment of his life. As long as Cristina behaved herself, the arrangement worked for her very well, took care of her pressing financial needs and gave her a coveted role among the elite. She liked the city, which she found more inspiring than the endless beachscapes of Rio de Janeiro, which had finally started to pall. She was growing up.

For a while she enjoyed this new bourgeois life, presiding over Claude's dinner parties, firing orders at the staff and throwing her weight around. He paid all her bills without a murmur, liked her to be expensively dressed, even found her tantrums amusing since they usually climaxed in bed. For a man of his age, he remained very fit. There was little that she could justifiably complain of.

At first she resented his weekends with his wife but soon came to see them as the benefit they were; she had the run of his house and driver and slowly started to build a life of her own. Love had never been mentioned between them; what they had was a business alliance that amply suited them both. And since love was something she had almost never known, it was not a commodity she missed.

*　　*　　*

195

After twelve years, though, of being Claude's mistress, Cristina was feeling distinctly jaded and yearning for something she couldn't quite specify. Security she had in abundance, as well as social recognition of sorts, since Paris was very worldly about such things. But that, she now felt, was no longer enough. At forty-six, she craved something more, was beginning to feel that this static life was making her listless and staid. And so, on the pretext of homesickness, she returned to Rio for Carnaval and a chance to soak in some sunshine and see a few friends.

Marie-Hélène was long since gone, married now to a minor prince and living in Salzburg, so they said, in fading rococo splendour. The rest of the pack had also dispersed, to wherever such party girls end up, and Cristina found herself even more lonely than in Paris. In the end, she called Madame Zarco who expressed herself pleased to hear from her and invited her round for a soirée the following night. It was better than hanging around in bars and she owed the woman a favour or two so Cristina dolled herself up and went on the razzle.

And, like Cinderella's, her life changed at midnight when Rocco Pereira and a bunch of drunk cronies belatedly burst into the room.

And now she was faced with a life-threatening dilemma. To marry Rocco she would have to tell Claude, which would put her immediately in the wrong and meant that Claude, if he chose to, could evict her. She had few illusions about his affection;

there had been a time when he doted upon her but that was ten years ago. She had watched his admiration wane with every temper tantrum she threw and, in her saner moments, she knew that her days in this house might be numbered. Which was, if she were honest with herself, the greater part of Rocco's attraction. Not only was he sexy and younger but he earned a fortune as a racing driver and could, if she played her cards skilfully enough, take her away from all this.

Which was where the main complication arose. Without the house and the façade of Claude's wealth, she was realistic enough to know that she lacked the wherewithal to catch and hold him. Such knowledge had only come slowly to her, after a lot of hard knocks. She no longer considered herself a world-class beauty. Hence the dilemma which she had to face up to: she couldn't afford to lose him. And there was the rub.

On cue, the door was gently pushed open and Fifi, on delicate paws, pranced in. She shivered and grovelled till Cristina swept her up and smothered her muzzle with lipsticky kisses, glad for a few mindless seconds to have something to love.

'What do you think I should do, chérie?' she whispered in the dog's bat-like ear but Fifi merely whimpered and licked her nose. With a heartfelt sigh, Cristina acknowledged that this latest mess was of her own making and that she had some urgent decisions to make.

When she married Cal, they had both been high and Cristina had only faint memories of the occasion. She recalled the heat and her shimmering dress and walking barefoot across baking sand, with her arms full of flowers he had recklessly bought at the road-side. She also remembered how handsome he looked, with his golden tan and his sparkling blue eyes, dressed entirely in white, including his shoes. He always had been a bit of a ham, with one eye cocked for the paparazzi who seemed to be drawn to his presence whatever he did. She remembered also the ring he had bought her, platinum studded with five carat diamonds, which she'd hurled through the window during one of their spats and never found again. What she couldn't recall, though, was who else had been there; if anyone traceable had witnessed the event.

She realised now she had one simple choice, either to try to locate the paperwork or else to let sleeping dogs lie. For twenty-three years, since Cal walked out, she hadn't given the subject a thought, not even when she first hooked up with Claude. Her marriage had been and gone in a blur and no longer seemed relevant to her life. Until she met Rocco, the thought had never struck her that she might want to marry again. If she chose to do nothing, as was her inclin-ation, the odds were that no one would ever find out. After two decades, and on another continent, the chance of a witness turning up seemed laughably remote. She had no idea where Cal was now, nor even if he were still alive, though she felt her heart would have somehow known if he weren't. He was only three years older than her which, even though she lied about her age, made him no more than forty-seven now.

Had there been photos? She couldn't remember, had certainly never seen any since, did not possess a treasured wedding album. Yet the paparazzi had been out in force, tipped off by somebody in the know, most probably Cal himself. Since she was, at that point, the queen of the catwalk, both of them A-list celebrities, it was hard to believe they had not hit the tabloids at least. After the wedding, they'd driven slowly through Rio, she standing up in their open car, throwing handfuls of flowers to the cheering crowds. Cristina smiled; it was all coming back. She remembered how happy she had been. The start of an idyll she had thought was for ever, though the truth was it lasted for less than eighteen months. And if she remembered, then others might too. It was too much of a gamble to take the risk.

But then she considered the ramifications and was once more struck by colossal doubt. If marrying Rocco meant losing Claude's patronage, she risked messing up the rest of her life should it ever emerge, at some future date, that she hadn't been legally free. More than anything else in the world, Cristina valued her independence. Since the days of scavenging and sleeping rough, she had done much of which she wasn't proud but her main achievement was to have survived and, by anyone's standards, remarkably well, considering. She glanced around her luxurious bedroom, with its walk-in closets and chandeliers, and knew that she dared not risk mucking things up and losing this lifestyle on one simple roll of the dice.

She had to protect what assets she had, so she picked up the phone and put in a call to her lawyer.

27

By the time Frankie got off the train in Bruges the weather had worsened to driving sleet, so dense she could hardly see anything at all. Magda's mitts were completely sodden so she'd peeled them off and stuffed them in her backpack, and her chilblains throbbed within her inadequate boots. She splurged on a cab to the centre of town and had it drop her at the tourist office, which seemed the logical place to start her quest. The woman there, though, had no knowledge of Chad and even less interest in helping her. The tourist invasion had not yet begun and the town, unusually, was more or less deserted. So it shouldn't be hard to track him down; it was all much smaller than Frankie had thought and he couldn't have just been passing through, since Bruges was the end of the line.

In a state of considerable agitation, she decided to follow the tourist route and stop off at likely places to ask if they either knew Chad by name or had seen someone answering his description. In her temporary state of dementia, it never occurred that his striking looks might have gone unnoticed. From the fleeting glimpse she'd had of him, it appeared he had not aged in any way. As the sleet grew heavier, she skidded on the cobbles as she ducked in and out of every café and bar, asking – pleading – if they knew where he was, the man she knew must be somewhere near, whom she desperately needed to find. But the people, though kindly, looked at her askance, discomfited by her sodden state and the madness in her eyes.

'If I were you, I'd go home, my dear, before you catch your death of cold.' The weather was growing dramatically worse. They were mostly closing early.

Frankie, having drawn a blank, wandered aimlessly along the canals, too distraught to absorb the beauty of the unspoilt medieval town. She was soaked right through and frozen to the bone, on top of which it was now growing dark and she had almost no money. She couldn't afford to stay overnight or even buy anything to eat. As it was, she would have to walk back to the station, if only she could remember where it was.

'Come home,' said Magda when Frankie called, still sounding quite demented. 'Let me know once you're on the train and I'll pick you up in Antwerp.'

Her heart went out to her fragile friend who had surely suffered enough without this, though from long experience she knew not to try to stand in her way. When Frankie set her mind on something, she listened to neither reason nor logic and this weird hallucination had clearly unhinged her.

202

'Come home, dearest,' said Magda, more gently, 'and we'll talk things over together.'

'I have to find him. I know what I saw. Please don't keep saying I dreamed it all up.' Wrapped in a blanket beside the fire, with a mug of hot chocolate clasped in both hands, Frankie was slowly thawing out and her teeth had at last stopped chattering. From the kitchen came wonderful cooking smells. They were preparing a pheasant casserole as a treat and had all discreetly left her alone with Magda.

'It's time to give up, love. You know it wasn't him. Don't be so hard on yourself. Chad has been dead for thirty years. After all, you were at the inquest. It isn't healthy to torture yourself in this way.'

But Frankie stubbornly shook her head. In this sort of mood, she refused to listen. Magda could only keep quiet and hope that, after she'd had a good night's sleep, she would get things back into perspective.

28

The flat, Charles argued, was a snip at the price and, when Cassie came to see it, she had to agree. Queen Anne style in ornate red brick, built in the 1880s, 'Pont Street Dutch' as Osbert Lancaster dubbed it. The owners, a diplomat and his wife, were moving permanently to Hong Kong and keen to make a swift sale. It was roomy and comfortable, though their décor was drab and would need some sprucing up. But Cassie liked the size of the reception rooms which would mean that Charles could entertain in style; also the fact that, with four bedrooms, each of the children would have claim to their own space. Not that Daisy and Tim would ever use it, but it might make a nice London pad for Rose, now articled to a solicitor in Penzance.

For years Charles had angled for a base in town but, since it was Cassie's money they were spending, she naturally got to have the final say. Aidan, at eight, was becoming a handful but would shortly be going to prep school in Knightsbridge so the Pont Street flat would be just the thing since Cassie considered him far too young to be boarding. The Elwes males always went to Eton so his name had been down for Sussex House before he could even crawl.

It would mean a bit of a sacrifice for her, having to forsake her beloved Cornwall for eight weeks at a stretch, three times a year. The grandchildren occupied much of her time but now it was natural for her son to take precedence. She would put her energies into the flat and act as a full-time wife for once. She felt guilty at having neglected Charles so much.

'At last we can do some proper entertaining. I look forward to meeting your London friends.' For the past few years Charles had travelled so much, he only ever got home at weekends and even then on a very sporadic basis. When not off visiting wealthy clients, he stayed in a hotel. He liked his work as a private dealer, which now took up most of his energy. Life as a country squire was all right but wheeling and dealing more his style. The light of challenge shone bright in his eyes whenever he felt he had pulled off a coup; he certainly seemed to have found his natural niche. Cassie often wondered where he had got his flair and taste.

Much of it, of course, he'd absorbed from her, though Cassie would never acknowledge that. Moderation in all things was her creed; the Cornish house and, later, the flat were models of studied understatement.

Daisy's children, Willow and Sam, were miniatures of their mother. With their huge brown eyes and angelic smiles they were good enough to eat, Cassie said. She could not have too much of them, was always content to babysit and get to play the role of doting granny. Since they lived only five minutes away, Daisy often dropped them at her mother's house where Willow kept her Shetland pony. Charles was teaching her to ride.

'He looks good in the saddle. I'll grant him that.' Sybil still viewed him with slight mistrust, though she liked the way he dealt with her brother's grandchildren. She and Tremayne were leaning on the gate, watching Charles, sleek in breeches and boots, putting Edwin's hunter through its paces. Whatever his antecedents might be, he had taken to riding like a real pro. Willow, enraptured, clapped her hands and begged to be hoisted up into the saddle and Charles, with his usual good humour, cheerfully obliged. Sam, the baby, gurgled with joy and stretched out his arms towards the horse. In a couple of years he'd be up in that saddle himself.

'We still don't know where he came from,' said Sybil. 'His past continues to be a closed book which he seems reluctant to open.'

Tremayne, still harbouring a grudge against Charles, viewed him through deeply cynical eyes. 'Superficially he's just too perfect.' He was jealous of the man's charisma. It seemed he had every woman in his hand. Even Sybil now, which really unnerved him.

'I'd like to know what he's up to,' he said, 'in all the time he is not at home, leaving poor Cassie here on her own. It isn't right.'

'Hardly on her own,' said Sybil, 'with so much family around her.' She shot him a shrewd incisive glance. 'I hope you're not suggesting he plays away.'

Not that it hadn't occurred to her too. He was ten years younger than his wife and oozed sex appeal. He would have to be pretty much of a saint not to give in to temptation at times and saintliness wasn't something that sat well with Charles.

'What precisely do we know about him? He must have some sort of a past.' He'd been twenty-four when he'd married Cassie. What had he done with his life before that? It certainly seemed, to Tremayne's jaundiced eye, that a lot had never been explained.

'I'm not exactly sure,' said Sybil. 'I believe his parents lived abroad. They were always travelling, according to Cassie, and the poor boy was sent home to boarding school at far too early an age.' One reason Aidan was going to a day school, so that his mother was there when he came home. She would be on hand to help with his prep and generally make a fuss of him. Both her daughters were now off her hands; in her heart she hated the thought of losing Aidan too.

'He is going to have to board at Eton.'

'But by then he will be thirteen.'

'Still too young, if you want my opinion.' Tremayne had never left this part of Cornwall, except for his two years' National Service, and still showed no signs of restlessness or any desire to move on.

'Cassie's father and brothers all went there. It's an Elwes family tradition.' Her own brother, Edwin, had

207

been privately tutored because of his dicky heart, which had clouded his life.

'So what was Charles doing,' Tremayne persisted, 'in the years between school and marriage? Did he go to varsity – he seems the type who would?' But even that they had to take on trust.

Sybil admitted she didn't know. She had tried asking Cassie who was equally vague. They had met not long after Edwin's death and fallen for each other on the spot. It was something Cassie rarely mentioned, at least to her former husband's sister, though there was no disguising the light in her eye whenever Charles entered a room. Without doubt it had been a genuine love match; Sybil had no problem with that. The only emotion she secretly felt was envy.

But what *was* known about the man? Tremayne continued to chew on that as he went about his daily duties, running the Hawksmoor estate. Charles Buchanan was a very smooth talker whose appealing smile and extreme good looks had an effect on everyone who met him. Not only the women, the men as well, which was what most troubled Tremayne. He had watched Richard Elwes, Cassie's brother, usually very much down to earth, pay serious attention to what Charles was saying, as if he had any knowledge at all of running a country estate. You really don't like him, he had to admit, confronting himself in the shaving mirror. But he also acknowledged that whatever it was went deeper than simple jealousy. His main concern was Edwin's legacy and safeguarding the family's interests.

*   *   *

Pont Street would be ready for occupation a month before the start of the autumn term, which put Cassie under considerable pressure to get things shipshape before they could move in. Charles, as always, was whirling around, buying pictures and delivering them to clients. Since he spent so much of his time on the road, he had lately invested in a fancy car, a Bentley convertible with ample room to stack paintings in the boot. Also it made the right impression on his clients. He had turned a hobby into a prosperous sideline and now found artworks for private collectors whose specialist interests he knew. The galleries well acquainted with him allowed him to have the pictures on loan and then cold call on appropriate clients, where he usually pulled off deals. He was endlessly popping over to Jersey where some of the biggest collectors were based and, as his social circles increased, so did his reputation. These days what he principally did were total renovations.

'By rights,' chuckled Cassie, as she showed him cloth samples, 'it's you who ought to be doing up the flat.'

'I don't have the time,' said Charles disarmingly. 'Besides, you couldn't afford me.'

The first thing she did, once the diplomat left, was have the living room walls repainted a lovely luminous antique white in place of the dowdy dark green. That, with diaphanous ivory curtains, totally transformed the room and made it seem a lot larger. Next on the list was Aidan's bedroom which she decorated to his specifications and turned into a cave-like schoolboy den. With his football pennants and personal computer, it was soon the image of the one at home, with a spare bunk bed so a schoolfriend could sleep over.

Although Cassie missed the Cornish routine and the daily visits of Daisy's children, for all sorts of reasons she'd felt it important that Aidan get right away. Though normally equably tempered, like his father, there were times when his behaviour had begun to alarm her. At first his nose had been put out of joint by the arrival, in quick succession, of Daisy's children, just eighteen months apart. When Willow was born he'd shown no curiosity but acted as though she were just a toy that failed to hold his attention very long. Once, though, Cassie had caught him by her crib, pulling the covers up over her head then down again in order to shout in her face. He was playing peek-a-boo, he explained, but Cassie suspected him of darker motives. She never mentioned the episode to Daisy or left him alone with either baby again.

Aidan was six then; now he was eight and Daisy had caught him undressing Willow in order, he said when she screamed at him, just to look. Cassie had defended him: he was just a growing boy displaying a healthy interest in living things. But, from then on, she kept them apart and was relieved when they took him at Sussex House. She still shuddered to remember the incident of the frogs.

* * *

210

With new connections through the school and the growing momentum of her husband's career, life developed a frantic pace to which Cassie was not accustomed. Her Cornish existence was very sedate, especially now that both girls had left home and Charles spent most of his time away. Her idea of a perfect night in was kitchen leftovers from the fridge, and perhaps a concert on Radio 3 while she read by the fire. She had lost the habit of trivial small talk, not that she'd ever excelled at it, and privately felt that the other mothers, all considerably younger than her, were uniformly lightweight. During term-time the invitations flowed in and she couldn't use Aidan as an excuse, since all the other parents were in the same boat. Most had nannies or else didn't work and all had space for a child to sleep over which here, in fashionable Knightsbridge, was much encouraged. Cassie's feeble protests about doing his homework fell upon deaf ears. The boys were bright, their futures assured, so let them play and make social contacts before they had to knuckle down for the tough stuff.

Charles was as bad as the other parents. 'He's only a kid,' he said. 'Wait until he moves on to Eton. That's when he'll really have to sharpen his act.'

It was at the opera house one night that they ran into Millicent Ferneyhough. An insipid-looking woman in, perhaps, her mid-thirties, she stood alone in a corner of the Crush Bar, nervously sipping a lemonade and looking uncomfortable and lost. Her mousy hair was pulled tightly back and anchored with an Alice band, a style too young for a woman her age that didn't do anything for her. Cassie became aware of her first, feeling herself being watched, and glanced around to see whose eyes were on her. Not on her, it turned out, but on Charles; the woman looked as if she were seeing a ghost. The wife of an out-of-town client, no doubt, though she lacked any visible style.

'It seems as if that woman knows you,' she said, nudging Charles, who was casing the room. 'Perhaps you should go over and say hello.' Though leave me out of it, she nearly added. She saw so little of Charles, as it was, the last thing they needed tonight was a hanger-on.

Charles glanced over then grimaced and shrugged. 'Never seen her before in my life,' he said.

He carried their glasses back to the bar, leaving Cassie alone and undefended, still uncomfortably aware of the woman's stare. When she looked again, the stranger was advancing with a very determined look.

'Excuse me,' said the woman, 'but the man you are with. Do you mind if I ask who he is?'

'My husband,' said Cassie with a sinking heart. Exactly what she dreaded was happening again. This insignificant country mouse was about to attach herself to them when company was the last thing they needed. She wished people would learn to leave him alone. Especially on a rare evening like this when, for once, she had him to herself.

'And his name . . . ?'

'Why do you want to know?' Cassie was suddenly

212

on her guard. Drawing herself up to her full five foot ten, she locked eyes with the smaller woman.

At that moment Charles returned, bearing two more flutes of champagne, whereupon the stranger switched her attention to him.

'It's Millie,' she squeaked, almost spilling his drink as she frenziedly grabbed at his sleeve. Handing both glasses to Cassie to hold, he carefully blotted the moisture.

'Charles Buchanan,' he said, offering his hand, 'and this is my wife, Cassandra. I don't believe I have had the pleasure . . .' Already his attention had drifted off; he was looking around again.

'But,' said the woman, clearly confused, 'you look so much like him. I thought . . .'

'Excuse me,' said Charles, relieving Cassie of his glass, 'but there's someone over there I need to talk to.'

He vanished back into the tightly pressed crowd, leaving Cassie alone with the stricken woman, who now seemed extremely distressed. Her hand shook and her face was pale, with two bright spots of colour on her cheeks.

'Are you all right?' asked Cassie, concerned, offering a steadying hand. 'Let's sit down and I'll fetch you some water. It's pretty stifling in here.'

Millie feverishly flapped her hands and shook her head in embarrassment. She had made a mistake and now felt a fool; words appeared to have failed her. It was rude of Charles to have been so abrupt and Cassie was far too kind to abandon her too. She spotted an empty table in the corner to which she carefully propelled her. The least she could do was stay and chat until the woman was less distressed. But never again, she silently vowed, would she let Charles get away with such gross behaviour.

The five minute bell rang and Charles was no longer in sight. He was out there somewhere, working the room, and would, presumably, come back to claim her in time for the final bell. Millie's high colour was slowly subsiding as she sank back into her mouse-like state, in her drab brown silk and old-fashioned tippet and, Cassie now noticed, truly dreadful shoes.

'Who, might I ask, did you think he was?' she began, but at that moment a man hurried up, muttering something about the impossible traffic. He nodded to Cassie and took Millie's arm; she was clearly more cherished than it had at first seemed. This portly man with the florid complexion appeared to be very possessive.

'I have to know,' repeated Cassie before they walked away. 'Who was it that you thought he was?'

Millie turned and smiled at her, safe now and almost coquettish. 'Oh, no one special. Just someone from my past.' Cassie could swear that she almost smirked. 'Cosmo Banbury, my first husband. Haven't seen him in yonks.'

'Right,' said Cassie, once they were home and Charles was pouring himself a whisky. 'Who was that woman and where does she fit in? It was obvious that she knew you.'

'She's the Countess of Rochester and that was her

214

husband.' He dropped an ice cube into the glass before slumping into his favourite chair.

'So you did know her after all,' said Cassie sharply.

Charles merely grinned and slowly savoured his drink. 'You are looking very fetching tonight,' he said. 'Once I've knocked this back, let's get off to bed. I have to make an early start in the morning.'

'Enough!' said Cassie, suddenly furious. 'Kindly stick to the point. Why did she think that you might have been her husband? And who is Cosmo whatever-it-was? I've never heard him mentioned before. What was she on about?'

He shrugged then flashed her that roguish grin that worked every time with the ladies. 'Who knows?' he said. 'She was clearly deluded. I met her once at a debutante ball the night she came out, simply aeons ago.'

'And?'

'And nothing. As I recall, we had a brief fling and then ran away. And, yes, since you ask, we may have got hitched but only as part of a drunken lark and under other names. Her daddy made certain that things went no further, you can bet your life on that. The fellow was loaded.'

Cassie's anger had turned to suspicion. 'And are you still married?' she asked.

'To her? Don't be daft. You're the only wife I've got and, furthermore, the only one I want.' He blew her a kiss, which she disregarded, and hauled himself to his feet. 'I'll tell you the rest in the morning,' he said. 'Right now I'm bushed and really must turn in.'

*　　*　　*

On the whole, though, Charles was a satisfactory husband. Cassie had few complaints. He was fun, he was sexy and, when he was around, still treated her like a princess. He might, on occasion, be careless with the truth and she'd learnt to take what he said with a strong pinch of salt. She had had one husband who was honest to the core but Charles, she had to admit, was a lot more fun.

She settled into the new regime, the week during term-time in the Pont Street flat, driving to Cornwall every Friday, returning Sunday night. It meant a great deal of driving for her but it was important that Aidan should have his mother around. She put much of her energy into doing up the flat and was more than pleased with the result. Instead of her solitary walks with the dogs, now being exercised by Tremayne, she bustled around the backwaters of Chelsea, picking up bargains like a magpie. Charles, who erred on the flamboyant side, was impressed by how little she spent.

'If every client was as thrifty as you, I'd go out of business,' he said.

When Aidan was eleven and apparently doing well, Charles and Cassie were summoned to the school to discuss, the headmaster said, a serious matter. His face was grave when he greeted them and he instantly came to the point. The boy stood accused of petty bullying; two sets of parents had complained. His behaviour in general was getting out of hand. He was becoming a subversive influence and needed to be controlled.

'What absolute tosh,' said Charles, quick to rise. 'The kid is only eleven. He is simply being high-spirited. At his age, I was the same.'

'He's been threatening them and stealing their sweets. On one occasion, he blacked a boy's eye. A younger boy, I might add.'

'Playground scrapping is par for the course. Self-defence is a necessary skill in order to survive.'

Cassie placed a restraining hand on his arm, but Charles impatiently shrugged it off. His volatile temper was quickly aroused when his son was criticised.

'I don't think you quite understand,' said the head, his manner increasingly frosty. 'Unless Aidan learns to behave, he will be suspended.'

'Keep your fucking school,' cried Charles, leaping to his feet. 'I'll be damned if I let him grow up a sissy. I'm removing him forthwith.'

'Now what will we do?' asked Cassie as the three drove home in muted silence. She saw her son's outrageous behaviour reflected in his father.

'No problem,' said Charles, his good humour restored. He always thrived on a fight. 'All we need now is to get him into a crammer.'

29

There seemed no point in returning to Bruges while the weather was still this bad. Magda suggested that Frankie try surfing the net.

'What exactly am I looking for?' asked Frankie, who had zero computer skills. It might help occupy her mind, thought Magda, and stop her falling apart.

'Anything at all remotely connected. You'll be surprised at what you find. It's simply a question of working out how to locate things. Start with Google.'

Under Magda's direction, Frankie typed in Chad's name then waited apprehensively to see what, if anything, emerged. And when, within seconds, his name popped up, she gasped in disbelief. There were several references, from two separate sources – the *Middlesbrough Evening Gazette* and the *Daily Mail*. With trembling fingers, she brought up each one in turn.

The *Gazette*'s report was from 1975 with details of the fatal fire. It included a grainy picture of Chad from the centre's personnel files. The headline was 'Death by Misadventure' and Frankie's name wasn't mentioned at all. The *Daily Mail* had covered the inquest and, later, Frankie's arrest and trial. Overwhelmed, she began to sob and Magda put her arm around her.

'Are you sure you want to continue?' she asked, alarmed at how fragile Frankie was.

'Yes,' said Frankie, 'I have to know.' There could be no turning back.

There was an earlier item from the *Daily Mail*, about Chad's knifing of the bully, for which he had been sent down.

'That's what he was in for,' said Frankie. 'Murder.' He had looked angelic but was ruthless underneath; after all these years, she acknowledged that, though it hadn't stopped her loving him at the time. It was not his fault. He'd had a tough beginning, with no one to give him unconditional love. Even his temporary foster parents had turned their backs at the first sign of trouble and returned him to the institution to rot. Small wonder he'd later gone on to kill. He had never really stood a chance.

'He certainly led an eventful life,' said Magda, 'in such a short space of time. I wonder how he'd have turned out had he survived.'

'He did survive. I know that now.' Frankie practically bit off her head. 'It was him on that train; I am certain of it. Or, if not him,' she added defiantly, 'someone who looked just like him.'

Magda attempted to hug her again but Frankie shook her off. Instead of consoling, she wanted a result. They had come this far on the internet, there might be other stuff there if they dug around.

'Could it have been a close relative, a brother or cousin, something like that? Shall we look up other Barnabys?' There must be a logical explanation or else Frankie was going bonkers.

'The name wasn't real; they made it up. The gardener's boy discovered him so the vicar named him for the boy and the church. They do that with foundlings.'

'But everyone comes from somewhere,' said Magda. 'He must have had parents once. Think.' Though she disapproved of this crazy obsession, she could never resist a puzzle.

For most of the morning they tossed it around instead of doing their scheduled chores. It was far too wet for working outside but Magda had the accounts to get through and Frankie was hogging the computer.

'Make a list,' Magda said to her, 'of anyone ever close to him. There must have been someone before you came on the scene.'

Frankie stared blankly then shook her head. 'Nobody I know of,' she said. 'At the time I met him, he hadn't a friend in the world.'

'Barnaby, the gardener's boy? What do we know about him? Put him on the list as well as the vicar. Have we any idea where St Chad's church was? Yorkshire, I think you said.'

'That's all I know. I'm not good at this. We simply never discussed that sort of thing.' She remembered most the passionate sex but refrained from mentioning that. There were certain areas still out of bounds between them.

Magda made a pot of coffee to help them focus their minds. 'After they found him, where was he sent?'

'Barnardo's.' She did remember that. Though not which branch of the home it was, presumably the one nearest to the church. With a sudden surge of renewed energy, Frankie put that on the list.

'And then what happened? At what point was he fostered?'

'Round about seven, I think he said. By a well-heeled family with a fancy name. One of those poncey ones that sounds made up.'

Magda waited, her pencil poised, but Frankie's memory failed her. 'I know they were pretty mean to him. With luck, it will come to me later.' She added it to the list and went on thinking. The tears had gone and her eyes now shone. Magda certainly seemed to know her stuff.

'In what way were they mean to him?' she asked, as she poured more coffee.

'They sent him off to public school. Then, when he stepped slightly out of line, took him away and returned him to the home.'

'Do you know when?'

'I could work it out.'

'And which was the school?'

'I think Repton.'

Frankie's cheeks had begun to glow as her optimism came flooding back. At last she felt they were starting to get somewhere.

'What was the terrible thing he did,' asked Magda, 'to deserve such a drastic punishment?' The way people behaved sometimes made her feel sick. To send a child to a privileged school, then turn their backs on him for bad behaviour. It was like returning a rescue puppy because it messed on the rug.

'Smoking in the playground,' said Frankie, remembering Chad had made a joke of it.

'That's all?'

'It was dope.'

Which did make a difference. 'And after that?' Magda asked.

'Borstal,' said Frankie. After he'd killed that boy.

Not exactly a saint, thought Magda, but who could blame him, with a background like that? If a child went wrong at an early age, it was often hard to go straight.

'Can you think of anything else?' she asked.

Frankie shook her head. 'That brings us up to when we met. From that point on we spent our time together.'

Magda woke in the middle of the night with Frankie shaking her pillow.

'Tewson-Finch! It just came to me. I told you it was a poncey name. Chad always used to laugh about it, reckoned he was lucky they didn't adopt him.'

'Stick that on the list,' said Magda, only partly awake. That should be enough, at least, to make a start.

30

Life for Jenny could not have been better. The Coot and Hern was doing really well and she dearly loved her new role as chef, though found it sapped her energy, the more so because she was also still acting as manager. She had never worked harder in her life which, after Condé Nast, was saying something, but this work was more on the physical side, leaving her healthily tired and able to sleep. Even Toby had quietened down and rarely interrupted her nights any more. Her daily routine was orchestrated to move as precisely as clockwork. Up at 6.30 to feed the child, then a brisk hour's run in the neighbouring fields while Hamish, the resident barman, acted as nanny. Back by 8.30 to be ready for the drayman and then to walk Toby to his school nearby before returning to the pub to make order out of chaos. Mrs Jones, the cleaner, was in every morning but Jenny took charge of the grate; swept out the ashes from the night before and carried in logs from the outhouse. The fire was a pivotal point of the bar; it had to be properly tended. Hamish was there to lend a hand but most of his mornings were spent with his books. With Jenny's encouragement, he was working part-time for a catering diploma.

'I never thought I could be this happy,' said Jenny to Vanessa as they made tomato chutney. 'I seem to have everything on my plate: my son, the pub and now Clive.'

Vanessa, who was slim and fair, smiled as she scalded preserving jars. 'Where is he, by the way?' she asked. 'I don't think I've seen him in weeks.'

'Working extra long hours, poor love. Sales conference followed by recruitment drive. They really make them slave at Osborne and Cole.'

'But he still enjoys it?'

'Loves it,' she said. 'And he's building his own consultancy on the side.'

'Which means?'

'He couldn't be happier either,' said Jenny, with new-found confidence.

'Has he got plans to quit?' asked Vanessa, whose expertise was interior design and who lived, these days, entirely off freelance work. She had finally given up on marriage, though she always kept a boyfriend around to share the bills, which made sense.

'I think so,' said Jenny. 'Though I'm not entirely sure. These days there's never enough time to talk.' What they mainly discussed, when they did get together, were farmers' markets and seasonal dishes and the past month's profits. They had taken a gamble but one that paid off. By carefully sticking to a limited menu, they were making their stamp on the local community, as well as pulling in diners from further afield. Joyce was still content with her role of sous-chef, preparing vegetables, making sauces and keeping a simmering stockpot on the go. The team was effective: two in the kitchen, Hamish and Simon behind the bar and two girls from the village who came in part-time to lend a hand. On alternate Thursdays, when Clive was there too, acting host from behind the bar, they now had the highest turnout of the week.

'I miss him a lot when he's not around. I wish he had fewer commitments.' Even after two years together, Jenny was still starry-eyed about Clive and Toby lived for the alternate Thursdays when he swept back into their lives.

But she couldn't grumble. It beat churning out articles and meant doing something she really enjoyed, while living a healthy and productive life. As well as making money. The kitchen door stayed open on all but the very coldest of days, and the fragrant smells of the verdant garden mingled with those of the cooking. Whenever she felt like taking a break she would stroll across to the waterwheel, lean on the railing and watch the brook chattering below.

'Do you ever think about Douglas these days?' Vanessa, who remembered the worst of all that, occasionally checked it out.

'Not any more.' Jenny shook her head. She was prettier, lither, somehow younger too and her brown eyes sparkled with vigour. Despite the amount of cooking she did, forever tasting and adjusting flavours and trying out recipes on family and staff, she still didn't gain any weight. She was proud of the fact she was still a size eight, though she did run five miles every day. 'That part of my life seems so long ago. To think, I wasted six years on him.' And his son, who had never even met him, would soon be five.

'It's odd he doesn't seem to want to see the baby.' Vanessa, whose children came first, above everything, had never been able to understand that. Though she'd never liked Douglas.

'That was the deal. The baby or him. He made that clear when I told him about it, though I never believed he would carry things through to this extent.' It was just as well he had, however. If he'd stayed in touch, it would have complicated things. Though she hadn't known that in those months of bleak despair.

'Does Toby ever ask about him?'

'He doesn't even know he exists.' Clive was the father figure in her son's life, which added to Jenny's quiet contentment. Two years of his unfailing support had made a huge difference to her morale. Never in her life had she felt more secure.

Most of her energies went into the pub. Their reputation was growing fast so that practically every night they had a full house. The brewery was pleased and her debt much reduced. If things kept up at this rate and they were careful with their spending, she hoped soon to be able to pay it off in full.

It was Clive's idea to have matchbooks printed, giving details of the pub and where it was, which he promised to hand out to his business contacts.

'Advertising never hurts,' he said. 'If you leave a supply of them on the bar, it will help spread the word and increase your clientele.'

She occasionally asked him about the sleeping partner, the golfing acquaintance who'd provided the loan. He had never been over to look at the place nor, as far as she was aware, even asked to see the accounts, which seemed unusual.

'Isn't he, at the very least, curious to see it?' she asked. In a way, she felt slightly snubbed. She had worked so hard to get things right. She couldn't believe he was so detached, unless he was very rich indeed, which was not something Clive had implied.

'Don't worry about it. He's just very busy. Has loads of other irons in the fire. I am sure he will come by when he's good and ready.' Clive was always so re-assuring and, after all, the man was his friend. She knew he was right: there was no point in fretting when apparently nothing was wrong.

'I don't even know his name,' she said. 'I'd like the chance to thank him.' Without the loan, she couldn't have done it. The least she owed him was a meal some time or even a Christmas card.

'It's not important. I really mean that. You have more urgent things to occupy your mind.' He firmly shooed her back to the kitchen while he popped upstairs to settle Toby and check that the television wasn't still on. It was only much later, after Clive had left, that Jenny remembered he still hadn't told her the name of her mysterious benefactor.

*   *   *

On Mondays she drove round the local suppliers, sourcing produce for the week ahead and planning her menus according to what was in season. They were a nice community, the smallholders around Bath, doing something they really believed in and trying to stay afloat in a tightening economy. On every level Jenny sided with them: the food was fresher and tasted much better than the big suppliers' and she sympathised with their aims. The supermarkets were killing them off; they needed solidarity to win through. She tasted cheeses and home-cured hams, watched them bottling pickles and lemon curd and bought jars of fresh honey for cooking and the overnight guests. Much of what she bought was organically grown, except in cases where she suspected too much hype and went instead for the outward appearance of the vegetables.

Each morning she spoke to her suppliers and put in orders for the day, a lot of her choices depending on the weather. If the seas were choppy, the fish wasn't fresh, and when the weather was hot people's appetites changed. It all became obvious once she had worked it out.

'How come you know so much?' asked the bar staff.

'Just natural talent,' said Jenny cheerfully, not bothering to tell them that, for all those years, she'd had her own culinary column in a major magazine. Then she had started to find it a drag; now everything she had learnt was emerging and serving a useful purpose. Nothing in life is ever wasted after all.

She liked the community and, as she got to know them, more of them came crowding into the bar. One of them, Alistair, dropped in most nights, still in waxed jacket and muddy boots, bringing her samples of leeks and beets and the wonderful cabbages he grew. Originally he had been an accountant but had packed it all in when his marriage fell apart. Now he tended a couple of acres and was building a whole new life for himself with an optimism that equalled Jenny's own.

'He's nice, that fellow,' said Joyce with approval. 'He lives in that lovely stone cottage down Newbridge way. I knew his mother from the WI until she passed on, poor soul. Now I believe he lives there all on his own.'

'Now, now, Joyce,' called Vanessa from the pantry, where she was checking stock and making lists. She loved the activity at the Coot and Hern and was down there, helping out, whenever she could. 'Don't start trying to matchmake, please. You know it never works.' Though privately she agreed with Joyce. Alistair Grey was a lovely guy, funny, nice-looking and obviously bright, and about the right age for Jenny. She knew enough from experience, though, not to start trying to sell him to Jenny. She never really listened to advice: where men were concerned, she was oddly naïve and resolutely blinkered.

The other locals were a colourful crowd, some of them straight out of central casting. A group of old men who played darts every night and sat and grumbled about the weather; four elderly ladies who gossiped in a corner, and a mixture of the local youth. Even the vicar was a regular patron who liked his gin and tonic at opening time. It helped him to do the

Lord's work, he explained, before he started his evening rounds. He often came back for a second when he was through.

Since the Coot and Hern had been serving food, the clientele had upgraded. People came now who had never been regulars, drawn by the ratings and word of mouth, and found the cooking so good that they came again. And, more to the point, brought their London friends. Jenny's celebrity was growing fast. Practically every night they were fully booked. Something was certainly going right; Clive's match-books were proving effective.

'We don't want too many or the standards will drop,' she occasionally told Vanessa.

That was the beauty of the place, not so large it could fit in a crowd but with sufficient covers to make a good profit. Sophisticated in an understated way, it retained a lot of its original charm with the beams, the woodsmoke, the crooked doors that had been that way for centuries. When people went upstairs, you could hear the boards creak.

Sex with Clive remained thrilling and intense. The gaps between their reunions kept it hot. With Douglas it had to be done on the sly for, somewhere in the background, a wife was watching. With Clive, though, things were entirely different. He was there as often as he possibly could be and the sheer anticipation was worth the wait. And, in between, he was always on the phone. They spoke, on average, several times a day which meant the excitement of it never wore off.

'I feel like seventeen again,' Jenny reported to Vanessa. 'What with the regular leg-wax, pedicure, the lot.'

Vanessa laughed. 'I envy you,' she said. After a while, even in the steadiest relationship, romance was inclined to pall. Jenny was looking her absolute best which, considering her strenuous workload, was a real achievement. 'Clive is obviously good for you. Has he said anything yet about settling down?'

'No,' said Jenny, 'though I must confess I would quite like another child. Toby will soon be five. He could do with a sibling.' At thirty-six, she was starting to cut things fine. Clive, who was considerably older, still showed no signs of committing himself. Vanessa was puzzled; it didn't entirely add up. When he was there, he appeared besotted; all the pub's regulars could vouch for that. His charm and devotion were frequently remarked on. 'Make an honest man of him,' they all said.

'Just how old is he?' asked Vanessa. Whatever the answer, he looked pretty good. Surely he must be having similar thoughts.

'I don't know for certain,' Jenny confessed. 'It isn't something we've ever had reason to discuss.' After the trauma she had been through with Douglas, she was frankly scared of putting pressure on Clive. Was content with the status quo without rocking the boat. Though his absences were becoming more frequent, a fact that secretly worried Vanessa. There came a point when the music stopped and the seesaw went either up or down. She couldn't bear to see Jenny hurt again.

'Why not throw a surprise party for him? When's his birthday?' she asked. It could do no harm to make some sort of statement, help him to make up his mind. All he needed, if Jenny was right, was an appropriate nudge. Otherwise Jenny might just as well call it a day.

Jenny, however, remained unconvinced. What could she lose? Vanessa asked. The answer was: the lot, if she got it wrong.

Alistair Grey, who was in most nights, eventually raised the courage to ask her out. The Young Farmers were having their annual June bash, to tie in with the summer solstice, and he wondered if Jenny would like to come as his date.

'Sorry,' she said, without even checking. 'But my boyfriend is usually here at weekends. Perhaps we could fit something else in during the week.'

Fool, thought Vanessa, swapping glances with Joyce, but neither presumed to make any comment. Jenny knew her own mind and resented interference. It didn't stop them conferring, however, once she was safely out of earshot.

'I worry about her at times,' said Joyce. 'She spends too much time on her own, just working. At her time of life, she ought to be having more fun.'

'I couldn't agree with you more,' said Vanessa, relieved to know she had an ally. 'Clive's okay but he isn't here enough. She is letting her youth pass her by.'

Joyce was very much of the same mind and still

favoured Alistair Grey. Having known his mother and seen where he lived, she felt he would make a perfect partner for Jenny, who ought to snap him up before she missed the boat.

The weekend of the Young Farmers' Ball approached and Clive called, late on the Wednesday night, to say he wouldn't be there that weekend; he had to be somewhere else on a business call.

'Where?' asked Jenny, suddenly annoyed. Other things lately always took precedence over her.

'I am sorry, my darling. I hate to let you down but our global president will be in town and wants to meet all the salesmen on Saturday night.'

Saturday was the night of the ball; it was too late now to let Alistair know. She tried not to let him hear her irritation. 'And you can't get out of it?' It reminded her of Douglas; she knew what he would say before he spoke.

'Absolutely not, my sweet. More than my job is worth. I will try to call if I get the chance. I'm as disappointed as you are.'

'So I'll have to wait another whole week,' she said, blinking back sudden angry tears. 'I was hoping to spend some quality time with you.'

She knew immediately, from his silence, that she wasn't going to like what was coming next. She heard him flick through the pages of his diary and hesitate before he broke the news. 'Next week I'm on my cricket tour. This year we've been invited to Corfu. Surely I told you that?'

'You didn't, no.' She was suddenly mad. He had

started to take her too much for granted. In the early days he'd been here without fail, every other Thursday night, on his way through to visit his West Country clients. Apart from anything else, it wasn't fair on Toby, who had learnt to look forward to his regular visits almost as eagerly as she did. But, rather than having it out with him, which was what she knew she ought to do, she simply muttered something abrupt and rang off.

They knew her well enough now to sense her moods, the loyal regulars in the bar, who were used to her greeting them with a smile on her face.

'What's up with you, girl? Cat got your tongue?' Mrs Dawkings, a lunchtime regular, never pulled her punches. She said whatever was in her mind, usually with an expression of stone, though Jenny had learnt that her bark was far worse than her bite. She sat in the corner with three of her friends, all widows who'd lived there most of their lives and liked to discuss the goings-on in the village.

'Sorry,' said Jenny, handing them menus, though they knew the contents off by heart. 'I'm a bit rushed off my feet today. There's a crisis in the kitchen.'

'What's happened to that man of yours?' There was no fooling Mrs Dawkings. 'I haven't seen him for a week or more. I hope there hasn't been a falling out.'

'No,' said Jenny, managing a smile though inside she felt like snarling. 'He's off playing cricket with his friends. It's a regular fixture every year. This time they've gone to Corfu for a week, lucky sods.'

'Corfu without you? That's disgraceful,' they said, the four of them shaking their heads. 'You should have gone too and spent some time in the sun. You work far too hard as it is.'

'I couldn't leave the pub,' said Jenny. 'Someone has to do the cooking and at this time of year, as you know, we are always busy.' The bar was filling up with tourists; it was still only just after twelve. By one she would have people waiting to be seated.

'Still, it's a shame,' said Mrs Dawkings. 'A pretty girl like you. Serve him right if you found someone else while he's gone.'

'Though he's awfully charming,' she heard them say as she hurried back to the kitchen. They all adored Clive; he had them eating from his hand. They just couldn't understand why he didn't pop the question.

And neither could she. She banished the thought and turned up the heat to sear the scallops. Joyce had already made the pea purée to go with them. Working this hard was sometimes a bind. Without her full-time commitment to the place, Clive might, indeed, have invited her to go too. But then, of course, she couldn't leave Toby. It was all so complicated. There were times, like this, when she longed to quit and settle down to have another baby.

The telephone rang; it was almost two.

'Get that,' she said as she sliced the duck breasts and poured on the rhubarb sauce. A party of six had arrived unannounced but they'd manage to squeeze them in. Trade was roaring, so she couldn't

235

complain, and it did help to keep her mind off Clive in Corfu.

'It's Vanessa,' said Joyce. 'Shall I tell her to call back?'

'Please,' said Jenny, preoccupied. This last bit was the trickiest part. She had to get it just right.

'She needs to talk to you right away,' said Joyce. 'She says to tell you it's urgent.'

'Blast!' said Jenny. 'She'll just have to wait. Tell her I'll be there in a tick.'

When at last she got to the phone, Vanessa sounded terribly hyped up. 'Are you watching the tennis?' she wanted to know and when Jenny said no: 'Switch it on.'

'Why?' asked Jenny, exasperated. Not in the middle of lunch, for heaven's sake. But it wasn't like Vanessa to interrupt without a very good reason.

'It's Wimbledon. I've just seen Clive. He's sitting front row, Centre Court.'

Jenny, abandoning Joyce to finish up, fled to the bar and switched on the set, regardless of the few drinkers still sitting there. She watched and waited and raked the crowd but none of the close-ups revealed his face so, in frustration, she switched the thing off and hurried back to the phone.

'You must be mistaken. He's in Corfu, playing cricket with the boys.'

'It was him. I swear it. They showed him up close. Relaxed and smiling like he always is, looking unusually spruced up.'

Jenny went silent. Then: 'Who was he with?' She couldn't believe this was happening.

Vanessa paused. This was hard to say but she knew it was important that she didn't chicken out at this stage. 'A woman,' she said. 'Much younger than him. Pretty and blonde and well dressed.' Looking quite radiant, she could have added, though she didn't out of deference to Jenny's feelings. She had thought very hard about phoning at all but felt she had the right to know. Since he'd said he was off playing cricket with the boys, he deserved to be caught out. On prime-time television, too, for the whole of the world to see.

Jenny's head was reeling; she couldn't take it in. Could she have got the dates wrong? Had the cricket tour not started yet? Pride came to her rescue.

'It'll be a business thing,' she said casually. 'The global president was over last week; Clive's probably entertaining a visiting VIP.' Though she knew from Vanessa's voice that it wasn't the case.

'There is one thing more you ought to know,' she said in a gentler voice. 'Neither was paying much attention to the tennis. They were far too absorbed in each other.'

They hadn't heard of him, of course, when she telephoned Osborne and Cole. No one of that name had ever worked there. Also, there was no global president. The company had always been solidly British, still owned and run by its two original founders.

'What are you going to do?' asked Vanessa, who'd come speeding over when she heard the news, appalled to have been the cause of so much grief.

'I haven't a clue,' said Jenny in despair. 'All I have is his mobile number. The awful truth is, I don't even know where he lives.'

31

Frankie was frustrated. They were getting nowhere. She decided to go back to Bruges. At last the fan-belt had been repaired so she'd fit it in when she went to the market and take a detour from Mechelen on the way home. The weather was slightly better now, no longer driving sleet, but none the less she put on several layers. She didn't want to tell Magda for fear she might want to come too. And this was something she had to do on her own.

'I might be late back,' was all she said. 'I'll let you know if I'm delayed.'

'Drive carefully,' said Magda calmly. She hadn't known Frankie all these years without figuring out how she ticked.

She shifted the vegetables very fast and drove on to Bruges with an empty truck, arriving early in the afternoon and parking close to the ring road. It wasn't raining but the sky was dark; it might start again at any minute. She headed first for the tourist office because it was so central. This time, however, she didn't intend to go in. She more or less retraced her steps, and when the downpour started, ducked inside a cosy-looking bar she didn't remember seeing before. It was warm and panelled, with a wood-burning stove, and she suddenly realised how hungry she was. She looked around for someone to serve her but the place appeared deserted. Yet the door was open and the lights were on; the clock stood at twenty to three. She decided to wait so pulled up a chair as close to the stove as she could get, then unwound her very long scarf and peeled off her mitts. Moules would be good, she thought, studying the menu, perhaps with some frites on the side. She was feeling flush from the vegetable sale and, although the money was not strictly hers, she knew the others would say she had earned a meal.

Footsteps entered the room from behind her and when she turned, there he stood. A tall, fit man with glossy black hair and the most arresting blue eyes. The one she had glimpsed from the train; there was no mistaking. The shock of seeing him face to face made her positively dizzy; for one awful moment she thought she was going to faint. She closed her eyes and clutched the table but the pounding blood in her ears made her deaf so that when he gently touched her shoulder, she jumped.

'Are you all right? You look ghastly,' he said, going behind the bar to fetch her some water. When he returned, she was shaking so hard she very nearly dropped the glass on the floor.

The voice was his, there could be no doubt, though he showed no sign of recognition. He was like a ghost, unaltered by time, yet his hand, when he'd touched her shoulder, had been flesh and blood.

'Is there anything else you need?' he asked, sincere concern on his face. 'Did you come in here for something to eat?'

Frankie, still stunned and unable to speak, simply gawped at him and nodded. Moules and frites, she tried to say but her voice seemed frozen in her throat so all she could do was point at the bar and a bottle of the house red wine.

'A glass of wine?' Perhaps he thought her mute, but took it all in his stride. He carefully filled a heavy goblet, wiped its stem and brought it across, then asked again if she wanted anything to eat.

This time she managed to croak out the words and watched him react when he realised she was English. From the way she was dressed, in old workman's clothes and boots so worn they were falling apart, he must have taken her for a Flemish peasant. These days she wore no makeup and her hands, without the mitts, were swollen and cracked. She looked a total wreck, she could see it in his eyes, but all vanity had deserted her years before. Yet now she was suddenly face to face with him, self-consciousness swept over her, filling her with unaccountable shame. He hadn't altered, not in any way, but she was totally changed. Worn out and defeated; unmistakably old. In sudden panic, she looked around, seeking somewhere to hide.

'Moules and frites coming up,' he said, wiping her table with his cloth before placing before her a great steaming bowl of mussels. It was years since she'd eaten as much as that, and had now lost all trace of appetite, but she made a valiant effort to pick in order not to offend him. 'More wine?' he asked, proffering the bottle again and she silently allowed him to top up her glass. She very rarely drank at all and it went straight to her head.

'Nasty weather,' he said conversationally, resuming his place behind the bar and polishing a row of newly washed glasses.

'Who are you?' asked Frankie, still deeply in shock, wondering if she was going mad or, at least, in the early stages of dementia.

She saw from the way he looked at her that he'd no idea why she'd asked the question. His gaze was direct and guileless; he didn't know her.

'Me?' he said, taken by surprise. 'My name is Aidan Buchanan.'

All afternoon Frankie sat in that bar in a stupor of mindless shock. Now and again Aidan wandered over, to wipe the table or freshen her drink, and each time stayed on to chat. The bar was empty, he had nothing to do and something about her intrigued him.

'And the name Chad Barnaby rings no bells?' She just couldn't leave it alone.

'Sorry.' Aidan shook his head. She could see from his eyes that he thought her crazed; either that or drunker than she appeared. Yet something about her attracted him. After thirty years of working outdoors,

242

a vestige of her former beauty still lingered. She must have been more than twice his age, pushing fifty would be his guess, yet he found her presence slightly unnerving. His sexual curiosity was aroused. Whatever it was that was driving her lent her a kind of pathos that got to him. Now that her hair was almost dry, it framed her face like a raven's wings, and beneath the shapeless mannish clothes her body was firm and well honed.

'Who are you, Aidan,' she asked again, 'and where are you from? I need to know.'

'Originally Cornwall,' he replied. 'Though my parents now have a place in London.'

'And they are?'

'Charles and Cassandra Buchanan.' His eyes were wary. He was suddenly on his guard. She was asking too many questions for a drunk. So he didn't add that they were divorced or that his father had recently married again.

The bar was slowly beginning to fill as time moved on and the workers came in to escape the relentless rain. Aidan's shift would shortly end so he brought her a final glass of wine and refused to give her a bill. He looked at her as she sat there, slumped, no longer watching, just blankly staring, lost in some desolate hidden despair of her own. A strange, gaunt woman with a secret sorrow. He longed to ask her questions but didn't dare.

'I'm leaving now.' He touched her shoulder, rousing her from her reverie. 'I think it's probably time that you left too.'

Frankie considered then meekly rose and followed him out of the bar.

The night with Aidan was electrifying and released in Frankie a torrent of raw emotion. Despite the quantity of wine she had drunk, she was totally sober and in the grip of an overwhelming passion. When she slowly removed her clothes, he was staggered by her beauty. All the years of punishing work, combined with a very frugal diet, had kept her body in perfect shape with no superfluous fat. Also, she knew what she was about even though she had been celibate for so long. Aidan had never known anything like it, had stepped aboard a rollercoaster that propelled him along at incredible speed and left him gasping for more.

'To hell with who I am,' he panted at last. 'Who in God's name are you?'

She didn't answer; she wanted him again. Their bodies fitted together so well that the next time she hit a high she screamed out, 'Chad!'

'Enough,' said Aidan, mortified at being called by another man's name. He rolled away and lit a cigarette.

'I'm sorry,' said Frankie, leaping from the bed. 'It has all been a terrible mistake.' She rapidly dressed, splashed water on her face, picked up her backpack and moved towards the door. She'd been out of her mind. She was forty-seven while Aidan was still just a kid.

'I'm sorry,' she repeated. 'It was all a mistake. I took you for someone else. I hope you'll forgive me.'

'Wait,' he said, not wanting her to leave. 'You can't just walk out on me like that.' His eyes looked bruised, and he was fighting obvious emotion. Something extremely powerful had happened. And yet she was leaving, without a backward glance. Aidan had never been treated that way. He found he didn't like it.

Frankie turned and looked at him, then smoothed his hair beneath her hands and kissed him full on the mouth.

'Who is this Chad?' He looked ready to fight. She thought a moment then made a decision: she pulled out her locket and showed him the picture inside.

'Christ,' said Aidan, turning pale. 'Where on earth did you get this?' It was like a mirror; he couldn't believe it. He turned to Frankie for an explanation but all she did was shrug.

'The love of my life. He died long ago. I am sorry I had to involve you. But now I think I have managed to lay his ghost.'

'You can't just leave.'

'I have to,' she said. 'I live in a closed commune outside Antwerp and it isn't possible to see you again. I only hope you will find a way to forgive me.'

'Hang on a sec,' he said, thinking fast. 'In case you should ever change your mind.' He scrabbled around in the various pockets of his clothes, still strewn across the floor, then scrawled on the back of a half-used matchbook the number of his mobile.

He stood at the window and watched her leave, tall and gaunt with a kind of dignity; she didn't even turn to wave. He waited until she was out of sight then found his phone and dialled an overseas number.

32

Pippa was not at her optimistic best. She was fretting again about Jack. The nursery school had dropped quite a hint that his behaviour there was not all it should be. There had been a couple of screaming fits which upset the other children. Tom, however, remained quiet and placid; though identical to his brother, a model child.

'Well, they certainly didn't get their temperaments from us. Neither of them,' said Pippa's mother. 'You were always such a happy little girl, though you also knew your own mind. Jack seems to have some demon in him and, as for Tom, I am not quite sure. Sometimes he seems to be on another planet.'

They were still quite ravishingly beautiful, though, attracting attention wherever they went. Strangers stopped Pippa in the street to get a closer look.

'You should sign them up with a model agency,' was something she grew tired of hearing.

'No thank you,' was her stock reply. 'They are vain enough as it is.'

Part of her malaise was due to the fact that Charles

was travelling more and more and these days, it seemed, was scarcely ever home. It was hard enough raising a couple of small boys, especially when one of them was hyperactive, but having to do it virtually on her own was beginning to take its toll. She had entered this marriage with such high hopes and, although she still adored her husband, she did feel a little let down on the family front. She was lucky to have her mother around to help out when she was needed. Now that she was semi-retired, she had more time on her hands.

Pippa was working shorter hours and worried about the effect on trade. The girls were great, and reliable workers, but it wasn't the same as being there full time herself.

'Where is Charles now?' her mother often asked and the truth was Pippa didn't always know. When he gave up Cornwall, having split from Cassie, she had fondly imagined he'd be home at weekends to help her out and be a proper father.

Even Aidan had defected now, off doing bar work before settling down. Pippa was quite surprised at how much she missed him. From being a thrusting young businesswoman, these days she felt dull and out of date. It was months since she'd last had a girls' night out or any real fun at all.

When he did come home, Charles was still her dashing lover and it gave her a lift just hearing his key in the door.

'Daddy's home,' she trilled to the boys. 'Let's get you bathed and ready for bed and then he will come upstairs and read you a story.' Then she slapped on some makeup and tripped down the stairs, giving a show of being a dutiful wife.

'How are you, my darling?' He crushed her in his arms and she breathed in the welcome scent of expensive cologne. Once Charles was there, things were always better; there was nothing he couldn't sort out. Her loneliness and slight claustrophobia, her grievance at having to cope on her own. The latest alarm from the nursery school about Jack's increasingly aberrant behaviour. If only he'd take the time to listen, which he did less and less.

While she checked the casserole in the oven, Charles poured them both a drink, then came to watch her make the salad and whip up his favourite dressing.

'More balsamic,' he said, licking his finger. 'And a tad more lemon, I would suggest.'

'How do you come to know so much?' she teased him as she did his bidding and had to concede, when she tasted it, that he was right.

'I get around. It's a bit of a bore but with all this travelling even I occasionally eat.'

'Like where?' she asked. She really wanted to know but his answers, as usual, were annoyingly vague. A lot of his business was still in the West Country where, since the divorce, she had not expected him to go. He mentioned a place called the Coot and Hern where the food was especially good.

'The where?' she said.

'The Coot and Hern.'

'What sort of a name is that?'

'Tennyson, actually,' said Charles rather smugly, liking to feel superior.

'And when did you start reading poetry?'

'I am more romantic than you think.'

Once he'd changed his clothes and tucked in the boys, they settled down to a cosy meal and Charles sniffed with appreciation when she lifted the casserole lid.

'Smells wonderful. What is it?' he asked and she told him beef cooked in beer. One of Delia's reliable perennial classics.

Charles tasted it and seemed suitably impressed. He half closed his eyes as he savoured the first mouthful and gave it his full concentration. 'More garlic,' he said, 'and a handful of wild mushrooms would make this a dish truly fit for the gods. Bravo! You have done it again, my dear.' He leaned across and kissed her.

Pippa, enraged, though she wasn't sure why, suddenly went for his jugular.

'What do you mean, *bravo*?' she screeched. 'What in fuck's name have *you* ever known about cooking?' He came and went, took it all for granted, left her to run the house and take care of his sons, when all the time her own business was losing ground because she wasn't there and couldn't give it the attention it deserved. *That* was her baby, which she'd started from scratch, and not these demanding twins she had never really wanted. A voice in her head told her that was not true, that she'd been willing to be a single mother, but now was no time for rational thought so she

250

ignored it. Charles, transfixed, watched her sudden rage then told her quietly to calm down. Whereupon she went off like a roman candle, an accident all too ready to happen the minute he crossed the line and the time was right. ·

Women. She saw the look in his eyes as she bit back her tears and gulped down some wine, too fast to enjoy the fragrance of the bouquet. She shakily picked up her knife and fork and tried to enjoy the meal she had cooked while Charles implacably watched her with distant eyes.

'Hard day?' he asked, with a hint of the cool sarcasm she'd finally learnt not to rise to.

'Normal,' she said as she picked at her food. He was right; it could have done with more garlic, which didn't improve her mood.

They ate in silence while Charles cleared his plate then graciously allowed her to give him some more.

'What gets into you, babe?' he asked later, when they were in bed. 'I have tried to give you whatever you wanted, the house, the children, even marriage.'

'Don't start on that again. What a wonderful wife Cassie was.' What bugged her more than anything else was the condescension in his voice, as if it was her fault alone that she had got pregnant.

Charles simply gave a theatrical sigh and switched off his reading lamp. 'If that's the way you want it,' he said. 'Let's talk when you're in a better mood. I have had a really tiring day. I've been driving all afternoon.'

Cassie, that was the secret, thought Pippa; he had never really got over her. She saw that very clearly now it was too late. The mother of his oldest son whose place the twins could never usurp; a woman with charm, integrity and class, not to mention money. Pippa had never been able to understand why Cassie had let him go just like that after the twenty-two years they had been together. She was ten years older than him and perhaps had had enough. Maybe had simply run out of steam. She had certainly preferred the remoteness of Cornwall to whooping it up on the London scene the way, until the twins arrived, they had done almost every night.

As Charles nodded off, Pippa lay in the darkness, wide awake and thinking about her life. She was not yet thirty, only half Cassie's age, yet the former wife, she was certain now, still retained a hold upon her husband. What, she wondered, was Cassie's secret except that, by letting him go, she had somehow won. She had liked what little she had seen of her and respected her decision to walk away. She wondered if, at some future time, she would ever have the guts to do the same.

'Where is Cassie these days?' asked Pippa, serving an extra special breakfast to compensate for last night's hissy fit.

Charles looked up vaguely from the paper. 'Venice, I think,' he said. 'Why do you ask?'

'Just wondered,' said Pippa as she stirred his eggs

to just the consistency he liked. 'Do you ever hear from her?'

'Very rarely and then only about Aidan. She worries about him travelling abroad on his own.'

As well she might; despite the charm, Pippa would never trust that boy, would not want to leave him alone with the twins. There was something about him that had started to alarm her.

'I'm surprised she can bear to be away from Cornwall.'

'Nothing to do with me,' said Charles, returning to the day's news.

Charles, however, turned out to be wrong. Cassie was back in London. Pippa ran into her several days later by chance. She was having her hair washed when Cassie walked in and crossed the salon to greet her.

'Pippa?' she said. 'What a lovely surprise. How are your beautiful twins?'

'Holy terrors and wrecking the place. About to hit the Terrible Twos.'

Cassie laughed. 'I sympathise. I remember Aidan at that age. All you can do is run for cover. I promise you that it gets better.' Though not for some time.

'But when?' Pippa laughed. 'That's what worries me. I am not at all sure I can stand it for very much longer.'

Emilion was waiting with scissors ready so she made her excuses and shuffled away, but she kept an eye on Cassie in the mirror, impressed by how well she looked. Divorce appeared to be suiting her. She'd lost years since the last time they'd met. Trimmer, happier, far more stylish, she had even finally cut her hair, which complemented her classic bone structure and magnificent eyes. I'd guess she has a lover, thought Pippa, inexplicably jealous.

She was at the desk, paying her bill, when Cassie approached her again. Even in a gown, with her head swathed in a towel, she still contrived to look chic. 'I hope you don't mind my asking you this but I'd love to see them one day,' she said. 'Aidan says they look just like him and I must confess I find that thought beguiling.' She was smiling warmly and quite sincere. Pippa was touched and grateful. Not many women in Cassie's position could bear to hold out the hand of friendship to the person who had actively wrecked her marriage.

'Any time you care to,' said Pippa. 'Come over for tea or whatever. Charles is away so much these days, we'd all be glad of the company. The boys are always delighted to be admired.'

Cassie already had the number and promised to call very soon. Since Charles was off on his travels again, Pippa never got round to telling him.

'How is Aidan?' They were drinking tea and the twins were playing with the toys that Cassie had brought. Cassie was dressed in something soft and draped that suited her tall and willowy figure, with pearls that must have cost an arm and a leg. Pippa, who hadn't had time to change, was wearing a raspberry pink velour tracksuit that could have done with a wash.

'Aidan's fine,' said Cassie brightly. 'Though I'm not

entirely sure where he is.' The poor little soul looks worn out, she thought, and I'm not at all surprised. The twins had started to squabble loudly and Pippa went over and picked one up. She brought him back to sit between them, trying in vain to calm him down.

'May I?' asked Cassie, holding out her arms, and when Pippa, defeated, handed him over, he almost immediately stopped his bawling and instead started sucking his thumb. 'Now which one are you?' asked Cassie gently, stroking the coal-black curls that were so like her son's. 'I am sorry,' she apologised to Pippa, 'but I still can't tell them apart.'

'Tom,' said Pippa. 'Normally the quiet one. Lately he's been acting as disruptively as Jack.'

That figures, thought Cassie, who'd researched the subject since Aidan had started reporting back. It very much seemed, from what she had heard, that Jack might have some sort of behavioural problem and, since identical twins are just that, sooner or later what was wrong with Jack was likely to show up in Tom. Poor Pippa. Cassie didn't envy her one bit.

The child, who had spotted Cassie's pearls, removed the thumb and reached out for them, flashing his radiant smile in pure delight. Cassie deftly kept them out of harm's way and cuddled him till he relaxed.

'Now how on earth did you manage that?' asked Pippa, greatly impressed.

'Practice,' said Cassie. 'Don't forget that I have been through it all too.' Though Pippa, poor thing, had a double dose and the sooner she sought professional help, the better. She cast around for a lighter topic to avoid getting on to trickier ground. 'Aidan tells me that Jack is a genius at art.'

Pippa's careworn face lit up. 'They say at the school that his drawing skills are exceptional for a child his age. The only time he settles is when he is drawing.'

'It's a wonderful gift,' said Cassie. 'You must help bring it out. I think he must have inherited it from his dad.' Charles, who had spent his adult life relying mainly on charm and fast thinking, also possessed that unerring eye for spotting a really good painting. Such a talent must have come from somewhere; it wasn't something you just picked up. If only he'd be more open about his background.

'Well he definitely didn't get it from me,' said Pippa, pouring more tea. 'I couldn't draw anything to save my life and neither could my mother.'

Having Cassie here had brightened her up; she liked the woman a lot. Being able to discuss the twins with someone who listened and empathised was a tremendous relief, especially now that Charles was so seldom around.

'I really ought to be going,' said Cassie. 'But thank you for letting me come here. Your boys are gorgeous, a lot like Aidan at that age.'

'Well, I hope they grow up to be like him,' said Pippa, pleased with the praise. 'They couldn't hope for a nicer older brother.'

'Yes,' said Cassie, avoiding further comment. There were things about Aidan that Pippa didn't know and Cassie hoped she would never find out.

*   *   *

Cassie's stories about life in Venice filled Pippa with wistful envy. She made it sound so colourful and romantic. She had taken to dropping in fairly often, bringing small presents for the twins and sometimes even pushing them out in their stroller.

'I am sure you could do with a break,' she said, with her gentle and tentative smile. 'I know how overwhelmed I often felt when my own children were this age.'

Pippa was grateful for Cassie's concern and glad of a break from the mind-numbing tedium. It gave her a chance to catch up on correspondence and get up to date with her various suppliers, something she found hard to do with the twins always under her feet.

'Are you sure you can trust her?' her mother had asked, jealous of another woman encroaching on her turf.

'Absolutely,' said Pippa with scorn. 'What do you think she's going to do? Take them back to Italy with her or push them under a bus?'

'You never know,' said her mother darkly. 'She certainly owes you no favours.'

'She's a warm and generous-hearted woman, which you'd know if you'd ever bothered to meet her, and, after all, Aidan is half-brother to the twins.' Also, in London Cassie seemed a bit lost. She was staying alone at the Basil Street Hotel even though Charles had magnanimously suggested that she use the Pont Street flat. It had, after all, once belonged to her, bought with her former husband's money. If anyone really owned it, it was Cassie.

'Why is she here?' he was curious to know, slightly suspicious of his former wife's motives. It irked him that she had become so self-sufficient.

'She is renovating a Venetian palazzo and doing research in the British Museum in order to get the period details right. But most of her time she's in Cornwall with the family. She misses Aidan very much.'

'Hmm,' said Charles, still a little concerned, not at all certain that he liked the idea of his two wives palling up.

Pippa, every weekday morning, dropped off the twins at the nursery school, then drove on into Fulham to open the shop. In the old days, when she was unencumbered, she'd stay there at night until seven or eight. Now she had to leave mid-afternoon to pick up the boys, except on those days when her mother would do it for her. She found it frustrating since, on the whole, the more serious buyers came in later and she wasn't there to greet them with her sales spiel. The girls were good but not in her league. When Pippa was there it was rare that anyone left the shop empty-handed. There was nothing, however, that she could do except patiently wait for the twins to grow up. At least when they were four they could move to a proper school.

On this particular afternoon she was talking to a rich American when the phone in the stockroom started to ring and one of the salesgirls answered it.

'It's for you,' she said, thereby breaking the rule that a customer must never be interrupted. And this particular one, skilfully played, might well turn out to be a winner. She had bought a house in Virginia Water and was planning to refurbish it right through.

'Not now, please,' said Pippa tersely. The girl knew better than that. 'Tell whoever it is that I'll call them back.'

The girl went back to talk to the caller then hovered anxiously in the doorway, clearly undecided what to do next.

'What now?' said Pippa, overly impatient. The girl should be able to handle something comparatively simple like that. When she was that age and temping at Liberty's she could juggle three customers all at once, with a bright and friendly smile for each one, and not keep them waiting too long. She'd maintained those standards throughout her career which was why the shop was doing so well; her name had become a byword for efficient reliability.

'I'm sorry,' said the girl, 'but it sounds rather urgent. It's somebody calling from the school.'

'Please excuse me,' said Pippa, turning pale. 'Alison here will take care of you while I am gone.'

'Don't worry,' said the American lady. 'I know what it's like with kids. Mine are all grown up by now, thank the Lord!'

A teaching assistant was on the line, telling Pippa not to be alarmed but that they thought she probably ought to come.

'What's happened?' asked Pippa, instantly panicking, convinced the woman was about to tell her something catastrophic.

'It's Jack, I'm afraid,' said the motherly woman, in a voice designed to soothe. 'He is having one of his little turns and we can't seem to calm him down. He's been screaming now for fifteen minutes and nothing we say or do has any effect.'

'I'll be there as fast as I can,' said Pippa, all thoughts of the affluent customer wiped from her mind. 'Sooner or later he will scream himself out but tell him that Mummy is on her way.' As if he was likely to listen, poor little beggar.

She reached the car in a matter of seconds and set off into the early rush hour, her heart pounding in her mouth. These little seizures were becoming more frequent and no one knew what was causing them. The word epilepsy had even been used, though not, so far, by a doctor, and each time Pippa thought about that, she broke out in a cold sweat. The traffic in the Fulham Road was even heavier than usual. There must be either an accident ahead or else some afternoon function going on at the hospital or the football ground.

'Come on,' she muttered impatiently, wondering whether she ought to call Charles or wait until she knew just how serious things were. He was off again, she had no idea where, but would presumably answer his phone, though she hated to appear to be checking on him. When the traffic still refused to move, she broke another of her rules, only to find that his mobile was switched off. So, agitated and close to tears, she called her mother instead.

* * *

They had moved the child to the first-aid room and his tantrum had more or less passed. The teaching assistant, looking somewhat tense, greeted Pippa at the school's front door, apologetic at having disturbed her at work.

'He is a lot calmer,' she assured her, 'but we felt it best that you should come.'

Pippa strode past her with barely a word and into the small clean room that was pointed out.

Holy smoke. She stopped in her tracks and one hand flew to her mouth in disbelief. For the small tear-stained figure tucked up tightly in the bed wasn't Jack at all but his brother, Tom.

33

Frankie couldn't get Aidan out of her head. Whatever had happened between them had shaken her up. He might be younger but was very much a man; the memory of their frenzied lovemaking had left her fractious and dissatisfied. Something deep inside her had stirred and now refused to go back to sleep. She slumped into a deep depression and turned her back on the world. Magda, with her built-in radar, sensed there was something seriously wrong and waited for Frankie to open up, which she didn't. Whatever had happened the night she stayed away appeared to have cut very deep.

Fate, however, then intervened. Within the week a letter arrived informing Frankie that her mother's estate had now been settled, leaving everything to her. Not enough money to make her rich but sufficient to give her some independence, should she choose to take it. Magda feared she might leave the commune but, as Frankie had often observed, where else had she to go?

Except, she now realised, to England in search of

Chad. With Aidan she seemed to have drawn a blank yet she couldn't let the matter rest. She had the list she'd drawn up with Magda; now she could afford to take the next step. If she systematically traced Chad's roots, she might discover where Aidan fitted in. She regretted now leaving him so hastily, but also knew it would have been wrong to stay. She would go to England and track down his parents. She knew their names were Charles and Cassandra and that they lived in London. Not a lot to go on but a start.

Rather to her surprise, the other women were in favour of her plan. She had never been to London before but now could afford the fare.

'Take Eurostar,' said Sister Agnes. 'It's the fastest and most efficient way.'

'And go first class. Why not treat yourself?' They all knew she hadn't had much of a life and richly deserved a bit of spoiling.

'You can act as our emissary,' Magda suggested. 'Make yourself useful while you're there.' It would help give some purpose to the trip; she couldn't bear to think of Frankie tilting at windmills. She also worried what she might do when she saw there was life beyond Antwerp. This way she'd have a reason to come back.

'An excellent plan,' said Sister Agnes, whose pottery lately had been winning awards and who very much hoped to find a market for it. 'We will put together a portfolio to demonstrate what we're doing here. Who knows, this could be our major breakthrough, put us all on the map.'

They got together in the barn to draw up a plan of action. Between them they were impressively productive. Magda's lace was quite exquisite; they all agreed that it needed a proper showcase. She worked in the old traditional way, which had hardly changed since the fourteenth century when Flanders had been a world centre for lace.

'Take some samples as well as pictures and show them around the specialist shops. They might be persuaded to order in bulk.'

'Not too much bulk,' protested Magda, though it was obvious that she liked the idea.

'How on earth do I start?' asked Frankie, scared at what she was taking on. Bruges was the furthest she had ever travelled. London suddenly seemed a daunting prospect.

'Common sense,' said Magda briskly. 'You'll know what to do when you get there. Be glad, at least, that you speak the language. And get your passport renewed.'

Armed with a slim portfolio, her backpack and a single bag, Frankie embarked on her daring expedition. Magda, who dropped her at Antwerp station, hugged her with controlled emotion. 'Take care,' she said, 'and keep in touch. And don't stay away too long.'

'Just as long as it takes,' said Frankie, her fighting spirit restored. She was nervous about the actual journey, at having to go through the Channel tunnel, but suddenly keen to get on with it and see what she could unearth. It had crossed her mind to contact

Aidan but she had mislaid his mobile number, which was the only personal data she had. Doubtless it was all for the best; she shouldn't have done what she did with him, felt ashamed because he was still so young. His parents, though, were another matter. If she could find them, she might get a clue as to where he had got his astonishing looks. Chad remained her lasting obsession; she would not rest until she had traced his roots.

"Bye,' she said, kissing Magda briefly. 'Thanks for everything you've done.'

'Take care,' said Magda again, suppressing all emotion. 'Bon voyage and good luck.'

34

Luise Barras was taken aback when he got Cristina's call. It had been a good ten years since she'd been in touch. The husky, petulant voice hadn't changed though; he could well imagine the discontent on her face.

'Luise, cheri, how are you?' she said and then, without pausing for his reply, launched straight into her request. Less a request, more of an order. She clearly hadn't improved much in patience or manners. She was planning to marry again, she explained, which would require written evidence of the divorce. A tiresome matter, to do with French law, but she needed it right away.

'Divorce?' said Luise, for a moment confused. Ten years was a very long time.

'My divorce from Cal Barnard,' she said. 'We married in '77.' Or thereabouts; she was typically vague. Could obviously not remember the details herself. Not surprising, the way she'd lived then, perpetually fuelled by drink and drugs. He hadn't even known she was now in Paris.

'My dear,' he said, 'you have caught me on the hop. I will need a little time to look up the papers.' He had no recollection of a divorce but wasn't going to say so until he was certain. Cristina had always had an ugly temper, would fly off the handle at the least excuse. The difference was, she was no longer a big star; Barras, along with the rest of the world, no longer jumped at her bidding.

'Well, make it snappy,' Cristina said, ending the call without a word of thanks or even a goodbye.

Damn, she thought, even more depressed, having heard the hesitation in the lawyer's voice. It looked horribly as if her premonition might be valid. In which event, what should she do next? Unless she managed to pin him down, Rocco was not a man to hang around. As it was, she couldn't be more aware of the age gap.

Barras rang back in a couple of hours to report he had turned up her personal file but there was nothing to indicate a divorce. 'Are you sure it took place in Rio?' he asked. 'As far as I recall, he was not Brazilian.'

'He was English, I think.' The truth was, she'd never known much about Cal apart from the fact that he turned her on. In those days they'd lived for the moment and little beyond.

'So what should I do now?' she wailed, gripped by sudden panic.

'The only person to answer that is the man himself,' replied Barras.

'Whom I haven't heard from, or of, since the day

he walked out. I don't even know if he's still alive.'
Things would be much simpler if he were not.

'After he left you, where did he go?' She was every
bit the flake she always had been.

'I have no idea. We parted badly. Please, Luise, you
have got to help me. It's a matter of life and death.'

At least it had served to improve her manners.
The Brazilian moved heavily in his chair and
checked the pages of his appointments book. 'By
chance, it so happens I shall be in London at the
end of next week. Leave it with me and I'll see what
I can find out. But I'll need a copy of the marriage
certificate. Perhaps you could fax it to me before I
leave.'

'The marriage certificate? Do I have that?' Cristina
was back in a state of panic. She had no idea where
to look for such a thing, assuming she'd ever even
had it.

'Where do you keep your birth certificate?' Barras
was losing his patience. He was bored with the endless
fecklessness of this child/woman.

'In my jewellery box, I think.'

'Well, that's where I would look first.'

He was certainly going to make her pay through
the nose for this, but he had been her on and off lover
for years and he'd never forget what a knockout she
had once been. He would put a London associate on
the case who could sift through papers at Somerset
House or wherever it was the Brits kept such records
these days.

'Don't hold your breath, though,' he warned as he

rang off. Even for such a sensational beauty, there was only a limited distance he would go.

The Public Records Office revealed very little, not even a copy of the marriage licence. Barras's man, who went there in person, could not even find a birth certificate for Cal.

'You are certain that was his name?' asked Barras, bored with the situation already and regretting ever having taken Cristina's call. She had always been trouble.

'Of course,' she screamed. 'I married him, didn't I?' Though the truth was she didn't even know what Cal was short for. Calvin, maybe, or Caliban; even Calamity Jane.

'It doesn't sound very English to me. Are you sure he wasn't American?' asked Barras.

'Not sure, no.' She was quieter now, recalling the doubts she had always had and the strong suspicion that he'd never been straight with her. 'There must be something you can do,' she wailed. 'Where else can you look?' At any moment, Rocco might show up. She dreaded to think what he'd say when he heard this latest news. He'd be off again at the slightest hitch. She had sensed all along that he wasn't wholehearted about it.

'Leave it with me,' said Barras, softening. 'I promise to let you know as soon as I can.'

Cristina ran through what knowledge she had of the dashing youth she had married and realised it amounted to not very much. She had been so dazzled at that first erotic meeting that nothing else had mattered at all, so that, after he'd dumped her and then returned, they had whirled into wedlock with barely a second's pause. She had always assumed that there'd been a divorce, though it hadn't much mattered till now. All she had wanted, when the music stopped, was to be shot of him once and for all; it drove her crazy just having him hanging around. In those days, still at the height of her fame, she had had no shortage of would-be suitors, could take her pick of the crème de la crème of Brazil.

Now she racked her brains for any small detail that might help throw light upon where he had gone. Having claimed to be a traveller of the world he could be almost anywhere at all. She vaguely remembered having had the impression, though now she couldn't remember why, that he'd already been through a quickie first marriage, despite the fact that, when they wed, he was still only twenty-two. It might explain his reluctance to commit as well as the undisclosed source of his wealth. At no time had he ever claimed to have come from an affluent background.

All of this she passed on to Barras, who dutifully noted it down. It was a measure of her desperation that this time she remembered to thank him, though made no suggestion that he should send her a bill.

The lawyer's associate in London, however, was made of sterner stuff and had all sorts of contacts in different strata, some only inches above the gutter, which was exactly what seemed to be called for in this case.

'He sounds to me like your typical chancer,' said a tabloid journalist in the pub. 'If I were you, I would flick through the headlines and the court reports for that year and the one before.'

The newspaper headlines for 1977 revealed nothing at all that seemed to match up with the very few facts he had. But when he moved on to the court reports, something caught his eye that immediately clicked: an account from 1976 of a society divorce where the bride had eloped from her coming-out ball and fled to Paris without her parents' consent. The father, a heavyweight property man, had pursued the couple across the Channel and paid off the youthful bride-groom on the spot, provided he got out of town. Once the settlement had been agreed, the marriage was quietly annulled. The bride was a certain Miss Millicent Hoare; the bridegroom, one Cosmo Banbury, whose profession was given in the report as barman.

Same initials, C.B., thought our sleuth, mentally striking his forehead. A very long shot but, what the hell, it might just be worth looking into.

'Go for it, boy,' said Barras, amused. He was starting to be intrigued by the story himself.

When Rocco Pereira burst into her life, the world rocked on its axis. It was years since she'd found a man so intensely exciting. Though he was drunk and boorish in his behaviour, Cristina was thrilled by his brutish allure so that, without further ado, they had fallen into bed. Twelve years behind her made him thirty-three, with a lean hard body running slightly to flab because of the decadent lifestyle he led. Still feted as a racing driver, although no longer top of the league, he spent his time moving from track to track and taking part in the international rallies. He had girls in many ports, but Cristina had reached a stage in her life when she found it expedient to turn a blind eye on all that. What she didn't know, she need not grieve over. She had learnt her lesson with a series of sharp knocks since falling from the top of the modelling tree.

The subject of marriage had come up quite casually, during a night of sensational sex that had left them both sated and reeling. He was drunk, of course, and Cristina was coked; together they made the most exquisite music and the light that shone in their slightly glazed eyes was pure love. He also assumed, since she lived in Paris and had once been queen of the international catwalk, that she was a lot better off than was actually the case. Pereira had expensive tastes, not all of them admissible to the taxman. Motor racing was very well paid but only as long as you continued to win and thirty-three was cutting things rather fine. He was slightly over the hill already and looking for a haven in which to drop anchor. Cristina Calväo was an enviable trophy until he could luck out with somebody younger. At which point, as was his wont, he would move on.

None of this did Cristina suss out; she thought she had stumbled upon the real thing. Though at an age when she ought to know better, emotionally she was still adolescent and hadn't felt like this since she'd met Cal. The torch she had carried for him all those years ago was now rekindled for Rocco Pereira. Insane, maybe, but she'd go to any lengths to satisfy her urgent carnal needs. She carried on with her wedding plans, without telling Claude, assuming that somehow, in her usual way, she would manage to muddle through.

The Countess of Rochester received him in the kitchen where she was trying to bath a dog. She stood there in her dowdy clothes, water all over the linoleum floor, nervously drying her hands on her apron before extending one to him.

'Yes?' she said, in a slightly squeaky voice, but her pallid cheeks turned to brightest red when the young man mentioned the name of Cosmo Banbury. 'Yes,' she repeated when her heart had stopped fluttering. 'He was, indeed, my husband once, though not for very long.'

The nice young man seemed harmless enough so she made them both a pot of tea and they sat side by side at the scrubbed pine table to drink it. Her straight brown hair was pinned tightly back and her face could have done with a lick of paint. Other than that, apart from the clothes, she was not unappealing, he thought. And, now that she had regained her composure, keenly engaged in what he had come here about.

The story he'd read in the papers was true. She made no protest; in fact, seemed shyly proud. The romance had been sudden and very short-lived. By the time they had reached the Paris hotel, her father was hot on their heels like the wrath of God.

'He was most unsuitable but, oh, if you had seen him.' The light in her eyes enhanced her face, making her almost pretty. 'The handsomest man I have ever known and, for one glorious month, he made me very happy.' She challenged him now but was back in control. 'You probably think me silly,' she said, 'but may you one day find such happiness yourself.'

She quickly regrouped and returned to reality. What was it he wanted to know? Time was passing; the family would be home. Though grown up now, they still expected to be fed.

'Where is he now? Have you any idea? It's urgent that I find him.'

'I don't know,' she said and he saw she told the truth. Her father, cold-bloodedly though probably right, had paid him off like the cad he undoubtedly was, on condition that he went abroad and stayed away for a specified time, until the marriage had been annulled and he could do no more harm to Millie. Towards which end, the money agreed on was paid over in instalments. Into a nominated foreign account.

'In Rio,' she said without his having to ask.

After some thought and a glass of dry sherry, she made the decision to tell him more. 'As a matter of fact,' she virtually whispered, 'I saw him again some years ago. He appeared not to recognise me but I knew him.'

Still handsome, still charming, still the centre of

things. Still working the room with a gleam in his eye. Her heart had almost stopped in her chest when she'd glimpsed him across the crowded bar that night at the opera house. Then she remembered the wife and her face lost its glow.

'He was with a woman, his wife he said. She was tall and elegantly dressed. When I called him Cosmo he didn't even flicker. Said I was mistaken and walked away.'

The sleuth was perched on the edge of his chair; this was better than anything he'd hoped for.

'Do you know what name he goes under these days?'

'Yes,' she said, with quiet satisfaction. 'I wrote it down in case I ever forgot.'

No chance of that, it was etched into her heart, the name of the man she had worshipped at seventeen, who had wooed and won her then tossed her aside like a foolish and frumpish rag doll.

'These days he styles himself Charles Buchanan. Charles and Cassandra, he said.'

At this point Luise Barras took over, now that things appeared to be hotting up. He had not hoped for such a speedy result. Charles Buchanan was easily found, with business premises in Walton Street and a residential address in nearby Pont Street. The man had clearly done well for himself, despite the fact that he seemed always to be on the move. The person who answered the office phone said Mr Buchanan was currently travelling and could she take a message? The lawyer said no. Instead he tried the private number.

The phone was answered by a man. He was, he said, Charles Buchanan's son and what was this about?

'It's a slightly delicate matter,' said Barras. 'I wonder if we might meet. I won't take up too much of your time, I promise.'

'Come here,' said Aidan. 'My father's away.' And his mother was safely in Venice. Something sounded intriguing here, and he was curious to know more.

'I'll be there at six,' said Barras, his mission achieved.

When Aidan saw the marriage licence a sudden chill shot through him. Although it was written in Portuguese, he saw immediately what it was though neither of the names was familiar to him. 'What's this to do with my dad?' he asked. 'Who is this Cal Barnard?'

'Who indeed,' said the silky lawyer. 'I was rather hoping that he might tell me that.'

The bride, he explained, at the time of the marriage had been a world class model. The groom had since mysteriously vanished, though his bank in Rio had now confirmed that the money he'd kept in his savings account had been transferred to a London branch. In the name of Charles Buchanan.

'I suspect you see what I'm driving at,' said Barras, a highly civilised man.

Just at that moment his mobile rang and, with an apologetic shrug, he turned his back and walked out of the room, to take the call in private. With lightning speed, Aidan grabbed the marriage licence, attached to a letter with a Paris address, and scribbled down the sender's details before the lawyer returned.

'Great,' he said, with his dazzling smile. 'I am sure

my dad will be riveted. I am not sure where he is right now but I'll certainly leave him a message to contact you.'

That night Aidan went to say goodbye to the twins. He had to go away again, he said.

'But you're only just back,' protested Pippa. 'Couldn't you wait at least till your father gets home?'

'Sorry,' said Aidan. 'There is something I must do. Just tell him from me, if you will, to watch his back.'

'Sounds intriguing. Won't you please fill me in?'

'Can't,' said Aidan. 'It is strictly between me and him.'

He played with the boys until one of them screamed and Pippa hurried over and gathered him up. He was tired, she said, it was time they were in bed. She tried to get Aidan to read to them but he said he hadn't got time.

'At least stay and have a drink with me. Your father will never forgive me if you don't.'

Aidan flashed his bewitching smile, so reminiscent of Charles. 'I'd like that more than anything,' he said. 'But I have to get going or else I'll miss my train.'

More than that he would not divulge, not even where he was going. But he hugged the twins tightly before he left and told them both to be good to their mother.

'You never know what may happen next,' he said.

Cristina was puzzled by Barras's call; puzzled and very frustrated. He had found out what she wanted to know: that there hadn't been any divorce. Cal was alive and living in London, under the name of Charles Buchanan, and had at least one other living wife, Cassandra. It was up to Cristina what she chose to do, confront him or turn a blind eye. His own advice, more as friend than lawyer, was to take the latter course.

'I can't see what you'd achieve,' he said, 'by blowing the whistle on the man. From all accounts, he is very successful and carries considerable clout. If it came to the crunch in a court of law, it could be a lengthy and painful business, initially based, without documentation, on nothing more than your word against his.' And he knew which side he would back, though didn't say it.

'You are saying I'm still his legal wife?'

'I'm afraid so, chérie,' he said.

She had no idea who to turn to now; Barras was reluctant and too far away and she also sensed he was washing his hands of the case. But she had to act fast before Rocco showed up. She had seen enough of his violent temper not to want to tell him the painful truth. She almost considered appealing to Claude, who was good at sorting her problems out, but even she could see that was going too far. She fleetingly thought about contacting Cal, had a strong desire to see him again, but the time had come to be realistic; he had dumped her at the height of her fame, and now had another wife.

So, in the end, she chose to do nothing and take the chance that things would never come out. If she moved to Brazil once she'd married Rocco, she'd be safe. It meant turning her back on all she had now but that was, in any case, likely to happen once Claude found out about the approaching wedding. He had taken his wife on a luxury cruise to celebrate their ruby wedding. It might, she thought, mean a total reconciliation.

'Yvette,' she screamed, 'come and run my bath. And tell the chauffeur that I'll need the car.' At a time like this only one thing could calm her. Cristina was going shopping.

35

The surging crowds at Waterloo station were almost enough to turn Frankie round and send her straight back to Antwerp. Brussels had been bad enough but there she had only been passing through; here she had to confront an intimidating city. She grabbed her bags and followed the flow towards the taxi rank outside. She had heard about the underground but had no desire to try it. She had booked a room in a Chelsea hotel where her mother had stayed when she came down to shop. It was also handy for Walton Street, where, she'd found out from directory enquiries, interior designer Charles Buchanan had his offices and showroom. Beyond that, she wasn't sure how to proceed. For the first time ever in her life, she found herself having to cope on her own and wasn't sure that she liked it.

She arrived quite late so called it a day. Once she'd checked in and unpacked her bag and had a drink in the small friendly bar, she found herself too pent up to want to eat. So she went back upstairs, took an early night and willed herself to sleep, which wasn't easy. She tossed and turned, disturbed by traffic and the voices of people passing in the street. She was here, in one of the world's great cities, for the first time in her life but was too intimidated to venture outside. In the morning, though, she would give it a go. Her determination to track down Chad remained undiminished.

Over breakfast she studied the map and worked out how to get to Walton Street. She was almost on the King's Road, said the waitress, but Frankie had no desire to look at the shops. She sat there, in her austere grey suit, with her short straight hair and sensible shoes and not a trace of makeup on her face. All she cared about was this mission; the faster she could get on with it, the better.

She found the showroom easily enough, then walked up and down the street several times before she had the nerve to go inside. It was somehow smarter than she'd expected; Aidan, for all his dazzling looks, had struck her as unassuming. But this place was the epitome of chic; when at last she found the courage to enter, a smart young woman looked up from her desk and asked if she could help.

Frankie got a grip on herself. 'I'd like to speak to Mr Buchanan.' She had no idea what she'd say to him, though had brought the portfolio as a calling card.

'Mr Buchanan isn't here.' She hadn't expected that. 'May I ask what it's about?' asked the girl politely.

Frankie stared blankly back at her, uncertain how to proceed. The plan that had seemed so simple in Antwerp had already come unstuck. 'I have some samples I want to show him.' She remembered Magda's contingency plan. 'I represent a small Beguinage in Belgium.'

The girl clearly didn't know what that meant. 'We don't deal with the trade,' she said. They were, she explained, a small design group, working solely for private clients, and got everything they needed from their own suppliers. Seeing Frankie's obvious disappointment, she politely offered to take a look. There might be someone, she said, she could pass her on to. She was clearly taken by what she saw, especially Magda's lace.

'I know just the person you should show it to.' She scribbled down an address. 'It isn't far, just along the Fulham Road.' Then took her to the door and showed her the way.

Pippa was alone in the shop when the doorbell clanged and a stranger walked in, tall and dark and looking slightly forbidding.

'Hi!' said Pippa with a welcoming smile. The twins had lately been behaving better which meant she'd been able to get a little more sleep. 'What can I do for you?'

She was blonde and pretty and slightly overweight; Frankie warmed to her instantly and felt far more at her ease. 'I've brought these samples,' she said rather gauchely. 'Someone suggested that I should show them to you.'

Pippa watched as Frankie opened the case and gasped when she saw the lace. 'Exquisite,' she said, really meaning it. 'And yes, I am definitely interested.'

They spent very nearly an hour together while Pippa ordered several lengths of lace, dependent on how much Magda could make and how quickly. Workmanship of this calibre was well worth the wait, she said. She already had several buyers in mind, was pretty certain she could easily shift it.

'I'm glad you found me,' she said, hugely pleased. 'Now is there anything else you need help with?'

Frankie showed her pictures of Agnes's pottery and the filigree silver that Sylvia produced. Pippa looked at it all and was very impressed. 'What a talented bunch you are,' she said. Then she suggested that since it was almost lunchtime, Frankie should stick around.

'My husband will be here any minute. Wait and I'll introduce you. It's very possible he'll be able to help you with contacts.'

Frankie hesitated then said no; she was anxious to be off. She had done her bit and got orders for the lace; now it was time to get on with her quest. Out there somewhere Chad's ghost beckoned. She had left it long enough.

'Do stay in touch,' said Pippa, when she left. 'I am sure we can do more business.' Strange woman, she thought, and rather sad. I'd love to know what her story is.

Three minutes later Charles arrived and whisked her away to lunch.

36

Ten days in Venice, facing a blank future, empowered Cassie in unexpected ways by opening her eyes to things she'd not thought about before. Here she was, on the brink of turning sixty, having never had to fend for herself or worry about the harsher realities of life. An adoring father, two husbands and two brothers; men had always looked after her and played a supervisory role. Even Tremayne had done his bit in helping to shield her from the daily grind by running the estate so efficiently on his own. Her childhood had been comfortable and Edwin very well off. Even Charles, with some help from her, had built a healthily flourishing business which meant that neither now had financial worries. She had graciously allowed him full use of the flat while she went to ground in Cornwall to think things through. Daisy was there, with her teenage children, and Rose, now an established solicitor, often turned up at weekends. Aidan was at Oxford, and hardly likely to want to live at home again. She had managed, by putting up no resistance, to keep the marital break-up civilised. In the eyes of the world, whatever else they thought, she was truly a dignified loser. What she felt inside was much more complex. She had not yet come to terms with that at all.

After the first annihilating blow, she had reeled for a while like a headless chicken. Despite her astuteness, she had not seen it coming, had turned a blind eye to her husband's obvious faults. In the twenty-two years they had been together, she had only been mildly aware of the fact that his devotion to her was imperceptibly cooling. His absences had grown longer and more frequent but she had put that down to the boom in his new career. Each fresh client took up more of his time so that Cassie no longer expected him home every weekend without fail. It was part of the price they were paying for success and made their reunions that much sweeter. One thing she'd never even wondered about; she had always known she possessed his heart and that he was totally faithful.

She was weeding the edges of the croquet lawn when she heard the purr of his fancy car at a quarter past four, three hours before he was due. She rose to her feet and wiped her hands, then pushed back her heavy hair in delight. His visits home were all too infrequent; it was like an unexpected birthday treat. He parked outside the front door and she watched him swing his long legs from the car and reach in the back for his briefcase. Time sat very lightly on Charles; from this distance he was still the dashing young buck who had wooed and won her in that hotel all those years ago.

She ran to greet him with a radiant smile, untying the apron she wore to collect the weeds.

'What a lovely surprise!' They'd have tea together, out on the lawn within earshot of the waves. All three dogs had appeared from nowhere, wagging their tails and wriggling in ecstatic welcome. When the master of the house came home, all attention was switched to him. Somewhere back in the kitchen the maid would be boiling the kettle and laying a tray with a laundered cloth especially for the occasion.

'Cassie, my darling.' He took her in his arms but his swift embrace was peremptory. She was aware he wasn't kissing her which spoke volumes.

'What's wrong?' she asked, picking up the vibes as she saw the sudden evasion in his eyes.

'Nothing, my dearest, but we do need to talk. I cancelled the afternoon and came straight home.'

He strode ahead of her into the house, tossed his briefcase on to a chair, then hurried upstairs to change his clothes and escape her incisive probing. All too soon it would have to come out; throughout the week he had dreaded this confrontation. The more he could do to delay it, the better for him. But not for her; she was there already, wringing her hands as she supervised the tray, trying to keep her breathing steady and not give too much away. Freshly baked scones and homemade preserves. The maid had done it all perfectly. She rinsed her hands and tidied her hair, then went back into the garden to wait. Whatever it was, she wasn't going to like it.

*   *   *

A younger woman; she should have guessed. Cassie covered her eyes for a second, then sat up straighter and carefully poured the tea.

'Do I know her?' she asked and he silently nodded, but when she heard it was Pippa Harvey, she froze.

'Pregnant, you say?'

'With twins,' he said.

'How long?'

'Three months.'

'No, not the pregnancy. The relationship, I meant.' She took deep breaths and tried hard to keep calm but the saucer rattled when she handed him his tea. 'Well?' she said, a shade more sharply, watching him visibly squirm.

'Five years,' he said.

'You louse,' she cried as, all of a sudden, things started to fall into place. His absences, his slight abstraction; the guilt, she saw it now clearly, on the girl's face. She had taken it then for appealing shyness but all the trollop had actually been doing was casing the joint and eyeing the lie of the land.

For a while they sat in uncomfortable silence, neither wanting to say the unthinkable words.

'You must marry her,' said Cassie calmly, with sudden resolution. 'Those babies will need a legitimate father and I'm far too old for you anyway.'

With quiet dignity, she rose and left him and walked down the lawn to the rocks at the edge of the sea. The sharp salt breeze swept the tears from her eyes and she stood there, facing the restless surf, knowing that life, as she'd known it till now, was ended. She had loved him completely but had feared this day might come. In a way, she was almost relieved that the waiting was over.

Venice had been an impromptu decision once the papers were signed and she knew there was no going back. She had to get away from home, could not bear to watch her marriage dissolve and all she had worked so hard for fall to pieces. She thought about Pippa, whom she'd rather liked, was disappointed that it had to be a person she knew. But if not Pippa, it would have been someone. She realised now how blinkered she had been. She remembered the incident with the Countess of Rochester and how, even after that, she'd suspected nothing. He had shrugged it off and she'd totally dismissed it; the woman was clearly demented, he'd said, and she, the older sophisticate, had believed him. She wondered now about other women. He was away so often these days she couldn't tell. Enough; such thoughts were purely erosive. There was absolutely no going back and the years were running out fast. On an impulse, she rang the reception desk and extended her stay for a few more weeks. She had nothing to hurry home for now so would make the most of the trip.

Venice became Cassie's new obsession, reminder of happier times and an earlier life. From that point on, when she could get away from the pressures of family and the Hawksmoor estate, she travelled back and forth at least once a year. She found the Danieli too imposing for her needs so moved instead to a family-run hotel with a quiet courtyard, shaded by massive trees, where she could sit and read between her excursions. Sometimes she took the vaporetto and travelled the length of the Grand Canal, absorbing the breathtaking scenery that had remained unchanged since medieval times, soaked in art and history and intrigue. Time had stood still here for centuries and little had altered in the thirty-eight years since that first idyllic honeymoon trip with Edwin. She recalled the earnest girl she had been, fresh out of school and with few expectations except to grow old with a man she had always revered. When she thought about him and compared him with Charles, words could not begin to describe the difference. But though Edwin had always been staunch and fair, as reliable as the stable clock, she still would not have missed a moment of her turbulent second marriage. She had known when they married about Edwin's heart; he had suffered with it mildly throughout his life. Though his passing had been sudden, it was not unexpected, and she'd never thought she would ever find love again. Nor, at the time, even wanted to. At thirty-three, she'd believed that all that was over.

She spotted the palazzo entirely by chance, a decaying ruin, crumbling into the canal, its painted façade like the face of a whore who had been out too long in the rain. Beautifully sited close to the Ca' Dario, the Palazzo Dandolo was elegant, though worn, and listing slightly to one side, which made it look tipsy. Several times she passed it, up and down, until its fading charms began to ensnare her. Without help and extensive capital investment, it looked too fragile to survive much longer, even though it had stood there for almost six hundred years. She wasn't rich, not to that extent, but she suddenly knew what she wanted to do; she had to have it. She made up her mind on the spot. This was the dream she'd been searching for, a beautiful ruin in dire need of rescue, a project to take the place of her shattered marriage.

'I have to have it,' she said to the agent, once she had tracked her down. No messing about with fake business finesse; when Cassie went after something, she was relentless. From the look of the place, it had been empty for years, a neglected ruin that nobody wanted despite its prime position on the Grand Canal. She'd worked wonders in Cornwall and also in Pont Street, had honed her talents to a very fine edge and was now prepared to take on the challenge of a life-time. No more marriages, she was through with all that; from this point on, a woman on her own, she would do as she damned well pleased. And finance herself.

'I'll give you whatever you ask,' she said. 'As long as it falls within my budget and providing you don't renege. You have just five days to talk to the owner or else my offer will be withdrawn.' Greener pastures was her implication though, privately, her heart beat fit to burst.

The Italian agent, jaded and weary, looked at Cassie with renewed respect, liking this sort of fighting talk, which she hadn't expected at all. The woman she'd taken for a dowdy widow was now revealing nerves of steel and virtually flashing her chequebook as she spoke.

'Three days,' she promised, suppressing a smile. There was no fool like an old one but business was business.

'He will meet you there,' she reported next morning. 'The owner won't consider selling until he has talked to the buyer.'

'That's fine with me,' said Cassie, slightly daunted, having not expected her crazy whim to draw such an instant response. What she would do about money, she didn't yet know. All she did know, without hesitation, was that she had to have the place and do all she could to restore it to its glory.

'Ten o'clock outside,' said the agent. 'I would come myself, but . . .'

'No need,' said Cassie. The last thing she wanted at this delicate stage was this woman messing things up. 'All I need to know is his name. The rest I can handle myself.'

'Why, the Count Dandolo,' said the woman, surprised. 'I thought you understood it was still in the family.'

'Great,' said Cassie, her spirits sinking. Just what she needed right now, the Count himself. But, having started, she was not turning back. For only the second time in her life, Cassie was doing her own thing.

It was drizzling slightly, as it does in Venice, a fine cool rain that was more of a mist, which swept in from the lagoon and shrouded the sun. Cassie, nervous but simulating calm, arrived at the palazzo at the appointed hour, cautiously looking around for this formidable man. Knowing Italians, he would doubtless keep her waiting; she resigned herself to a wasted morning and started to wander about. Viewed from all angles, the property was daunting, four storeys high with a water entrance and obvious subsidence into the canal that needed fixing fast. The only other person not hurrying past was a silver-haired man quietly studying the façade. That's him, she thought, and strode purposefully over before she could lose her nerve and scuttle away.

'Scusi,' she said to his motionless back. 'Would you, by chance, be the Signor Contino?'

'You've been listening to too much Mozart,' he said, turning to her with an affable smile. 'Mario Dandolo, at your service. I prefer Professor to Count.'

The hair was silver but the face was not old, with inquisitive eyes behind rimless lenses that looked at her with appreciation as she offered him her hand. Younger than her but older than Charles; to Cassie an excellent omen. And the softly modulated accent was pure mid-Atlantic.

'Professor of what?' she asked as he juggled with the keys.

'Architecture mainly,' he said. 'Here in Venice.' But also at Harvard where he spent the main part of the year.

Which was why, with reluctance, he'd decided to sell. The palazzo, his family's home since the

Renaissance, was more than he could afford to maintain any more. He had sunk what inherited money he'd had into the basic structure, renewing the piles and shoring up the walls to prevent its total collapse from sheer neglect. The interior, though vast, was cavernous and gutted. It would take many years of devoted work to restore.

'Though it breaks my heart, it has got to go,' he said. 'But only to a suitable buyer. One who will cherish it as much as I have and give it a new lease of life.' He looked at Cassie appraisingly and seemed to like what he saw. His children, he explained over coffee, were now all grown and had gone their separate ways, while his wife, an American, preferred her own country. Would not consider forsaking New England to live in a mosquito-ridden swamp, which was how she liked to describe the Venetian lagoon.

'How sad,' said Cassie, thinking of Cornwall. Though now she knew that the die was cast and her fate about to be sealed. Provided, of course, she could find some way of raising the requisite capital fast. It might be a ruin but didn't come cheap; it encapsulated six centuries and was an important part of Venetian history. She would be hard-pressed to find the money but was resolved that nothing should stand in her way.

It's only money. She had often heard him say that, but when Cassie confronted Charles his jaw visibly sagged.

'You want to *what*? Let me try to get this straight.', For a second, he placed his hand on his forehead, then looked at her again with incredulous eyes. He had aged, she reflected; it was doubtless those twins. The glimpse or two she had had of them had kept her awake at night. But they, thank goodness, were not her problem. Pippa had brought this all on herself and would have to deal with it. She had, after all, been the catalyst of the break-up.

'I want to sell the flat,' she repeated. 'I need the money for something else.' He had, after all, his Walton Street showroom as well as the villa in Barnes. And the flat had been paid for by Edwin's estate, was actually nothing to do with Charles though Cassie was far too well-bred to mention that. She'd already discussed it with the family and they'd leapt at the idea. A Venetian palazzo, how very romantic. The ideal setting for Cassie, they felt, and a project to stretch her innumerable talents which they, if not her husband, fully acknowledged. She was every bit as gifted as Charles, though no one had dared to say so before, and had mouldered too long in the country in semi-retirement. Rose was prepared to risk her career and come out and help for as long as it took, while Sybil's eyes gleamed as she quietly considered what might be in it for her. A summer school for aspiring sculptors; something she'd always wanted to do. From the surveyor's plans, which Cassie brought home, there was more space than she could ever dream of using.

'I definitely think you should do it,' she said. 'Edwin, I know, would approve.' The studious child he'd so lovingly nurtured was finally finding her wings at last. Not before it was time, after all she'd been through.

Charles was wholly incensed with fury, his customary suavity totally gone. Never, in all these years, had she seen him like this.

'You don't even speak the lingo,' he said, his blue eyes blazing, his mouth in a snarl, his fists, she noticed, clenched as though he might strike her.

'As a matter of fact, I do,' she said calmly, resisting the urge to argue. There were things about her he still didn't know. His own career had always come first and she had done what she could to encourage it. Now she saw she had nurtured an egotist, and took full blame for that, but was reluctant to provoke an uglier mood. The money she wanted belonged to her, though he was acting now as though she were trying to rob him.

'You don't need the flat any more,' she said firmly. 'Your house is plenty big enough for your needs.'

'That's not the point.' He was shouting now. 'I need it to entertain business contacts. I can't expect them to trek all the way out to Barnes.'

Cassie couldn't help smiling at this; he looked so like Aidan in one of his snits. Though normally equable, the boy had a tendency to fly through the roof at the slightest cause even when he knew he was in the wrong. But Aidan was only just out of school; his father was almost fifty and should know better.

'Why are you laughing? It isn't funny.'

'Indeed,' she said. 'I only want what is mine.' She'd behaved impeccably over the divorce, removing all obstacles from his way in order that it could go through fast and legitimise his twins. She had kept the house, which had always been hers, but allowed him sole use of the Pont Street flat and asked for nothing at all from his burgeoning business. Over the years he had borrowed large sums, to plough into the business, he'd said, but so far she hadn't seen a penny's return. Had she turned nasty, which was never the intention, she might well have gone for fifty per cent. As it was, she had walked away with nothing of his. But now she needed to sell the flat in order to buy the palazzo. And if he attempted to stand in her way, she would bring in lawyers without hesitation. She had been a loyal and forbearing wife long enough.

As his anger grew, he began to shake and Cassie was instantly sickened, for she recognised in his contorted features the face of the son they shared. She had started to wonder if Aidan might be unbalanced; there were certain things she had never told Charles. His year away, spent travelling in Europe, had come as a secret relief to her. She had seen his behaviour echoed in the twins and knew that Pippa had a problem on her hands. But never before, in their twenty-two years, had she ever seen Charles quite like this.

'Pull yourself together,' she said coldly and left.

He was waiting for her at an outside table close to the Rialto bridge when Cassie arrived to sign the final papers. She had raised the money, completed the deeds; now all that was left was her signature and a final handshake to solemnise the deal. It was a clear bright morning in early spring and the chill had gone from the air. The sky was a deep cerulean blue, straight from a Renaissance painting, and the sunlight sparkled on the waters of the canal. Mario, as he had asked her to call him, wore jeans and an open-necked shirt and was staring wistfully at the palazzo that any minute would cease to be his, always assuming he wasn't about to rescind. This was the moment she had lived for for months, too superstitious to enter the date in her diary.

'Cassandra,' he said, taking both her hands and looking as though he was about to kiss her. 'These past few months have meant much to me, spending so much time with you, even though it means having to forfeit my birthright.'

Cassie blushed like a bashful maiden and lowered her eyes from his gaze.

'Mario,' she said. 'I give you my word that I'll do everything in my power to honour your trust.'

The architectural details he would handle himself on his occasional visits back from the States. They'd already spent many evenings together, poring over his intricate drawings, discussing the future of the palazzo as if it were to be a home they shared. Cassie had promised he would always be welcome; she would keep a suite of rooms for his sole use.

'And you,' he said. 'How will you manage here alone? In summer it will be hot and the streets over-crowded.'

'I'll manage,' said Cassie. 'My daughter is coming.

And my sister-in-law, an eminent sculptor, has plans to visit us too.'

'But not your husband?' The question was loaded. They'd steered clear till now of discussing their private lives.

'I have no husband,' said Cassie simply, seeing the wakening interest in his eyes. 'He moved on,' she explained, 'to a younger wife. And now has a whole other life.' I am redundant, she reflected silently. Even my son is no longer around.

'Cassandra,' he said, 'you're a beautiful woman who should not be living alone. If it weren't for Harvard, I would stay here like a shot and hope to get to know you better.' He raised her hands to his mouth and kissed them and the look in his eyes sent a shiver down her spine. She was not too old to feel something, after all. 'I'll be back,' he promised, 'after the next semester. I will give you what help I can in restoring my home.'

'But your wife . . .'

'My wife doesn't care,' he said. 'She prefers to play tennis and meet her friends. The reason I moved to the States was because of her.'

He said little more but she felt she understood him; he still had the Dandolo blood in his veins and Venice was the home for which he pined.

'I'll be back,' he repeated. 'Just as soon as I can.' And she knew that this was a man whose word she could trust.

37

The place to start would be Middlesbrough where they met, which was also the town where he'd died. She fingered the locket she never took off though she could no longer bear to look at his picture. She felt what had happened with Aidan had defiled it; felt bad about betraying the love of her life.

She bought a road map and rented a car; though not accustomed to driving on the left, she thought it simpler than the train, and once she hit the north she'd be more at home. She would bypass the Wirral; there was nothing for her there. Even her earliest memories had been spoilt. So she'd head for the detention centre where she'd gone straight after the fire. It was an unbelievable twenty-eight years since she was there.

She enjoyed the drive, found the motorway easy. She was used to driving a heavy truck so the rented Toyota just skimmed along and put her into a more relaxed holiday mood. The legacy had freed her to enjoy herself a bit; she even stopped for lunch and a cigarette. She remembered the sulky child she had been, fifteen years old and full of hate for the man who had done her so much damage. Chad's intervention had been very timely; if it weren't for him, she might not even have survived.

She arrived in Middlesbrough mid-afternoon and went in search of the old detention centre. The town had grown vastly bigger since those days and she couldn't identify any landmarks but did eventually, aided by the map, track down the right location. The building still stood but its windows were broken and coils of barbed wire were there to repel intruders. She stopped outside and lit up again. The shock of being back moved her profoundly.

She got out of the car and rattled the gates but no one came; the place was obviously deserted. A sharp breeze blew some old rubbish around; it was nothing more than a desolate wasteland. Eventually Frankie was forced to give up, return to the car and think about what to do next.

The social services, once she found them, were pleasant and willing to co-operate, though, faced with them, she wasn't quite sure what she was after. Anything they could tell her about Chad before he was sent to this horrible place; Borstal she already knew about and, before that, Barnardo's. The woman provided the relevant details and wished her success with her quest. It would mean another long drive to Yorkshire but at least she was on her way.

Barnardo's were not at all proud of Chad. His name was not on their roll of honour. At first they seemed

300

reluctant to talk to her at all. Frankie's persistence, though, finally paid off. The man checked the records and gave her chapter and verse. Chad had spent two spells with them, from his birth in 1955 until 1962 when he had been fostered. The foster parents had sent him to Repton, whence he had been expelled at fifteen, after which they had washed their hands of him and sent him back to the orphanage.

'Shocking behaviour, I know,' said the man. 'People like that have a lot to answer for. No community spirit or conscience. They should not have been allowed to foster at all.'

'And after that they'd deserted him?'

'Well, he knifed a lad. Some argument in the play-ground. He always had a volatile temper. He ended up in Borstal.'

'Do you have the address of his foster parents?' She knew she was fighting against the odds. But Frankie, inspired, could also be very persuasive.

'This is most irregular,' said the man. 'I'd be much obliged if you wouldn't mention my name.'

Frankie knew, from his complicit smile, that privately he approved of what she was doing. She didn't explain her connection to Chad, just that he was a distant family member. The Tewson-Finches lived in Derbyshire which was why, presumably, they'd sent him to that school. What a waste of effort and money, they must have felt.

She loathed Yolande Tewson-Finch on sight, from the moment she opened the door. Nouveau from her bouffant hair and the spastic smile on her lifted face, she was X-ray thin and wearing expensive cashmere. Frankie hadn't bothered to phone; thought she might find out more if she simply turned up.

'Yes?' said Yolande, expecting a delivery. She must be at least in her early eighties but was very well preserved.

Frankie smiled and charmed her way in. 'I'm here to talk about Chad,' she said and watched the sudden wariness in her eyes.

'Chad? He's been dead for thirty years. What about him?' the woman said. Cold, just as Frankie had assumed she would be; a woman without a heart.

Frankie looked round the opulent house, with its fake antiques and rococo mirrors, and reflected that, on the whole, Chad had turned out well. What polish he'd got must have come from the school. He certainly hadn't got it here. And this vile old woman could well have destroyed him by turning her back at the time he had needed her most.

'Why did you get rid of him? I know the story,' said Frankie.

'He was out of control,' Yolande snapped. 'Threw back in our faces all we'd done for him by getting expelled from the school.'

'For smoking?' said Frankie. 'He was only fifteen.' She had been that age herself when she set the fire.

'Precisely,' said Yolande, through tightened lips.

'So why take him on in the first place?' she asked. If you weren't prepared to be a proper mother and offer unconditional love.

Yolande considered and her fish-eyes softened. 'He was the cutest child I had ever seen. At seven years old, with those great blue eyes, he looked like a little angel.'

'And yet you dumped him just like that,' Frankie virtually spat.

'It turned out he was a natural delinquent and that we were well shot of him. He later killed someone. Tainted blood. There was nothing else we could do.'

Except to love him and back him up. Frankie was suddenly feeling sick. The sooner she got out of this house, the better.

38

'Calm down,' said Clive, 'or you'll make yourself ill. I still don't understand why you're so upset. What do I have to do to convince you that it wasn't me at the Centre Court? Apart from the fact that I rarely watch tennis, I was in Corfu with the lads who can vouch for that.'

'But Vanessa saw you . . .'

'She was mistaken. Tell her to go and get an eye test before making any more false accusations. She meddles too much, as it is.'

'She only wants what is best for me,' said Jenny, still not entirely convinced though he hadn't turned a hair when she'd brought it up. Just laughed and asked if she was having him watched. She had yet to tell him about Osborne and Cole, did not want him thinking she was turning into a snoop. But that was the thing that baffled her most, the fact that they'd claimed not to know who he was. There had to be some sort of logical explanation; maybe she'd simply misdialled. She felt ashamed of doubting his word. She would talk to him later when both were less stressed; right now, she didn't want to rattle his cage. So instead she asked about the cricket tour and he filled her in on scores and things, although she had never really seen much point in the game. In the Welsh valleys where she had grown up, rugby football was a second religion and, since childhood, she had screamed from the stands along with her father and his friends. She still tried never to miss an international.

Now Clive was back, looking tanned and relaxed, he reclaimed his place behind the bar. The locals all told him how much he'd been missed. Thursday nights were not the same without his benevolent presence. He laughed and offered free drinks all round. He wasn't the landlord but knew that Jenny would approve. He had always emphasised the importance of goodwill; she might never have got off to such a good start without his intervention.

'You spend too much of your time away,' said Mrs Dawkings darkly. 'A girl like that needs a man around. It doesn't do to leave her too much on her own.'

'And there are plenty here who would take your place.' Mrs Bailey, one of the clique, was in total agreement. She glanced significantly along the bar to where Alistair Grey stood drinking alone, a thoughtful man in boots and a waterproof jacket.

'Ladies,' said Clive, at his most beguiling, 'I can't disagree with what you say. If it weren't for the fact that I have a living to make, I assure you I'd be here all the time. Please don't hold against me my need to work.'

He left them and moved along the bar, twisting down glasses and flicking them in the air before concocting his exotic cocktails, an innovative feature he had introduced.

'Well,' said Mrs Bailey, with a heartfelt sigh. 'He certainly knows how to chat up the ladies. I don't mind admitting, I wouldn't turn him down.'

'All mouth and trousers,' growled Mrs Dawkings, though she couldn't disguise the glint in her eye as she watched him strutting his stuff.

'It was him,' said Vanessa. 'Without a shadow of doubt. How many men have that rakish charm and those luminous cobalt eyes?' Though not enamoured of him herself, she could quite see where the attraction lay, was secretly glad that her heart was otherwise taken.

'He says not,' said Jenny tiredly. 'And that your eyes need testing.'

'Me and forty million other television viewers? I don't think so,' said Vanessa, incensed. She had never completely trusted the man and now he had started playing games.

'I'm afraid I have to believe him,' said Jenny. 'He has given me his word that he wasn't there.'

'And what does he say about the job? Did he manage to wriggle out of that one too?'

'I haven't got round to asking him yet,' said Jenny, unsure of what he'd say. She wanted, more than anything else, to trust him.

The memory of Douglas's evasiveness still made her slightly sick. Clive was an altogether nicer man who always treated her extremely well and had shown his solid devotion right from the start. Take the way he behaved in the bar: he made no secret of their attachment so that all the regulars knew that he was her man. He would not risk putting his neck on the line if he were not totally straight. Yet Vanessa was a loyal friend who would never risk hurting her in any way unless she was pretty sure of what she'd seen.

'I'll talk to him later, after closing time, and find out the truth about Osborne and Cole.' Which was something she didn't look forward to in the least.

'Look, my darling,' he said to her later. 'We have to talk about these jealousy fits. It isn't like you, you are usually so well balanced. What is it – your time of the month or something like that?'

'No,' said Jenny, profoundly annoyed. 'What I asked was a perfectly reasonable question. I called your office and they claimed not to know who you were. Can you blame me for being confused? For the past four years, since we very first met, you have told me about your strenuous job.' Principally to explain his regular absences.

At first he looked deeply put out. He picked up his drink and paced the room, then stepped out into the cool night air and the sound of the babbling brook.

Cripes, thought Jenny. Now I've really done it. She had gone one step too far this time and ran the risk of driving him away.

But when he returned, he was smiling again; he took her in his arms and held her close. 'I'm afraid you're a little too smart for me,' he said, once he'd smothered her with kisses. She was right about the job, he confessed; it wasn't quite what he'd said. He hated himself for not being straight with her but his hands, at least for the present, were tied; he wasn't entirely his own man. The story about Osborne and Cole had been only a front.

'But they do exist?'

'You spoke to them. And I've had dealings with them in the past, even if they don't remember me now.' They made a convenient front for him while he got on with his real work, the nature of which he wasn't allowed to divulge. At least, for now.

'You mean you are undercover?' she asked, slightly incredulous yet intrigued. This man was far deeper than she had ever suspected.

'Something like that,' said Clive, relieved, since she seemed to be taking it all so well. 'It's the reason, my darling, that I travel so much and haven't been able to give you a fixed address. Soon, I hope, it will all be in the open and you, I promise, will be the first to know.'

'I think he's a spy,' she reported to Vanessa. With all that charm, she should have known he was more than just a travelling salesman. Parts of that story had simply not added up.

Pull the other one, said Vanessa, but only to herself.

Meanwhile, Jenny was cooking up a storm, growing in confidence every day and constantly adding to her repertoire. She stuck to the staples, like cottage pie,

308

but boldly advanced on the gourmet side until she began to get write-ups in the papers. Not just the papers local to Bath but the *Sunday Times* and the major glossies. A couple of her old colleagues even came down. She entertained them in her private snug and they caught her up on the London gossip. Douglas, they told her, though cautiously, had now embarked on a new affair and appeared to be treating the girl in the same casual way.

'Anyone I know?' asked Jenny, willing it not to hurt.

'No, she's only been there a matter of months.'

She was younger, they said; in her middle twenties. Exactly my age at the time, she thought, but kept her mouth firmly shut and said not a word. So he hadn't changed; in a way she was glad. It would have hurt her considerably more if he'd finally left his wife.

And how was she? they wanted to know. Was there anyone new on the scene? Yes, she said and told them about Clive, though not the bit about what he did for a living. They seemed impressed by the meal she laid on and promised her, off the record, an excellent write-up. She was making quite a name for herself which was why they had bothered to come at all. She felt optimistic as she showed them out. Things at last appeared to be really working.

Clive was off on his travels again but now she knew not to ask where to or when to expect him back. Since he had told her his need for caution, she tried not to talk about him much at all except, of course, to Vanessa, who already knew.

'So what does he claim to be?' she asked, the disbelief quite clear in her voice. 'A plain-clothes cop or
a customs man? Insurance investigator? What?'

'I am not allowed to know,' said Jenny, 'but it
certainly must pay well.' He never seemed short of a
bob or two and his car was a Bentley convertible which
she'd always thought rather plush for a travelling
salesman. That, and his mastery of perfect martinis,
elevated him to James Bond status. Which made the
spy theory plausible; she adored him all the more.

'What has he said about the mystery financier?'
Vanessa was still very much on his case. She knew
the damage that Douglas had wrought, was determined Jenny should not go through that again. She
had never really been sure of Clive; he was much too
good-looking to be kosher.

'Not a word,' said Jenny blithely. 'But now I realise
it doesn't matter. Whoever it is has obvious faith in
what we are doing here at the Coot and Hern.'

Alistair Grey asked her out again but Jenny was reluctant to go in case Clive suddenly returned without
notice. It was two whole weeks since he'd last been
here; he hadn't even called.

'You're crazy.' Vanessa and Joyce agreed. 'When did
he ever consider you? He comes and goes but only as
it suits him. And doesn't show much remorse if he
suddenly cancels.'

'Are you sure he isn't married?' asked Joyce, her
innocent tone belied by her searching look.

'Of course I am,' said Jenny impatiently, wishing

310

they'd let the subject drop. Lately she had the feeling they were ganging up.

'Why?' asked Vanessa, leaping straight in. 'Has he actually spelled it out?'

'Of course not,' said Jenny. 'He knows I trust him. That kind of interrogation isn't for us. We're already much closer than that which is really what matters.'

A significant glance, not lost on her, passed silently between the other two before they let the subject drop. Are you thinking what I am, it said quite clearly.

'Leave it alone and get on with your work. In less than an hour we'll be opening up.' Joyce still had the sauces to prepare and Vanessa should really get home to her kids. She was good to give them so much of her time but, right at that moment, Jenny would rather she left. She was starting to grate on her. Clive was right when he said she interfered.

The secret backer was on Vanessa's mind; she still thought it awfully strange. Who would invest such a sizeable sum yet show no interest in the profits? Jenny told her sharply to shut up.

'You are always interfering,' she said. 'Clive's right. It's none of your business.'

'Have it your own way,' said Vanessa, now cross. 'But don't come crying to me when it all goes pear-shaped.' She drove off home in a bit of a huff, leaving Jenny feeling miserable and contrite. She gave her time to reach her house, then phoned and apologised.

'I don't know what's got into me,' she said. 'I must be over-working.'

Or worrying about things unspecified. Vanessa had a shrewd idea but wisely made no comment.

Jenny tried asking Clive again but only made him angry. 'What is it with all the questions?' he asked. 'It's that bloody Vanessa sticking her nose in. Tell her to stay out of our lives. She only gets in the way.'

Jenny, of course, didn't pass this on; Vanessa was her dearest friend. But she also didn't want Clive upset. She tried cooling the friendship but that didn't work. Vanessa was no fool and knew exactly what was going on.

'Listen, my sweet,' she said to Jenny. 'If you don't want me around, I'll shove off. But I'll always be here if things go wrong. Don't let that bastard wreck your life just because he can't be honest with you.'

Undercover work, my eye. Far more likely to be another woman.

Toby was growing fast and was now almost seven, an intelligent child with a questioning mind to whom Clive was a father figure, the only adult male he had ever been close to. While Clive was away, he longed for his return and greeted him with a barrage of questions the moment he walked through the door. Clive would sweep him into his arms and swing him up high above his head and the child would cry out with joy and feverish excitement. On these occasions Jenny's heart lit up and she wondered whether the time had come to suggest giving Toby a brother or sister. She was almost forty and cutting things fine, yet didn't want to upset the applecart.

'Did you never want children of your own?' she cautiously questioned Clive. 'You seem to be a natural, certainly with Toby.'

'It's really a matter of timing,' he said. 'Yes, some time I would like a family, especially if they turned out like this little lad. But I need a more stable lifestyle before committing to that extent. It simply wouldn't be fair, the way things are now.' He looked at her with his bright blue eyes as if appealing for understanding. She moved silently over, with a brimming heart, and enclosed them both in a hug.

'I really think he is coming round,' she confided to Joyce as they cooked. 'Toby certainly regards him as his dad.'

'Well, he'd better get a move on,' said Joyce, pessimistic as always. 'That is, if it's you he's planning to have them with. You may look good for your age but you're no spring chicken.'

'Thanks,' said Jenny, by no means offended, swiping at her with a cloth. 'You sure know how to make a girl feel good.'

Clive was here for a long weekend; nothing could spoil her mood right now and, since he was starting to share his secrets, almost anything could still happen. She badly needed to talk to Vanessa but hesitated about ringing her. They weren't on the best of terms any more since their slight contretemps over Clive. If only he would get on and pop the question, she would do what she could to restore the friendship.

Providing, of course, that the two of them promised not to fight.

The following Saturday, when Clive wasn't there, Alistair Grey turned up in the bar with a woman. They stood at one end and he ordered gin and tonics while the bar staff craned to get a proper look.

'Don't tell Jenny,' said Hamish to Simon. 'I've a hunch she might not like it.'

She was in the kitchen, preparing the meal, when Joyce popped down to bring the bad tidings; always the albatross of doom, she just couldn't help herself. 'I think you should check the bar,' she said, trying to keep the glee from her voice. 'There is someone there I think you should know about.'

Jenny, preparing the venison salad, scarcely gave it a thought. 'Not Clive?' she said, but when Joyce said no, she kept her mind on the task in hand and showed no further interest. Clive would be gone at least another week; her mind was exclusively on the job. Whatever was disconcerting the staff left her unconcerned.

'Just go upstairs and take a peek,' said Joyce. 'I'll finish that for you.' She practically elbowed Jenny from her place, made her remove her chef's whites, comb her hair and stick on some lipstick.

'Why?' asked Jenny, mystified, but Joyce could be as annoying as Vanessa.

'Take a break and go up to the bar. Have yourself a glass of wine. They need to see you from time to time; you work much too hard as it is.'

'Hi,' said Alistair, when she appeared, and introduced her to his date. A big-boned woman, taller than him, with ruddy cheeks and a lusty laugh, dressed in the countrywoman's uniform of boots and a sage-green Barbour.

'Hi,' said Jenny, extending her hand. 'Welcome to the Coot and Hern. I don't believe I have seen you before. Are you from these parts?'

'I hope I shall be soon,' said the woman, fairly obviously gloating.

'Well?' said Joyce, when Jenny returned.

'Seems nice,' replied Jenny vaguely. 'It's probably time he settled down. Now where did you put the langoustines and have you finished the garlic mayonnaise?'

'It's useless,' said Joyce when she bumped into Vanessa. 'Nothing we say does any good. She is stuck on the fellow even though he treats her like dirt.'

He seemed to be away a lot but that was the season, he pointed out. In the summer months what it was he did was always extraordinarily busy. Jenny didn't really care. The tourist trade was in full swing and she had enough on her hands as it was without also having to worry about Clive. She was working flat out all her waking hours and the place was fully booked, with a waiting list that extended for weeks in advance. She had to bring in extra help yet still had no time to relax. Toby was dispatched to Neath, where her parents could make a fuss of him and he could connect with another adult male. Perhaps he would pick up

315

a smattering of Welsh and learn about rugby from his gramps. Jenny knew he'd be spoilt to death which, at that age especially, was important.

'I miss him, of course I do,' she said. But she couldn't object to the amount of trade they were doing. Almost more than Toby, though, she found she missed Vanessa. But still hadn't quite the courage to give her a call.

Joyce frequently met Vanessa in town, often by arrangement. Vanessa worried about Jenny a lot and didn't want to lose touch. She could always call her but that wasn't the point. She knew she was not a favourite with Clive who resented the closeness of the two long-time friends.

'It's almost as though he is jealous,' she said. 'Which is crazy when you think of it. We go back almost twenty years, have always been there for each other.'

'He begrudges anyone close to her, even me at times.' Joyce had watched Clive following Jenny around, disliking how friendly she was in the bar, breaking up any conversation he deemed to have lasted too long. It was an odd conundrum; he neglected her yet, when he was there, appeared to want to possess her. 'It's a matter of dogs and mangers,' she added. 'Doesn't want her enough himself but is keen no one else should have her.' Like Alistair Grey who still looked wistful when his Amazonian girlfriend wasn't there. 'If I were Jenny, I'd snap him up and not waste any more time on that sweet-talking rogue.'

Vanessa wholeheartedly agreed with her. One of

these days, she sincerely hoped, they would finally catch the bastard out red-handed.

When Clive came back after three weeks away, he seemed unusually tired. He had lost a lot of his natural bounce, was less keen to serve in the bar but spent more time at the back with Toby, newly returned from South Wales. As Toby got older, the pair grew closer. It warmed Jenny's heart to watch them talking like a couple of ancient buddies.

'He's great with kids,' she remarked again. If only she could persuade him to have some of his own.

'When are you going to settle down?' she asked one night as she sat on his knee, her arms round his neck.

'When my life is more stable,' he said, carefully extricating himself and going to the bar to get them both drinks. It seemed to suit him, this peripatetic existence, belonging nowhere, constantly moving around. Whatever it was that absorbed his life, she knew she was only a part of it. Occasionally, in her darker moments, she wondered what awful secret he might be concealing. The girls had asked how she knew he wasn't married and she'd almost bitten their heads off. The truth was, she knew nothing of the kind, feared to find out from some neutral source that the dream of happy-ever-after she clung to was no more than pie in the sky. Provided that she never found out, she could continue to dream. It was a pathetic way to live, a throwback to the Douglas years, but while she was working this hard, she had no other choice. Maybe, once the season was over, she would pluck up the courage to confront him. But then, on the other hand, she might not. She was scared of what she feared was the truth, that he'd never loved her at all.

39

From Derbyshire Frankie drove on to Yorkshire, in search of the church where Chad had been found. She was fired up now with a new incentive; her encounter with that hateful woman had made her doubly keen to track him down. St Chad's was somewhere in the Hull environs. She bought a map of the neighbourhood and tried to find it without asking. In a tree-lined enclave in a tiny village she finally located the Norman church, square and rough-hewn with a vaulted roof, unchanged throughout the centuries it had stood there. The morning was bright, and there was no one about. She locked the car and strolled across the grass, still fresh with early dew.

She stood in the porch and looked around. It was here the baby had been abandoned. She imagined him swathed against the night air and wondered how long he had lain there. The door was ajar so she stepped inside, inhaling the musty aroma of beeswax and wood. The flowers at the altar were freshly done; the church appeared to be still in regular use. She wandered in search of some tangible sign that the boy she had loved and lost had once been here. If she closed her eyes and focused her mind, perhaps she might even make contact with his spirit. It had been so long, she was parched by her desire.

'Can I help you?' She hadn't heard his approach; he seemed to have sprung out of nowhere. Surprised, Frankie turned to face a smiling verger.

'I was looking for the parish records. I wondered if you kept them here in the church.'

'Only those for recent years. The rest are kept under lock and key. If you tell me what it is you want, perhaps I can help you look.'

The man was small and quite affable, too young, she thought, to have known about Chad who had never even lived in this village at all. But his offer of help appeared genuine and he seemed not to be in a hurry. So she explained her reason for being there and said she'd like to see the documentation. When asked about her motivation, she lied and said she was an archivist. Someone had asked her to trace his family roots.

'The best thing I can suggest,' said the verger, 'is that you stop by at the vicarage and ask if you may look at the relevant records. The vicar's hobby is genealogy. I am certain he will be only too pleased to assist you.'

He pointed her in the right direction, towards an attractive, ivy-clad house with gables and a beautiful flower-filled garden. Frankie thanked him and did as he suggested. It was just before ten; the vicar would still be at home. Her pulse was working overtime. She was apprehensive about the next connection.

She was greeted by the vicar's wife who was outside, pruning the roses. Yes, she said; her husband was home. She wiped her hands, put down her secateurs and went to call him through the open window.

The vicar's interest was immediately caught; he invited Frankie inside. His wife obligingly made them coffee and they all settled down in the panelled study where Frankie explained in more detail why she had come.

'Fifty years is a very long time. There are few people hereabouts that go back that far. The name, you say, was Chad Barnaby? I don't believe that's a local name. Do you have any more information to narrow the field?'

Frankie told him all she knew. The baby had been abandoned in the porch and found by the gardener's boy, who heard him crying.

'Ah,' said the vicar, recognition dawning. 'I think I do remember the case. Barnaby was the gardener's boy so they named the baby after him.'

'Right!' said Frankie, exhilarated. Things were proving easier than she had hoped. The vicar unlocked a huge wall cupboard in which some leather-bound tomes were stored and very easily turned up the relevant year. 'Nineteen fifty-five,' he said. 'Almost half a century ago. Have you any idea of the time of year?'

'June,' said Frankie. 'And also full moon. He was found around the summer solstice.' It all came back, what Chad had said, and how he had been named for the church and the boy.

The vicar found it very quickly, the handwritten entry for 23 June in which the baby's name was recorded as of 'unknown parentage'.

'And there's nothing more?'

'I'm afraid not,' he said. 'This book is simply a record of births, marriages and deaths.'

But then his wife piped up and said: 'There's a resident in the village almshouse called Barnaby Corbett. Perhaps he's the one.'

Barnaby Corbett was gnarled and frail with bad arthritis and obvious cataracts that made him look much older than he was. Frankie feared that he might not understand her. She sat beside him in his sunny room and explained what she was after and a jolt of excitement shot through her when he smiled.

'The baby,' he said, his expression softening. ''Twere me that found him, that's the truth. A right little cracker he were and no mistake. Someone had dumped him in the porch and I heard him crying when I was tidying up.'

'Can you tell me anything about him?' asked Frankie, on the edge of her chair with anticipation. All this was helping to bring Chad closer to her.

'Just that he was right bonny,' said Corbett. 'With the bluest, brightest, most knowing eyes. He looked to me like an ancient soul who had been around a number of times already.'

'And his mother never turned up, is that right? Nor even left a note to explain?'

'He was certainly never claimed,' said Corbett. 'In the end he had to go to Barnardo's, even though the vicar asked questions from the pulpit for several Sundays in a row. But there was a note, which the vicar kept to himself.'

'I don't suppose you remember what it said?' She could hardly bear the suspense. The mother must have been at her wits' end to take such a drastic and final step. Frankie couldn't help but pity her.

Corbett fell silent and stroked his chin, looking back into the past. He hadn't remembered that baby in years but now, despite his sightless eyes, he could see it as clearly as if it were here in this room. Raven black curls and those brilliant eyes that seemed to conceal some inner knowledge. Devil's spawn; he remembered the poor girl's note.

40

Things were looking serious. The doctors were wary of making a firm pronouncement. They had taken Tom in – both twins, in fact – and were giving them extensive tests before they could decide what should be done. Cassie, who'd come at Pippa's request, sat with her in the visitors' room, holding her hand and trying her utmost to calm her.

'It will be all right,' she said constantly, treating her just like one of her own. It was hard to believe, a shattering truth, but Rose and Daisy were older than Pippa by very nearly a decade. And yet this was her ex's child-bride and the hand she held so firmly in her own had done unimaginable things with her own former husband. It made the mind boggle; she tried not to consider it until the door swung forcefully open and Pippa's mother stood on the threshold, looking as vengeful as the wrath of God.

'What's she doing here?' she practically barked, the once peroxided hair now muted to a more becoming shade of tarnished brass. She was something in PR, Cassie thought, though only worked part-time these days. If it weren't for the scowl, she'd look very much like her daughter. Slimmer, though, and better dressed but, then, poor Pippa was going through very bad times.

'She's here because I asked her,' said Pippa, defiantly clinging to Cassie's hand and daring her mother to make any sort of scene. The mother, whose name Cassie couldn't remember, hovered before them with a face of doom until Pippa, wailing, begged her to try to calm down.

'It isn't the end of the world,' she said. 'But I need Cassie here because she is Aidan's mother.'

Cassie, ever the diplomat, invited the woman to join them, letting go of Pippa's hand as she did so. 'We are all in this together,' she said. Well, you two are; I am not. 'And since our boys all share the same blood, it makes absolute sense that we all pull together until we know the best thing to do for them all.' It wasn't any kind of joke; far from it. She'd been through it all herself. But, from what she had seen of those babies, they did require help. And she was here to do what she could. She was, after all, only human.

The mother glared but took it in; she sank on to an adjacent chair like a deflating balloon. The stress was getting to all of them; no wonder, considering the implications. Cassie would either stay or go, whichever seemed for the best. A nurse came in and offered them tea and told them the wait would soon be over.

'Don't worry,' she said, with an optimistic smile. 'I am sure things aren't nearly as bad as you probably think. This is always the worst time, the waiting part.'

They were calming down and making light comments about the weather and how the evenings were growing shorter, when the door to the room crashed open again and Charles Buchanan strode in.

'What's *she* doing here?' he asked apoplectically, pointing at Cassie with a shaking finger and looking as though he might expire on the spot.

As Pippa went through it all again, Cassie rose gracefully to her feet, held out her hand to her former husband and invited him to sit down. It was time, in any case, that she went, she quietly explained to Pippa. Her presence was clearly not welcome here after all.

'But I want you here.' Pippa was growing desperate, scared of what the prognosis might be. Cassie said she had things to do and asked her to be in touch when she knew the results.

'I am sure the nurse is right,' she said, her magnificent eyes full of genuine concern. 'But it's better to be safe than sorry at this stage. Don't you agree?' This last remark was addressed to Charles who looked as though he would gladly throttle her.

'Get the hell out of it,' he snarled. 'You don't belong here at all.'

'Charles!' said Pippa, deeply shocked. 'That's no way to talk to your former wife. Especially as she is only here because I begged her to come.'

'Don't worry,' said Cassie, stooping to kiss her. 'I have to be going in any case. I have a meeting at four with my accountant.'

Pippa's mother conceded defeat; Cassie had class to the nth degree and had handled the situation with consummate grace. 'I hope we'll meet again,' she said, rising to her feet and offering her hand. 'I know you have been a huge support to my daughter.'

'Anything I can do,' said Cassie, acknowledging with charm the other's climb-down. 'While I'm in London, which won't be for very much longer.'

'You must come to the house before you leave.' Pippa was also now on her feet, reaching out to the woman she had grown to admire. 'Perhaps for tea with my mother one day?'

'Over my dead body!' hissed her husband.

The medical report, when it finally came through, could possibly have been worse. Yes, they were almost certainly autistic but had been caught at a young enough age to allow for something to be done, with careful handling.

'Both of them?' said Pippa, stunned.

'Identical twins,' said the doctor gently, 'which means their genetic imprint is the same.'

'But Jack . . .'

'Has a very developed talent. His drawing skills are extremely advanced.'

'And Tom?'

'Still lacks the manual skills but will learn to compensate.'

'And how do we cope?' Pippa's mother stepped in, having pulled herself together now Cassie had gone. Charles was pacing and muttering to himself. He showed great signs of agitation but didn't seem able to listen constructively. Something Cassie had done had driven him wild. Pippa had neither the time nor the inclination to find out exactly what, at least for now. The twins were what mattered, not their aberrant father. From the expression on the doctor's face, they were yet to hear the worst.

'Diet and discipline are mainly what counts, though tantrums are unavoidable. The children must be forced to observe a regular routine.' No running around with food, he explained. They must not be allowed to leave the table until they had finished eating.

'Mainly it is old-fashioned common sense.' He looked to Charles as an older man. 'The way we were obliged to behave by our parents.'

'But how did it all come about?' asked Pippa's mother. 'It isn't something I've ever encountered before.'

'It's largely genetic,' the doctor said. 'The genes are found on an area of the sixth chromosome, known as human leucocyte antigens. The tendency is inherited from the father.'

They all looked at Charles who appeared not to hear. He was still in a white hot rage about something else.

Something was clearly rattling Charles though he didn't say what it was. He seemed to have serious matters on his mind. Not just the health of his infant sons; some of their symptoms he had seen in Aidan who had turned into a fine and engaging young man. These days Pippa found Charles hard to talk to; he appeared to be drifting away from her, which only succeeded in adding to her general gloom.

'Just when I need his support,' she complained, 'he

seems to be off on some tangent of his own.' Despite his frequent absences, till now he had always been at her side, loving and supportive when she was down. She wondered if he had business worries; if so, he had never said a word, but these days he rarely discussed such matters with her.

Her mother, as always, sympathised, aware that Charles was now moody and detached, no longer the charming seducer he had once been. His thunderous mood had to do with his first wife who had jerked the rug from beneath his feet by going ahead with the sale of the Pont Street flat.

'Not that I blame her,' said Pippa's mother, won over by Cassie's charm. 'She had a basinful when he dumped her, yet did nothing to stand in the way of a speedy divorce.' A lady, that was what Cassie was, with old-style morals and standards. In her position, she'd have taken him to the cleaners, though she judged it inappropriate to mention that.

Cassie needed the money to finance a project, entirely reasonably since it was hers, left to her in trust by her prosperous first husband. Besides, Charles still had the house in Barnes as well as his plushy Walton Street showrooms. Neither she nor Pippa could understand his sudden rage, which seemed to stem from Cassie's new-found independence.

'I think he still loves her,' said Pippa despondently. 'I was only ever meant to be a fling.'

'Where is Aidan these days? Do you know?' Despite his sometimes erratic behaviour, Pippa missed her stepson's high-spirited company. She loved to watch him playing with the twins, the three of them all so much alike with their glossy curls and luminous eyes and irrepressible laughter. She found his presence a constant tonic, remembered the comment her mother had made about how she should have chosen the younger model. The way his father was acting now, her mother might well have been right, though she wouldn't admit it.

'I assume still on his travels,' said Cassie, who had dropped in for tea and to say goodbye. She was off to Venice at the crack of dawn, having raised the necessary cash. 'He hardly ever contacts me now. Has always been closer to his father.'

It was true the pair were as thick as thieves on the rare occasions they got together yet Charles hadn't mentioned Aidan for quite a while. If they were still in regular contact, he never bothered to tell her. She sometimes wondered if he might be jealous; Aidan was just that bit too close to her own age. Not that Charles seemed to care either way; lately his mind was fixed on other things.

'Do you think he'll visit you in Venice?' asked Pippa, wishing that she could be going there too. She was sick of Barnes and the daily grind and her constant worrying over the twins. She longed to be like Cassie, fancy free.

'I shouldn't be at all surprised,' said Cassie, drawing on her gloves. 'The last I heard he was heading for Paris on some urgent mission for Charles. I am sure, as soon as his money runs out, he'll be back to Mama like a shot.' She smiled and said she really must go. She still had a lot to do before she left.

'Well, if you do see him, please give him our love. And tell him he's always welcome here. We could even put him up, now the flat has been sold.'

Cassie paused and regarded her shrewdly. 'That's kind of you,' she said, 'though don't make a fuss. He's a grown man now and can stand on his own feet. The more we pander, the less he will do towards knuckling down to a proper job and thinking about a career.'

Dino was thoughtful as they pounded round the park. He hated to see Pippa's spirits at such a low ebb.

'So what's with this Aidan?' he wanted to know. He featured a lot in the conversation though he was just the son of the elderly guy she had married. Dino had never really understood why she'd settled for Charles in the first place. She was sparky, vivacious and as smart as they come, or had been till she had fallen pregnant. Her reputation as an entrepreneur still dazzled his other clients. In the gossipy circles in which he moved, few people's private lives were safe. The upwardly mobile and super-rich mingled anecdotally through their trainer.

'Aidan is Charles's oldest son. Half-brother to the twins,' she said. 'He used to drop by on a regular basis. Now we've not heard from him in months.'

'So?' asked the trainer, still not understanding. She ought to be glad not to be encumbered. From the stories he heard from his other clients, the children from an earlier marriage were to be avoided at all cost.

'It's just that he's good with the boys,' sighed Pippa, not fooling him for an instant. 'If I knew where he was I would beg him to come home but even his father says he hasn't been in touch. Which is fairly unusual because they have always been close.'

'And you fancy him like mad,' said Dino. 'Don't even try to deny it.'

Pippa, with glowing cheeks, confessed that she did.

'So what do you plan to do about it?'

'There is nothing I can do,' she said. The marriage, she saw now, had been a mistake. She had been content with just the affair and Dino had counselled her then not to get more involved. Him and her mother; she should have listened. Before she had even hit thirty her life was screwed up.

'Have you talked to your husband?'

'What is there to say?'

'The truth, maybe. That you made a mistake and would now like to call it a day.'

'And be left on my own with the Terrible Twins? I don't think so,' said Pippa in horror. She found these sessions an immense relief, therapy as much as exercise, and regarded Dino as one of her most trusted friends. While he kept his eye on her rising heart rate, she poured out her daily troubles to him and usually felt a lot better when they were through.

'The gym is cheaper,' Charles had said but Pippa would not be fobbed off with that. Though she'd sacrificed many of her little extravagances, it would take a lot to persuade her to part with Dino.

'So what's the story?'

'I still don't know. I just wish he would come home and help out with the twins.' And let me know where he spends his time; in the face of an emergency, I'd be lost.

Pippa's friends weren't a lot of help either when she summoned them, on a whim, for Saturday lunch. Her mother had valiantly taken the twins and would entertain them till she got the signal. Pippa was grateful but her mother didn't need to be thanked. They were in this together was the way she saw it; she still felt guilt at not having intervened before Pippa committed herself. If only Pippa's father had still been around, but she'd seen him off when Pippa was small; it must run in the family, this wayward streak. Pippa offered the nanny too but her mother assured her that she could cope. Keep them active and tire them out. It had worked like a dream with Pippa.

Charles was away for a couple of days and had seemed rather vague when cross-examined. Business combined with a country sojourn might be all very cosy for him but left his wife feeling boring and neglected. So she bought in some salads and a case of good wine and told the girls to convene at half past twelve.

They ooh-ed and aah-ed about the house; most hadn't seen it since it was finished, and none seemed to care very much that the twins weren't there. They were seven in all, and of the group only Pippa was married, though a couple of the others had live-in partners. The dining table was covered in dishes and a floral arrangement sent by Charles, who had seemed relieved that Pippa would not be alone. When he'd rung to wish her a good weekend and she'd asked exactly where he was, the line had gone suddenly crackly so he'd ended the call. There had been a time when she wouldn't have cared, would have put it down to the luck of the draw, would have shouted her love and gone back to preparing the lunch. Not any more. She gritted her teeth and wondered whether she should reveal that her marriage was up the spout.

As it happened, there wasn't enough time for that; everyone was talking at once, each of them keen to put across her own viewpoint on matters germane to them all. When Pippa went to fetch more wine, she smiled to hear the unbroken babble and realised how much she'd been missing her female friends. They were all in fairly prominent jobs, one a rising young politician, two of the others journalists, had a lot to say that was interesting and shouted to get it across. By the end of the afternoon, when they left, Pippa found herself quite worn out. It would almost be a welcome break to go and collect the twins.

'The grass,' pointed out her mother wisely, 'is nearly always greener. It's a lesson in life that few of us ever learn.'

When Charles eventually came home, he still seemed out of sorts. He'd been doing a lot of driving, he said, and hadn't the energy to talk. Pippa, who had bought them a ready-made meal which she planned to heat in the microwave and then pass off as her own, poured him a whisky. Sooner or later, his mood would improve, and then she would try to find out where exactly he'd been. He kept on saying that business was booming, so he had no excuse to be quite so grumpy when he staggered in after all those days on the road.

The twins, on the whole, were being reasonably behaved, quietly bickering in the corner but not yet declaring war. The afternoon with their granny had proved effective.

'How've they been?' he asked at last, pointing at them with his glass.

'All right,' she said, 'all things considered. Though my mum took them off my hands for most of today.' She skirted round the subject of the lunch; did not want him to think she'd been having fun. Once she'd have told him every detail and he might even have listened. Those days, though, were long since over. He picked up the evening paper and started to read.

Somehow Aidan had to be the key, if only she knew how to find him. Pippa brooded as she microwaved the meal and wondered what on earth to do next for the best. If Cassie were still around, she'd have called her. She felt that they now had a real connection, based, to some extent, on the plight of their sons. But Cassie had left no contact number and was back in Venice, getting on with her life. Suddenly Pippa saw how ironic it was.

'Why are you laughing?' He raised his head as she carried in their steaming plates and indicated that he should open the wine.

'At nothing, I'm afraid,' she said, 'that you'd ever understand.' Then she pulled up her chair and silently started to eat.

'Do you happen to know where Aidan is?' she asked him next morning at breakfast.

'No,' he said, suddenly alert. 'Not exactly. Why do you want to know?'

'No particular reason,' said Pippa. 'It's just that we haven't seen him in a while and it's nice for the boys to have an older brother.'

Charles looked at her long and hard before returning to the paper. Conversation between them these days had reduced itself to a minimum. After breakfast she caught him talking on his mobile but he clicked it off the moment she entered the room. Something was going on, though she didn't know what.

Later she found him burrowing through the bureau, hurling stuff to left and right, apparently in a frantic search for something. He barely looked up when Pippa entered but continued to yank out drawers and make a mess.

'What are you looking for?' she asked him idly, by now indifferent to his varying moods. He often acted as though she wasn't there.

'My passport,' he said. 'I may have to go away. Something has suddenly come up in France. A client with a private collection, keen for me to try to locate a Stubbs.'

'I have never seen your passport,' she said. Since their marriage they'd barely been anywhere together because of his constant travelling and the twins. 'But you might look upstairs in the chest of drawers. That's where I always keep valuables. The bureau is far too obvious to a burglar.'

He checked the time. 'I have to be off. I've a meeting in Walton Street in twenty minutes.'

'Do you want me to have a look for it?'

'Don't bother,' he said. 'I'll be back by noon. But you might lay out a couple of ironed shirts.'

He treats me like a skivvy, she thought, as she cleared the dishes and dumped them in the sink. The cleaner would be in today which meant one less chore for Pippa. No wonder Cassie had let Charles go so meekly.

She went upstairs to shower and dress, though she left the bed for the cleaner. She hated to give her such menial tasks but Pippa's own time was so overcrowded that she hardly ever got to the shop these days. Remembering the shirts, she opened the drawer and flicked through a pile that had just come back from the laundry. She loved the smell of freshly starched linen; Charles had never stinted himself and everything he owned was top-notch quality. Beneath the shirts her hand brushed against something small and compact in an envelope. She pulled it out; perhaps she'd unearthed his passport.

Eureka! At least she could do something right. She

opened the envelope to check and found not one but three matching passports tucked in a rubber band. Pippa examined each one of them, staring in baffled confusion.

41

The sky was dimming; it was growing late. She had reached the end of her list. She had thought about going to visit the school, which would have involved another wide detour, but the odds were against there being anyone there who had been around in Chad's day.

She got back on to the motorway and stopped at a service station. She was tired, dispirited and suddenly hungry, with a terrible urge to cry. The unloved child she had always been took over, her agony unresolved. She should never have come in the first place; it was madness. All of a sudden, she longed for the only place where she now belonged, with Magda and the Antwerp sisters who had charitably taken her in.

She sat within a circle of light, alone at a grimy Formica-topped table, a defeated woman, past her best, who had lost all traces of beauty. Her mission had failed; she could only go home. She thought fleetingly of nice Pippa Harvey and regretted that she had been so abrupt. If she'd stuck around and met the husband he might have produced some more business contacts but she'd gone off on a wild goose chase of her own.

London was still several hours away and Frankie was daunted by the volume of traffic, the more so since it was now almost dark and the motorway lights had come on. After the byways of rural Belgium, she wasn't accustomed to traffic like this; also she hated having to drive on the left. Over a meal of burger and chips, she got out the atlas and studied the route, working out how she could drive only on minor roads. She had nothing at all to hurry back for; London continued to scare her stiff.

She groped around for a cigarette and then found, to her mild irritation, that she'd lost her lighter. It was only a cheap one but she couldn't be bothered to join the queue and ask for a box of matches at the till. Instead she dug deeper into her backpack to see if she had another and found a half-used matchbook she hadn't known was there. After she'd lit up, she saw that it was the one on which Aidan had scribbled his number. In her state of confusion at the time, she must have stuffed it away and then forgotten it. She stared, transfixed, at the row of figures and wondered whether to give him a call. It was weeks now since that ill-fated encounter but she hadn't been able to get him out of her mind. She had used him badly, which he hadn't deserved; the least she could do was apologise. With luck, he would still be in Bruges.

Anxiously she punched out the number and was

almost relieved to find the line was dead. She fingered the matchbook thoughtfully and pondered what to do next, then slowly focused on the advertisement on its printed cover. The Coot and Hern, on the outskirts of Bath, was precisely what she felt like: an anonymous haven in a country backwater where she could go to ground. The idea of Bath had appealed to her since her childhood addiction to Georgette Heyer. She had the car and unlimited funds and nothing to hurry back for. Without further delay, she called the number and booked herself in for the night.

42

The great carved doors of the house stood wide open as a bunch of workmen and domestic staff unloaded spindly-legged gilded furniture and relayed each piece inside. The butler, Gérard, stood anxiously watching, ready to pounce should anything go wrong. A scratch on the woodwork, a mark on the marble; this house, in the sixteenth arrondissement, was not accustomed to such barbaric treatment. It was most irregular, this sudden invasion, at a time when the master was off on a cruise, beyond even satellite reach. The Slut, however, would not listen to reason, was hell-bent on doing this sacrilegious thing of marrying a stranger in the master's own home, presumably without his knowledge or consent.

'Shut up, Gérard,' Cristina said rudely, whenever he attempted to have his say. It was her house now and he mustn't forget that, not if he wanted to keep his job. She made all the decisions here; there was nothing more to be said. There was not a lot that the butler could do, though the rest of the staff were all on his side. It was true the Slut had presided here for

342

the past twelve horrible years. But she wasn't the wife, had no formal standing, though Madame Daumier must certainly know. Why else had she not set foot here in all this time?

The Daumier marriage was typically Parisian; they had an understanding. And the country château, where Gérard spent half his time, was sufficiently luxurious to keep her contentedly at home. Monsieur spent three days of each week with her there and four back here, with the Slut. Gérard, though respecting his energy at an age when most men were beginning to fail, nevertheless could not condone his taste. The only good thing was, once he knew about the marriage, Monsieur would undoubtedly throw the bitch out which was something everyone in the household awaited. Meanwhile the travesty continued right under his nose.

'You are sure you can't get him by email?' asked Serge, enjoying every second of the sleazy charade, even though it would mean a probable end to his hours of voyeurism up the convenient ladder.

'Non. He is on a private yacht and does not wish to be disturbed. His wife's decision; she wants him all to herself.'

The gardener sniggered and the butler smiled. The two men knew each other well enough not to need to spell out too much detail. They had put up with so much abuse from this woman that the only reason both were still here was solidarity with the master, whom they liked as well as respected. Admittedly, there was a certain amount of private amusement. And now she'd transcended her own worst excesses by planning this vulgar wedding.

'What is she wearing?'

'We have yet to find out.'

Yvette, their normal source of gossip, had been unusually silent on the subject. 'You will simply have to wait and see,' she said, with a twinkle in her eye, relishing what they would say when the secret was unveiled. One thing Yvette was pleased about: she had not given in to her wish to resign but had hung around to witness the dénouement. And, if everything went to plan, it should certainly prove well worth the wait. She didn't want to spoil the spectacle for them.

'And what of the bridegroom?' Serge asked Gérard, once the chairs and tables were all safely stowed and the vanload of shabby workmen had driven away. 'It seems he hasn't been heard from yet. He is surely cutting things rather fine. What time is the ceremony scheduled to take place?'

'Seven o'clock tomorrow,' said Gérard. 'The string quartet is booked to be here at six.'

The two men strolled to the rear of the house where a swarm of gardeners were trimming dead flowers and manicuring the lawn. 'Shouldn't you be out there helping?' asked Gérard.

'I have only the hanging baskets to arrange,' said Serge with a nonchalant shrug.

It was all the most colossal upheaval, principally suffered by Yvette, who was, of course, always first in the firing line. The shouting, the swearing, the hurling of abuse; occasionally also of plates. Cristina was at her foulest worst. No one would ever have suspected that, in fact, she would shortly be a bride. She stomped around with her phone glued to her ear, gabbling in Portuguese or imperfect French. Part of the sluttishness of her behaviour was that, in her long sojourn in Paris, she had never bothered to learn the language properly. She screamed at everyone she could think of, the manicurist, the hairdresser, the maid, the caterer, the party planner, the butler. Most of all she screamed at the airlines because they couldn't tell her when her bridegroom was due.

'I think maybe he's not coming at all.' Despite the abuse and the extra work, there was very much merriment downstairs in the kitchen. The bridegroom was now a full five days late and, as far as anyone knew, Cristina still had not heard a word from him.

'She is out of her mind. She should just give up and go back to where she came from.' Though Serge would still be prepared to take her on, but only at a knockdown price as very damaged goods.

The gown that Yvette was so secretive about was a frothy meringue of sugar pink satin, trimmed with strawberry lace. The neckline was tastefully slashed to the navel and similarly down the back, while the sleeves were more of the same pink candyfloss. She looks like a female impersonator, thought Yvette, as she struggled to zip it up.

'Merde,' shrieked Cristina, 'you clumsy cow. You pinched my flesh. Watch out!'

Only because she had put on weight; the bodice bulged beneath her bust and, should she happen to sneeze, she would burst right out.

'Perhaps Madame should go without breakfast,' Yvette said diplomatically, itching to get her hands on the seams which should be let out by half an inch at least.

'No,' screamed Cristina. 'I need a tighter bustier. Go through my closets and find one, you fool.'

She flounced, half dressed, across the room and scowled at herself in the full-length mirror. Downstairs the hairstylist patiently waited to get his hands on that unkempt mane which the bride, in her middle forties, refused to have cut. There were hours to go before the deadline but a huge amount still to do. The alterations to the gown which would, for certain, have to be made once the termagant shrieking into her phone could be persuaded to agree. The hair and makeup, which often took hours; the selection of the jewellery. All these details had been left till now while Cristina paced and worried and cursed, waiting for any word at all from the man she was planning to marry.

One of the maids was walking the dog, after which it would fall to Yvette (who else?) to groom and gussy it up. For this occasion, the pathetic mutt would be decked out with a huge pink bow of the same material as the bridal gown. And, in place of a bouquet, the bride intended to carry it in her arms.

'I only hope she remembers,' said Serge, 'to hurl it into the crowd.'

* * *

Behind her bluster and extreme bad temper, Cristina was in a secret panic, scared of losing not only face but everything else as well. She was still appalled at not being divorced but, since this was something she dared not admit, could not discuss it with anyone else and thus took it out on the staff. Part of her longed to see Cal again but when she called the number in London that Barras had told her belonged to him, the phone was answered by a letting agent who told her the flat had just been sold. She seemed to be up against brick walls all round; no Rocco and now no Cal. There would, however, soon be a Claude; his cruise was to end in a couple of days. With her customary care-lessness, she had cut it fine but now it looked as though everything might backfire. The thought of Claude's arriving home before she had managed to tie the knot filled even fearless Cristina with something like dread. She could charm her way out of most situations but Claude's sense of humour regarding her had been on the wane for some time. If only that blasted Rocco would call and put her out of her misery. If this was how married life would be, perhaps she should back out right now.

She called everyone she could think of in Rio but nobody seemed very sure where he was. One of his pals, a habitual drunk, vaguely thought he might be in France but seemed unaware that he was about to marry.

'Who's the lucky girl?' he slurred; Cristina banged down the phone without saying goodbye.

She swallowed her pride and called Madame Zarco,

mortified to have to admit that she didn't know where Rocco was. Somehow their wires had got crossed, she said, and now she appeared to have lost his itinerary. Of course, he would soon be arriving in Paris for the wedding.

'A wedding, chérie? How exciting for you. I wasn't aware that Daumier had become free.'

'Not Daumier, Rocco. I assumed that you knew.' He obviously hadn't broadcast the news, which magnified the dread in her heart about a hundredfold.

'Chérie! How delightful. No, I hadn't heard. I haven't even received my invitation. It must have got lost in the mail.'

Cristina mumbled a feeble excuse: they were keeping it small, it was very low-key. They loved each other too much to be able to wait. The only thing was . . .

'You don't know where he is.' There was no disguising the note of pure malice in Madame Zarco's voice.

So, instead, she took out her anger and frustration on any poor innocent who stood in her way. The whole house, metaphorically, shook with Cristina Calvão's black mood.

The party planner had now arrived and was supervising the floral arrangements that were being carried in from another van. The marble foyer had a vast creation, to match the colours of the bridal gown, and silver bowls of sugared almonds were being distributed. The grand piano in the main salon had been

348

unveiled by the string quartet and would be used to herald the bride's triumphant arrival down the stairs. Balloons and ribbons festooned the stairway down which the glamorous figure would glide to Handel's 'Arrival of the Queen of Sheba'.

'*Tiens!*' said the butler, with distaste. 'They are turning the whole performance into a circus.'

After the ceremony was over, dancing was planned outside on the lawn so paper lanterns had been hung in the trees and the sound engineers were annoying the gardeners by stretching their cables across the lawns that had just been so carefully mowed. From somewhere in the background came a crash; a table of glasses had been pushed over so now they were out with their brushes and brooms, clearing it up before Cristina appeared.

The couturier had been persuaded to come and artfully loosen a few of the seams and now Yvette, with her nimble fingers, was sitting upstairs in Cristina's room, carefully redoing the delicate stitches.

Downstairs, in the kitchen, the caterer's staff were getting under the housekeeper's feet while a couple of waiters were sampling the wine and becoming noticeably tipsy.

Five o'clock and still no sign of Rocco. Gérard, by now, was ringing the airlines. No more flights were due in from Brazil, certainly not in time for the wedding; unless he was coming from somewhere else, it didn't look as though he could possibly make it.

'Ought we to tell her?' They took a secret vote and

the consensus was to let things proceed. By now they were all having too much fun to care.

'Who's going to get to pay for all this?' Serge was curious to know.

The butler shrugged. He had no idea. The way the Slut always ran her affairs, the bills would undoubtedly stay unpaid until she was taken to court. Or until the master stepped in, as he usually had to. Not this time, though; she had properly blown it. Unless Rocco arrived in the nick of time, made her his bride and bore her off, Cristina was well and truly stuffed. To put it at its mildest.

'Madame,' said Yvette, rubbing her eyes, 'the alterations are finished.' She lifted the gown with reverent care and laid it across the untidy bed. Despite the basic contempt she felt, the spirit of the occasion was getting to her. Cristina, lying on crumpled sheets, was still in an ugly, belligerent mood. She had had her bath and was taking a rest before she allowed the stylist in to sweep her hair up into a fancy concoction.

'Aren't you going to try it on?'

'No point,' said Cristina sullenly. 'If it doesn't fit now, it never will. There isn't time for any more adjustment.' As usual, as though it were Yvette's fault. The maid said nothing as she bustled around, tidying up her sewing things, but mentally she looked at Cristina and spat.

The stylist came in, with his sidekick in tow, and Cristina settled before the glass to allow them to do their best. The makeup girl was waiting outside until it was her turn to work her magic and turn this overblown former beauty into a semblance of what she once had been.

'Rather her than me,' said Yvette, when she popped down to the kitchen to get her more tea.

Quarter to six and he still hadn't come. By now the bride was fully dressed and her hair was finally being tweaked into shape. Her caramel skin was glowing with health and her eyes were great globes of enticing fire. Her waist was compressed, the seams were still holding and the petulant scowl upon her face was starting to fade as she looked at herself with delight and appreciation.

'Pop downstairs and check with Gérard in case there is any news,' she said and Yvette, who hadn't relaxed all day, wearily did her bidding. As if he wouldn't have let her know; the whole thing hinged on the groom's being there. Gérard, who had also been ceaselessly working, was standing now in the main salon, surveying its finished splendour. The house was looking its glamorous best; inside he swelled with proprietorial pride. He almost wished the master might see it now. These fine old houses dressed up very well, the perfect setting for such an occasion, if only the bride were not a slut and the groom apparently missing.

'Of course there's no news,' he said to Yvette, his eyes glued to the rococo clock. 'And I'd wager a thousand euros he isn't coming.'

The string quartet were tuning up; they were due to start playing in fifteen minutes, or such had been their instructions from the bride. Soon the guests would start to arrive, the handful of B-list celebrities Cristina had managed to rustle up among her soi-disant friends. The champagne corks had begun to pop and the first few glasses were being poured. Downstairs the staff were taking a break and prematurely toasting the happy couple. They had worked hard and were feeling no pain. Whatever else might happen tonight, this certainly was one wedding they'd never forget.

When she'd married Cal, it had been so simple. They had walked barefoot along a beach, Cristina with her arms full of freshly picked flowers. She'd been beautiful then, only just nineteen and the toast of the international catwalk. How far she had tumbled since those halcyon days that she'd lived through in a coke-fuelled haze and only barely remembered. When she'd married Cal, it had been for life yet had lasted less than two years. This time she meant to make it work, provided the bastard showed up in time. The scowl returned to her botoxed face and she jerked away from the stylist's hands in sudden irritation.

'Get me a glass of champagne,' she snapped and the man went scurrying to do her bidding. She would force herself into a party mood and wait for the doorbell to ring.

Which it did, right on cue: a resounding trill that instantly halted the sound of music from below.

'Wait!' she yelled. 'Don't open the door! Leave it for me. I am coming.'

She took one last twirl in front of the mirror then, satisfied with what she saw, picked up the skirts of her voluminous dress and headed for the staircase. Down she tripped in her satin slippers, dyed to precisely the right shade of pink, and across the marble hallway, strewn with petals. Gérard was waiting but she gestured him aside.

'Go!' she said. 'And allow me to greet him alone.' She turned and waved the musicians away, and the waiters lounging with their laden trays. When she greeted her bridegroom, finally arrived, she wanted to be on her own.

The bell rang again, more peremptory now, as if the caller were growing impatient. If she didn't hurry he might go away and then where would she be? Cristina studied herself in the glass and tweaked one strand of her burnished hair, artfully tousled by the fashion industry's finest. Her lips were glossy and pneumatically plumped. She looked the image of innocent love, eagerly awaiting her future husband.

'Coming!' she cried, sounding almost coquettish as she crossed the last few paces to the door and fumbled with the intricate locks she'd rarely ever had to deal with before.

Upstairs in the boudoir, straightening the bed, Yvette heard the sound of the heavy door opening, followed by total silence and then a gasp.

'Cal?' she heard her mistress say on a rising note

that rapidly turned into a terrified scream that brought them all running.

The front of her dress was soaked with blood and the knife that had punctured her heart was still in there, quivering.

43

The Coot and Hern, when she finally found it, was even more delightful than Frankie had hoped. Ivy-clad and built of grey stone, it stood by the side of a boisterous brook, with a waterwheel that had been restored and now was working again. It was almost eight and the place was packed; the car park was jammed solid. A steady buzz issued from behind the doors and the bottle-glass windows twinkled in friendly welcome. A picture from a Christmas card; for the first time since she had left the commune, Frankie felt at home.

The main door led into a narrow hall, oak-panelled and furnished with real antiques and an opulent Turkish rug in glowing colours. The beams were low and the genuine thing; the whole place smelt of cooking and woodsmoke, reminding her faintly of the barn in Lier. She tapped the polished brass visitors' bell and looked around with appreciation. Now this had certainly been worth that night-marish drive.

A door at the end of the corridor opened, emitting

steam and a strong whiff of garlic, and a flustered woman, done up in chef's whites, peered out.

'Can I help you?' she asked though she obviously had her hands full.

'The name is Wilde. I booked a room. I am sorry to have arrived so late but I've just driven down from Middlesbrough,' she said. By a wildly circuitous route.

'Oh yes. I'm sorry, we are understaffed. If you don't mind waiting another two ticks, someone will be out to check you in. Let me order you a drink from the bar and you might like to look at the menu. As it's Thursday night, we are pretty full up but I've kept a table for you. You were lucky to get a room at all but we had a last-minute cancellation. By the way, I'm Jenny Matthias.'

Nice, thought Frankie, flopping into a chair and picking up a copy of *Country Life*. Five minutes later someone else appeared, a dowdy woman in sensible shoes, who checked Frankie in, then led her upstairs to a pretty room with a dormer window and a teddy bear on the bed. 'The bathroom's through there. We'll expect you down by nine. If you've had a chance to look at the menu, I can take your order now.'

Everything on it looked simple and scrumptious. Frankie, nostalgically, settled for pheasant then stretched out on the bed for a ten minute nap. The trip, so far, had been disappointing. Now, perhaps, things might start looking up.

She had brought few clothes so didn't change, just washed her face and combed her hair, then went downstairs with some trepidation, to confront the crowded bar. The dowdy woman came hurrying over, with a glass of red wine and nuts in a bowl, and steered Frankie to a corner table, close to the blazing fire.

'We'll let you know when your meal is ready. The dining room is through those doors. We always used to eat in here but have recently expanded.'

'Thanks,' said Frankie, stretching her legs, relieved to be out of the car. She settled down to enjoy her wine and watch the general activity at the bar. She was so unaccustomed to social life, to her it was like living theatre.

Most of the drinkers were young and trendy, though a group of stalwart older women sat at a table across the room from her. They were clearly regulars, in their down-to-earth clothes: ancient Barbours with wellington boots, contrasted with single-strand pearls and shapeless tweeds. One of them even wore a hat, a battered felt that had seen better days. It was clear from the rhythm of their conversation that they all knew each other very well. And, from the glances they shot at her, they recognised Frankie as somebody new, presumably just passing through. A group of old men played darts in a corner; what was most attractive about this pub was the natural interaction of new and traditional. A bunch of younger women, loud and brash, obviously on a girls' night out, were clustered around an older man with a shock of silvering hair. From the way they screamed and jostled for position, he was clearly a magnet to the ladies. Born to the job, that was obvious, as he skilfully mixed them cocktails and kept them laughing. Mein host, she thought, though the chef was a woman. She wondered where he fitted in.

It was decades since Frankie had been in a pub, not since her teens on the Wirral. She thought back to her stepfather, the colonel, who sometimes, when they'd been out with the guns, treated her to a half of shandy, on condition she didn't tell her mother. They had been conspirators in those days; he had thought of her as the son he'd never had, with the dogs and her pony and that glorious open air life. She wondered now how things might have been if she hadn't burnt his house down. But he'd had it coming after what he'd done, which she'd never been able to tell her mother, nor even Magda or anyone else, come to that. His unexplained death in a shooting accident still seemed like divine retribution, though, despite her years in a spiritual commune, she had never believed in stuff like that.

There was a small commotion by the open door as a fair-haired boy, around six or seven, ran in and clasped the landlord round the knees. Laughing and full of bonhomie, he swept the child up into his arms and swung him high in the air till he squealed with delight. The women all cooed and petted the child, a wholesome scene that Frankie envied. Perhaps she too might have had a normal life if she hadn't fallen so obsessively in love. And if he had survived.

A waitress summoned her to her meal so she left

the heart-warming family scene and moved to a table in the adjoining room.

The meal was superlative, out of this world; certainly worth the drive and the wait. Frankie had never eaten so well in her life. After the pheasant and honeyed parsnips, she had raspberry crème brûlée and some local cheese.

'My compliments to the chef,' she said when the waitress came round to clear the plates and ask if she'd mind moving back to the bar for her coffee. Through the long, drab years she had lived in Belgium her diet had been adequate but sparse. The vegetables she had diligently tended had helped keep her healthy and underweight but the spartan regime had long ago started to pall. Home cooking was better than prison fare, but that was the most she could say. The commune's ideals were on a higher plane; they ate in order to stay alive and never even thought about fleshly pleasures.

What with the wine and the warmth from the fire, combined with the hours she had spent on the road, Frankie, lulled by the excellent meal, found herself dozing off. She would certainly sleep well tonight and might stay on for a few more days, if they could fit her in and her room was still free.

'Would you care for a nightcap?' The landlord was hovering as he went around picking up glasses. It was late; the place was emptying fast. Soon he'd be calling for final orders though she, as a resident, was under no pressure to leave. She was half asleep but comfortable so ordered one more glass of the excellent wine. He smiled down at her then walked away, a handsome man with twinkling eyes that dimly reminded her of someone else.

Aidan's eyes, she realised. That same compelling blue.

'Chad?' she said, jerking wide awake, but the man was no longer in the room.

44

The first thing Cassie did, as soon as she could, was move out of the hotel and into the palazzo even though, at first, it meant having to camp. She was used to old buildings with cavernous rooms; had spent so much time on her own in Tintagel that even the echoing silence failed to alarm her. She missed the dogs and the sound of the sea which had always helped her to sleep at night, but the constant busyness of the canal more than made up for that. Whenever she paused to take a break, she would stand at one of the tall arched windows and never grew tired of the moving pageant below. It was almost like having gone back in time; the restless scene could have changed very little in all the years the palazzo had been standing.

The ground floor storerooms were no longer in use but the first floor *piano nobile* was still partially furnished. Vast old cabinets, with faded paintwork, loomed inside each of the family rooms and some of the ancient mosaic floors were still in remarkably good nick. Mario, over the years, had done much to protect the structure from the weather, so at least she didn't have problems with leaking roofs. Most of the walls were flaking and cracked and the floors that weren't tiled were very creaky. To do the work properly would mean huge investment. Cassie determined to do what she could by herself.

She bought a bedroll, a hurricane lamp, and a primus stove which she hoped not to use, then set herself up in one of the smaller rooms. In order to keep the draughts at bay and give herself some privacy, she hung a baize curtain over the entry arch. She indulged herself with a battery radio and a pile of books she had brought from home. Then she found an old trestle table and unrolled her plans. The years with Edwin were paying off; she knew more about Renaissance architecture than she had even remembered. During the mornings she simply wandered, enjoying the city and seeking inspiration from the many and varied buildings all around her. She also looked for local craftsmen to help her with the heavier work. Mario had been generous with introductions; just the mention of his name instantly opened doors. At night she would eat a simple meal, then settle down by her hurricane lamp to swot up on the relevant details before she embarked on the actual renovation. The weather was warm, so she needed no heating, was glad to come in from the mugginess outside in order to cool off. She wore cut-off jeans and cotton shirts and her skin acquired a becoming glow, though she shaded her face beneath a wide-brimmed straw hat.

'Aren't you lonely?' asked Daisy, when she phoned, alarmed to think of her mother there all on her own.

'Not in the slightest,' said Cassie cheerfully. 'I have far too much on my plate to think about that.'

Once they knew that she wasn't a tourist, the Venetians were very friendly. Her fluent Italian and natural charm won them over immediately and soon she knew a handful of locals by name. She bought her food in the nearby shops and picnicked, perched on a wide window ledge, though at night, since she couldn't be bothered to cook, she nearly always ate out. She had her mobile, which she seldom used, calling the family instead every week from the landline in a nearby neighbourhood bar. The family had that number too in case they should suddenly need her. Cassie found it all hugely exciting; by marrying young she had missed out on college yet here she was, at almost sixty, living the life of a student.

'In England I'd soon be drawing my pension,' she marvelled to herself. But she hadn't felt this youthful and fit in years.

She missed her daughters and they missed her, but they promised to visit as soon as they could, though she warned them the place was still just a ruin, not even remotely habitable. She tried to get them to understand that that was all part of the massive challenge. 'It's like being a Guide all over again,' she said.

Rose was hoping to come out and join her and didn't mind roughing it in the least. She was sick to death of her stolid legal life and fancied a change of scenery. If she liked it enough, she might even quit the job and risk finding casual work in Venice. If her mother could turn bohemian, so could she. She was taking Italian lessons at night as well as studying her father's art books. He had left his children a rich and compelling heritage. Rose was a lot like her father's sister, with the same gaunt features and forthright manner. She lacked Aunt Sybil's artistic flair but shared her sharp tongue and fertile brain.

Daisy was still being comfortably domestic and Sam and Willow were now in their teens. Roughing it on a building site was not their idea of a family holiday; the kids would prefer to go somewhere where they could surf.

'I can't see why they need a holiday at all,' grumbled Daisy, who was always chasing after them. 'All they ever do as it is is spend their lives loafing about.' With a husband who played golf when he wasn't working, she did rather get the rough end of the deal. Besides, she still had to walk the dogs and keep an eye on her mother's house. Tremayne was constantly in and out but plants needed watering, rooms kept aired and the weekly cleaning supervised. It was interesting how Daisy had turned into a hausfrau. Nothing genetic on either side explained that.

'We will come,' she promised, 'when it's up and running and we don't have to live in a slum.'

'Which won't be for many years,' said Cassie, 'the way the place is looking now.' She promised to keep a photographic record of the step-by-step progress she made.

From Aidan lately there had been not a word. None of them knew where he was.

'He'll turn up. He usually does.' Though secretly Cassie was starting to worry. He had not been in touch with her for several weeks.

In May, at the end of the spring semester, Mario Dandolo returned. He maintained an apartment in Santa Croce and strolled across to the palazzo within minutes of getting in from the airport and dropping off his bags. He discovered Cassie in workman's overalls, industriously scraping down a wall.

'*Bene*,' he said with admiring approval. 'I hadn't understood you'd be so hands on.'

'It is harder than I had thought,' admitted Cassie, pushing back the hair from her sweating forehead. 'But at least it's a start before the workmen move in.'

Mario strolled around in deep thought, savouring the timeless atmosphere of the place that had been his family's home for the past six hundred years. It was obviously a moving moment and Cassie had the tact to leave him alone. It must be like parting with the Cornish house, only worse.

'I think,' he said eventually, when he wandered back to join her, 'that I made a very wise move selling out to you. I feel it is now in the proper hands. My ancestors would approve.'

'Thank you,' said Cassie, touched and pleased. It meant a great deal to her to have his blessing. 'I feel it's the challenge I have waited for most of my life.'

To celebrate, he asked her out for dinner locally

that night. Cassie, sick of her own company, accepted with delight. She found him enormously *sympathique* and wanted to get to know him better; it seemed a shame that he now lived so far away. The problem was what to wear. She had brought few clothes, and the primitive way she was living at present was not conducive to looking her best, though the manual work she engaged in daily had firmed her figure and brought a new colour to her cheeks. Feeling positively decadent, she took a shopping trip to San Marco and finished up with a hair appointment at a fashionable salon in that area. It was years since she'd had a proper date and she felt as excited as a debutante, though she knew that, of course, all he wanted to do was talk. They had quite a lot in common, she sensed; it was a real treat to be with such a cultured man.

'My dear, you look enchanting,' he said when he called for her at the palazzo. The dress was chic and understated, its simple cut belying the extortionate price. She had teamed it with fashionable strappy gold sandals which emphasised her long tanned legs, but what he most admired was the up-to-date hairdo. 'You have cut your hair! I like it,' he said. 'If you will permit me, it takes ten years off your age.'

'It's the first time I've had it cut since my teens,' confessed Cassie, suddenly bashful. 'Both my husbands preferred the old-fashioned look.' Also her son, though she didn't mention him. She had been, she realised, for far too long under the yoke of meeting male approval.

'Both husbands! We have a lot to discuss,' said Mario, taking her arm.

The meal was perfect and they sat outside, an echo of that lonely night when Cassie had first arrived in Venice after Charles exploded his bombshell. Then she'd been timid and quite at a loss, not knowing what she would do with herself or how she could possibly face the future without him. Now, three years later, she had come into her own, had adjusted to being a woman alone and not just somebody's wife or somebody else's mother. She was independent, healthy and well off, with a brand new start in the city of her dreams, and only on the brink of her seventh decade.

'Tell me about all these husbands,' said Mario, quietly refilling her glass. He seemed to be genuinely captivated by her.

'There's not a lot to say,' she said, warmed by his obvious admiration. 'At the time they seemed all important, now less so.'

It wasn't that she hadn't loved them; she had, both times, with all her heart. With Edwin she'd been the receptive pupil; with Charles, the indulgent mother figure, once the initial exuberance of sex had worn off. She had turned a blind eye to his numerous faults though saw them quite clearly now in his son. Which was why she had started to feel she had somehow failed.

At last, however, she had found her match. She looked across at her dinner companion and saw recognition mirrored in his eyes.

*   *   *

No matter how happy she was in Venice, Cassie still had commitments at home so hoped to get back there at least every two or three months. For a start, it wasn't fair on Tremayne to expect him to run the estate single-handed, even though he'd been doing just that since Edwin's death. She sometimes wondered why he stuck around, then remembered he had been born in those parts. In some ways it meant as much to him as the palazzo did to Mario, even though his forebears had never actually owned it. Land and property were very important; Cassie now understood why Charles had objected so strongly to losing the Pont Street flat.

But Charles and Pippa had a life of their own that no longer impinged on hers. Since the property row Charles had kept away though Cassie couldn't resist making contact with Pippa.

'How are the twins?' she wanted to know and Pippa, touched that she still seemed to care, was keen to pour her heart out. Not so good, though she hesitated to say that.

'Can we meet?' she asked and Cassie said yes and invited her for lunch at Harvey Nichols.

'I daren't risk asking you to the house. He hates the fact that we get along and still can't forgive you for getting rid of the flat.'

'Too bad,' said Cassie, unconcerned. What a spoilt little boy he had turned out to be. Perhaps her fault, but he'd always been such a charmer.

Pippa was looking pale and drawn, a shadow of her former self. She had lost some weight but her eyes were dull and her hair quite lustreless. She no longer resembled in any way the foxy minx who had snared and run off with Cassie's husband. But how were the twins? Cassie truly cared, especially so since there'd still been no word from Aidan.

'Good days, bad days. Things are much the same. Jack is still excelling at drawing while Tom, on the whole, is sweeter-natured except when he's having one of his bad turns.'

'What do the doctors have to say?' Cassie had read up everything she could but, nevertheless, still wanted to know. Whatever it was was hard to put a name to.

'They say if they catch them early enough, they can take them from being under-performers to mainstream students at school.'

Aidan had had no problems with learning. He had sailed through Eton and, later, Oxford. His character flaws had been mainly behavioural. She remembered the tantrums and later the fights. More than once he had been on detention for bullying but had never, ever displayed the slightest remorse.

'What does their father have to say?' He had always taken Aidan's side and seemed to find his boorish behaviour amusing.

'He doesn't appear to be worried at all. In fact, to tell the truth, I don't think he cares.'

They kissed and parted; Pippa had to get back and Cassie promised to call before she left. She would love to take those children in hand and give them the benefits of country air and space enough to be able to work off their demons. She couldn't ask but felt fairly sure that the marriage had taken a turn for the worse. A less nice person might have gloated but Cassie was genuinely concerned.

Sybil, though now in her early eighties, had lost none of her sharpness or bite. She still had plans for the sculpture school and had had some good feedback from the city of Venice. Mario had offered to lend it his patronage.

'Who is this count?' she asked, intrigued and not a little suspicious.

'Oh, just the man,' said Cassie vaguely, 'from whom I bought the palazzo. He is hardly ever there these days, spends most of his time in the States.'

Her casual air did not fool Sybil, who had known her too well for so long. Cassie looked positively radiant these days, with her stylish clothes and becoming hairdo. A glow like that did not come just from working one's fingers to the bone. But she knew enough not to interfere. Cassie would tell her in time. And if it meant a new man, then good luck to her. The way that bastard had treated her, she deserved all the happiness she could get. She had been an exemplary wife to Edwin and that was what counted with Sybil.

But Cassie's concern was for Sybil's future. She felt she should no longer live on her own. She was still very strong and could wield her chisel but the St Ives studio was up steep steps and worryingly remote for a woman her age. Suppose she should have a fall or something; she wouldn't be able to let the neighbours know. But try telling that to Sybil Hawksmoor. She was every bit as stubborn as Rose. Still, it was worth a try.

'Why don't you move in here full time? You'd be company for Tremayne. We could build you a workshop in the grounds and you'd be a good guardian for the house. You could even help Daisy walk the dogs if you ran out of things to do.' Cassie stopped; she must not overdo it. They were all entitled to their independence. And far be it from her, a new recruit, to tell an old campaigner how to live her life.

Sybil looked at her, long and hard. 'I'll think about it,' she said.

This time, now she was a resident of Venice, Cassie eschewed the motor launch and came in instead, as the natives did, by train. The experience was worth it for the aesthetic pleasure alone. The scene that greeted her, as she issued from the station, was enough to stop anyone in their tracks. She stood and gloated at the panoply before her, more like a painted stage set than a living city. Then she briskly wheeled her single bag down to the vaporetto, to take the boat eight stops along the Grand Canal.

She was coming home. Her heart was light as she dragged the bag from the landing stage and along the narrow path to her own front door. Shopkeepers shouted and waved to her and she couldn't wait to get inside and back to work on her mammoth project, now the focus of her life. She had done her duty and checked up on her girls, had seen that everything was in good hands and that life still continued serenely without her there. Tim was a bore but Daisy was fine and the children, in their separate ways, delightful. Rose was the prickly character she'd always shown signs of becoming, close in looks and attitude to her aunt. Once she'd made her choice and taken that daring leap, there was nothing to stop her achieving whatever she wanted. There would always be room for all of them here as well as in Cassie's heart.

Pippa, who wasn't in any way hers, yet still preoccupied her thoughts, had a long and difficult journey yet to travel. Cassie wished her only well and would always be there for her. She planned to keep in touch on a regular basis.

She let herself through the palazzo's street door with the gigantic iron key and stood in the sun-streaked atrium, imbibing the place's echoes. It smelt of dust and mould and time, spiced up by drying plaster. She was back in the place she wanted to be, where she hoped to remain for however many more years she had left. A huge task lay ahead of her but Cassie wasn't afraid. She stood and let the place wrap itself around her.

One small niggle, though, teased her mind as she lugged her bag up the mighty staircase and into the small cosy nest she had made for herself. The girls were okay; the grandchildren too. But what, in heaven's name, had become of Aidan?

45

'Where is he?' asked Frankie, almost crazed with agitation. 'The man who was here before, I presume the landlord?'

A woman she recognised as the chef had taken his place behind the bar, small and trim with bright dark eyes and a most infectious smile. She wasn't smiling now, however; her expression clouded the moment Frankie appeared.

'He's gone,' she said, 'and is not coming back. I don't know why but he suddenly said he had something urgent to do.'

'What?' asked Frankie, disbelieving. 'We only spoke a few minutes ago.'

'That's how long it took,' said Jenny, undisguisedly hostile now. 'And, by the way, he is not the landlord. That's me.'

'Sorry,' said Frankie. 'Only I assumed . . .'

'Perhaps you assumed too much.'

Frankie had no idea what to do. She had to catch up with him fast and find out for herself. It was like the moment she'd seen Aidan on the train. Only this time she had a gut reaction that told her it really had been Chad.

She tried, more humbly, to win Jenny over. She'd been perfectly affable earlier on, when Frankie had arrived.

'Might I ask what name he goes under these days?' The age was right, she just hadn't been thinking straight. And she couldn't have mistaken those eyes. 'I think I knew him many years ago. Before you would have come on the scene.' Perhaps before she was even born, though she wouldn't go into that.

'He's called Clive Barclay,' said Jenny, less fiercely. 'And he's my live-in partner. We have been together five years.'

'And the child?'

'Not his, if that's what you're wondering. Though Toby looks upon him as his father.'

Desperate now, Frankie thought very fast. The nightmare was happening all over again, only this time she was determined not to lose him. She thought of telling the whole story to Jenny but caution warned her not to. It was late and if he had really gone, there wasn't a lot she could do tonight. In any case, she'd had too much wine to drive.

'Could I stay on for a couple more days?'

'No,' said Jenny, 'we are fully booked up.' She showed no sign of wanting to talk so Frankie went meekly to her room.

All night she smoked and paced the floor, trying to figure things out. This strange encounter had not been accidental but engineered by Aidan. If he hadn't given her the matchbook in the first place, she wouldn't have known where to look. But why would he do it; she could see no point, though it did prove there must be a connection. Someone was playing games with her but now she'd make sure that they stopped. She had wasted her whole life on Chad, mourning a man she'd believed to be dead and now found was very much alive. A man in his prime, with a family setup as well as a thriving business. When she thought of all she had sacrificed for him, she very nearly choked.

First thing in the morning she settled her bill then went straight out to the car. She was through with dreaming; it was time for action. No more meandering along leafy lanes, admiring the English countryside, but straight back on to the motorway and to Middlesbrough by the fastest route.

And this time she had only one port of call: the police.

46

The first thing Jenny did after Frankie left was get on the phone to Vanessa.

'I'm sorry,' she started, 'it was all my fault.'

'Bollocks!' said Vanessa. 'I'll be right over. As long as you guarantee that that man isn't there.'

'He's not. He's gone. I don't know where or even if he'll ever be back.' She felt as though she'd been punched in the head, could not believe this had happened. The man she'd thought she could trust with her life had suddenly bowled her a googly. When Vanessa's car drove into the yard, Jenny was out there waiting for her and the pair embraced like the soulmates they'd never stopped being.

'You look ghastly,' said Vanessa bluntly. 'What you need, I feel, is a drink.'

'At ten a.m.?' But she didn't resist and allowed Vanessa to make them both Bloody Marys. They sat outside by the weeping willows. It was Friday morning; she should be cooking but, hell, could not have cared less. Piece by piece she narrated the story of how this strange woman had turned up and the shock she'd glimpsed on Clive's face the instant he saw her.

'Who was she?'

'I still don't know,' said Jenny. 'She booked in under F. Wilde. Tall and sort of ravaged-looking, wild by name and by nature. A throwback from his past, she said, no one he's ever mentioned to me, though he certainly didn't greet her with any warmth. Acted, in fact, as if they were strangers though I could see, as the evening progressed, that he practically never took his eyes off her.' She'd been moving, as usual, between kitchen and dining room, so had only seen a little of what went on.

'In what sort of way did she look at him?'

'Hardly at all, which was also strange. She seemed to be totally self-absorbed and only spoke to him briefly, to order drinks.'

The bastard was up to his tricks again; Vanessa was secretly pleased, though she hated to see her best mate suffer and Jenny had clearly not slept at all. Her hair was matted and her eyes were like pits in her normally cheerful face.

'So why did he go?'

'I don't know,' said Jenny. 'He just upped and left while she was still in the bar. Muttered something about things he had to do, then vanished into the night.'

'Will he be coming back?' asked Vanessa, hoping the answer was no.

'I really don't know,' said Jenny, eyes brimming. 'Oh, why,' she asked, grabbing Vanessa's hand, 'do I always get it so wrong?'

'You don't,' said Vanessa. 'It isn't your fault. All you

377

have been is unlucky. Let me make a couple of quick calls and I'll stay here all day and help out.'

There were strangers in the bar at lunchtime, among the regular crowd. Nothing unusual in that, though they caught Jenny's eye. A man and a woman, inconspicuously dressed, they stood close together and spoke in low voices as though unwilling to be overheard. So why don't they go outside? she thought. There were plenty of empty tables there. There was simply no accounting for people's stupidity.

'Keep an eye on those two,' she muttered as she pushed past Vanessa, who was manning the bar. 'I feel there is something slightly fishy about them.'

'Are they regulars here?'

'I've not seen them before. And I don't believe they have made a booking for lunch.'

The pair edged their way to a corner table and proceeded to order a number of drinks, presumably expecting others to join them.

'Will there be more of you?' asked Vanessa. 'I can try to clear you a larger table.'

'No thank you,' said the man. 'It's just us two.'

'And will you be wanting lunch?' she asked. 'The kitchen is fairly busy right now so I suggest you put in your orders soon or else you may not get served.'

'Thanks,' he said. 'We're just passing through. But I would, if I may, like to take a look at the menu.'

Vanessa brought it, along with their drinks: four glasses of wine, two white, two red, as well as a dry martini, American style. Odd, she thought, for a couple like that, who she would have guessed might have been teetotal. The woman, in particular, seemed very uptight. And the wines were all different, which also seemed strange. Well, each to their own, she thought as she bustled away.

'On reflection,' said the man when they left, 'we would like to book a table for tonight. I hope we haven't left it too late. You are obviously very busy.'

'Let me check it out,' said Vanessa. 'I need to talk to the boss.'

Jenny, harassed and over-heated, was searing scallops with one eye on the clock. By this time of day she was working at fever pitch.

'I don't believe we can fit them in unless we get a cancellation. Tell them that if they care to chance it, they can go on the waiting list.' It was the best she could do but not her fault that they hadn't bothered to book. There had been no word from Clive and her heart was breaking.

'Are you okay?' asked Vanessa quietly.

'Not really but I'll cope,' said Jenny. 'Be a pal and call Toby down for his lunch?'

Clive returned in the early evening, just as Jenny was opening up, as suave and relaxed as he usually was, exactly like the night he had first walked in.

'Hello, my sweet. Sorry I'm late. I would have called but I hadn't got my mobile.' He kissed her as if there was nothing wrong, though she felt him tense when Vanessa appeared, ready to start on the evening shift and stand in for Clive behind the bar.

'What's she doing here?' he asked Jenny sharply, almost losing his cool.

'Helping out,' she told him firmly. 'After you left me in the lurch.'

In the circumstances, there was little he could say so he greeted Vanessa with a degree of warmth which didn't fool her one bit; she knew he detested her. But the early drinkers were drifting in so they both knuckled down to the job in hand, while endeavouring to stay as far apart as they could.

'Who was that woman?'

'What woman?' he asked, as he took off his jacket and rolled up his sleeves in readiness for battle to commence.

'The one who was here last night,' said Jenny. 'Who had booked a room and stayed down here till we closed.' The one with the crazy staring eyes and the tragic look of a drama queen. Who had behaved as though she had seen a ghost and needed urgent sedation.

He paused and shrugged. 'I have no idea. You can't expect me to remember them all.' Then he whipped down some glasses and gave them a rub, ready to mix his famous cocktails.

Jenny, feeling decidedly brighter, popped upstairs and spruced herself up, then returned to the bar her usual smiling self. For a while she lingered on in there, chatting with the regulars, something she always liked to do to make them feel really at home. Joyce was valiantly manning the kitchen, ready to step aside when Jenny came down.

The bar was full, with a few new faces, which usually happened on Friday night when strangers from out of town swelled the regular crowd. She spotted the couple who had asked for a table and had their names on the waiting list. They appeared quite content as they chatted together in a corner. They must have liked what they saw at lunchtime or else they would not have come back so soon. There were also two men who had just come in, formally dressed for a weekend night, who ordered halves of beer and stood looking around. Jenny was feeling cheerful again. Her man was back; there was nothing wrong. As usual, she had just overreacted and jumped to a false conclusion. The place was buzzing; they were fully booked. She felt enormously proud of the Coot and Hern.

She was just about to return to the kitchen, when the door swung open and the Wilde woman stalked back in. Entirely different from how she'd been last night, with flashing eyes and a flush to her cheeks, she pushed her way through the crowd to the bar and confronted Clive head on.

'Hi, Chad,' she said. 'Remember me?' She fumbled at her throat and pulled out a locket. 'See, I still have your picture round my neck.'

There was a sudden hush as everyone listened. Something dramatic was going on and they had ring-side seats. Clive, in the process of pouring a beer, glanced up briefly without recognition then handed the glass, with a smile, to the waiting punter.

'Don't pretend you don't know me,' she said. 'You

tried that last night and it didn't work, though I must admit you very nearly got me. You are going to tell me next that you don't know Aidan.'

The crowd pulled back to allow her space and she stood there, openly challenging him, an imposing woman with mixed emotions in her eyes. In a flash her sad, wan look had gone; overnight her ancient beauty had revived. Jenny, watching quietly from the doorway, experienced a frisson of fear. Whoever she was, she wouldn't be going quietly.

'I'm afraid you're mistaken,' said Clive, without a flicker. 'I don't believe we have met before. Apart, of course, from last night,' he added. 'When I have to say you were somewhat the worse for drink.'

'Don't give me that,' said Frankie, snarling. Jenny stepped forward to intervene but Frankie impatiently shrugged her off, looking as though she would like to break his neck.

'I've already told you,' Jenny explained, 'that this is Clive Barclay whom I've known for years. We all have, isn't that right?' she said and everybody nodded.

Frankie never even glanced at her, acted as though she hadn't heard; just continued to stare at Clive with impassioned eyes.

'His name is Chad Barnaby,' she said. 'Something I can prove. Or will do once he has taken the necessary tests.'

The two of them continued to lock eyes; she certainly had his attention now. Vanessa, watching from a corner of the room, could swear that he turned perceptibly paler. Blimey, she thought, for once he has run out of words.

'See,' said Frankie, in a quieter voice, removing the locket and passing it round. 'That's how he used to look when I last saw him. Younger, yes, and a great deal fitter. But if you look closely, you will see it is indisputably the same man. He was on remand,' she added. 'We both were. Me for arson and him on a murder charge.'

Total silence. Nobody spoke. Now everyone's eyes were on Clive.

'Well,' he said, his composure restored. 'The very least I can do, I suppose, is offer you a drink on the house.'

'How much of this is true?' demanded Jenny, once she had shunted the three of them out of the bar and into the privacy of the snug where they wouldn't be over-heard. Vanessa had wanted to be there too, feeling that Jenny needed backup, but someone had to run the bar. On Fridays they brought in extra help.

'Call me if you need me,' she said, aware of the smouldering hostility. There was no doubt now in anyone's mind that what Frankie had said was the truth. Even Clive didn't try to deny it. He had stopped protesting, had gone unusually quiet. All the more reason to watch him, thought Vanessa. She had never trusted him in the first place and now was being proved right.

'All of it,' admitted Clive. 'I won't deny that I used to be Chad. But, heavens, that was so long ago I can't believe it still matters. All we were was a couple of kids having a bit of a lark.'

'I loved you,' said Frankie, 'and you let me down.' There was no disguising the tremor in her voice. 'I helped you escape and then waited for you. You never came so I turned myself in and later confessed to your murder.'

'Well, more fool you,' he said, slightly sneering, having recovered his savoir faire. 'I owe you nothing. You should have run when I did.' He had brought a bottle of malt whisky through and was now topping up his glass.

'Tell me the truth, did you ever love me?' Frankie almost pleaded. The look between them was enough to cut glass but he didn't so much as waver.

'I've told you,' he said. 'We were simply kids. What did we know about life or love? I'll tell you, the best thing you did for me was help me get out of that place and I'm grateful. I guess I still owe you one.'

'But I went to jail for your murder,' she said. And have spent the rest of my life in mourning for you.

'Well, thanks. What more can I say?' he asked, raising his glass in a mock toast.

Back in the bar, Vanessa was coping though she longed to know what was going on. Joyce, alone in the kitchen, was holding her own. She had popped in there a couple of times, to check that things were under control, to find Joyce positively cheerful and quite unfazed.

'Are you all right?'

384

'I am better than that.' The homely woman in the sensible shoes appeared to be having a ball as she cooked the whole meal. For years she'd stood back and watched Jenny do it, yet her culinary skills were just as great as Jenny's. All she had lacked was confidence and the guts to go it alone.

'So dinner is served as usual?'

'It is.' Joyce relished the thought of being, for once, in control. There were a couple out there who were taking more than the usual interest in how the place was run; she had watched them closely as she'd scurried through with assorted hors d'oeuvres. Joyce might be frumpy but she wasn't a fool and had been in this business for most of her life, never a star but the eyes and ears of the place. She knew what she thought, and she wouldn't divulge it. She was just extremely glad that it was tonight of all nights that she, at last, would get the chance to demonstrate what she could do. Thank you, Clive, she said to herself. She had never remotely trusted the man, but at least he had helped to brighten things up. And, in all fairness, had always been lovely to her.

They were still in deadlock with hackles raised, like a couple of cats set to fight to the death. Jenny, alarmed, was scared of what might happen.

'Who is Aidan?' Frankie spat at him, stopping him in his tracks.

'What do you know about Aidan?' he asked.

'Just that he's some sort of sociopath. Without whose intervention I'd never have found you.'

'Leave Aidan out of this,' said Clive, with a new grim note in his voice. He rose to his feet and moved towards the door.

'So tell me who he is,' she said. 'He looks exactly like you.'

'He's my son,' said Clive, shocking Jenny to the core. 'And I won't have him getting involved.'

'Too late, he's involved already,' said Frankie. 'More or less up to his neck. And, by the way, I know what you did. You killed a gypsy and dumped him in the fire, so that everyone thought the body was yours. Ingenious, I will give you that. It even fooled the police.'

'How did you find out, then?' he asked, intrigued and slightly admiring.

'At first I didn't. I mourned your loss and sacrificed my whole life for you but then I met Aidan and the pieces started to fit.'

Clive, suddenly silenced, did not say anything, and nor did Jenny who'd been listening, stricken, throughout.

'I have just been back to Middlesbrough,' said Frankie, 'to talk to the police. With the help of the local newspaper, we finally figured out the truth. A gypsy boy was reported missing at the time.'

'Really,' said Clive, with a sudden sneer. 'You girls are certainly full of it.' He picked up his bottle and started to leave but Frankie stopped him with one last question.

'I have to know. Did you ever love me?'

Jenny was waiting for his answer too.

386

He turned and stared at both of them with no compassion in his ice-blue eyes. 'I never learnt the meaning of love,' he said.

'I'm off,' he said, a few seconds later, taking his jacket from behind the door and nodding to Vanessa as if they were friends.

'One moment, sir,' said a man in a suit, who'd been quietly drinking a half at the bar. 'I wonder, before you go, if we might have a word?'

47

All Frankie desperately wanted now was to get ou of England as fast as she could and turn her bac on the whole unsavoury business. Had she been abl she'd have gone straight to Waterloo station, droppe off the car and caught a train to Brussels that nigh without even stopping in London. But the trains didn run after nine p.m. and she still had a two-hour driv So, she'd check back into the Draycott Hotel and hop to get on Eurostar in the morning.

It was raining on the motorway, just as it alway did at home, which made her nostalgic for Magda an her friends. She was through with sex and perfidiou males; in future she planned to spend her time onl with women. She should never have come here in th first place, stirring up trouble best left undisturbe but the trip, at least, had knocked on the head an unfulfilled dreams she might still have. She hadn completely taken it all in, except that Chad was aliv after all and appeared to be having a whale of a tim within his different personas. Someone had died bu it wasn't her fault. The gypsy boy's body had been i the hostel before the fire was even set. Chad had gambled on her witless devotion to make her do just what he wanted her to and never to question the outcome.

Now she saw clearly that he'd never loved her, had only ever used her as a pawn. All his life he had been a killer, which now explained her own stepfather's death. The colonel had been a sexual pervert but hadn't deserved to die in that way, shot by his own gun in front of his dogs. Chad killed casually, without compunction or any thought of the repercussions. She'd trusted him yet he'd slipped away, leaving her to carry the can and serve a sentence for something she hadn't done. In all the years she had suffered and grieved, he had been out in the real world, living off other women, it seemed, without a thought for the one he had betrayed.

She was grateful to the Middlesbrough police for listening courteously to her story and not dismissing it out of hand as the loony ravings of a sad old spinster. Instead, they had shown her the newspaper archives and helped her search through the relevant files until they'd unearthed the brief paragraph which mentioned the missing traveller. The rest was up to the forensic squad; they still had the boy's remains in the unmarked grave. And, more to the point, they now also had Chad, in custody without bail.

First thing in the morning, she spoke to Magda and said she would get on the next available train. But, being Saturday, it wouldn't be easy. Weekend breaks were top premium with Eurostar. Magda told her not to worry if she couldn't get a seat, there really wasn't any need to hurry back. She had come so far and spent so much, it seemed a waste not to stay on a while and, at least, see a little of the London she'd never known. She worked so hard throughout the year, she was long overdue some sort of break and Magda sensed that she needed to sort out her head.

'We are thrilled with what you have done for us.' The orders for lace alone made the trip worthwhile. She knew, without asking, that something was wrong, that Frankie was far from being herself, but she would wait until she felt like opening up. She offered to meet her in Brussels with the truck but Frankie told her that she could manage. She knew she had bridges to mend with Magda, was aware she'd been brusque and withdrawn. All that would keep, however, till she was home. They had the rest of their lives together to come to an understanding. From this point on, she would open up and try her hardest to love again. It would take some doing and a lot of pain but she still had a great deal to give.

She wished she'd been able to get to know Jenny whom, in other circumstances, she felt she would have liked. She had obviously worked wonders with the pub, while also raising a child on her own. She deserved a genuine happy ending instead of the shit she'd had flung in her face. When, some weeks later, news filtered through about Jenny's winning a Michelin star, the note that Frankie sent her was warm and sincere.

* * *

Frankie took Magda at her word and picked up some leaflets at the desk about tourist attractions in London. First, however, there was one more thing she felt she would like to do. The sisters had been so good to her in encouraging her to take this trip, the least she felt she should do in return was try to drum up some more business. Pippa Harvey had been very helpful and given her much of her precious time. After she'd finished a leisurely breakfast, she would stroll back along the Fulham Road in the hope that she might be up for ordering more lace. This time she might even meet the husband; she felt guilty at not having stayed around before.

Pippa, however, was not in the shop. A nice young woman stood in for her and said she would not be back that day, owing to a family crisis. She asked if she could help but Frankie said no.

'I only wanted to say goodbye. I am leaving this afternoon on Eurostar. Perhaps you'd tell her that I'll definitely be in touch.' A pity, she thought as she walked away. That was somebody else she'd have liked to know better.

48

The news was totally devastating; Pippa still hadn't fully taken it in. Charles had been arrested on undisclosed charges.

'I don't even know where he is,' she wailed. 'Or why they can't let him out on bail. They won't even let me see him. They say I'm not really his wife.'

Dino was seated at her kitchen table, patiently listening as she poured out her woes. He normally didn't approve of coffee but was willing, on this occasion, to turn a blind eye. She was clearly distraught; he would do all he could to help get her over the trauma. He had grown enormously fond of her in the years she had been his client.

'Tell me again what happened,' he said, reaching across and taking her hand. In all the years she'd worked out with him, he had never known her this tense.

It started with finding the duplicate passports after Charles had asked her to lay out his shirts. 'He was going away on a sudden trip but didn't say where to. Only that it involved a client and a Stubbs.' She blotted her eyes; her nose was running but she seemed quite unaware of that. In her dirty tracksuit, with unwashed hair, she looked the picture of desolation. What would do her most good was a run round the park but Dino was wise enough not to mention that. Her spirit was more important than her body; right now she could use all the comforting she could get.

'And the passports were all in different names?'

She nodded and finally blew her nose. 'All CBs, that immediately struck me. His own name, Clive Barclay and Cal Barnard. I had no idea what was going on but assumed he'd explain when he came to fetch them.'

'But he didn't come?'

'He called instead. To say there had been a change of plan and he had to go back to the West Country for a meeting.'

'And you didn't ask him about the passports?' It didn't surprise the trainer one bit that the man had turned out to be a crook. He hadn't much liked him, the few times they'd met. He was too good-looking and far too cocky, besides being much too old for Pippa; talk about cradle-snatching. He agreed with what her mother had said, that she should have held out for the son. From all accounts, he was simply a younger version.

'And then what happened?'

'The police arrived. To say they were holding him pending inquiries. He is wanted in connection with several incidents which is why they won't let him out on bail. It sounds pretty serious, don't you think?'

It did indeed, no question of that, but Dino was paid to counsel and not to alarm. He looked at Pippa's tear-stained face and wasn't sure what advice to give, except that she get herself a first-rate lawyer. Which, having considered, he kept to himself. She was quite upset enough as it was without his adding to her grief.

She didn't tell her mother about it, could not face having her on her case. When Dino left, she went upstairs to try to make order out of chaos. The next workout session they had together would be in another two days. Because he hadn't remembered his diary, he had promised to call ahead of time to check that the hour they had fixed was still all right. The twins, meanwhile, were at nursery school. She had until four to pick them up, by which time she hoped to have got a grip on herself. How could he have done this to her, she asked herself tragically in the mirror as she brushed the tangles out of her hair and plastered on some warpaint.

Pippa had been a star in the making when she'd completed her Courtauld course; had remained that way till she'd got enmeshed in the life of Charles Buchanan. And, even then, she had made it work, had milked him for contacts and all he could give; had been content, at that stage of her life, with being his bit on the side. Few of her friends had understood. They had urged her to make the break while she could and find somebody who was nearer her age and could offer her a future. But at that time Pippa's prime concern had been to make her shop a success.

Charles had given her loads of support; even now, she wouldn't deny that. And, without the unplanned pregnancy, she'd have been content to leave things as they were. At twenty-seven, with the world at her feet, marriage had been the last thing on her mind, until the pregnancy was confirmed and she'd felt she had no other choice. She had ended up as Charles's wife and, incidentally, mother to autistic twins. End of story as far as Pippa was concerned and she still hadn't yet turned thirty.

The thought only made her cry again so she stepped into the shower instead and then had to start the makeover process from scratch. The person she longed to talk to most, certainly more than her own mother, was Cassie, in Venice embarking on a new life.

There was no word from Cassie or Aidan but the police were back in a couple of days, keen that Pippa should answer more of their questions. They remained non-committal, were still 'making inquiries', but Pippa sensed, from their brusqueness of manner, that she herself was by no means out of the frame. They cross-examined her for several hours about intimate details of her marriage and how she had first met up with Charles. Whom, disconcertingly, they called Mr Barnaby: not a name she had ever heard before.

She answered their questions as far as she could, trying hard not to lose her cool. It might only make things worse for Charles if she did.

Was she aware he'd been married before?

'Yes,' said Pippa; she knew Cassie well. They'd

become good friends because they had children in common.

So did she know where Cassie was now? Or Mrs Hawksmoor, as they styled her.

'In Venice,' said Pippa, not understanding why Charles hadn't told them that.

He was not being very co-operative, they said. They were here to check out certain facts. They mentioned an 'incident' in Paris and asked if she knew the name Cristina Calväo.

'No,' said Pippa, thoroughly puzzled, asking what it was all about. They refused to give away any answers, simply took copious notes.

In the end, when she was about to explode, they closed their notebooks and called it a day. They would be in touch, they told her politely, and asked her not to leave town.

There were business matters to be arranged so, since Pippa was still the boss's wife, she drove to the Walton Street showrooms to sort things out. No need to let them know what had happened; the press would get wind of it soon enough. The main thing was keeping the business up and running. Pippa, wearing her largest dark glasses, told them that Charles had been called away – family matters she vaguely implied – and asked if there was anything she should do. Nothing, they said, all was under control; he had trained a highly capable staff, which was how he had managed to move around so freely. They asked if she knew when he would be back and, when she said no, didn't seem concerned. Things were ticking over as usual; business was still very brisk.

'I'll let you know as soon as I hear.' She couldn't wait to get out of there. It was almost beyond her capabilities to put a good face on things. Part of her wanted to kick and scream; how could he have landed her in this mess? And, furthermore, how was it possibly true that she wasn't his legal wife? That was the part that puzzled her most, once she'd calmed down enough to think it through. Cassie had agreed to a quickie divorce to ensure that the twins were legitimate. Her marriage, she knew, had been rock solid. So what was this they were saying now? None of it added up.

Even more reason to talk to Cassie, but she hadn't left Pippa a contact number. She was back in Venice, in her famed palazzo, which had brought new happiness into her life and made Pippa frankly jealous. The only person who knew how to reach her was Charles, who was now incommunicado. If only Aidan were still around. This family mess was his as much as hers.

On the way back to Barnes, she dropped into her shop and they gave her Frankie's message. They had missed each other by half an hour but Pippa barely took that in. 'She wanted to say goodbye,' said her staff. 'She leaves this afternoon on Eurostar.' The last thing on Pippa's mind right then was Frankie, whom she barely remembered meeting.

She was slowly beginning to feel less stressed, telling herself there had been some mistake, when the doorbell rang again; she instantly stiffened. She was scared to death the police were back; the thought of going through all that again appalled her. They had made her feel like a criminal when, in fact, she was the injured party. As soon as Charles was home, she would file a complaint. She stood in the hallway, uncertain what to do, until the bell stopped ringing and somebody peered through the letter box.

'Pippa, it's me. Please open up. I know you're in there. I saw your car.'

Aidan! She couldn't believe her ears. 'Wait!' she shouted and rushed to open the door. 'Where on earth have you been?' she cried, falling into his arms with relief. The person in the world she most wanted to see.

'Abroad,' he told her, smoothing her hair. 'What on earth has been going on here? I've never seen you like this.'

'It's your dad,' she said. 'They've arrested him. And they won't even tell me why. Just that they've taken him in for questioning. Some confusion over his passport.'

She wasn't sure she should tell him the rest; he was, after all, Charles's son. Then she realised that he was fully adult, scarcely younger than her, in fact.

'Come on through and I'll fill you in,' she said.

First he checked that the twins weren't there, then poured her a massive drink. He looked fit and tanned and more mature, with those compelling eyes, as blue as his dad's.

'They wanted to speak to your mother, too, but I don't have a contact number.'

'Here,' said Aidan, scribbling it down. 'Though I can't understand why they didn't just ask my dad.'

'They said he wouldn't co-operate. Which is why they won't let him out on bail.'

'It all sounds rather extreme to me. Proper Gestapo tactics.'

'They mentioned the name Cristina Calvão but it rang no bells with me,' she said.

Aidan's sudden change of mood surprised her. 'And did they mention Frankie too?' He ceased his restless pacing.

'No,' said Pippa, taken aback. 'But, oddly enough, someone else just did. She came into the shop just now and left a message for me.'

'Frankie's in London?' He seemed surprised. He grabbed Pippa roughly by the shoulders. 'Where is she? I need to know,' he said. 'It's vital I catch up with her. We have unfinished business.'

'I believe they said she was leaving today.' She shrugged him off and checked the note on the pad. 'On Eurostar this afternoon. I think there is only one. But how on earth does she fit in? I only met her once, peddling homemade lace.'

The phone rang. He told her not to answer but Pippa had picked it up. It was only Dino, confirming their workout. Pippa told him she couldn't talk.

'Tell me more about the police,' said Aidan, obviously rattled now. 'What exactly did they say about Cristina?'

'You know her?'

'Maybe.'

'They told me nothing. Just mentioned her name,' said Pippa.

Aidan's mood had perceptibly darkened; he looked just like his father on a bad day. Pippa hated these temper tantrums, so reminiscent of the twins.

'So what did they want?' he almost shouted. His eyes were turning red.

'Only something to do with his passport,' she said, hoping to placate him.

'Are you sure you're not holding anything back?' He moved towards her menacingly and, as she tried to back away, grabbed hold of her by the throat.

Someone banged sharply on the kitchen door and Pippa struggled to break away but Aidan's fingers were like a vice. 'Keep quiet,' he hissed in her ear.

'Help!' she screamed as she fought like mad and heard the door crash inwards.

'In here!' she yelled as her legs gave way and Dino came bursting in.

'Go after him!' she begged, but Aidan had gone.

49

Lulled by the rhythm of the wheels, Frankie nodded off. Eurostar had been virtually empty and the leisurely lunch had helped to ease her tension. At Brussels she had switched to the Amsterdam train, to a first class carriage from a bygone age where, at least until Antwerp, she could be fairly sure of remaining undisturbed. If her mother's legacy had bought anything, it was privacy. She waved away the refreshments trolley; there was nothing further she needed. Soon she'd be home and back to her spartan regime.

She was deep in a dream that featured Chad when the sliding open of the compartment door awakened her abruptly. The man who stood there, blocking the light, was tall and she couldn't see his face. Instinctively Frankie fumbled for her ticket.

'Hello,' he said. 'Remember me?' unconsciously echoing her own fateful words. He remained there, swaying, as she stared in shock: Chad – at his best from those far off days – the embodiment of her dream.

'Aidan?' she whispered as her senses cleared. God, but he had scared her. She had not expected to see him again, even though their first encounter had been on a train. Too much had happened in the past few days for her to be able to face him now. The sharp emotion she felt was predominantly guilt.

'The same,' he said, with that dazzling smile. 'You've been leading me quite a merry dance. For a while, I confess, I thought I had lost you in London.' In one hand he carried a styrofoam beaker from which he now started to sip. 'Mind if I join you? It has been one hell of a day.'

He seated himself across from her, his long legs pressing against her knees, and when the trolley returned on its rounds he nonchalantly waved it past. They had forty-five minutes, approximately, until the first stop which was Antwerp. Frankie, awake now, was fully alert. She saw, from the gleam in his restless eyes, that he hadn't just come here to talk.

'I am sorry—' she started but he cut her short.

'As well you might be, bitch,' he said, a visible twitch in his lower lid, his face no longer smiling. He was just like Chad, with the same stunning looks. But now she saw, with a frisson of fear, that Aidan was totally out of his mind. As she must have been on that wild night of their first meeting.

'I am sorry,' she repeated, 'for what I did.' He was half her age, she should have shown more restraint. 'I realise now I must have hurt you. My only excuse is that I was under great stress.'

Tentatively she touched his knee but he smacked away her hand. Don't mess with me, the cold eyes said, and now she saw he trembled with bottled fury.

He finished his coffee and crumpled the cup, grinding it under his heel. All trace of affability had fled; she was face to face, she knew, with a seasoned killer.

'What is it you want from me?' she asked, as calmly as she could. She was tall and fit from a lifetime of hard toil but he was taller and younger.

'To shut you up once and for all,' he said, searching inside his inner pocket. 'And stop you doing something really stupid and spilling the beans on my dad.'

His dad. Of course. It was obvious now and should have been so from the start. But then she hadn't known that Chad was alive.

'Who,' she asked quietly, in order to gain time, 'is your mother?' Certainly not Jenny, who had been as shocked as she was when they'd both heard the news.

'My mother, Cassandra, is a very fine lady, too good to mix with the likes of you or that slut at the pub who was carrying on behind her back.' Now he drew out what she thought was a pen then realised, with a jolt, was a spring-blade knife. His face was a solid mask of hatred; there was little doubt what he had in mind. She tried to slither along the seat but he blocked her with his knees.

'Not so fast,' he said, brandishing the knife. 'You are not getting out of it this time. When I called him to tell you were on his track, he asked me to keep an eye out for you and said he'd fix things when he had the time.'

'He loved me.'

'Oh yes?' He was gloating now and the dazzling smile returned. 'You mean like all the others who tried to trap him? It all began with you,' he spat. 'If you'd never come snooping, we'd all of us still have been happy.'

'Dad,' he'd said, when he'd made the call. 'What have you been up to?' And later, when he'd met the Brazilian lawyer, he'd known he had to act. No one must know about the other marriage, which was why he'd had to kill the Brazilian bitch.

Frankie listened as he rambled on; there was no doubt now that he was mad. It was twenty-five minutes until they reached Antwerp; if she kept him talking, she might still hold him off.

'I don't understand,' she told him calmly, 'what difference that can have made to you.'

'It makes me a bastard,' he virtually screamed. 'Along with those fucking twins.'

She had to do something. This wasn't going to work and Frankie was damned if she'd sit there and let him slit her throat. After all she had suffered because of Chad, things weren't going to end like this. She tensed herself then sprang at him, sticking two fingers into his eyes and knocking away the knife.

The corridor, when she wrenched open the door, was disconcertingly empty. The downside, she realised grimly, of travelling first class. She sprinted towards the dividing door that led into the adjoining carriage, but as she tried to open it he grabbed her round the neck. She could feel the knife-blade under her ear but managed to turn and grab at his crotch then stepped across the dividing gap to the safety of second class.

'Damn you!' he hissed as he doubled with pain and she heard the clatter as he dropped the knife. She was ready for him when he leapt at her and she socked him sharply on the jaw, then recoiled as he lost his footing and slipped through the gap.

The train was travelling at maximum speed and would soon be arriving in Antwerp. By the time they found his body, she ought to be home.

Magda was waiting beside the truck, solid and dependable, just as she always had been.

'Good journey?' she asked as the pair embraced.

'Uneventful,' said Frankie.